The
Black

Stiletto

Secrets &
Lies

The Black Stiletto

Secrets & Lies

The Fourth Diary—1961

A Novel

Raymond Benson

Oceanview Publishing

LONGBOAT KEY, FLORIDA

ISBN: 978-1-60809-161-4

Published in the United States of America by Oceanview Publishing,
Longboat Key, Florida
www.oceanviewpub.com

10 9 8 7 6 5 4 3 2 1

PRINTED IN THE UNITED STATES OF AMERICA

For Judy, My Sister

ACKNOWLEDGMENTS

The author wishes to thank the following individuals for their help: Mike Christensen, Dan Duling, Susan Hayes, Helmi Hisserich, David Kahn, James McMahon, Pam Stack, Grace Stewart, Bert Witte, Pat and Bob Gussin, and everyone at Ocean-view Publishing, Peter Miller, and my family, Randi and Max.

AUTHOR'S NOTE

While every attempt has been made to ensure the accuracy of New York City, Los Angeles, and Las Vegas in 1961, the Second Avenue Gym, the East Side Diner, the Krav Maga Studio, and Flickers nightclub are fictitious.

The
Black
Stiletto

Secrets &
Lies

I
Martin
The Present

It was bad news, and to be honest, I expected it all along. Maggie and I both knew that Mom had grown worse over the past couple of months, so I was a little anxious when March rolled around. That meant it was time for Mom's biannual evaluation.

Maggie was now the sole physician who monitored her at the nursing home. A neurologist had come in to give Mom tests, and two days later Maggie called me in to discuss them. Sandy, the head nurse, and Melissa, the director of the dementia unit, were also in the room.

"Your mother is experiencing a rapid decline. I'm afraid you're going to find the Alzheimer's symptoms getting worse. We'll have to resign ourselves to, well, just making her comfortable from here on out."

The room was silent for a moment as my mind refused to register her words. Was Maggie saying Mom was going to die soon? My mother? Judy Talbot?

The woman the world once knew as the Black Stiletto?

Sometimes I forgot Maggie and I were the only ones who knew that.

"I'm sorry, Martin," Maggie added.

"I'm afraid I agree, Doctor," Sandy said. "I've been observing Judy a lot." She looked at me and also said, "I'm sorry, Martin."

I'm not sure exactly what I felt. Shock, sure. Anger, absolutely. The disease was cruel, brutal, and unfair. Was I sad? Of course. But there was also a little guilt for being relieved. "Happy" wasn't the right word, but I was glad she wouldn't have to suffer through the indignity of it all much longer.

"What kind of time frame are we talking about?" I asked, but my throat was dry and my voice cracked.

"It's difficult to say," Maggie said. "We've talked about it before, Martin. At this stage, although it's entirely possible she could live another year, it's probably more realistic that she has only a handful of months, maybe just a few weeks. If you're using a three-stage model for the disease's progression, she's definitely in stage three. With the Reisberg Scale, she's at six and will soon be at seven."

I looked at Maggie and almost said something I would have regretted. It always amazed me that she became so businesslike and matter-of-fact when she was playing her role as a doctor. I was no longer the boyfriend, but rather the patient's son. It was easy to think of her as "Margaret" rather than "Maggie."

"You've seen her yourself. Her ability to speak is extremely limited. Since I've been treating her, she was never much of a talker, but three months ago she could have had something of a conversation. Now she's very quiet; it appears that it's a great effort for her to say anything."

"She called me Little Man Martin the other day," I interjected.

"What?"

"Mom called me Little Man Martin. It was something she used to call me when I was little. Uh, *real* little."

"You never told me that," Maggie said, laughing a little. "That's cute."

"So doesn't that mean there are still memories in her head?"

"Sure there are. They're all in there, but she can't get to them. You know all this. Alzheimer's is like a computer virus, only in this case the computer is the human brain. Even in this late stage, your mother will continue to remember things, but they will usually be out of context. She may pull something out of nowhere and surprise you, but it's almost always spontaneous and not a result of conscious thinking on her part."

"The more serious developments are the physical impairments," Sandy said. "More and more the staff has to hand feed her. She can't bathe or dress herself. She lost control over toilet habits months ago."

I knew that. Things were diminishing at a rapid rate.

"I'm sorry, Martin." Maggie squeezed my hand. "I know it's hard."

"So what do we do?"

"Like I said, we try to make her comfortable. Just do what you've been doing, Martin—take it one day at a time. It's all we *can* do."

When I arrived at the office for another round of scintillating tax returns, I mumbled a hello to Shirley, the receptionist and legal aide, and went straight to my desk. I guess you could say the morning meeting with Dr. Margaret McDaniel really bummed me out. It wasn't like it was a surprise. I've always known Mom would die eventually. It was just a question of when. Lord knew she deserved to be spared such an ugly death; I supposed she was fortunate in that the disease worked uncommonly fast on her. She went through in three years what most Alzheimer's patients suffered in ten.

Damn it, whenever I seriously considered Mom's mortality, I was invariably reminded of her old alter ego. Since Christmas I hadn't thought much about the Black Stiletto. That was by choice, too. My anxiety disorder flared up if I thought about her too much. It's why I stopped reading the diaries. I read through the third one and stopped. It upset me too much, I just couldn't do it. There were two more books, one covering 1961, the other, '62—the year I was born. Was my birth the reason for the Black Stiletto's disappearance? I knew I'd learn something about my father if I continued reading. He was supposed to be Richard Talbot, killed during the first year of the Vietnam War, which was a little odd because nothing too serious was really happening over there that early on. I don't know how he died or what he looked like. Mom erased every sign of his existence. She never talked about him.

I had the feeling she hated him, whoever he was.

"Why so glum, Martin?" The voice startled me and I jerked. "Sorry, didn't mean to scare you."

Sam Wegel was my boss and owner of Wegel, Stern and Associates, Inc., the little accounting firm where I worked. He was standing right in front of me and I hadn't noticed. Sam was in his seventies and he said he was going to retire soon, *every single day*.

"That's okay, Sam. Just lost in my thoughts. Sorry."

"You talked to your mother's doctor."

"Yeah."

"Not good?"

I shook my head.

"I'm sorry, Martin. What can I tell you? It's a horrible thing."

"Yeah, I know, Sam. I've been getting used to it for a few years now, but you know what? I'm still not used to it."

After a respectful beat, Sam sat in the client chair in front of my desk. "I want to ask your opinion on something, Martin."

"Sure, Sam."

"What do you think of this place being called Wegel, Stern, Talbot and Associates?"

At first I thought I was supposed to answer, "I don't know," and then get a punch line. But then I saw by his expression that he was serious.

"Really, Sam? You're making me a partner?"

"I think it's time. I'm going to retire soon."

I was pleased, but in all truthfulness, being a partner in the tiny two-man firm wasn't much to talk about.

"Thank you, Sam. I appreciate it. You mean I get my name on the stationery?"

"Wegel, Stern, Talbot and Associates."

"That's great, Sam. I'm honored." I said the name aloud, too, to try out how it felt on the tongue. "Can we drop the word 'Associates'? I mean, it's just us, Sam."

"All right. But we can't drop 'Stern,' it would be disrespectful to Mort."

"Of course not. Wegel, Stern, and Talbot it is."

We shook hands. When he didn't get up, I knew Sam had more to say.

"I really *am* retiring, Martin. Probably at the end of this month. Doctor says I have pancreatic cancer."

Crap. Another medical blow to someone I admired. "No, Sam. Really?"

"Yeah. First Mort, now me. I got to take the chemo. Rose says I should be at home. We're okay financially. Anyway, I want you to have the business, Martin. It's yours. My kids don't want it. They're not accountants." He shrugged. "So what do I do?"

"You could sell it, Sam. *I'd* buy it from you if I could, but you can't give it to me. I can't accept it."

"Yes, you will. I'll leave it to you in my will so you might as well take it now. We can work out something, I'll continue to get a piece of the profits while I'm alive, but after that, it's yours, fair and square, as long as Rose benefits in some way. You can even change the name if you want."

"I doubt I'll do that. What about Shirley?"

"Don't you want to keep her here?"

"Sure. Gee, Sam. I don't know what to say. Thank you. Wow. I'm really floored. But what about you? You feeling all right now? Are you in pain?"

"I'm fine. Just tired, you know." He slapped the arms on the chair, stood, and walked a few steps before turning back to me. "Now let's do some work. It's tax season!"

I was planning to stop by Woodlands to check on Mom, but before I left work I called Gina in New York. After digesting Dr. Schneider's news that morning, I wanted to hear my nineteen-year-old daughter's voice. She was a student at Juilliard, studying dance and acting. She was also involved in some kind of martial arts thing that scared the hell out of me. Carol—her mother—and I don't hear much from her. Usually, one of us had to call *her* in order to find out how she was or what she was doing. We hadn't seen her since she was here for Christmas. She seemed happy and fine then. I'm glad about that, but it was a little surprising. Carol and I both thought Gina would have a hard time after the assault she suffered last year at the beginning of the school term.

Gina picked up after two rings. "Hello? Dad?"

"Hi, honey. What's up?"

"Oh, I'm at Krav Maga class. I meant to call and tell you I already got my yellow belt and pretty soon I'll get the orange one. For most people it takes about nine months to get the yellow, and I got it in four!"

I had no idea what she was talking about. "That's great, honey. How's school?"

"School? Oh, uh, *eh*. It's just school."

"Are you doing any acting or dancing?"

"Nah, I didn't get cast this semester. Look, Dad, I gotta go. I was kind of in the middle of a drill. Josh doesn't like us to have our cell phones on."

Josh?

"Well, call me more often. I miss you. Have you talked to your mother?"

"Not any more than I've talked to you. I don't think she notices, her being newly married again and everything."

That was kind of a sore subject with me, although I've accepted it and moved on. I have my own leading lady now by the name of Margaret McDaniel.

And as if she'd read my mind, Gina asked, "How's Maggie?"

"Just fine. I'm going over to her house for dinner right after I stop in and see your grandmother."

"Why don't you and Maggie just live together?"

"I don't know, Gina, it's just the way we like it for now. I have my house and she has hers."

"Whatever. How is Grandma Judy?"

"Not too good, sweetheart. The doctor says she's entering the last stage of the disease. I'm afraid it's going to get rough. That's one reason why I called."

"Oh, no."

"Yeah. I'm sorry."

"Shoot, that's terrible. Oh, Dad."

"I know."

"What can we do?"

"Not much, I'm afraid. Just love her. You think you can come visit again sometime soon?"

"I don't know."

"You'll come home when the semester lets out, won't you?"

"Uh, Dad, I gotta go. Tell Grandma I love her. I'll call soon!"

And she hung up. Short and sweet.

Well, at least I knew she was breathing.

It was snowing when I left Deerfield and drove to Riverwoods. March in Chicagoland. Third worst month of the year, after February and January.

As I pulled my BMW E90 into the Woodlands parking lot, I suddenly realized that nearly twelve months had gone by since I first learned my mother was the Black Stiletto. I'd never forget Uncle Thomas handing me that letter and strongbox. Thomas Avery was the lawyer who handled Mom's estate ever since I was little, and as long as I've known him he was probably Mom's best friend. Come to think of it, she didn't have many friends when I was growing up. I imagined she and Thomas were romantically involved a bit in the sixties, but I didn't know for certain. He was a few years older than my mom, but he was still working. Even though he wasn't related to us, really, he was the closest thing to an uncle I ever had.

I don't know why, but I never quizzed Uncle Thomas about Mom's finances. She never worked, but she always had money. Uncle Thomas *had* to have known something, wouldn't he? How she had managed? I believed Thomas when he said he didn't know the contents of the strongbox that my mom kept in trust for me until she became incapacitated. Now I wasn't so sure. I supposed I was afraid to find out too much of the truth. Out of sight, out of mind, as they say.

What a bombshell that was. After reading Mom's confession, I started exploring our old house in Arlington Heights—which was *still* up for sale—and found her costume and the diaries in a secret closet in the basement. I learned how fourteen-year-old Judy Cooper ran away from her mother, brothers, and an abusive stepfather in Odessa, Texas, and ended up in New York alone and penniless. There, she was befriended by Freddie Barnes, the owner of a gym in East Greenwich Village, and moved into a room above the facility. She worked as the gym's cleaning woman, but after hours Freddie taught her how to box. A Japanese trainer named Soichiro instructed her in martial arts before stuff like *judo* and *karate* were in the public consciousness. It was her first serious boyfriend, a Mafia soldier named Fiorello, who taught her how to use a knife. After Fiorello's murder, she became the Black Stiletto and took it upon herself to fight crime and social injustice in the city. Law enforcement didn't like it. Soon she was wanted by the police and the FBI. Nevertheless, the Stiletto fought social injustice, petty criminals, the Mafia, and Communist spies. She was even responsible for a handful of deaths, but they were truly bad guys and probably deserved what they got. That wasn't for me to judge.

I tried to push those thoughts out of my head when I stepped into the dementia unit's dining room and saw Mom at the table, sitting in a wheelchair. One of the staff was helping her eat. Mom held a fork and lifted bites to her mouth, but it was obvious she forgot what she was doing at times. Some days were better than others. I'd witnessed meals when she couldn't feed herself at all. It was true; her health had declined since Christmas. She was much thinner, the muscle tone in her arms and legs had disappeared, and her skin color was paler.

"Hi, Mom!" I said with as much cheer as I could muster. "Dinnertime?"

Her eyes brightened a little when she saw me. She still knew I was someone she loved, although aside from the "Little Man Martin" incident, she rarely called me by name anymore.

I sat across from her and said, "Guess what, Mom? I've been made a partner in the accounting firm. It's going to be all mine when the boss retires. Isn't that cool?"

Mom attempted to say something while chewing and she swallowed badly. She coughed and the nurse had to pat her back until she recovered.

"Sorry, I didn't mean for you to answer with a mouthful of food," I said.

"Oh, that's all right," the nurse spoke for her. "We're okay, aren't we, Judy?"

Mom nodded as the nurse gave her a drink of water.

Unbelievable. *This* was the Black Stiletto. The world wouldn't know what to make of it. It was why I had to keep her secret safe. It made me want to cry.

And, as if she had switched on that empathy thing she possessed, tears formed in my mom's eyes. In fact, she inexplicably cried more than usual on a daily basis. It was a normal symptom of the stage she was in.

"I talked to Gina a little while ago. She said to send you her love."

At the mention of my daughter's name, Mom managed to smile. "I... me, too," she said. Wow! That was an appropriate response! She always seemed to know who Gina was. Ever since my daughter was born, the two of them had a weird psychic connection I couldn't explain. And Gina was so much like my mother, it was scary.

"Maybe she'll be able to come home from college again soon to see you."

"That's... nice."

Another score! It was a good day for Mom.

I reached over and took her free hand. She squeezed mine and smiled at me again.

As the doc said—one day at a time.

Maggie handed me a glass of red wine that I nearly chugged. It tasted like heaven. After such an emotional day, I felt a little drained.

"Here, have another, Little Man Martin," she said as she poured.

"Thanks. I needed that."

"I know. How are you, darling?"

"Aw, am I your darling?"

"Of course you are. Aren't you?"

"Yes, ma'am. I'm your darling. Just don't call me Little Man Martin." I sat at the table, where she had placed plates of steaming spaghetti and marinara sauce, with broccoli and salad on the side.

"I asked how you're doing."

"I'm okay." I shook my head in admiration. "How is it you can work all day seeing patients, witness me taking some bad news hard, see more patients, and then have dinner on the table when I come home?"

"I try to be Superwoman, Martin, and I thought you handled today very well."

"Really?"

"Yes."

We ate in silence for a while until she said, "I know how hard it is for you."

I had no reply to that, so I just sighed. Then—"Hey, I almost forgot. I have some news. You're looking at the new partner of Wegel, Stern, and Talbot!"

"Oh, Martin, that's fabulous! Congratulations!"

"Thank you, my dear."

"Maybe that means you should move in with me," she remarked.

"You think so?"

"We haven't talked about it in a while."

"Gina said the same thing today." I related how the phone call went. Then I told her about my visit to Woodlands and Mom's verbal responses.

"It's amazing she relates so well to her granddaughter."

"Yeah. I just worry Gina's going to be—like her."

She wagged her finger at me. "Martin, you're not supposed to think about *her*, and I don't mean Gina. You've been doing so well."

"I know. No anxiety for three months. I've stayed away from the diaries. And I appreciate it that you have, too."

She snorted a little. "Frankly, the suspense is killing me. I've been dying to read the fourth and fifth diaries, but I haven't for your sake."

"Now, now. We can't have you knowing more about my mom's story than me."

"I realize that. That's why I've respected your wishes."

Then I said something that surprised me. "Maggie, the truth about my father has to be in those last two books. I'm—I think I might be ready to look at them again."

"Martin—"

I held up my hands. "Come on, we both know we'll have to eventually, right? How can we not? The prospect scares the hell out of me, but at the same time, it's *crazy* that I haven't plowed through all five of those diaries. Any other person would have read them all in one sitting."

"Martin, it's perfectly understandable why it upsets you to read them. Are they still locked up in the safety deposit box?"

"No, they're at my house. I never put them back."

"Well, you should, so you won't be tempted."

I put down my fork and wiped my mouth with the napkin. I took another long gulp of wine and stood.

"Where are you going?"

"Hold on." I went over to where I'd draped my sport jacket over a chair, reached into it, and pulled my Mom's fourth diary out of the inside pocket. I went back to the table and set it in front of Maggie.

"They're all at the house except for this one, which I picked up before coming over. Maggie, I want to read it. I think I'm ready. There are still too many questions, too many—"

"Martin, I don't think it's a good idea."

"I have to face it, Maggie. Come on, you know I do. You want to as well. Right?"

She narrowed her eyes at me and tilted her head. "Are you sure? Should you talk to your psychiatrist first?"

"And tell him what? He doesn't know about the Stiletto. 'Hey Doc, better monitor me more closely because I'm going to read the rest of the Black Stiletto's diaries.' He'll have me committed."

She snickered and shook her head. "I don't think he'd do that."

"Let's do it, Maggie. We'll read it together. We can read it to each other. It'll be romantic."

"Romantic is not the word I'd use, but if you really think you can handle it, then all right."

"Awesome. Shall we start after I wash the dishes?"

"If you wish-es."

That made me laugh. I felt better, grateful that there was someone with whom I could share the bag of secrets my mother had buried so long ago.

I knew the rest of the story would be a very rough ride.

2
Judy's Diary
1961

JANUARY 8, 1961

I've been lazy, dear diary. After New Year's I just didn't feel like writing anything in my new diary until I had something to say. Well, I don't really have anything to say *now*, ha ha, but I thought I'd better put *something* down on paper or I'd get out of the habit.

It's been business as usual at the gym. Despite the cold weather, the guys come in regularly for training and workouts. I expected to see Clark the other day, but he didn't show up. Maybe he's on winter break. I would have thought school was back in session by now, though. Freddie has been grumpy lately, not his normal self. I asked him about it last night at dinner, and he admitted that he wasn't very happy. Ever since his heart attack last year—gosh, it was around this time exactly a year ago!—he's had to cut down on his physical activity, and he doesn't like it. He used to get in the ring and box with the boys, do his own workouts and more training and lessons; but all that ended. Now he sits behind the cash register and watches everyone. No wonder he feels bad. It's like being kicked out of your own club.

For the first time, he also confessed to being lonely. At first I said, "What do you mean, Freddie? I'm here. You've got tons of friends." But he shook his head and said, "I'm talking about a woman, Judy.

I haven't had a *date* in, well, longer than I can remember." I felt embarrassed after that. Of course, he meant his love life. As long as I've known Freddie, he hasn't seen many women. So I asked him about it.

"I was engaged once," he said. "It didn't work out."

"What happened?"

He shrugged.

"You don't have to tell me if you don't want."

"It's okay. It was a long time ago. It was when I was a professional boxer. Her name was Giulietta, spelled the Italian way, with a *G*. She was the daughter of a mobster who had a hand in the boxing business. Back then, the mob ruled boxing. They controlled everything. Still do, a little. You had to play by their rules. Anyway, Giulietta and I were sweet on each other, and her father thought he could use our relationship to maneuver me into some shady deals. I told you that story before, didn't I?"

"You once said they shut you out of your career because you didn't obey them, or something like that."

"Giulietta's father wanted me to throw a fight, and I wouldn't do it. I was blackballed after that. Her father forbade her to see me, and the engagement ended. Basically, I was threatened with my life if I tried to contact her again."

"Gee whiz, Freddie. That's awful."

"So, I guess you could say I'm a little bitter about women."

"It wasn't her fault, Freddie."

"In a way it was. She went along with her daddy and ridiculed me for not playing the game. She turned pretty nasty."

"Well, then, she wasn't the right girl for you. That's plain to see."

He shrugged again. "Maybe so. Anyway, since then I've dated only sporadically. There was one girl named Virginia who I took out for a while. I don't know what happened; it just kind of fizzled out."

"Well, we're going to have to get you fixed up," I said, but Freddie held up his hands.

"Don't you dare, Judy. I mean it. I don't like being 'fixed up.' I hate blind dates, and believe me, I've been on plenty. Besides, I'm damaged goods. I've got a bad heart, I can't do anything strenuous. What good would I be to a woman?"

I knew what he was talking about. "Oh, Freddie. There are ways you can—" I felt myself blushing. "Freddie, talk to your doctor! Plenty of people have had heart attacks and still have a love life."

With that, I got up from the table. I was too flustered to continue the conversation. It was like talking about sex with a father or uncle. Yuck.

In other news, Kennedy and his family will move into the White House soon. President Eisenhower cut off diplomatic relations with Cuba. I wonder if that had anything to do with those Cuban and Russian spies I caught trying to kill Kennedy and Nixon last October? It's so strange there was nothing much in the papers about those characters. Did the government cover up the plot? Why would they do that? Maybe they don't want to give anyone else ideas. I was tempted once to call John Richardson to see if he knew anything about it. But I decided I didn't want to talk to my FBI agent former boyfriend.

And that reminds me—the Black Stiletto hasn't made an appearance in a while. It's cold outside, freezing, in fact. That's never stopped me before, but when that icy wind blows down the avenues, it feels colder than it really is. Everyone here calls it "wind chill." I never heard that term until I came to New York.

Big deal. The Stiletto can take the chill. I feel too cooped up. The sun is down. It's time to hit the streets.

LATER

It's nearly 3:30 in the morning and I'm miserable. I was frozen to the bone, so I took a hot bath and now I'm drinking hot tea. With my luck, I'll probably get sick.

I'm lucky I'm not dead.

Dressed in my outfit, I slipped out my bedroom window, climbed to the roof, and ran across the tops of the buildings on 2nd Street, as I always do. The wind *was* strong and cold. I had the fleeting thought that maybe I should turn around and go back to the warmth of my room, but my stubbornness won that battle.

Down the telephone pole and on the street, I noticed the lack of humanity, and it was only 9:00 or so. Smart people. They weren't stupid enough to be out in the arctic wasteland like the Black Stiletto was. Nevertheless, I went on patrol and ran around the streets more for the exercise and to keep warm rather than to find crimes in progress. I didn't see anything but a few hapless souls all bundled up and hurrying for home. After nearly an hour, I'd had enough. Even though my heavy leather winter outfit blocked the worst effects of the cold wind, I still felt like an icicle. I was near Washington Square Park, so I turned east along 4th Street to head home. As I neared Broadway, I saw three guys outside a furrier's shop. One of them stooped and started working on the steel pull-down grate that covered the entrance. The other two appeared nervous, looking up and down the street. A white van idled directly in front of the storefront. I ducked into an alcove and watched them. I was sure they hadn't seen me; I tend to blend in with the night. Steamy breath issued from their mouths. I heard one of the standing men say, "Hurry!" and the crouching guy reply, "I got it." The three of them raised the grate and then loudly smashed the plate glass window on the ground floor. No alarm went off.

The three men stepped through the broken window. A fourth man sat in the van while his buddies did the dirty work. I emerged from my hiding place, sprinted toward the back of the vehicle, ducked, and slithered along the driver's side. When I was directly below his window, I reached up and opened the door. Boy, was *he* surprised! I grabbed him before he could honk the horn or issue a warning to his friends, and I pulled him out to the street. I then used one of my invented *wushu* maneuvers that was a combination of what I learned in Chinatown and the *karate* I learned from Soichiro. I suppose it was a modified *Mawashi-geri*—roundhouse kick—followed by circular punches. The fellow went down for the count. I left him there and moved around the van to face the building. The burglars had flashlights; the beams jerked here and there in the darkness inside. Otherwise, I couldn't see anything but dark shapes.

Maybe it was because I was cold. Perhaps I was out of practice and just wasn't thinking. It could be because I'm headstrong and impulsive. Whatever the reason, I barged in there without a plan of action. Dumb idea.

My vision is better than most people's, so I got used to the darkness pretty quickly. Only then did I comprehend how crowded it was in the shop. Racks of fur coats were on either side of me, blocking easy access to the sides of the place. "Hey!" one of them shouted. Flashlight beams swung in my direction and temporarily blinded me. My brain should have registered that there weren't only two. The duo was directly in front of me, but I didn't realize the third guy was off to the side, out of sight. I rushed toward the brightness as one burglar shouted, "The Black Stiletto!" Feeling cocky, I blurted, "No applause, please!" as I slammed into him and knocked him over. Not very elegant, but it worked. He dropped the flashlight and it skittered across the floor. I turned my attention to the other beam of light and struck the dark oval shape above it with my fist. The man yelped in pain as my knuckles crushed the cartilage in his nose. He, too, dropped his torch and curled up, holding his face. A swift kick to his chin sent him to Dreamsville. By then, the first guy had gotten to his feet, but he ran past me toward the broken window. I turned to chase him, but—*bam!* A gun fired from behind the rack of coats to my right. That third guy I'd forgotten about was back there. I swear I felt that hot bullet zip a mere inch or two from my face. My survival instinct kick-started like a motorcycle, and rather than attempt any kind of offensive maneuver, I had to save my life first. I fell to the floor and stretched as low as I could, figuring he'd either come out to see if he'd killed me or he'd run for the van.

He did the latter—and before I could get up and follow him, the burglar turned and fired another shot into the shop, cutting a parallel line only a few feet above the floor where I'd flattened myself. Then he jumped into the passenger seat of the van. The other one that had run out of the store got in the driver's seat, and off they went, the tires screeching loud enough to wake the neighborhood. They'd left me with two unconscious gang mates, one inside the fur store and the other guy on the street.

Sirens pierced the frigid night.

I absolutely did not want to be caught, since the NYPD has standing orders to arrest me. They'd probably shoot me on sight instead. There *are* some good guys wearing the blue uniform; I know, because I've encountered some of them. But a majority of the police force believes I'm a criminal. They call me a *vigilante* in the press, and I guess in the minds of the cops that's a sin. But if what I'm doing works to some degree, why can't they accept it? I'm on *their* side, for Pete's sake.

Even so, the sirens' shrieks grew louder. There was nothing to do but get the heck out of there. I got to my feet and prepared to leap out of the broken storefront window, when I saw that a patrol car—lights flashing—shot past me in pursuit of the van. A few lights popped on in the windows of the buildings across the street, but there were no other cars. All clear.

I stepped outside and stood over the man I'd pulled from the driver's seat. He was groaning, starting to come to. As the cops' siren receded from me, I became aware of a different one growing louder. Backup was about to turn the corner at the west end of the street. I started to run—and the guy on the ground grabbed my leg! He was *strong*, too!

The patrol car rounded the corner, blazing a bright red and blue and white. I felt like a deer caught in the headlights. I was practically in the middle of the street and was held there by a fur burglar. That sounds funny, but it wasn't at the time.

I kicked and struggled, but that man held onto my leg for dear life. Wasting too many seconds trying to pull away from him, I

finally did a little leap with the one leg that was on solid ground—
and while I was a foot or two off the ground, I kicked the guy in the
head.

He let go of my leg.

I darted across the street and ran east on the sidewalk. I sensed
the police car slow and finally stop in front of the storefront, its headlights illuminating my leg-grabbing friend. Was I safe? No, for even
more sirens blared, this time ahead of me. But 4th Street is one way
going in my direction; I was pretty sure I could make the intersection
before the new cars arrived.

To my surprise, a patrol car turned onto 4th from Broadway,
heading the wrong way straight toward me. I was trapped between
Broadway and Mercer, with policemen at both ends. So I ducked
into the nearest dark doorway and pressed myself small into the alcove. The patrol car *stopped* before it went by. My heart nearly
stopped, dear diary. I thought they'd seen me. As much as I hated it,
I knew I'd have to fight my way out of the situation.

I expected cops to appear on the street in front of me at any moment. But it didn't happen. *Nothing* happened. I stood there in the
shadows for several minutes. Finally, I dared to inch forward and
find out what was going on. The police car to my east was just sitting
there, its colorful lights going round and round. To my west were
more cops pouring over the crime scene. Unless the guys to my east
got out of their car and joined their team at the shop, I'd have to stay
where I was.

And it was really, really cold.

That's what happened, dear diary. The cops never got out of the
car or moved it until the other policemen finished their job at the
store. I guess they were told to watch the street.

It took *hours*. I suffered. I really did! It was so darned cold. I sat
there in that wet, frigid doorway until 2:38 a.m.

The two burglars I'd pounded were eventually taken away. I
kept my fingers crossed that the cops would call it a night and not

bother with searching the rest of the street. Thank goodness, they just left. Maybe the two under arrest told them that the gang's other half made off in the van. I wonder if they got caught.

I was frozen stiff. It hurt to make my way home. I was afraid I'd gotten frostbite on my lower face, the part that's not covered by the leather mask. All my energy was depleted, and it was a huge effort to climb the telephone pole and trek across the roofs to the gym. Once I was in my room, I looked in the mirror and saw that my lips were *blue*. That scared me, so I took a hot bath and soaked for a half hour. I laid a warm, wet washrag over my mouth and nose, and after a while, my face looked normal again. Then I made some hot tea, and here I am.

Now I can barely keep my eyes open.

3
Judy's Diary
1961

JANUARY 10, 1961

I've got a bad cold and a fever.

It's no wonder, after what I went through the other night. I got so cold and wet, and for such a long period of time, too. And what did it accomplish? Well, no big fat thanks to the Black Stiletto. A lot of good it did me, stopping that robbery. Besides, I was only half successful, and it got me sick as a dog in the process. There was nothing in the papers about me. The *Daily News* said the two burglars arrested in front of and inside the fur store had been left behind by their own gang members, who had gotten away. Surely, the two guys told the police the Black Stiletto was there. I bet the cops withheld that information on purpose just to spite me.

I feel so crummy. I went to see Dr. Goldstein today. He said I had an ear infection, something I don't think I've had since I was a kid in Odessa. He gave me some medicine, and then I thought about something Lucy and I had discussed recently.

It was a little embarrassing, but I didn't know of any other way to bring it up but to just ask. "I've heard there's going to be some kind of birth control pill?"

Dr. Goldstein shot me a look a parent might give. He must have thought—*What? A nice girl like Judy Cooper?* He went back to his note writing and said that it was approved, but only for married women. I felt like he was disappointed in me somehow. Well, I'm not his daughter. As for this new pill they're talking about, I don't know if I'd take it. Gosh, the way my love life is going these days, there's no *need*, ha ha.

I suppose some people would think I'm a slut for even thinking about it. Why would any unmarried girl want to take the pill unless she's easy? That's the mainstream viewpoint, but it seems to me there's a kind of underground position, especially among women, that it's really okay for us to like sex as much as men do. We should have more choices in what we, as women, do with our bodies, such as whether to have kids or not. There's a growing sentiment that it should be legal for women to safely have abortions. I don't know what I think about that, but I do admire there is something happening in this country with regard to equal rights, whether they're for women or Negroes or whomever.

After the doctor appointment, I went home, took my medicine, and went to bed. Got up a little while ago to have some chicken soup Freddie brought in from the East Side Diner. He's a great nurse.

Now I'm going back to bed.

JANUARY 15, 1961

I'm feeling better. I stayed in the last two days and did nothing but watch TV. On Friday nights it's always a toss-up between *Route 66* and *77 Sunset Strip*, followed, of course, by *The Twilight Zone*. Seems like Saturday nights are filled with westerns—*Bonanza*, *Have Gun-Will Travel*, and *Gunsmoke*. That's okay, I like westerns all right. I went to work yesterday and today. I still have a congested nose and my hearing is a little muffled, but my strength is coming back. I'm taking it easy, though. I do training for my individual clients, but then sit with Freddie the rest of the time.

Yesterday, Clark, the Negro teenager I train, got into a rumble with a white boy who's new to the gym. His name is Kraig, and he's a little older and a little bigger than Clark. Maybe he's eighteen or nineteen. Anyway, I saw Kraig shove Clark as they were coming out of the locker room. Clark turned to Kraig and pushed him back. Kraig suddenly walloped Clark with a right hook that knocked the teenager down.

"Hey!" I shouted, and then I went over there. All the other guys stopped what they were doing and stared for a second; then they went about their business as I confronted Kraig.

"What's the idea?"

"Nothing," Kraig said. "It was an accident."

"No it wasn't, I saw the whole thing." Clark got to his feet as he rubbed his jaw. "You all right?"

Clark nodded. "Yeah."

Kraig tried to move away. "Hey, I'm talking to you." He stopped, but I could tell by his expression that he didn't put much stock into taking orders from a girl.

"Yeah?"

"The only fighting allowed in here is the kind in the ring, with gloves."

"Okay."

I wanted to say more, but then he *did* walk away. I turned to Clark. "What was that all about?"

"He lives near me. He's one of the guys I've had trouble with all this time. He's one of the reasons I started coming here."

"Well, he's nothing but a big bully," I said. "Ignore him."

"I can't. Him and his friends hang out on the street corner I have to pass every time I want to go somewhere. I live on Avenue C. I'm forced to go around the block the long way to avoid them."

"That's what you've been doing?"

"Yeah."

"Then they've already won, Clark. You shouldn't have to do that in your own neighborhood."

"I don't think they like Negroes much in my neighborhood, Judy. We're thinking of moving up to Harlem."

Clark was a trooper, he went out on the floor, avoided Kraig, and did his training anyway. I know his jaw hurt, but he wasn't about to show it. As for Kraig, he just glared at me a lot, every now and then grinned like the Cheshire Cat.

Guys like him make me grind my teeth.

JANUARY 16, 1961

I got together with Lucy and Peter tonight. We went to see *Exodus* starring Paul Newman. It was long and kind of dull, but both Lucy and I think Paul Newman is quite the man. I *love* his blue eyes. "Quite the man." Lucy and I have started saying that lately as a running joke. "Well, he's *quite the man*, isn't he?" "I'd say *he's* quite the man!" We sound like a couple of schoolgirls. Speaking of men, I asked Lucy about what she does to keep from getting pregnant. I think I'm frighteningly naïve about such things. She told me about the diaphragm, and that most women use one of those. Lucy said I should get one before next month and I asked why.

"Silly, maybe you'll meet Paul Newman," Lucy said. I looked at her like she was nuts, and then she reminded me about the trip to Los Angeles they had planned for February. I'd forgotten about it! She wants me to come along so she'll have someone to play with while Peter works. He's got some kind of business conference there. They've offered to buy my plane ticket and hotel room. I told her I'd have to make sure with Freddie. I'll talk to him in the morning.

Disneyland! Hollywood! Oh, that's going to be exciting!

JANUARY 17, 1961

This morning Freddie said I could go in February. Yahoo! I called Lucy and told her the news, so Peter's going to make the reservations. I told her I'd pay my way, but they won't hear of it. That's so sweet of them.

"Will I meet Paul Newman?" I asked Lucy.

"Well, I wouldn't get your hopes up," she said, laughing. "Besides, he's married to Joanne Woodward."

"So maybe I'll meet someone else."

"I hope you do, Judy," she said.

Who knows, dear diary, I might meet *quite the man*. I hear they have *some* men in Southern California. Some muscular and tan beach guy who surfs, perhaps?

Gosh, I'm going to need a swimsuit!

4
Leo
THE PAST

I ordered my third vodka martini just as Bobby Darin took the stage. Phyllis, the long-legged redhead I picked up at the bar an hour ago, was already on her fourth. I'd seen her around the club. The word was that she was an open-minded girl if you got her drunk. That wasn't too difficult. The problem was I didn't know what I was going to do with her when Mookie arrived. I glanced at my watch and saw that he was a half hour late. Too bad, he was missing a great show. That Bobby Darin has some pipes. He started right in with "Splish Splash," and the crowd in Flickers went nuts. I guessed he'd save "Mack the Knife" for last. That's what I wanted to hear. I hoped Phyllis didn't pass out on me before then.

My uncle appeared to be enjoying the show, too. He was lucky to get Darin and book him at the last minute. Darin's so popular now that a club like Flickers might not be on his radar, but Charlie had done pretty well for himself. I'm proud of him. I always looked up to Charlie. When he opened Flickers right off of Sunset Boulevard, I knew he'd be a success. Now he hobnobbed with Hollywood royalty and singers like Darin and Jerry Vale and Ricky Nelson. Dean Martin sang at Flickers once. If only Charlie could get Sinatra, he'd establish Flickers as *the* Hollywood hot spot. Maybe it already was. Seemed like it.

It's helped me, too, I had to admit.

Whenever I came to Flickers, everyone treated me like one of those celebrities. Not only did the entire staff know me by name, I could go anywhere in the joint. I was part of the family. To tell the truth, though, I didn't make it a regular thing to come to Flickers because Charlie never let me pay for my own drinks. I tried and he wouldn't let me. When I did show up, I liked to dress nice, in a suit. Sometimes I get filthy at some of the warehouses, so I like to clean up when I go out. The chicks like me better that way, too. Charlie always said I was the handsome one of the family, but I didn't think that was true. Christina held that position, and by that I meant *she*'s the one who got the looks.

Phyllis gave me the droopy-eyed gaze and showed me her empty glass. "Hey, Larry," she slurred, "how about another one?"

I took the glass from her. "The name's Leo, not Larry. And I think you've had enough for now, darling. I don't want you counting sheep before we skip this joint and find someplace more comfortable to get to know each other."

She wrinkled her brow. "Counting what? Why would I want to count sheep?"

"Never mind." Suddenly she wasn't as attractive as she'd been an hour ago. Maybe I could pawn her off on one of Sal's guys. I could see them occupying their usual two tables, close to the stage but against the wall, near an exit. Salvatore Casazza liked to be able to leave in a hurry if he had to. He sat there, all three hundred pounds of him, with his signature black cigar and pin-striped suit. Once I suggested he should lose some weight, and I thought he was going to have me whacked. We get along okay, though. He was a good friend to have in this town.

Next to him was some broad I'd seen him with before, Rachel or Ronni or Rosie or something like that. Dark hair, great figure, kind of looks like Liz Taylor. His two goons, Mario and Shrimp, sat at the adjacent table, ready to put the muscle on anyone who might want to approach Casazza. I think I could take them both. On the other side, at a different table, sat two new guys in his crew. Paul

Faretti and Mike Capri had come down from Vegas to help with Casazza's gunrunning operations. They weren't very friendly. Maybe I just have to get to know them. Or maybe I could take *them* both, too.

They knew I was at the club to meet Mookie Samberg. The Jewish counterfeiter came highly recommended from Sal's contacts in New York. Me, I would have preferred we hired someone I knew. But Casazza said the word came down from Vegas that we needed to talk to Samberg first. If his price was agreeable, then that's who DeAngelo wanted. And whatever Vincent DeAngelo wanted, Vincent DeAngelo got. Hell, pretty soon he was going to own all of Las Vegas, the way he was going. Even Casazza, the L.A. boss, was small fry to DeAngelo.

Everybody worked for DeAngelo.

What I wouldn't give to have his job. Jesus, what a life. The guy was richer than sin, he owned one of the big casinos in Vegas, he lived on a ranch on the outskirts of the city, and his crew would do anything for him. I understand Sinatra sang at one of his parties. His daughter, Maria, was a spicy little number, too. Blonde, brown-eyed, delicious figure. A bit spoiled for my liking, but I wouldn't mind a roll in the hay with her. I could tell she liked me, so I might have to consider getting to know her better. Getting in good with DeAngelo couldn't hurt my career, either. My pop and him were pals and business associates. I grew up knowing the DeAngelo family.

"How about that drink, Larry?" Phyllis slurred in my ear just as Darin launched into "Beachcomber," one of my favorites. I almost smacked her, but instead I gave her the old Kelly charm smile and said, "My name is *Leo*, baby, and if you call me Larry again, I'm going to have Charlie show you the door. Shut up and listen to the music, okay? As soon as I meet with this guy, we'll leave and go have ourselves a good time. Okay?"

Phyllis looked surprised. "You know Charlie?"

"He's my uncle, darling."

"Charlie Kelly is your uncle?"

I held my hand out to her for the second time that night. "Leo Kelly, ma'am, glad to meet you." She dumbly shook hands with me and grinned.

"I didn't know you knew Charlie!"

That did it. As good looking as Phyllis was, she was starting to annoy me. I looked around the room, caught my uncle's eye, and jerked my head. He came to my rescue. Phyllis beamed at him and said, way too loudly for Bobby Darin's comfort, "Hi, Charlie! Remember me?"

"Uncle Charlie, could you ask Boone to take Phyllis home? She needs to leave right away, she has an appointment." I shot him a look that he interpreted correctly. He was to *get rid of her*. My driver would know what to do. "Tell Boone to come right back."

"Sure, Leo." He held out his arm for her. "Come with me, dear, I'll take good care of you."

"What? Where are we going? I don't need to go home."

He got her to stand and escorted her toward the bar. I looked over at the Casazza boys, and they were all laughing, even Rachel or Ronni or Rosie. I rolled my eyes at them and pretended to wipe the sweat from my forehead. *Close call*, I mimed. And at that moment I saw Mookie Samberg enter the club. Looking at Casazza, I jerked my head at the Jew. Sal subtly gave me a nod. I half rose in my seat and waved at the guy. Samberg saw me and headed toward my table.

Mookie Samberg was in his fifties and had worked for one of the New York families for a long time. As I said, he came highly recommended, and DeAngelo knew his work. Supposedly he was the best counterfeit artist in the world. He engraved plates that made very convincing bills, but he was also known to be a pain in the ass. And expensive, too.

"Leo, how are you doing?" he said in my ear, over the music, as we shook hands.

"Good, Mookie, have a seat. What can I get you to drink?"

"Club soda and lime, please, thank you."

I thought that was odd, but I got Melinda's attention; she came over and took my order. Samberg's eyes went up and down her figure and then raised his eyebrows when she walked away. I didn't blame him. Melinda and I had a thing a few months back.

"Nice waitresses you got here," he said.

"You bet. Flickers is top shelf. Melinda's a honey. She might even go out with you if you're nice."

"Maybe you can put in a good word for me, huh, Leo?"

"Sure, Mookie. Sit back and enjoy the show."

Darin really worked the crowd. Women in the audience were ready to throw themselves at him. If I could sing, I knew that's what would happen to me, too. A lot of 'em tell me I look like that guy in *Cat on a Hot Tin Roof*.

As expected, Darin ended the set with "Mack the Knife." The crowd went crazy. Mookie and I stood and applauded with everyone else. Great song.

We got down to business after the music was finished. I explained to Samberg that I ran a warehouse business in Los Angeles, and I did import, export, and storage work for Casazza, and, in turn, DeAngelo.

"I get it," Samberg said. "You're a smuggler."

That raised my hackles a little. "That's not very polite, Mookie. The word doesn't describe what I do at all."

"Sorry, Leo. Go on."

I said I'd be supplying Samberg with the space, equipment, and personnel he would need to make the counterfeit dough. I needed exact specifications of what he wanted and how much his fee would be. Samberg nodded, took a pen and small pad of paper out of his jacket pocket, and wrote down a figure. He then tore off the sheet and slid it across the table. I glanced at it and nearly choked, but I kept my poker face. No one I knew wanted to play poker with me— I was that good.

"I'll see what the boss has to say, Mookie. In the meantime, get me that list."

"You'll have it tomorrow. When do I get to meet DeAngelo?"

"You don't get to meet DeAngelo."

"What about Casazza?"

"That's possible." I didn't let on that Sal was right there in the club.

"Well, tell him the hundred dollar bills I'll make will be so perfect they'll pass anywhere. The plates will be beautiful. What do you do with the funny money you make now?"

"We sell it to the Mexicans. The bills pass all right down there, but they don't fly in the U.S."

"That's what I'm talking about, Leo. I guarantee you'll be able to pass my stuff here."

Out of the corner of my eye, I saw Christina enter the club, looking fabulous as usual. She went over to Charlie and gave her uncle a kiss on the cheek.

I held out my hand. "I'll speak to you tomorrow, then? We get the list, we talk, we figure out how much all this is going to cost, and we'll come to a decision."

He clasped my hand and said, "Don't take too long. Chicago is interested in hiring me, too."

After he got up and left, I stood and went over to Casazza. Sal told Rachel or Ronni or Rosie to go powder her nose for a minute, and she obediently vanished. Sal relit his cigar and said, "Well?" I showed him the piece of paper with the figure on it. Casazza grunted and said, "I'll have to take it up with Vince."

"I figured."

"What else does he need?"

"I'll get the list tomorrow."

Casazza nodded and then lightly slapped my cheek. "You done good, Leo." I hated it when he did that. "If this operation turns out to be a good earner, Vince will be very pleased. Your father, may he rest in peace, would be very proud. You set this up, Leo. Vincent won't forget that."

All I could say was, "Thanks."

"Your pop and me, and your pop and Vince, we go back a long way."

"Yeah, I know."

Then he dismissed me. "Speak to you later." I looked over at Shrimp and Mario, who nodded at me. Then I turned my head to Faretti and Capri. They had sneers on their faces, as if I was something they'd stepped in. I decided then and there I didn't like those guys. I wanted to break their noses. Uncle Charlie would have to clean their blood off the nice tablecloths.

I got up and found Christina at the bar. "How was your meeting?" she asked.

"Good. How was the range?"

"Fantastic. I beat my score. That semiautomatic you gave me for my birthday is becoming my weapon of choice."

She was talking about a Smith & Wesson model 39 I bought her. I think it was the seventh gun she owned. I've never known a girl who liked guns so much as my crazy sister. She was one tough cookie, too. That's not a surprise, since she did twelve months' time on an armed robbery rap. If it hadn't been for DeAngelo's lawyers, she'd have been slapped with fifteen years. That's the good thing about the friendship our father had with DeAngelo. The two were like brothers. They knew each other since they were kids. Ever since Mom and Pop died, DeAngelo had kind of looked out for us kids, and we looked out for each other. I still looked out for Christina. We shared a house in Hollywood and she had a job at Pop's company—now mine—in the Wholesale District. I owed her, and I always would. When she was popped, Christina didn't give up the names of her fellow armed robbers. She knew the score. That's why I loved her. As she was four years my junior, she would always be my baby sister, no matter what.

"I'm surprised you don't have some starlet on your arm, Casanova," Christina said. "What's the matter? You slipping?"

I laughed. "I had business, doll." I surveyed the bar and saw a shapely brunette finishing a glass of something. "But watch this." I went over to the woman and offered to refill her drink. She smiled and her eyes grew wide. I had to tell her I wasn't that actor, but I hoped she'd still allow me to buy her a beverage. She accepted. Her name was Carolee. I sat on the stool beside her and ordered two martinis. Then I looked back at my sister, who smirked, shook her head, and turned to chat to Gary, one of the bartenders.

Christina was used to staying on her side of the house at night.

5
Judy's Diary
1961

JANUARY 18, 1961

I'm feeling much better and am back to full strength, I think. It's still cold outside, but not as bad as it was. That freezing wind finally died down, so maybe I'll try going out again as the Stiletto in a day or two. Or maybe not.

When I went into the kitchen for breakfast this morning, Freddie showed me the newspaper. The police commissioner announced that a task force was formed to "catch the Black Stiletto." More police officers will patrol the streets, not only because crime is rising, but also to keep an eye out for the "vigilante." Squads are being trained to use "quick response and trap strategies" to catch me.

"I just don't understand it, Freddie," I said. "Why do they hate me so much?"

"You should know the answer to that by now, Judy," he replied with a sigh. "A: it's against the law to be a vigilante. B: you make them look bad."

"But I get results. Usually. You'd think they'd want me around. If Superman or Batman were real, they'd be welcome in the city."

"Real life isn't a comic book." He put the paper down. "Judy, it's going to get more dangerous for you out there. I worry about you."

"I can take care of myself, Freddie."

"You can't ward off a bullet. Or if you're captured alive and unmasked, you'll go to some women's prison. There's no telling how many other crimes they'd try to pin on you."

I tried to make light of the conversation. "You know any good lawyers?"

"It's not funny, Judy. I'm serious. Maybe it's time you should start thinking about retiring the Black Stiletto. It's just not worth it."

"It is for me, you know that. I don't know what I'd do without the Stiletto."

"You'd be Judy Cooper. You'd find a nice man. Settle down. Live a normal life."

"Are you kidding me, Freddie? You really think *I* could live a 'normal' life? After what I've done? The Stiletto is a part of me. It'd be like cutting off an arm."

He shook his head. "I just worry about you, Judy. If something happened to you—"

I placed a hand on his arm. "Try not to worry. I'll be okay."

"Don't you think someday someone will find out your secret? What will you do?"

I didn't tell him that's already happened. John Richardson knows who I am, and thankfully he has respected my privacy. "Freddie, I'd find a way to deal with it."

"But what about the people close to you, Judy? How will it affect them? Lucy? *Me*? Have you thought about that? They could arrest me for aiding and abetting a criminal."

"Look, I know I can't do this forever, Freddie. Times are changing. This newspaper article is proof of that. Maybe I'll be forced into retirement. It's possible. And I promise you, if and when I make the decision to retire, I will bury the Black Stiletto. She'll be a secret I carry to my grave. And I'll do everything in my power to protect you."

Freddie just made a grunting noise and sipped his coffee. I guess the conversation was over at that point. I made some scrambled eggs and we sat at the table in silence. Finally, when I was done, I said I was going downstairs to the gym to exercise before we opened for the day. I kissed him on the cheek and told him I loved him.

He didn't reciprocate.

JANUARY 20, 1961

John F. Kennedy is now our president! It's so gratifying that he and Jackie are now in the White House. After all the work I did last year on his campaign, it feels really good. I know he's going to be a great president. There's so much bad stuff happening in the world. The Communists want to take over. Everyone is afraid of nuclear bombs. I heard one guy in the gym saying how it was nothing compared to what we faced during World War II. That's probably true. My father was killed in the Battle of Midway. The threat of Germany and Japan was worse than what we have now, although there were no atomic bombs then. I guess that's the crux of the matter. Would someone be mad enough to push the button?

Oh, my gosh, they're playing a new Elvis record on the radio! It's *fantastic*! The song is called "Surrender." The DJ said the melody is the same one as Dean Martin's "Come Back to Sorrento," and I thought it sounded familiar, but Elvis changed the lyrics and it's more up-tempo. It'll be in the stores in a couple of weeks!

That just put me in a good mood. Good enough to go out. Talk to you later, dear diary!

LATER

It's taken me thirty minutes for me to catch my breath after barely making it home. The newspaper was right. There are a lot more cops on the streets. They're *everywhere*.

The night started off all right. I didn't see any policemen until I got to Washington Square Park around 10:00. There were so many! It was a regular cop convention, I counted at least ten. I avoided the spot, moved uptown, and put a lot of distance between me and the park. Maybe I should have taken that as a warning to give up and go home, but I kept going and got up into the 20s. I headed west; I don't know why. It's not too often that I have a plan when I go out as the Stiletto. Usually I just wander, and that's what I did tonight.

It was around 7th Avenue and 22nd Street that a patrolman spotted me. I was running along the street as I normally do, and suddenly, there he was on the corner. We practically bumped into each other. He shouted for me to halt. I called back to him, "No time, sorry!" and kept going, darting out into traffic. Horns honked. A cab almost hit me. The cop blew his whistle. There was no question that he'd call for a patrol car, so I didn't let a few moving vehicles stop me. I successfully made it across 7th and ran like the dickens to 8th Avenue, and then shot uptown.

Figuring I'd eluded the patrolman, I slowed to my normal sprinting pace. It's always the same when I run through the city. Pedestrians see me, point, and gawk. Every now and then a woman screams, but I certainly don't mean to scare anyone. Sometimes a man will do a wolf whistle. "Look, there's the Black Stiletto!" "Hey, Stiletto, want to go on a date?" I often get applause and cheers, and just as frequently attract boos and am called nasty names. I'm used to it, but this time, though, it really bothered me. Some guy yelled something I can't write down, dear diary, and it made me feel—*exposed*. That's the only way I can describe it.

A sense of great danger had crept up on me since I'd passed the policeman, and I suspected the cops were on my tail. Sure enough, a siren started blaring behind me. Turning, I saw the red-and-blue lights several blocks down 8th Ave. I had run up to 30th Street, so I hooked a right and sprinted into the shadows. A brownstone's stoop provided enough cover for me as I squatted and waited for the cop car to pass on by the intersection of 30th and 8th. The siren pierced my eardrums as the vehicle continued uptown. It didn't turn toward me. For a moment, I thought maybe they weren't chasing me after all and were on their way to another crime scene. Nevertheless, I waited a minute, caught my breath, and then continued east on 30th. So far, I'd spent the entire night running from the police. And it wasn't over. As soon as I got to 7th Avenue, more patrol cars shot through the intersection, heading south. Were they looking for me? I froze on the corner amidst a few pedestrians. The last patrol car drove past me, but the officer in the passenger seat looked directly at me and we locked eyes. The driver slammed on the brakes; the wheels screeched horribly as the siren and lights kicked on.

There were three options. I could dash across 7th Avenue into heavier traffic and maybe get killed by a speeding taxicab. Or I could run north on 7th, but I'd have to run past the cops. If I went south on 7th, they'd be in pursuit right behind me. The best alternative was to reverse my tracks on 30th and head west, so that's what I did. Within seconds, I heard the two cops shout at me to stop, and then they gave chase. I knew I could outrun them, but one of the guys was some kind of track star; he gained on me surprisingly fast. With only twenty feet or so separating us, I approached the intersection of 30th and 8th—and three cops appeared, guns drawn.

They had me hemmed in. It was the exact same thing that happened to me the night I'd caught my cold. Only this time I wasn't able to duck into a dark doorway and hide. They had already seen me.

Dear diary, my first thought was—*I wasn't having fun anymore*.

Throughout the three years of the Black Stiletto's so-called career, it was always an invigorating, liberating sensation to step out on the streets in my outfit and take the city by storm. Tonight, though, I felt like a mouse in one of those laboratory mazes. And instead of a piece of cheese at the end of the tunnel, there was a hungry cat.

Flashlight beams from both ends of the street jumped around, trying to put the bull's-eye on me. I darted back and forth across 30th and then headed east toward 7th again. There were only two patrolmen chasing me from that direction, whereas there were three in the other. I took the path of least resistance. But this was also the path occupied by that really fast runner, the cop who thought he was doing the 100-yard dash for a medal.

Looking back on what happened, all I can say is that there was no other way, dear diary. It was either do what I did or get caught.

I attacked the policeman. He was just catching up to me, running like a bull, and I reacted spontaneously and instinctively, like a wild animal. Right after it happened, I regretted it and felt really bad. But honestly, *I had no choice.*

The cops bearing flashlights couldn't keep them trained on me, so all they got were glimpses of me running through them, back and forth. The guy running toward me, though, didn't have one. I could see him, but he couldn't see me. My eyesight is better in the dark than most people's. So I charged and body blocked him, probably harder than I meant to. He *flew* as he emitted a loud, "Ooompf!" The cop crashed into the adjacent stoop, hitting the stone steps with a horrifying crack. Then he laid there motionless. Like a rag doll. I should have stayed to see if he was okay, but I didn't. I kept running east. The other cop had a light, but he hadn't caught me in it. I ran right past him on the opposite side of the street. When I got to the corner, I sped across 7th and kept going until I arrived in the East Village.

Now I'm concerned about the policeman. I really do hope he's okay, but oh my God, I think I killed him.

JANUARY 21, 1961

The story was in all the newspapers. BLACK STILETTO AS-SAULTS COP! My heart nearly stopped when I saw the headline. I read what it said and found out the patrolman was in the hospital. His injuries weren't revealed, but he was expected to recover. I was relieved, but still sorry that I had to do it. I wish I could apologize to him somehow. What really disturbed me was the venom directed at the Black Stiletto. She was being portrayed as a violent, dangerous criminal. The police commissioner pledged that catching the Black Stiletto was the NYPD's number-one priority.

Freddie could tell I was upset all day, but he didn't say anything. I'm afraid he thinks it's true—that the Black Stiletto *did* maliciously attack that cop—and I'm afraid he's right.

I'll have to talk to him, if he'll listen.

6
Martin
THE PRESENT

I started the fourth diary and took a look at the trinkets that Mom had left in that strongbox Uncle Thomas gave me. I knew what the roll of film was. The Kennedy campaign button made sense. There were two more items the diaries hadn't mentioned yet. One was a silver heart-shaped locket, the other a small gold key. I examined the locket again. There were three diamonds on it—one each on the two rounded tops of the heart, and the third down at the point. Inside the locket was space for a small photograph, but it was empty.

Another mystery.

I was as curious as ever to talk to Uncle Thomas again. I'd never pressed him for answers before, so I decided it was time for him to come clean. Foremost on my mind was what arrangements, if any, my mother had made regarding her funeral. That was a morbid subject and no one really liked to talk about it, especially when the person was still alive, but it's something we all needed to address, right? People who had the means and wherewithal to do so usually take care of their own arrangements before death so their children won't be burdened with the unpleasant task. Uncle Thomas had told me sometime after Mom had gone into Woodlands that I wasn't to worry about her financially. We basically had to get rid of all her assets so that Medicaid would pay for the nursing home stay. At the time she was basically broke anyway, living off the fumes of an empty gas tank, and I didn't realize it. I was too caught up in my own world to notice.

Thomas Avery's office was in Arlington Heights, not far from our old house. A new real estate firm was handling the sale of the house, and I recently decided to put a little of my newfound salary into sprucing it up so we could sell it. It's been on the market for a couple of years, but we never had any luck getting rid of the place because it was in such disrepair. I suppose it was a good thing it didn't sell right off the bat, otherwise Mom's Black Stiletto stuff would still be hidden in that secret room in the basement. I would never have retrieved it, and the new owners would be living with one of the world's most valuable treasures right under their noses.

I grew up in that house, went to high school in Arlington Heights, and then left for college. It was weird—I'd taken it for granted that Mom had money, because she always did. At least she got by, she was able to feed us, put clothes on our backs, and pay for my college tuition. She never worked. When I once asked her about it, she said we lived off a big inheritance that my father left. I never questioned it. I was a dummy, probably too absorbed in my precious existence that I was oblivious that anything could be, well, not *normal* about our family.

We moved into the house in 1970, when I was seven. I remember being relatively new to the neighborhood when I started first grade. Prior to that, we lived in an apartment in Arlington Heights for a year or two—going backward from there was where it started to get hazy for me. I had vague memories of being in the car a lot, staying in hotel rooms, living in a couple of different apartments for short durations, but I couldn't say where we were.

Uncle Thomas's secretary, Janie, greeted me warmly when I entered the office. She was nearly as old as her boss, so I've known her a long time, too. Janie really was on top of things at his office; it was like *she* ran *his* life. Thomas and my mom were pretty close, and I've always suspected they dated at one time. But since then, did Thomas and Janie ever have a thing? Uncle Thomas was once married to a woman named Martha, but she died a few years ago.

"How's that lovely daughter of yours doing?" Janie asked.

"When I *hear* from her, it sounds like she's doing great."

Janie laughed. "Don't take it personally, Martin. When kids go away to college, they want to spread their wings and fly. Some cling to their parents and are afraid to let go, but others become *very* independent."

"Oh, I know. She's definitely changing, she's—"

"Growing up?"

"I guess that's what you call it."

Uncle Thomas opened his private office door. "I thought I heard your voice, Martin. Come on in. How are you?"

He was dressed in his usual garb—white shirt and loosened tie, trousers with suspenders, and tennis shoes. Still had a head of wavy white hair, a bushy white mustache, and glasses. My mom's attorney and friend.

"I'm fine, Uncle Thomas," I said as we shook hands. "You look dandy."

"I don't feel dandy. My back is acting up again."

"Oh, I'm sorry."

He waved a hand to dismiss any pity. "Come on in. Can I get you anything?"

I declined and followed him into the little office where nearly a year ago he had handed me the biggest surprise of my life. When I closed the door myself, Thomas raised his eyebrow at me. It was going to be one of *those* kinds of talks.

"What can I do for you, Martin?" he asked as I sat in front of his desk. He moved to his own chair and lowered himself slowly into it, wincing as he went.

"Have you seen a doctor?" I asked.

"Yeah. I get these every once in a while, I'm just getting old."

"Maybe you're working too hard. Aren't you ever going to retire?"

"I'll retire on the day I die, Martin. I can't stand to do nothing." He indicated the piles of folders and paperwork. "Look at this, Martin. It's more work than I can handle. I'm a very lucky lawyer at my age. Now what can I do for you? You look concerned. How's your mother?"

I told him the results of Mom's medical evaluation, and Thomas nodded grimly. "I was wondering when it would come to this point," he said. He seemed truly broken up about the news and went into a spell of private grief.

"Uncle Thomas," I began, as gently as I could, "I came to ask you about any arrangements that might have been made. You know, for her funeral."

He snapped out of it and nodded. "Yes, Martin, she took care of all that. Once she realized she had Alzheimer's, she made all the arrangements with me. She paid for a funeral for herself. It was part of the process of eliminating her assets. You don't have to worry about it."

I nodded and then just gazed at him.

"What?" he asked.

"I think you know a lot more about my mom than you've admitted to me."

My statement surprised him. His eyes blinked rapidly for a second. When he didn't say anything, I continued. "I've never really asked you about it, Uncle Thomas. Last time you said you didn't know what was in that envelope and strongbox. But I have a feeling you really did know. You've been the only person I'm *aware of* that Mom trusted and was close to, and I've never ever talked to you about it. So tell me, Uncle Thomas, did you know what was in that stuff last year?"

He averted his eyes and stared at the desk for a long time. His silence was my answer. Then he said, "Martin, your mother made me promise not to let on that I knew her story until after she was gone."

"So you know—everything?"

He nodded. "I'm sorry. I should have told you."

"You've read the diaries?"

"No. She wouldn't let me. Those were for your eyes only."

"Why would she not want me to know you know? It doesn't make sense."

"All she said was that it would build character for you to deal with it on your own. I wasn't to interfere. It was up to you whether to tell the world her secret as soon as you could, or keep it under wraps as you're doing, or sell the life story after she's gone. My role has been to carry out her wishes, Martin, and that's all. And you should know that everything she did—everything she's done since the day you were born was for you. She went into hiding, as you probably know by now, to protect you. She loved you more than anything."

"Protect me from whom?"

He wrinkled his brow. "Don't you know?"

I shook my head. "I haven't read all the diaries. It's too painful. Well, it was for a while. I couldn't do it. I'm just now reading the fourth one."

"I see."

"So who is it?"

"They were people who wanted to harm her. And you."

"Who? Are they still out there?"

"I don't know. It's possible. It's been a long time, though. If they were going to find her, I think they would've by now."

"Uncle Thomas, *who are they*? And another thing. Do you know who Richard Talbot really is? Did you know my father?"

His expression said it all. He was a man who knew that question would come someday. "No, I didn't know him." Thomas closed his eyes as if it hurt him to tell me. "Please, Martin. Don't make me go against her wishes. I'm not to get involved. She wanted you to read her story in the diaries. All the answers are there, Martin."

"I was never a big reader."

He smiled. "I think that concerned her, because *she* was."

"Jesus." I slapped the arm of the chair in anger.

"Please don't be upset. All will be revealed, Martin. It's really not for me to tell you. I love you like a son. I've known you since you were a baby."

I paused before asking this one. "Did you and my mom ever—?"

Uncle Thomas grinned, and the familiar sparkle in his eyes returned.

"Martin, I asked her to marry me in 1964, but she turned me down. We stayed friends, though. That's all there is to it. I went on and married Martha, we had a long marriage, God bless her soul, and two beautiful kids."

"But?"

His eyes welled with tears. "But I always carried a torch for Judy. I never stopped loving her. She was quite a woman."

"Still is."

He smiled again and used a finger to wipe an eye underneath his glasses. "Yes. You're right. I'm sorry." He looked at me with kindness and asked, "How long did the doctor say she had?"

I shrugged. "No one knows. It could be another year. It could be just weeks."

Then he really started to cry.

7
Judy's Diary
1961

FEBRUARY 8, 1961

I'm in Beverly Hills!!

I'm in the fancy Beverly Hills Hotel, and I'm so excited and can't sleep. So here I am, dear diary. Maybe writing will calm me down. I haven't written much lately, I was kind of down in the dumps after that business with the policeman.

Anyway, the big day arrived and we flew from Idlewild Airport to Los Angeles on TWA. This was a very different experience from when I flew back to Odessa in '58. The airport was much busier. It's expensive to fly. Peter's company is sending him to a lawyer convention and went all out on expenses. Peter and Lucy paid for my ticket, but they won't let me offer any payment. Our plane was full of men wearing suits, except for a handful of ladies here and there, always accompanied by a man. I think I was the only single girl, but I felt like a movie star. TWA is supposedly the "airline of the stars," but I didn't see any celebrities on the plane. The stewardesses were cute and treated everyone like royalty. We had drinks and food. The flight lasted six and a half hours, so after a while the ride got a little old. One stewardess announced that beginning later in the year, the airline will show movies during the flight, and everyone applauded.

A taxi took us to Beverly Hills. Traffic was heavy. Peter told Lucy and me about the freeways, the big roads with no stoplights that were being constructed to help with the traffic congestion. We didn't see any on the way to the hotel. Peter thinks only two or three freeways are in operation, but we'll see and maybe drive on one when we go to Hollywood tomorrow.

The Beverly Hills Hotel is pretty ritzy and famous. And *gorgeous*! I can't imagine what it costs. It's like a palace. I have a room to myself, and Peter and Lucy are next door. There's a lovely swimming pool outside, and that's good because the climate here in California is wonderful. I can't believe it's February. Back in New York it's cold and wet. Here it's bright and sunny and warm and *beautiful*!

For dinner we went to the Brown Derby in Hollywood! Wow, was that ever fun. A lot of movie stars are supposed to eat there, especially at lunchtime. We didn't see anyone famous, though. The building is shaped like a derby hat. I once saw an episode of *I Love Lucy* that takes place there. The Cobb Salad was supposed to be the thing to get, so that's what I ordered. It was delicious—greens with roasted chicken pieces, bacon, hard-boiled egg, tomato, chives, and Roquefort cheese.

Peter and Lucy were real tired after the long flight, so we came back to the hotel after dinner. They went to bed, and I'm wide-awake. This is so much fun. Tomorrow I'm going to Disneyland! I'm like a kid waiting up for Santa Claus.

It feels good to get away from New York. I haven't been very happy lately. The policeman got out of the hospital in a couple of days after the "assault." He'd had several broken ribs and a punctured lung. That's pretty serious, so I felt bad about that. Freddie wouldn't speak to me for a week, but I think we're past that now.

So I'm very excited to be here in California, where I've never been. I'll have fun with Lucy, but at night it's kind of lonely here in the room by myself. I almost envy Lucy for having a great marriage. *Almost*. I'm not looking to join that club.

Okay, time to try and sleep. I have to get my rest and look my best when I meet Mickey Mouse tomorrow.

FEBRUARY 9, 1961

Oh, dear diary, magic, magic, magic! What a fabulous day. I was transported to another world, a fairyland, a place of dreams. Disneyland! It was everything I imagined it to be and more.

Lucy and I each got a "special season ticket book," which included admission and coupons for ten rides for only $3.75. It sounds expensive, but that's a good deal. If you bought tickets for rides separately, that would cost over $6.00.

I did see Mickey Mouse and told him—I think it was really a *her* inside that get-up—that I was in love with him, and I asked if he'd take me away with him somewhere, ha ha. There were other Disney characters walking around, too, and actors in costume, like Snow White. My favorite area was Tomorrowland, where we rode the Submarine Voyage ride and saw an incredible movie called *America the Beautiful* on a huge Cinerama screen. The monorail was amazing, I felt like I was in a science-fiction movie. The Western Mine Train in Frontierland was unbelievable. There were mechanical moving animals along the way that looked very real. We rode the Matterhorn Bobsled in Fantasyland twice. Lucy screamed like a teenager, it was so funny. I was a kid again, too, all day long.

I bought postcards, a Disneyland shirt, and a Mickey Mouse hat for Freddie, ha ha.

We stayed until nightfall—Peter had business—and saw the fireworks over Sleeping Beauty's Castle. The day went so fast, I couldn't believe it was over when the car Peter sent to pick us up met us at the front gates. I didn't realize how exhausted I was until I got in the car. After not sleeping so well last night, I was dead.

Tomorrow Lucy and I will explore Hollywood, then tomorrow night Peter gets off and is meeting us at one of the hot spot nightclubs.

What a vacation!

FEBRUARY 10, 1961

Well, dear diary, I had a very interesting day!

And this evening I met a man and we have a date tomorrow night, without Lucy or Peter!

This morning Lucy and I walked up and down Hollywood Boulevard. We saw Grauman's Chinese Theatre and all the hand-prints of movie stars. My favorite was seeing Marilyn Monroe. I wondered why Elvis Presley's prints weren't there, but I guess they don't consider him a movie star, even though he makes movies. Is there a place with singers' prints? I don't know. And, oh, my gosh, we went in Frederick's of Hollywood. I was turning all kinds of shades of red when I saw the sexy lingerie. I thought about buying a corset but I didn't know who I'd wear it for. That's not the kind of thing a girl wears when she's alone! Lucy told me the owner, Frederick, invented the push-up bra. There were plenty of those! I bought one, but don't tell anyone.

For lunch we went to Musso & Frank Grill, a Hollywood landmark, it's been there since the days of silent movies. We still didn't see any celebrities though! I thought for sure we'd see *someone* on this trip, but it hasn't happened.

I stood on the corner of Hollywood and Vine for a few minutes in case a movie producer spotted me and wanted to make me a star, ha ha. From there I had a great view of the Capitol Records Building, which looks like a stack of records. On the sidewalk are a few stars with famous names on them. Apparently this "Walk of Fame" is going to extend all the way down the boulevard.

After going back to the hotel for a swim in the pool and a rest, Lucy and I took a cab to Flickers nightclub, which was close to the Sunset Strip. The lights of the Strip were dazzling. It was just like on *77 Sunset Strip* except in color!

Flickers is a nightclub with a stage; they have popular music acts there. Frankie Laine performed tonight. The only thing I knew of his was the theme from *Rawhide*, which he sang. Everyone loved it.

The club wasn't very big. You had to have reservations to get in. The bar was separated from the tables and stage area, but waitresses moved around and got drinks for people. Lucy and I waited a half hour at the table before Peter finally joined us. He was glad to be almost finished with his conference.

Right before Frankie Laine went on, Lucy squeezed my arm and blurted, "Is that Paul Newman over there?" She indicated a well-dressed man across the room standing near the bar. He was talking to the guy wearing a tuxedo who had greeted us at the door. Sure enough, the man she was talking about did indeed resemble Paul Newman, but I could tell it wasn't him. This fellow was short, and his upper body was muscular. I've heard Paul Newman is shorter than he looks on screen, but this guy was probably 5'7". That's no big deal to me. I don't necessarily have to have men as tall or taller than me. It's usually *the men* that are bothered by it.

I said to Lucy, "He's not Paul Newman, but whoever he is, he's *quite the man.*"

He must have seen me watching him, for he caught my eye and kept turning his head to look at me. In a little while, the guy in the tuxedo came over with a tray of drinks for all three of us. He introduced himself as Charlie Kelly, the owner and manager of Flickers. He said his nephew Leo—and indicated the Paul Newman look-alike—had treated us to drinks and would like to come say hello. I knew then that it was me he was interested in. I was the third wheel at the table.

Lucy raised her eyebrows at me, letting it be my decision.

"Sure," I said.

The owner went back to the bar, spoke to his nephew, and then the man came over to our table.

"Good evening," he said. "I'm Leo Kelly. My uncle runs this place."

"Yes, he told us," Peter said. He introduced us all to Leo.

He then addressed me. "I couldn't help but notice this lovely young lady sitting without a partner. Are you waiting for someone, Judy?"

His blue eyes were dazzling and he had the nicest smile. I figured him to be maybe ten years older than me, early thirties. Oh, he was *definitely* handsome, and he had a glow about him that was infectious. There was something hard-edged about him that I couldn't quite define, though. "No, I'm not," I replied.

"May I sit a minute?"

I looked at Peter and Lucy. Peter beat me to it. "Please do."

Leo sat beside me and said, "You look like visitors. Am I right?"

"Yes, we're from New York," Peter answered. "I'm here on business. Lucy and Judy are here to have some fun while I'm otherwise engaged."

"We went to Disneyland yesterday," Lucy offered.

Leo laughed. "You can't come to L.A. without going to Disneyland. What else have you done?"

Lucy and I took turns telling him a little about our adventures. Peter asked him what he did, and Leo replied that he was in the warehouse business, whatever that was. His father had built a company located in the Wholesale District of Los Angeles and he ran it now. As he was saying this, I made a point to look at his left hand. No wedding ring. He was becoming more and more attractive by the minute, dear diary.

Leo was very charming. Not only was he terribly good looking, he spoke with confidence and as if he was worth a million bucks. He had light brown hair cut short like Paul Newman's. He was dressed in a pin-striped suit that looked as if it came straight from Italy. When that thought crossed my mind, I realized what it was my intuition had flagged. He wasn't Italian, I don't think, but he reminded me of gangsters I had come across in Manhattan. Leo had the same attitude, but not the menace. He asked us what our plans were for tomorrow. I said Lucy and I were doing more sightseeing. And then Lucy spoke up and said, "I'm going with Peter to a banquet at his conference tomorrow night. Judy, have you decided what you're going to do?"

"No, not really."

Leo raised his eyebrows. "You mean you're on your own tomorrow night?"

"Yes."

"May I take you to dinner? I would be delighted to keep you company."

My heart fluttered, dear diary. "Oh, I don't want to impose. I'm sure I can—"

"No, no, I insist. Please. It would be my honor to show you the town. I know a landmark Italian restaurant that's exquisite. It would be my pleasure, Judy."

I looked at Lucy. She was giving me the *do it! do it!* eyeball. "Well, all right," I said. "That's very kind of you."

With that, he reached into his inside jacket pocket and removed a business card, which he gave to me. It had his name, office address—Kelly Warehousing Enterprises—and phone number. I told him I was staying at the Beverly Hills Hotel. He seemed impressed by that.

"Why don't I pick you up there at, say, seven thirty?"

"Sure. That'll be fine."

He smiled and tilted his head. "You don't sound like a New Yorker. Are you from the south?"

"Texas. But I've been living in New York for almost ten years."

"I *love* your accent."

That made me blush. "Thank you."

All of a sudden, a gorgeous brunette approached the table. She was dressed in a cocktail dress and wasn't too bothered by the amount of cleavage she was showing. My first thought was, *Uh-oh, here's his girlfriend*. But no, Leo looked up and said, "Ah, Christina!" He stood. "Everyone, this is my sister Christina." Peter stood and shook her hand, and then Lucy and I did, too.

"Won't you join us?" Peter asked.

"No, thank you, I just came to collect my brother. Are you ready, Leo?" she asked. As soon as she spoke, my senses went haywire. This girl was dangerous. She was in her late twenties, but she exuded a worldliness beyond her years. She had seen some things. If I thought Leo had a mysterious hard edge about him, Christina Kelly had him beat in spades. It was an instant dislike, dear diary, and I'm not completely sure why. She seemed nice enough, but I felt as if she looked down her nose at me. Like I was not good enough for her brother.

Leo turned to us and said, "Ah, yes, Christina and I have an appointment. It was such a pleasure meeting you all." He shook hands with Peter and Lucy again. "Have a marvelous stay in Los Angeles for the rest of your trip." Then he took my hand in both of his. I swear I felt a shock run up my arm. This guy had overflowing charisma. "Judy, I'm so happy to meet you. I look forward to tomorrow evening. Seven thirty, in your hotel lobby?"

"Sure. Thank you."

"*Buona sera*," he said. Frankie Laine was just coming on, so Leo said, "Enjoy the show," and scooted off with his sister.

"Well, how about that?" Lucy said, giggling and grabbing my arm.

"Oh, my God, I have a *date*! What do I wear?"

"He's so handsome! Don't you think so? He's shorter than you, but does that matter?"

"Not at all. Yes, he's very good looking."

The music was going full swing by then, so we had to shut up. I sat there during the show, sipping my drink and thinking about the mysterious man I'd just met. Now *that*'s going to keep me awake tonight!

8
Judy's Diary
1961

I'm writing this on the airplane. We're on our way home to New York.

It was such an incredible trip. I had so much fun. Going back to cold, dreary Manhattan won't be fun. I loved L.A. I liked the sunshine and the climate. I liked the food and the sights. It's so different from New York, almost the antithesis. Life seems to move at a slower pace in L.A., so I felt more relaxed.

Which brings me to something Leo proposed to me last night, dear diary, and I'm actually thinking about it.

Yesterday began with breakfast at the hotel, Peter went off to the final day of the conference, and Lucy and I were turned loose on the town, ha ha. We went to Rodeo Drive and Santa Monica Boulevard and looked at really expensive clothes. I wanted to get something to wear on my date with Leo, and I told Lucy I wanted to look like a movie star. It was unbelievable how much the so-called designer clothes cost. But I found something I liked, and Lucy said I looked great in it, so I splurged and paid $30 for it. Highway robbery if you ask me, but it does look cute. It's a black chiffon cocktail dress with a sleeveless bodice and a low neckline. The bodice has satin cord floral "appliqués"—that's what the salesman called them. Fitted skirt.

I also purchased a cashmere scarf—a black one—that would go well with New York winters. It set me back another $9. Outrageous, but it's pretty and it'll be a nice souvenir of the trip. I'm actually glad I bought it.

After lunch at a little French café, the name of which I can't remember or pronounce, we discussed plans for the afternoon. I voted for the hotel pool. Lucy agreed. So that's what we did for three hours—we just reclined in our swimsuits and *did nothing*. It was heaven. We both had some white wine, too. We swam. We laughed. Men gawked at us. A few flirted with us; when they learned Lucy was married, all their attentions fell on me. I had to fight them off, ha ha.

Lucy brought up the date with Leo and pointed out something that I knew but never paid much attention to. She said I tend to be attracted to the "dangerous" types. Fiorello was an Italian mobster in New York. John Richardson was an FBI agent. And Michael Sokowitz was a Communist assassin! Of course, Lucy doesn't know that last tidbit; she just knew Michael was a jerk. Lucy also has no clue that my relationships with these men were so much more complicated than she thinks. I had to relate to each man *twice*—once as myself and then again, almost simultaneously and quite differently, as the Stiletto. Am I doomed to always have to conduct *two* separate relationships with the same man?

I replied to her, "Oh, Leo's not dangerous." What I saw was a dark attractiveness and said so.

"Just watch yourself, Judy," she said. "Be careful. I may have pushed you into that date, but afterward I didn't like the way he was so slick. I can't explain it."

"What does Peter say?"

"He had nothing to say. He thinks it's great you got a date for tonight."

"Look, I think you're just seeing the 'Hollywood' in Leo," I said, in denial that I really knew nothing about him. "That's just a Hollywood attitude he's got. I think he's very friendly."

"He is, and he's charming, but I feel like it's just an act. It's not really him." She waved the thought away. "Don't listen to me, I want you to have fun tonight."

Deep down, I know she's right, but I'm actually very excited about it. Danger or no danger.

So at 7:30 I was in the hotel lobby, wearing my new dress and heels. Peter and Lucy had already departed for the banquet, so they didn't get to see me. I think I looked pretty good, dear diary. I was a little afraid I was showing too much cleavage, but I just told myself I was in Hollywood. All the men in the lobby watched me while I waited, so I must have done something right. I probably could've snatched a date there if I'd wanted, ha ha.

Leo showed up promptly at 7:30 and was dressed in a different suit than he wore at Flickers. This one was a bright blue, and he had on a wide tie with a wild print. He reminded me of the *Ocean's 11* guys—Frank Sinatra and Dean Martin and those fellas.

When we stood next to each other, yes, I was taller. I didn't mind and I tried to gauge if he was bothered by it. He didn't seem to be. He said I looked beautiful and we went out to his car, which he said was a Karmann Ghia. It was a little thing, and only two people could fit in it. It was gunmetal gray and looked like a racing car. It was a convertible, too, but he had the top up. We couldn't help but sit *very close together* in that car, dear diary! I also felt like my bottom was just inches above the road as we drove. And oh yes, I *did* feel like a movie star.

"Do you drive?" Leo asked me as we sped through the city streets.

"No," I answered. "But I think I'll take lessons when I get back to New York. It's something I should know how to do."

"Definitely. Everyone needs to know how to drive. And you'll love it, too." He indicated the scenery that was flashing past us. "Isn't this fabulous? It's like we're in a little bubble and the rest of the world can't hurt us."

"It's breathtaking. I've never been in a car like this."

"Usually I ride in a big Lincoln and my driver is at the wheel. But I thought tonight I'd get the Karmann out."

"You wanted to impress me?"

He shot a twinkle-eye at me and smiled. "Maybe I did."

He took me to a place on the Sunset Strip called Villa Nova. It's a famous place that's been around nearly thirty years and known for being a hot spot. And guess what! I saw my first movie star! Bing Crosby and his wife Kathryn were there! They were sitting in a more secluded area of the restaurant, probably so no one would bother them. Leo whispered to me and pointed them out. I was thrilled!

Before we were shown to our table, Leo stopped to talk quietly with a big guy who was sitting at the bar. He was dressed in a suit, too, but he looked more like a football linebacker.

We then sat at a table that was lit by a candle. Leo knew the staff, and they greeted us warmly. They treated him like a VIP.

"You know that man at the bar?" I asked. An obvious question.

"That's Boone, my driver. He works for me, so he acts as a driver and assistant when I'm on business."

"What's he doing here?"

"He was supposed to meet us here. He… looks after me."

Aha! The man got more intriguing by the minute. "He's your bodyguard?"

Leo shrugged. "In my business, it's best that I travel with one."

"How come?"

So he explained to me what he does. He runs a company that leases warehouses to shipping firms and railroads. He called himself a "glorified landlord." He also dealt a lot with the warehousemen's and longshoremen's unions, because his warehouses were often used to store goods and stuff that come in from overseas. He asked me if I'd ever seen *On the Waterfront*, and I told him I had. "That was the East Coast, but the same kind of corruption can occur here. The unions, organized crime—it's a rough world. I have some powerful friends and some powerful enemies. I can't be too careful, so I keep

Boone around. Don't get me wrong, I can take care of myself just fine."

By the look of his shoulders, I could tell he was a fighter. "I believe it. You're not in the mob, are you?" I asked with a laugh.

He smiled broadly. I swear his eyes really do twinkle. There's a little light that sparkles at the edge of his pupil. It's simply enchanting. Dear diary, I didn't care about anything he was talking about, but I sure liked looking at him. Watching his mouth as he spoke drove me wild. I admit it! It sounds scandalous, but I really wanted to feel his lips on mine.

"No, I'm not with the mob. I'm not Italian. Well, my mother was Italian, but my father was Irish. But I know some of them, sure," he answered. "I grew up on the streets," he said. "That tends to toughen you up, and you meet a lot of interesting characters. My industry is full of guys from the streets. You know, warehousemen and long-shoremen, you gotta be pretty tough to do those kinds of jobs. So, sure, you get some corruption every now and then. I stay out of that part of the business."

I studied him to see if I could detect any hint of deceit. My natural knack of perceiving lies had benefitted me in the past, but there was only a slight tingle of doubt this time. He wasn't lying, but he wasn't telling me everything.

I didn't care. He had me captivated. The meal was *fabulous*. I had linguine in clam sauce that was out of this world. Leo had lasagna. I tasted it and it was great. We also drank a whole bottle of delicious red wine, so I was feeling pretty good, ha ha.

Our conversation was about all sorts of things. I told him a little about my upbringing, confessed that I ran away from home when I was fourteen, and that I currently work in a gymnasium. He found that unusual, which of course it is. He asked where in Texas I'm from, and I told him—Odessa. Leo said he had some business associates in Texas, and that he knew people in Odessa. He didn't elaborate, but I found that amazing.

When we were nearly done with the meal, he looked over at

Boone. The bodyguard/driver was talking to two other men, and they definitely looked like gangster types. They had the style and attitude I recognized so well from my interaction with "wiseguys" in New York. It appeared as if Boone was trying to prevent them from coming over and talking to Leo.

"Excuse me a minute," he said as he rose and joined his driver. I couldn't hear them, but the two newcomers seemed angry about something. Leo must have placated them, for he calmly and quietly spoke to the men, placing a hand on one guy's shoulder. After a moment, the men nodded and looked sheepish. They all shook hands, and then the two guys left. Leo returned to the table and sat. "Sorry about that."

"That's all right. Who were they?"

"More business associates."

"Everything okay?"

"Everything's just fine. How's your pasta?"

I studied his face and once again detected no dishonesty. But Lucy's right. I realized then and there that something mysterious, hard, and dark resided inside Leo, and that only made him more attractive to me. Part of me wanted to find out what it was; another part of me *didn't care*. I just wanted to feel his arms around me. He was *that* magnetic. I think he might be the most charismatic man I've ever met.

He asked me what I wanted to do with my life. "You're so young, Judy. Do you really want to work at a men's gym forever?"

I told him I might be ready for a change. Lately New York was getting me down.

"You should move to Los Angeles," he said. "The weather's always perfect here. You would love it."

"I do love it, at least what I've seen. But I don't know what I'd do in Los Angeles. I'm not an actress or anything like that."

"L.A. isn't all show business, although I must say you are beautiful enough to be an actress. Or a model. Have you thought about that?"

"No." I think I was blushing up a storm!

"I tell you what. If you came out here, I could convince Charlie to give you a hostess or waitress job at Flickers. Would you like that?"

It sounded glamorous. It would certainly be a complete change from what I was doing now. Would it be something I'd like?

"Maybe."

"I think you've got the looks to be a hostess. Just think of all the movie stars you'd meet. They really do come in the club all the time. And then there are all the wonderful men who drive Karmann Ghias."

That made me laugh. In fact, through most of the evening he said funny things. I can't remember them all now, but he had me in stitches at one point. He told me one story about meeting Jimmy Cagney at Flickers. Leo did an imitation of the actor and it was perfect.

After they'd brought the bill and we were about to leave, he said, "I'm going to be in New York in March or April. May I look you up?"

"Of course!" He then took one of his business cards and a pen from his jacket pocket and wrote down the gym's phone number as I recited it. I don't know why I never got a separate line; I didn't feel the need to.

We rode around in his little sports car for the rest of the evening. He drove up into the hills near the Hollywood sign that overlooks the city. We sailed along Mulholland Drive, a scary winding road in the hills, but the view of L.A. from there was breathtaking. It was very romantic. Then he mentioned ice cream and I fell for it. He took me to a place called C. C. Brown's, apparently another Hollywood landmark. Leo said they invented the hot fudge sundae, and that's what I had! Yum!

By then it was nearly 11:00. The time had flown. He drove me back to the hotel, and we said good-bye in the driveway in front of the main doors.

"I'm going to call you when I'm in New York," he said.

"You'd better."

And then he kissed me.

Oh, my gosh, dear diary. It was like someone had plugged me into a light socket. It was electric, it really was. It was a wave of energy. That kiss traveled through my body from my lips down to my breasts and into my ribcage. I felt it *down there*.

"We could continue our evening at the bar," he said softly. "Or in your room."

I really felt flushed when he said that. Dear diary, as much as I wanted to, I knew I couldn't just jump into bed with someone on a first date. That wouldn't be proper. I wasn't that kind of girl, and I told him that. He said he understood, that he couldn't help himself asking, and that he had enjoyed our evening together. He told me again how beautiful I am and that he can't wait to see me again. He wished me a safe flight home. And then he was gone.

There were clouds under my feet as I walked into the hotel. I went up to my room and called Lucy, but no one answered their phone. I guess they were still at the banquet. She said they might not be back until midnight.

I went to bed and, surprisingly, slept very soundly. This morning I filled Lucy in on my adventure last night, and she said it sounded like I had a better time than she did. She was one of very few wives at a stuffy old businessmen's banquet.

So that was my California trip. I've got memories of Disneyland and Hollywood Boulevard and sunshine and great food and drinks. But mostly I'm thinking about Leo Kelly.

I think I'm smitten again. Heaven help me!

9
Martin
The Present

"Martin, come here, quick!"

I was in the bathroom at Maggie's house. She was in the living room and the television was on.

"I'm a little busy!" I called.

"Well, hurry up, or you'll miss it! It's about the Black Stiletto!"

Looking at my watch, I noted it was that time of the evening when *World Entertainment Television* was on. They occasionally had stories about the Stiletto. I had something of a crush on the anchor, Sandy Lee. So I finished my business, washed my hands, and joined Maggie in front of the set.

Sandy was with an elderly woman who was displaying pieces of a costume that appeared to resemble the Stiletto's. The caption read: BETTY DINKINS—THE BLACK STILETTO?

"She says she's the Black Stiletto," Maggie said.

"*What?*"

"Listen!"

Sure enough, that's what the story was about. A woman in New York City named Betty Dinkins claimed to be the legendary Black Stiletto. I watched in shock as Sandy interviewed her.

"Oh, yes," the old lady said. "I'd put on this costume and go out in the streets. It was cold sometimes, but I managed."

"How did you learn how to fight and climb buildings?" Sandy asked her. "Did you have natural athletic ability?"

"I suppose I did. I didn't train or anything like that. I just did it. I was fearless in those days. Most of the time those criminals were cowards and couldn't defend themselves. It was surprisingly easy to subdue them."

Yeah, right. "What is this shit?" I asked aloud. "I don't believe this is happening."

Betty Dinkins was allegedly seventy years old, and said that she'd decided to "come clean" about her secret when she reached that milestone age. Of course, anyone doing the math would know that in 1958, she would have been about fifteen. As I watched her speak, I could see that she was a tough old broad. She hadn't kept her figure, was heavy now, and she spoke with a thick New York accent. You couldn't imagine her wearing that costume at one time.

Sandy asked her, "Ms. Dinkins, you have to admit, this is a spectacular claim you're making. Aside from the costume, what proof can you offer our audience that you're telling the truth?"

The woman got visibly angry. "Are you calling me a liar? I don't have any proof except what you see. You'll have to take my word for it."

"Other women over the years have stepped forward and claimed to be the Black Stiletto. It was quickly proven that they were not."

"That's because they *weren't* the Black Stiletto. I was!"

She went on to recount a few exploits that were widely covered in the newspapers. Anything she said could have been extracted from them. The woman also produced several black-and-white photos, supposedly of her wearing the costume. I recognized them. There were very few existing pictures of the real Stiletto on the streets of Manhattan or L.A., and these were some of those. Of course, the woman in those photos was my mother, not freaking Betty Dinkins!

"Why did you relocate to Los Angeles in 1961?" Lee asked.

"I thought I would be discovered by a Hollywood producer, and we'd make Black Stiletto movies. It was a crazy idea. I was there about a year, that's all. Then I retired the costume and came back to New York. I decided to become a normal person and put all the pretense behind me."

Dinkins appeared very sure of herself. Was she deranged? Crazy? I didn't think so. She spoke in complete sentences and acted like she knew what she was talking about. She was just a big fat liar. And then the crux of the matter was revealed.

"I understand you're entertaining some book deal offers." Sandy said.

Dinkins grinned broadly. "That's right. There are already two offers on the table. My agent says there will be more. We're talking six or seven figures. I should have told the truth about myself a long time ago!"

"You're going to write the book?"

"My son will. He's an author. He's written several books."

"Who's his publisher?"

"Oh, he hasn't been published yet. But when he writes *this* book, it will sell a million copies."

Sandy Lee addressed the audience. "We'll be talking more with Betty Dinkins in the coming days. She promises to tell us some hair-raising stories of her adventures as the Black Stiletto. Stay tuned. This is *World Entertainment Television*."

As the program went to a commercial, I turned to Maggie. "Who does this woman think she is, telling the world that crap?"

"Um, the Black Stiletto?"

"Maggie, it's not funny."

"I know it isn't. But what can you do about it?"

"I'll sue her, by God. I'll expose her to be the liar she is. I can't believe it!"

"Martin, think about what you're saying."

"What?"

"How are you going to expose her? You'd have to tell the truth about your mom, wouldn't you?"

That gave me pause. Of course, Maggie was right, as always. In the heat of the outrage, I wasn't thinking it through. "But there must be something I can do. Maybe I can contact her anonymously and tell her I know she's lying. Tell her to cease and desist or the *real* Black Stiletto will sue her."

"I doubt it would scare her. I imagine she's got herself a lawyer. She says she has an agent. And, frankly, she looks like she could knock someone's block off."

"What's she going to say in a book? Make up stuff and claim it's true? It'd be complete fiction. I wonder if someone put her up to this. Probably that son of hers. They thought it was an easy way to make a buck. Maybe they're going to split the profits."

"Don't get yourself all worked up. I bet once a publisher checks out her story, she'll be revealed as a fraud."

"I need a drink."

"Well, grab a bottle of wine. I'll have some, too. Dinner's almost ready."

Three glasses later, I was feeling much better, but I was still peeved. We had a lovely dinner of shrimp scampi—I don't know how Maggie does it. But Betty Dinkins was still wreaking havoc with my sense of justice, so I decided to call Uncle Thomas and get his take on it. I figured he was home from the office by now, so I called him there.

"Uncle Thomas, it's Martin."

"Hello, Martin. How are you doing?"

"Did you see *World Entertainment Television* just now?"

"No, I don't watch that stuff."

I gave him a capsule summary of what I'd seen.

"Martin, it's not the first time someone has said—"

"I know, but it's the first time anyone's done it since I found out the truth about my mother. Is there anything we can do? Can we send her a cease-and-desist letter or something?"

"And how do we explain what we know?"

"What if we don't explain anything? Just send her the letter.

You're Mom's lawyer. Just say you represent the interests of the Black Stiletto."

"Martin, that won't work. If the woman shows the letter to the TV people or her publishers, they're going to come knocking on my door. I can protect Judy up to a point, but a reporter with half a brain might be able to find her."

I grunted. "I guess you're right. Sorry. I got kind of excited there for a minute. It just made me mad."

"I understand."

"Sorry to have bothered you."

"It's all right, Martin."

"I'll talk to you later."

"Wait. Martin. I just thought of something else."

"What?"

"Remember I mentioned that there were bad people in the world who could harm your mother if they knew she was alive?"

"Yeah, but you also said that was a long time ago. They're probably old or dead, right?"

"But what if they're not? This woman could be in danger."

"Fine, it'll serve her right for telling stories."

"I'm serious, Martin. What's her name again?"

"Betty Dinkins."

"I think it's only right that we warn her somehow. Just in case."

"And how do we do that without revealing our hand?"

"Let me see if I can find out her contact information. I'll try to get in touch with the TV program people. The fact I'm a lawyer can cut through red tape. If I'm successful, then we can decide what to do."

"Fine."

We hung up and I sat and stewed for a while. I wasn't interested in watching television, and as much as I loved Maggie, I didn't feel like having company at the moment. She was settling into her comfy chair, ready to spend the rest of the evening in a vegetative state.

"Honey, I'm going back to my house," I announced. "I need to check the mail and do a couple of things."

"Are you coming back?"

"I'll call you. I need to let off some steam."

"Okay. Are you all right to drive?"

"Of course. I only had three glasses of wine."

"You're an easy drunk, Martin."

"I am not!"

I grabbed my jacket—it was still nippy outside—and got in the Beemer. It was a short twenty-minute trip to Buffalo Grove.

My house stood vacant and dark. There was two days' worth of mail in the box since I last checked it. I was spending less time there, so maybe I really should consider moving in with Maggie. Was I ready for that level of commitment?

There were the usual bills and junk-mail items, but also an envelope from Juilliard. I opened it and was surprised to find a check for the full amount of Gina's tuition for the semester.

It was a refund.

What the hell?

I immediately called Gina on her cell. Got voice mail. "Gina, I just received a refund from Juilliard for the spring semester. What's this mean? Call me back as soon as you get this."

The next call was to Carol. She was just as perplexed.

So what was our rebellious and reckless daughter up to now?

10
Judy's Diary
1961

MARCH 12, 1961

Hello, dear diary, and yes, I know I haven't written in a while. Coming back from California depressed me. Every day I did my job at the gym and then stayed in my room the rest of the evening, not socializing with anyone. I'd play my records and listen to the radio. "Surrender" is climbing the charts, as is "Blue Moon" by the Marcels. "Blue Moon" is cute, but I'm just not in the mood. I prefer Elvis's version, of course, and *that's* the mood I've been in!

I think I'm also disheartened that I haven't heard from Leo. He did say "March or April," didn't he? I can't remember. Maybe I should get used to the notion that I'll never hear from Leo Kelly again.

A fight broke out in the gym today between Clark and Kraig. Perhaps that's what prompted me to make a diary entry. I think I should keep track of altercations between those two. There's going to be a lesson learned at some point. I just hope no one gets hurt.

It was Kraig who started it. From what I understand, he "accidentally" slammed his shoulder into Clark as he passed his nemesis on the way to the locker room. Clark didn't ignore it. He turned around and punched Kraig in the face and knocked the much larger kid down. Kraig recovered quickly and attacked Clark. It went on for at least a minute before Freddie and I were able to stop it. We separated them; Freddie took Kraig into his office, and I tended to Clark. His lip was cut and he was going to have a swollen eye. I don't know how bad Kraig's injuries were, probably not as much as Clark's.

Both boys got stern warnings not to fight in the gym anymore. I pointed out to Clark that Kraig always visits the gym in the late afternoon.

"Why don't you come at a different time of day and avoid him altogether?" I suggested.

"But right after school is best for me," Clark replied.

"Could you come before school?"

"And get up *early*? No!"

"Well, it's either that or the evening hours. We now close at 7:00, you know. We open at 6:00 in the morning."

"That's awful early."

I kind of snapped at him. "If I can do it, Clark, you can do it." He looked surprised and then left. I suppose I was disappointed in him a little, too. He knew better than to fight back.

I'll be interested to see what he chooses to do.

Dear diary, I've been wondering a lot lately if this is the end of the Black Stiletto. Should I try going out tonight? I don't know. Maybe I should go join that new organization Kennedy spoke about. The Peace Corps. I'm good at keeping the peace, ha ha. And it'd get me the heck away from here.

LATER

Just after midnight.

I'm very shaken and scared to death.

I went out as the Stiletto. I thought maybe if I got out and had at least a good run I would perk up. Now everything is worse than ever.

It was dark when I slithered down the telephone pole. 2nd Street was mostly empty, but 2nd Avenue was crowded with pedestrians.

That was nothing new to me, so I took off uptown along the east side. I had no desire to go west and revisit scenes from my last outing.

There were the usual surprised reactions from people on the streets, good and bad. "Look, the Black Stiletto!" "Hurray for the Black Stiletto!" "Someone call the cops!" As usual, I'm friendly to everyone if I'm forced to stop at a light. Most people just get out of my way and gawk.

I made it up to 37th Street without any incidents. No crimes in progress. Nothing for me to do. But it was still early; I didn't want to turn back just yet. I kept going, and as I approached 38th Street I stepped into a mess of trouble. Cop cars appeared in front of me, blocking off the intersection, lights blazing. I did an abrupt about-face and started running toward 37th so I could slip east. But police cars appeared with perfect timing, blocking that intersection, too.

It was a coordinated plan, it had to have been. The only thing I can think is that the police have informers planted around the city. If they see me, they call it in, and then the task force that was set up to catch me goes into action. I now realize that's what the cops were attempting the last couple of times I saw them—cutting off the escape routes on both ends of a street or avenue.

If I crossed 2nd Avenue, I'd be wide open. They could easily shoot me. There was no fire escape on the building I stood in front of. Up was not an option. If I moved forward or backward, I'd run into cop cars and the men who ride in them. I didn't know what to do. Cops were advancing from north and south. Some stayed behind to guard the intersections. So I did what I thought was the less risky thing. I figured they wouldn't try to shoot me because traffic was heavy and there were too many pedestrians about. So I bolted west into 2nd Avenue traffic to cross to the other side.

It all happened so fast. A car slammed on its brakes to avoid hitting me. As a result, a taxi behind it crashed into the back. It then swerved into oncoming traffic and flipped. For some reason, a city bus was also moving at a ridiculously fast speed behind the cab, and it was full of passengers. It, too, collided with the now upside-down taxi and the first car, which I saw had two men in it. The bus plowed heavily through the disabled vehicles, nearly crushing the taxi, and then began to tilt. It careened on two wheels and fell over on its side and slid twenty or thirty feet. The noise the metal made on the road was like the roar of a gigantic, wounded beast. When the bus finally came to a rest, I heard the screams. Everyone heard them. I stopped running. My intention was to go to the bus and see what I could do to help.

"Freeze! Raise your hands!" Cops with guns drawn ran toward me from the east side of 2nd. I didn't hesitate; I turned back and continued my trek across the road to the other side, and then dashed south. One policeman fired his weapon, but I heard another shout, "Hold your fire!" Suddenly it seemed there were a million people swarming around the accident.

And one of them yelled, "It's the Black Stiletto's fault!"

I kept running until I got to 36th Street, then I turned east to disappear into the darkness. From then on, I zigzagged east and west and moving southward until I got to the East Village. It was no problem getting to the gym roof and through the window to my room.

It was horrible. How many people were hurt? Was anyone killed? The driver of the taxi must have suffered the worst. I don't think I'll be able to block the echo of those screams from my mind.

Oh, my God, dear diary, what have I done?

11
Leo
The Past

I was invited to Vincent DeAngelo's birthday party bash. It was always a big to-do and a spot on the guest list was coveted. I've been asked a few times, but I'm not on the list every year. I don't know why. This year the don remembered me. He didn't invite Christina, though. Maybe he didn't realize we lived in the same house. Maybe he thought she was still in jail. She pretended not to care, but I knew she was a little miffed that I got to go and she couldn't. You'd think we could just call up and ask if she could come, seeing as how our pop was good friends with DeAngelo and all; but that just wasn't done with the DeAngelos. I wasn't even allowed to bring a date. They kept a strict watch on the invitees. Sal Casazza, Mario, and Shrimp were always there. A couple of the other big shot wiseguys in L.A. got to go. Mostly the parties consisted of DeAngelo's extensive family, the Las Vegas crew, and rotating privileged close friends.

DeAngelo—I sometimes referred to him as "the don," although that's more of an East Coast Italian thing; no one called him that here—lived on a ranch on the north side of town. There were no cattle or anything like that; it's just a lot of desert acreage and a huge mansion and swimming pool. He had the place landscaped, so there was green grass—the kind they had on golf courses—on the huge back lawn, fountains, trees, and gardens. It was indeed beautiful. If it wasn't so damned hot outside, it'd be paradise. Well, there was supposed to be a little bit of hell in paradise, right?

They kept the riffraff out of Shangri-la with a big stone fence that surrounded the entire property. Armed men watched the front gate twenty-four hours a day. DeAngelo rarely left his castle except to go to the Sandstone Casino in town. He was always protected, no matter where he went. Vincent DeAngelo was probably the most important man in Vegas next to Howard Hughes.

The party was in full swing by the time I got there. The sun was just starting to go down, so the temperature was gradually dropping from what seemed like a hundred-and-ten degrees to a balmy one hundred. The food was indoors where the A/C was on. What a luxury. I just had A/C installed in my home in Hollywood. Don't know why I never had it before.

It was quite a spread. Carlotta DeAngelo, the don's wife, was famous for her pasta dishes, and there were plenty—spaghetti and meatballs, lasagna, and fettuccini Alfredo. Then there was veal and sea bass, lots of vegetables and fruit, plates of bread and cheese, finger food, and ice cream and pastries for dessert. They were going to top off the evening with a gigantic birthday cake for Vince. He was sixty-four.

The man was enjoying himself. He sat in a lounge chair by the swimming pool, decked out in swimming trunks, sunglasses, and a cowboy hat. Somehow that hat just didn't look right on him. DeAngelo wasn't as heavy as Sal, but he outweighed me by a hundred pounds at least. He was bald except for some gray hair on the sides of his head above his ears. I guess the hat protected him from the sun—he'd look pretty funny with a pink head.

DeAngelo stayed busy greeting friends and chain-smoking cigarettes. I liked tobacco, but they're saying it's not good for you. Now they tell us. Some of Sal's business was moving black market cigarettes. People craved the stuff. I couldn't imagine people were going to pay much attention to the surgeon general, whoever he was. As for DeAngelo, he would *never* give up smoking. They were going to have to bury him with a couple cartons of his stinky Italian numbers, or else his corpse would rise and demand them. I figured I'd go say hello a little later. It'd feel weird shaking his hand with me all dressed and him practically naked and looking a little bit like Humpty Dumpty in a cowboy hat.

DeAngelo's bodyguard, Rico Mancini, and the consigliere of the family, Luchino Battilana, stood close by. Everyone called Battilana "Lucky," although I didn't know why. He had his eye gouged out in Sicily during World War II, and he lost an arm in an automobile accident. Maybe he was Lucky because he was still alive. Rico caught my eye and glared at me. He didn't necessarily have anything against me, but he had some issues with Boone, of all people. I guessed there was some kind of one-upmanship contest going on in the bodyguard union. Maybe he thought he could beat Boone's ass, but if I had to bet real money on a fight, I'd pick Boone every time. Hell, I think *I* could take on Rico.

I meandered around the grounds, eyeing the various guests. Many of them I knew, most I didn't. I did business with quite a few. One guy was a client who paid me a ton of money to store some drugs he smuggled from Corsica to Los Angeles via the Port. I didn't normally like to get in the narcotics business, but at the time I needed the dough. With my warehouse leasing operation, it turned out to be pretty easy. They hid the junk inside engine parts, which was pretty clever, if I was to say so myself, and I leased them an old warehouse in the Wholesale District south of downtown L.A.

Casazza was in his element—eating all the food and drinking the booze. He appeared to be chumming it up with Tweedledum and Tweedledee—Faretti and Capri. I'd heard they had made new gun-selling deals with the Heathens and were now like crown princes or something.

I noted I didn't see a single guy wearing a Heathens leather jacket. DeAngelo hates those guys. He doesn't like doing business with outlaw motorcycle clubs, but he does it anyway. The money's too good.

The women in attendance were always breathtaking. I thought DeAngelo routinely hired a couple dozen party girls for decoration. That way, if any of the VIP guests wanted to try and get lucky, they had an opportunity. I figured I might as well give it a shot, too. I saw a very attractive redhead heading inside for the food. It'd been a couple of days since I nailed that blonde with the little mole on her cheek. I met her at Flickers, of course. She was a lot of fun. It was possible I'd give her another call some day, unless something better came along.

What could I say? I've been called a ladies' man more than once in my lifetime. It's something to be proud of. There were plenty of fags in Hollywood, believe me. You'd think the women would run away screaming for a virile man—*any* man—to rescue them. Well, I figured that was my job. Who was it that said, "Too many women, so little time?" It was certainly the goddamned truth.

Speaking of the opposite sex, I had to go to New York in a couple of weeks. Mookie wanted me to meet with a paper supplier for the counterfeit dough. Believe it or not, dollar bills were made of a special paper that's manufactured exclusively for the government. It had wood pulp, cotton, silk, linen, and I didn't know what else in it. Mookie was a genius when it came to stuff like that. Anyway, I had to go and work out an acceptable price for some rolls of the special paper. So while I was there, I thought I'd call that girl I met last month. Judy Cooper. What a dame. She was a lot of fun. Gorgeous, smart, and built like an Olympic track star. I liked 'em tall, too, and she had legs that stretched for miles. I charmed her pretty good. Didn't get her in the sack, but it was a first date. I got the feeling she could be persuaded to do it, but she was playing nice girl who had to be romanced first. She just might be worth the effort.

I made my way over to the gazebo, which stood on the far end of the lawn, near the trees. They had a bar set up there, so I grabbed a beer. It was then that I noticed a square hole in the floor of the gazebo. A waiter climbed out of it with a case of wine.

"What's down there?" I asked the bartender.

"Oh, that's an underground passage. It leads to the house, the wine cellar, in fact. Mr. DeAngelo had it built so the staff could easily retrieve food and beverages without having to carry them across the lawn, through the clusters of guests. He built the gazebo on the far side of the lawn to give people an incentive to spread out away from the house. Mr. DeAngelo likes to see every inch of his grounds filled with happy people when he throws a party."

"That's incredible. Can I go down and look?"

"Sure."

I entered the gazebo and climbed down a ladder ten feet to a paved tunnel. It was twenty degrees cooler down there. I walked a little ways into it. The passage was lit with a ceiling bulb every ten feet or so. I went all the way to the wine cellar and saw the staircase leading up into the house. Impressive.

When I was back outside, I spotted the redhead I'd seen earlier. She was walking away from the bar with a drink in hand, so I started to follow her. But Maria DeAngelo was also at the bar, and she said, "Leo!" I stopped. She gave me a pretty smile and asked, "Leo, are you an employee now?"

I laughed. "I was just having a look at that tunnel. I never knew it was there. That's amazing."

"There are all kinds of secret passages and tunnels on the property."

Maria was a swell-looking babe. Talk about a *blonde*; whew. We've known each other since we were kids, but didn't see each other very often. You could count the number of times on one hand. She was going to turn twenty-five this year, five years younger than me. Never married. She was still a virgin. No one could get in her pants unless he gave her a ring. And that was a challenge because she was daddy's little girl, and no one was good enough for her. DeAngelo would have a big say in who she ended up with.

"Say, Leo, didn't you promise me you'd take me to Disneyland?"

Had I? I didn't remember.

"Come on, Maria, you've been to Disneyland, haven't you?"

"Of course, but I love it. They're always adding new things, too."

I figured what the hell. Why not? "Sure, Maria, we can go to Disneyland. When do you want to go?"

"I'm free next week. Any day."

She was actually free every goddamned day. She didn't do a thing except lounge around the pool, unless she was in L.A. shopping on Rodeo Drive for expensive clothes. Daddy gave her a blank check. She drove a sweet 1958 Alfa Romeo convertible, one of many lavish presents from her father.

"It'll have to be next weekend, Maria. I work this week," I said.

"Saturdays are really crowded."

I shrugged. "I'm sure we'll manage. So, is it a date?"

"Sure. What do I do, come to L.A. Friday night? I could stay with my cousin in Santa Monica."

"Do I know your cousin?"

"She's here. Catherine. You've met her before. She's six years older than me. Has four kids."

"Oh, right. That sounds good, I can pick you up there."

"Get Boone to drive us. That car of yours is too small."

"Sure thing."

She leaned in close and kissed my cheek. Maria was my height, which was all right. Like I said before, I usually like 'em taller than me, and that's a group that probably includes most of the chicks in the world. "Thank you, Leo! I look forward to it."

Yeah, she liked me. Maybe I *could* develop something to my advantage. Romancing Maria might be a good business move. Was it possible to marry my way into the DeAngelo family? The idea was so fantastic, it was funny. Besides, she came with a lot of baggage. She was good looking, but I didn't like the way she felt entitled to everything. She always got her way. I believed women needed to know their place.

"Hey, Maria!"

We looked over and saw her older brother Paulie waving at her.

"What?"

"Mom wants you!"

"I'm talking here!"

He waved at her sternly. "Come on!"

She rolled her eyes. "Oh, dear. It must have something to do with the cake. Excuse me, will you?"

"It's all right."

Maria grabbed my hand. "Let's talk some more later." And then she was off, and I watched her sashay across the lawn to her brother. He chewed her out a little, but she brushed him off and went in the house. Paulie turned to me and shot me a dirty look. He wasn't one of my favorite people. In fact, he was a pain in my neck. I've known *him* all my life, too. He argued to his pop that I shouldn't be put in charge of the counterfeiting operation because I wasn't "experienced" in their ways. I didn't know why he was against me. He just didn't like me.

Paulie was the oldest kid in the DeAngelo family. He was thirty-five or thirty-six, I can't remember. Tall and skinny and had a face like a weasel. Had the temper of one, too. Someday maybe he and I'll get into it. I think I could take him.

After the sun went down, DeAngelo put on some clothes and stood near the gazebo, smoking a cigarette and telling stories to the numerous sycophants around him. I finally went up to him and said, "Happy birthday, Don DeAngelo. Thank you for inviting me."

"Leo, my boy! Leo, I'm so glad you could come. How are you enjoying the party?"

"It's great, sir. I always love coming here."

He addressed everyone. "You all know Leo? He's Philip Kelly's boy. I've known Leo since he was a baby."

The group nodded. Some of them actually did know and respect me.

"I've been meaning to talk to you, Leo. Excuse us, I need to speak with Leo for a minute." He put an arm around me and we walked away from the bar to talk in private.

"How's business, Leo?" he asked.

"Great. And that thing I'm working on is going well."

"That's what I understand. Mookie Samberg knows what he's doing, even if he is expensive." He belly laughed and lit another cigarette.

"I'm going to New York in a couple of weeks to talk to the paper supplier."

"Good, good. I trust you, Leo. I know you don't do a lot of work for us. I appreciate this initiative of yours. Everything all right? Do you need anything?"

"No, and thank you, sir. Listen, if there is *ever* anything I can do for you, please let me know. I have a whole warehouse operation at your disposal."

He laughed again. "Of course you do. Your father and I did a lot of business together. He was a wonderful man and a good friend."

"Yes, sir."

"And, it's funny you mention it, but I *did* want to ask you about something that maybe you could do for me."

"What's that, sir?"

"Stop with that 'sir' stuff. I don't like it. And that 'don' thing doesn't work either. That's what they say in New York. I'm not a New Yorker."

"I'm sorry."

"Don't ever apologize. Makes you look weak."

"Yes, s—um, I know."

"You know, Maria likes you, Leo. She talks about you a lot."

"I like her too. She's a lovely gal—er, girl. We're going to Disneyland together next week."

He paused for a second, registering that his daughter was going on a date with me. How did he feel about it? Well, apparently it was okay, because he said, "That's great. You'll have a good time."

"I'm sure we will."

"Now listen. What I wanted to talk to you about. Your sister—"

"Christina?"

"Christina. She did some time."

"Yes, she did, sir—damn, I'm sorry. What do I call you if you don't want me to call you 'sir'?"

"Call me Vince. My closest friends call me Vince."

"All right, Vince. Thank you. I'm honored."

"Forget it. Anyway, your sister—"

"Christina."

"Christina, she was in for armed robbery, right?"

"That's right."

"Is she still in the joint?"

"No. We share a house in Hollywood."

"Oh, I wish I'd known. I would've invited her to the party."

"It's all right."

He paused and looked at me, and then said, "I hear she's good. At armed robbery."

That surprised me. "Yeah, I'd say she is. Was."

"Does she know anyone else who could, let's say, participate in a job?"

This was getting better. I answered, "Sure. Me."

DeAngelo looked sideways at me. "You? You've pulled off bank jobs?"

"I helped Christina a couple of times."

"Are you good? Tell me the truth. Could I call you professionals?"

My sister was a pro, but I couldn't say I was. I'd helped her out a couple of times, and she got popped on the second one. "Sure, Vince. When Christina and I did that sort of thing, we were very good. We robbed this bank in San Diego—"

"Listen, I may have a job for you and Christina. Are you interested?"

Yeah, I was interested. If it was for Vincent DeAngelo, I was definitely interested. And Christina would jump at it in a heartbeat. I told him so.

"Good. I don't know anything yet, but if it happens, it's going to be tricky. I need someone I can trust. It's probably going to involve a Hollywood bank. I'll know something concrete in a few weeks. You want to talk to Christina and see if it's something she's willing to risk? I know if she gets popped again it'll be bad news."

"I'm sure she'll be all for it."

"Fine. As soon as I know more details, I'll let you know. We'll talk again."

"Thanks, Vince."

He shook my hand and then walked away. I was stunned. He wanted to give me an important job. Me and sis.

I spent the rest of the evening enjoying myself—gorging on the food, drinking some very nice booze, and dancing with Maria.

But I really had my eye on that redhead I'd seen earlier.

12
Judy's Diary
1961

APRIL 10, 1961

I heard from Leo this evening! He called and asked me on a date because he's in town this week. Suddenly I have something to look forward to. I know it's been a month since I last wrote. I began the last entry feeling sorry for myself. It's even worse now, or it was until just a few minutes ago. Seriously, I have not been a happy person for the past two months. I drag myself through the days, and I've certainly had no desire to go out at night as the Stiletto.

They blamed the traffic accident on me, of course. And they're right. If I hadn't darted out into the street, it wouldn't have happened. The miracle about it all was that no one was killed. I thought surely passengers had died in that bus. There were a lot of injuries, and some serious ones, too. The taxi driver is still in the hospital.

The newspapers were full of the story for a few days, and then it kind of died out. However, last week, one of the passengers was quoted as saying he was going to sue the Black Stiletto if he could find her.

It all made me feel terrible. Freddie has also been quiet. A week after the accident he tried to talk to me. I was too upset to do so. I think he was mad at me at first, but then he saw how shaken I was by the whole thing. I told him I didn't want to talk about it, because there's nothing to be said. I caused the accident, people were hurt, we're all lucky no one was killed, and I'm sorry.

I considered writing an apology and sending it to the *Daily News* or the *Times*. I wonder if they'd have printed it.

A week ago there was another altercation between Clark and Kraig. Kraig continued to visit the gym at his usual time, 2:00 to 4:00 p.m. Clark started coming early, as I suggested, at 6:30. But after a couple of weeks, he said it was affecting his performance in school. So he switched to the end of the day, from 5:00 to 7:00 p.m. There was always a chance he'd run into Kraig, and it finally happened. They got into a fight outside in front of the gym, on the sidewalk. Jimmy alerted me to what was happening, so I stopped wiping down the glass cases and ran to intervene. Freddie beat me to it and had already separated the boys. Clark had a bloody nose, but Kraig was none the worse for wear. Freddie had no choice but to suspend them from the gym for a week. Kraig raised his middle finger at us and walked on. I brought Clark inside so he could wash up and hold a rag on his nose. I wasn't as disappointed in him as last time, because I'm sure he was only defending himself against a stinking bully. But rules are rules and I told him so. He said he understood, thanked me, fixed himself up, and left.

Both boys were able to return today. Clark did his usual 5:00 to 7:00, and I was happy to see him. Kraig didn't come in until after Clark had left. I was in the middle of closing up, and I was the only person in the gym. Kraig came swaggering in, dressed in street clothes. I was behind the cash register. He had the audacity to jump up and sit on the counter.

"Hello, Kraig," I said. "Get down, please."

He did. "I just stopped by to tell you I won't be coming to your gym anymore," he announced.

"I'm sorry to hear that."

"No, you're not. You only want customers who don't mind working out with niggers."

His words made me bristle, so I looked him in the eye. "Get out,

Kraig. And don't come back. And if I hear you've done anything to Clark, I'm coming after you."

He raised his hands, bugged out his eyes, and did an insulting impression of a Negro stereotype, "Oh, you scarin' me, Miss Judy, you scarin' me to *death*!"

"*Get out.*"

He grinned and backed up. As he sauntered toward the door, he turned and said, "Oh, by the way, your little nigger is dead meat. Don't be surprised if he doesn't show up anymore."

"Kraig, I'm serious. I'll get the police involved."

He just laughed. "Too bad you're such a bitch, Judy, otherwise I'd let you _____ my _____." I can't even write down the words, but they had something to do with my mouth and his anatomy. I wanted to come around the counter and clobber the creep. Instead, I controlled my temper and just glared at him, shooting imaginary stilettos from my eyes at him.

That put me in a grouchy mood, so after I locked the front door, turned out the lights, and went upstairs, I got in the tub and soaked for thirty minutes. I would have stayed longer, but Freddie knocked on the bathroom door and said I had a phone call from Leo. Freddie knew about Leo, I'd told him all about the California adventure. I'd also complained that I hadn't heard from him, so Freddie knew I'd want to take the call. I told him to tell Leo I'd be there in just a minute, so I quickly got out of the tub, wrapped a towel around my body, padded a wet trail to my bedroom, and picked up my extension.

"Hello?"

"Judy? It's Leo Kelly."

"Leo! How are you?"

"I'm good. How are you?"

I lied and put on my best happy voice. "I'm good, too. Are you calling from California?"

"No, I'm in New York. I told you I'd call you, so here I am."

"Oh, wow, when did you get in?"

"Just today as a matter of fact. I'm staying at the Carlyle on the East Side."

I was impressed. That's a pretty fancy hotel. "I heard President Kennedy is buying an apartment there, or he's already got one, or the family has one, or something like that."

"Really? I didn't know that. Listen, I'd really like to see you."

"Me, too," I said, and I did want to see him. I really did. "How long are you in town?"

"All week. I leave on Sunday. What are you doing Thursday night? I have tickets to see Mike Nichols and Elaine May on Broadway."

"Really? Oh, I'd love to see them."

"Great. Let's have dinner first."

I thought about the gym schedule and decided it wouldn't matter. Freddie could cover for me if I left early. "Sure. Where do you want to meet?"

"How about I come pick you up?"

That made me hesitate. I really didn't want Leo to see me at the gym. For the first time in my life, dear diary, I was ashamed of my position in life. Leo was a successful, well-dressed businessman. I didn't want him to think I was just low-class white trash. "How about I meet you at the restaurant? Just tell me the place and time. I can get off early."

He thought a second and said, "How about Sardi's. Do you know it?"

"Sure, I've eaten there before, it's fun."

"Six o'clock then? I'll make reservations. That'll give us enough time before the show at eight."

We jabbered about nothing for the next minute or so, and then he said good-bye. Today's Monday. I don't know how I'm going to wait until Thursday!

The phone call from Leo put me in a better mood, so I decided to write this diary entry after I got dressed and had dinner. I guess I need to get back in the habit. I'm still bothered by what Kraig said to me. I fear Kraig and his cronies will gang up on Clark in the street. Kraig knows Clark's gym schedule. I could follow Clark home tomorrow as the Stiletto. Should I? Would it be safe?

It's funny, the radio is playing "Runaway" by Del Shannon. When I hear it I think about Odessa. My brother Frankie is still there, I suppose. I wonder if John is still in the army. Should I contact Frankie? Do I dare risk facing those awful West Texas memories again? It may be a selfish reason that I don't stay in touch with my brothers, but it's just too painful to be reminded of that time in my life.

I'll sleep on it.

13
Judy's Diary
1961

I'm mad and I feel like an idiot. I'm in a lot of pain, too. I think I sprained my ankle pretty bad, so I have an ice pack on it, a glass of Freddie's bourbon in one hand, and a pen in the other. Tough luck if I don't get up tomorrow morning in time for work.

Today after Clark finished his workout, I ran upstairs and dressed as the Stiletto. It was still light outside, but it would be dark in an hour. I quickly slipped out the window, ran across the roofs and caught up with Clark as he made his way to 1st Avenue. He lived on Avenue C, which is also called Loisaida Avenue. Pablo, one of our newer gym regulars, told me that the word is really English and Spanish mixed, is pronounced "Low-E-Side-a," and it means "Lower East Sider." The neighborhood is primarily Puerto Rican and Dominican, but there are some Negroes and white people, too. I rarely travel that far east.

Clark lived between 2nd and 3rd Streets on the east side of the avenue. Normally, he would walk west along 2nd Street to get to the gym, but due to Kraig and his band of bullies, who live on 2nd between Avenues B and C, he takes a detour and goes a short block out of his way on 3rd Street. It's not a big deal to him, but I believe it's the principle of the thing. He shouldn't have to do that. And after Kraig's threat, I wanted to make sure he was okay.

Tonight he walked along 2nd Street on the way home. I guess he figured it was too late for Kraig to be guarding his turf. He was wrong.

I didn't want him to know I was following him, so I stayed in building doorways until he was far enough ahead before I continued. After I crossed Avenue B, I climbed the nearest fire escape on the north side of the street using my pulley hook and rope. I then moved along the rooftops until I had a bird's-eye view of the entire block. Clark was now below me to my west, nearly to Avenue C. He looked so small. Clark's not a very big guy. Has he turned eighteen yet? He was sixteen when we first met. I don't remember when his birthday is.

Sure enough, I spotted a group of four boys loitering on a stoop in front of a brownstone at the other end, and south side, of the street. Kraig and his henchmen. I moved farther east along the roofs until I was directly across from their building. Dusk had turned into night, so it was unlikely anyone could see me.

As Clark approached, he saw the trouble ahead and casually crossed from the south side of the street to the north. At that point Kraig and his buddies noticed him and stood. Kraig held a baseball bat. I positioned myself above a fire escape so that I could slither down if I had to. The quartet stepped into the street and shouted at Clark.

"You're on our street, boy!"

"What the hell you doing, boy?"

And so on. Lots of N-word usage.

Clark, bless his heart, did his best to ignore them. He kept walking, eyes straight ahead. He passed directly beneath me. Kraig and his gang moved closer to Clark.

"I'm talking to you, boy!" He slapped the bat against his palm.

Clark just kept going. Kraig obviously wanted him to get mad and say something in return, which would give Kraig an "excuse" to attack him. Clark said nothing. Then, just as Clark approached the corner of C and 2nd, a police car turned onto 2nd from the avenue. It slowly moved toward Kraig and the other boys, who retreated so the patrol car could pass between them and Clark. By the time the cops were gone, Clark had reached the corner. He was safe.

"We better not see you on this street again!" Kraig shouted.

Clark could have turned and hollered a retort, but he didn't. I moved along the roofs to the building at the end of the street and watched Clark finally enter a brownstone apartment building.

I breathed a sigh of relief. It went better than I expected. If I had interfered, it may have turned out a lot worse. Someone would have gotten hurt. Clark had done a really smart thing by not responding to the white boys' taunts. He handled it maturely and responsibly. They're teenagers, and they need to work out their differences by themselves. They don't need me. I still don't trust Kraig to leave Clark alone, but maybe Clark will continue to use 3rd Street as his route instead of 2nd. I think I'll advise him to do that the next time I see him.

On the way back to the gym, I used a different fire escape to get down to the street at the corner of Avenue B. Unfortunately, there were some bolts loose, and the entire contraption broke away from the building in a few spots. I was on the top level of stairs and I thought my weight would cause the structure to fall. It wobbled like crazy. I made my way down slowly and carefully until I got to the second-floor landing. From there it was maybe a twelve or fifteen foot drop to the sidewalk. I'd jumped and landed on my feet from that height so many times in the past, it was like second nature. But this time, I don't know what happened. Maybe I wasn't concentrating. Perhaps I was too relieved not to have plummeted with the fire escape. Whatever it was, I jumped and I landed badly on my left foot. Even with my sturdy boots on, my ankle twisted and I felt a sharp pain. I yelped and fell, right in front of pedestrians—a couple. I think it scared them, for the woman shrieked. At first I thought I'd broken my ankle because it *hurt like the dickens*! I rolled onto my back, bent my leg at the knee, and held on to my leg as I gritted my teeth.

"It's the Black Stiletto!" the man said.

"Really? She's not an imposter?"

"Are you all right?"

What a dumb question, but I guess he was trying to be helpful. I shook my head and sucked in air.

"Are you the real Black Stiletto?" He had a Spanish accent. He and his companion were most likely Puerto Ricans.

I nodded.

"Did you twist your ankle?"

"Yes," I managed to say. I wanted to cry, it hurt so bad.

He knelt beside me. The guy was maybe in his thirties. "You need to take off your boot. If your ankle swells too much, you won't get it off."

I knew that, but I was too mortified by my clumsiness to think. There was no way, though, that I was going to get it off by myself. "Can you help me?" I asked.

The woman said something to him in Spanish. He answered her and they had a momentary conversation I couldn't understand. It seemed she didn't want him to get involved. After all, I was a criminal, right?

"Please, can you help me?" I asked again.

The man positioned himself in front of me and took hold of my left boot. "This will hurt."

"It can't be worse than what I feel now."

It was. I actually screamed a little as he tugged and worked that boot off my already-swelling foot. I examined my ankle and, sure enough, it was starting to balloon.

My first thought was: how was I going to get home? I couldn't limp on one foot all the way. I'd never be able to climb the telephone pole to the roof or enter my room through the window. It would have to be the gym's front entrance. It was only around 8:00 in the evening, so there were a *million* people on the streets. I'd be seen. I'd be caught.

A little crowd was already gathering around me. Mostly Puerto Ricans.

"Can you stand up?" the man asked.

I had to try, so I nodded and he helped me. I dared putting some weight on my left foot and *wham*—the pain made me wince and nearly cry out.

Everyone was jabbering in Spanish, but my savior snapped at them, and then repeated himself in English, "No police."

"Thank you," I said. Apparently someone's bright idea was to turn me in.

What was I going to do? I did have my trench coat in my backpack, so if there was a place I could unmask and put on the coat without anyone seeing me, I could probably hobble home. But how was I going to explain that to my audience? How did Clark Kent do it? On the other hand, if I tried to get home in my complete outfit, the cops could see me, I could be followed, no one would leave me alone, and no telling what else.

It must have been providence in action, for at that moment a taxi-cab traveling from east to west on 2nd Street stopped and let out some passengers, right there on the corner where we were standing.

"Please hold that cab," I said to my benefactor. He stepped to the passenger window and spoke to the driver. He then motioned for me to come. Carrying my boot, I shuffled to the car. My friend opened the door for me and I climbed in the back seat.

"You all right now, miss?" he asked.

"Yes. Thank you so much. *Gracias.*"

He smiled. "You're welcome. Be more careful next time."

"You said it."

I shut the door and then looked at the driver. He was staring at me with his mouth open.

"Yeah, I'm the Black Stiletto, and I hurt myself. Can you take me to the corner of 2nd Street and 2nd Avenue? I realize that's only three blocks."

"Sure."

As we drove, I counted what money I had on me. Exactly twelve dollars. The fare and tip wouldn't be more than a couple of bucks. I then got my trench coat out of the backpack and struggled to put it on. When he pulled over at our destination, I gave him the entire amount. "I'd like you to close your eyes. Please."

He saw the money and said, "Okay."

"Please don't watch me. As soon as I get out of the car, I want you to cross 2nd Avenue and keep going. Don't look back. Deal?"

"Okay."

Then, as smoothly as possible, I removed my mask and stuffed it into the boot I was carrying. I opened the car door and stepped out on my good foot. To anyone on the street, they would have seen a normal young woman wearing a trench coat emerge from the taxi. I watched the driver, and he kept his word and didn't look at me. The light turned green and he drove across the intersection as I'd asked.

No one paid any attention to me, even though I sort of hopped onto the curb. I was just another pedestrian, albeit one with a bad limp. It wasn't far to the gym's front door, but on one leg it seemed like a mile. I used my keys to unlock the door and went inside. Nobody had followed me. My secret was still safe.

So that's why I'm mad at myself. I went out for a stupid reason. Clark was just fine on his own. It was none of my business. I shouldn't have butted in. Look what it got me for my trouble. A sprained or broken ankle. Tomorrow I'll have to go to the doctor or hospital and get it X-rayed.

Darn, darn, darn!

Sometimes I wish I was more comfortable cursing like the guys in the gym!

Damn, damn, damn!

There. Did cursing make me feel better?

Nope.

14
Martin
THE PRESENT

I flew to New York City today. Jesus, how many times was I going to travel to New York in one year because of my unpredictable daughter? This was the third trip in six months.

After getting that tuition refund from Juilliard, Carol and I frantically tried to reach Gina on the phone, to no avail. We were really starting to get worried and I considered calling that NYPD detective, Ken Jordan, who had helped with her cases in the past; but then Gina finally returned Carol's call. I suppose it's a good thing she spoke to Carol and not me, or it wouldn't have been pretty.

Gina dropped out of school without telling us. Unbelievable. She had registered for the spring semester, I'd paid for it, and then she canceled everything before classes began. And that's not the worst of it. She moved out of the dormitory and was now living with a boyfriend. Her Krav Maga instructor. Some guy named Josh. She told Carol she wanted to concentrate on Krav Maga "full time" and become an instructor in martial arts.

On hearing the news, I had to take a tranquilizer and chase it with a glass of vodka. I was *very* angry. I loved my daughter, but I wanted to strangle her.

Maggie helped me cool down and suggested that Carol and I should maybe go back to New York and talk to Gina in person. Carol, however, couldn't get away from her job at such short notice like she did before, so it was up to me. I asked Sam if I could have a few days off, and he didn't mind. "Family always comes first," was his mantra. I didn't know what I was going to accomplish, but at least I'd see Gina, meet her boyfriend, and try to talk some sense into her.

I also figured I could take care of another mission while I was in the city. Before I left Chicago, I talked with Uncle Thomas. He located Betty Dinkins and gave me her address. The woman lived on West 47th Street, between 9th and 10th Avenues. It was an area once known as "Hell's Kitchen"—maybe it still was, although supposedly it was a lot nicer now than twenty or thirty years ago. In other words, despite being close to the Theater District, it was one of the more run-down sections of Manhattan. I figured that if Dinkins had lived there a long time, then she probably wasn't the richest woman in the city. No wonder she was claiming to be the Black Stiletto. She was just trying to make a buck. I still thought someone had put her up to it, that son or another relative. I intended to find out.

The Empire Hotel across from Lincoln Center was my usual stomping grounds when I visited the city. I checked in and immediately tried calling Gina. She knew I was on my way to see her, so this time she picked up promptly.

"Hi, Dad."

"Gina, honey, we need to talk."

"I know. You really didn't have to come all the way to New York, you know."

"Yes, I did. Where are you?"

"I'm at the studio. Why don't you come by? You can meet Josh and see what it is I'm doing."

"Fine."

She gave me the directions—it was a short walk—and I set out to confront my wayward daughter. The place was called, simply, "Krav Maga," and was located on Broadway between 69th and 70th Streets. It was a small place tucked between a pizza joint and a dry cleaner. Through the front plate-glass window I saw a brightly lit room resembling a ballet studio. There were mirrors on opposite walls, and a large mat covering the floor. Doors in the back led, presumably, to dressing rooms/bathrooms and an office.

Gina was on the mat, sparring with a young man with brown curly hair, a beard and mustache, and more muscles than I thought were humanly possible. She was dressed in sweatpants and one of those sleeveless sports-bra tops that exposed her midriff. She was barefoot and her long brown hair was tied in a ponytail. I'd never seen Gina look so buff before.

I stood and watched for a while as the couple went through some drills and exercises. I'd read up on Krav Maga before coming to New York. It was an Israeli self-defense system, and practitioners didn't really like to refer to it as a "martial art" because it existed solely for protecting oneself. There were no sporting rules with Krav Maga. Apparently anything went, for the goal was to quickly and efficiently neutralize an opponent. The Israeli Defense Forces trained with Krav Maga. Unlike the Asian martial arts, Krav Maga was intentionally brutal and aggressive, combining defensive maneuvers with decisive counterattacks. It was hard to believe my little girl wanted to do it, and she was demonstrating that she *could*. She'd never been particularly sporty, except with gymnastics when she was younger. Back then, what appealed to Gina was all the attention she'd get from being in show business, or so she thought. Whether or not she was a good actress or dancer, I couldn't really say. When I saw her high school things, she was okay. I wasn't big on that kind of stuff anyway. But there she was inside the "studio" learning to be a lethal weapon.

Why?

Even though it wasn't particularly cool outside, I felt a sudden chill.

Gina was becoming my mother.

The couple stopped what looked to me like a lot of choreographed grappling. As they took a breather, my daughter spied me through the window. She smiled and waved as if there was nothing wrong with that picture. I met her at the door.

"Dad, it's good to see you! Gosh, you've lost some weight!"

"Glad you noticed." I immediately hugged her. "Are you all right, honey?"

It was a genuine embrace. And I felt unusual strength in her arms.

"Of course I'm all right, I'm *great*."

I held her at arm's length and I must admit—she looked marvelous. A complete change from the last few times I'd seen her, especially post-assault. While she did a great job presenting to the world how quickly she "got over it," I'd known there was something still missing. With her standing before me, I figured out what it was.

She was beaming with happiness. Absolutely *glowing*. And she looked so pretty—despite the sweat and clothing—and I knew there was no way I could yell at this girl, make her feel bad for disappointing her mother and me, and bring her back to the real world.

It wasn't going to happen.

"Well, you look great," I managed to reply.

"Dad, I want you to meet Josh."

The young man stood nearby. Our eyes met and he approached me with an outstretched hand.

"I'm pleased to meet you, sir."

We shook and I said, "Likewise, Josh. Pardon me, what's your last name again?"

"Feldstein, Daddy," Gina said. "Josh Feldstein, meet my dad, Martin Talbot."

"How are you?"

"I'm fine, sir."

I had thought he was a young man, closer to Gina's age, but up close I could see the years in his slightly toughened skin and worldly eyes. This guy wasn't much younger than me. I could see why Gina was attracted to him, though. He was handsome and certainly fit. The muscles practically rippled over his body.

"How old are you, Josh?" I asked without thinking.

"Dad!" Gina blurted. "Gee whiz—"

Josh laughed and said, "It's all right, Gina, I don't mind. Mr. Talbot, I'm thirty-nine years old."

"He'd have to be, Dad, he's a Black Belt Dan Three."

"Is that good?"

"Dad, it's expert-level Krav Maga. It takes sixteen years to get where Josh is. He first started learning it during his military service."

"You're from Israel?" I asked him. He didn't have a foreign accent.

"I was born there, sir, in Jerusalem. But then my parents emigrated here when I was a baby. I actually have dual citizenship. I grew up in Yonkers, but I go back to Israel often to see family. I chose to fulfill my military service there. I'm glad I did."

"Are you hungry, Dad? We just finished our lesson. We could go somewhere nice."

"No, Gina, I'm not, but I was hoping I could talk to you alone for a bit." I turned to Josh. "If you don't mind, Josh."

"Not at all, sir. Gina, I'll be in the office." He gave me a friendly smile and then walked across the mat and through a door.

"Dad, that was kind of rude," Gina said.

"I'm sorry, but I think we need to talk about this, and not in front of him, Gina."

"All right. You want to sit down?" She motioned to some folding chairs along the side of one wall.

"Sure." We went over and sat. "Gina—"

"Dad," she held up a hand, "I'm sorry I didn't tell you or Mom about dropping out. I am. I was afraid you'd be really mad and I hate it when you're mad at me."

"Gina, honey, your mother and I love you, no matter what. You know that, right?"

Tears formed in her eyes. "I don't know. I guess."

"Of course, we do. But that said, *yes*, we're a little mad at you. We don't like being taken by surprise. No parent does."

"I talked to Mom and she's sort of okay with it now."

"When did you talk to her?"

"This morning."

"What'd she say?"

"That she hoped I knew what I was doing, but she'd support me in my decision." That was news to me. "But I am sorry I caused you any grief, Dad. I was afraid to tell you. I know you have that anxiety thing and I didn't want to make that worse. I don't know, I thought maybe so much time would go by and when I eventually told you then it wouldn't matter. It was dumb."

"But why, Gina? Tell me why you want to do—" I looked around the room—"*this*."

"I don't know, Dad, something happened to me last fall, and I'm not just talking about the assault. Well, that may have been the beginning of it, but I started re-examining my life and what I wanted to do with it. After I was attacked, school just seemed so pointless. Acting and dance—that's all wonderful, but I suddenly couldn't see myself doing it. I'm sorry, Dad, I know I put you through hell regarding my choice of college and my major, and here I am ditching it. But I assure you, what I'm doing now means a lot to me and I have a clear vision of the future."

"Really? Do you?"

"Yes."

"Then what is it?"

"Dad, it's too complicated to go into right here, right now. How long are you in town?"

"I'm not sure. It's supposed to be a quick in-and-out."

"Well, can we talk about it another time? Can't we just be together for now? I really want you to get to know Josh. He's a great guy."

"He certainly could give the Hulk a run for his money. I take it he's Jewish?"

"Does that matter?"

"No, of course not." I gestured to the empty studio. "Where are all the other students?"

"There aren't that many. Josh teaches a very specialized course. He trains us one-on-one. There aren't any classes right now, but I train eight hours a day, Dad. I'm serious about it."

"Eight hours a day? How can your body stand it? Isn't that like exercising all day?"

"Well, yeah, it is. That's what professional athletes do."

"So you're an athlete now?"

"No, Dad, but I'm training in a very physical skill. And guess what? I'm *good* at it. I've been progressing faster than anyone Josh has ever seen. I'm already a yellow belt, and it usually takes nine months to get one. I started six months ago, and I've been doing it intensively for only four. It actually won't be long before I'll have an orange belt, and that usually takes a whole year to get."

I was dizzy from all the information. It was totally foreign to me. She may as well have been speaking Swahili. "So, what, do you go to the Olympics or something? Join the Israeli army?"

She laughed. "No, but it's possible I'll be able to use my ability in my work."

"What do you mean?"

Gina shook her head. "Look, never mind, just know that this isn't costing me anything. I'm living with Josh, so my expenses are practically nothing. I help out here in the studio, and Josh pays me a small salary, too. I'm basically being paid to train."

"Your boyfriend is also your boss and your teacher?"

She shrugged. "It's not as weird as it sounds."

"And what happens if you two break up? Then are you out on the street?"

"I don't think that's going to happen. So, how about dinner? Are you hungry? I'm starved, and I'll bet Josh is, too. You won't have to treat, Josh will. He said he wanted to."

"That's not—Gina, this is all so sudden—and *different*."

She gave me the smile that melted hearts of males everywhere, including her own father's. "I know. But I swear to you, I'm happier than I've ever been."

"I can tell, Gina. That much is evident. You look beautiful."

"Aw, thanks, Dad. Should I call Josh out?"

"Yeah, I guess."

She did and her paramour emerged, now dressed in street clothes. Gina jumped up, saying, "I'm going to change. You two get acquainted." Then she ran off to her own locker room.

Josh joined me in the seats and said, "Gina is quite remarkable, Mr. Talbot. I've never had a student so determined and dedicated. Where does she get it? Are you or her mother athletic?"

"Not at all." I shook my head. "I don't know where she gets it." Of course that was a lie. I knew exactly where Gina got it. "Maybe her grandmother. She, uh, did gymnastics when she was a young girl."

"That could be it," he said. "Gina's told me about her. Your mother, right?"

"Yeah."

"I'm sorry to hear about her condition. How is she doing?"

It was a little weird having a total stranger ask about Mom. "As best as can be expected, given her illness."

"I had an uncle who had Alzheimer's. It's very hard on everyone. My sympathies go out to you, sir."

"Okay, thanks, but let's stop with the 'sir,' stuff. Just call me Martin, all right?"

He smiled again. "All right." There was genuine warmth about the guy. Despite his intimidating size, he seemed like a nice person. "She's the best student I've ever had, Martin, and I've been instructing Krav Maga for over ten years. She is going to set a record for learning and mastering the system in a relatively short time. She has exceptional speed and ability. It normally takes at least seven years to obtain a brown belt—that's one below the black—but I predict she'll do it in five, and that's unheard of. She's a machine."

"Great," I said, but it was obvious I had no clue what the significance of it all was. It was also apparent that I would have to just go with the flow when it came to Gina. It made my anxiety level jump a couple of notches, but what could I do?

I hoped Gina and Josh didn't mind if I had a few drinks with dinner.

15
Judy's Diary
1961

April 13, 1961

Be still my heart! What just happened tonight?

I had a date with Leo, that's what happened. He simply fascinates me. Oh, my gosh, I think I'm giddy from just being with him. Am I in love? He's so good looking and charming. He seems to have money, too, and that can't hurt!

It was a wonderful evening, despite the fact that I was on crutches. Yes, I found out yesterday that I sprained my ankle, but the leather boot prevented a broken one. I feel awkward and stupid and ugly, and you can imagine what it was like being seen with Leo in public and having to mess with crutches when you sit down to dinner or go to the theatre. It's an embarrassing bother.

A taxi took me to meet him at Sardi's and, surprisingly, I wasn't late. Traffic at that time of day is the absolute worst, especially in the Times Square area. I've never been much to frequent that part of town as the Stiletto because there are way too many people around. And way too many cops. But sometimes the place can be exciting whether you visit as a tourist or a native New Yorker.

Sardi's is a fun place to go. It's on W. 44th Street and it's been there forever as a Broadway hangout. I always enjoy it. The food is good and I like to look at the caricatures of Broadway actors and actresses on the walls. I don't go to the theatre as often as I probably should. Lucy and Peter go a lot. When I have gone, I've enjoyed it. It is more expensive than going to a movie, and that's a deterrent.

Leo was there waiting for me, and he looked like a million bucks. He was wearing a shiny gray suit I simply wanted to *touch*. I should have warned him I'd be on crutches, but I didn't have a way to reach him. He was surprised and I think a little amused. He was a real gentleman with regard to taking charge of the blasted things when I was seated. Still, I was mortified, everyone in the restaurant turned to look at me. That tends to happen, doesn't it? When you're in a public place and someone comes in on crutches or in a wheelchair, you notice, right?

I was nervous, obviously so. The place was very crowded since it was the dinner hour before the 8:00 start time for shows. It felt like everyone was staring at me, not just Leo, ha ha. He *was* looking at me like he'd just opened a present on Christmas morning. I wore a low-cut dress that revealed more of my bust than I usually do. He told me I looked "spectacular" and that I have "striking eyes." He asked me if I'd ever been a redhead, and I told him no. He thought I'd look good as a redhead. So right off the bat he made me feel self-conscious. I mean, I was flattered; I wasn't offended or anything like that. But he kept staring at me like he wanted to pounce.

But I relaxed as time went on and the food—and *drinks!*—arrived. We had champagne, dear diary, and some very nice wine with our sirloin steak and spinach cannelloni *au gratin*! It was a fabulous meal. It's a good thing we shared, or I'd be so full and uncomfortable in the theatre. The seats in those old theatres are too close together and allow no room for people with long legs, like me. But we make do.

Over dinner we talked about all kinds of things, but very little about his work because we covered that last time. He's in New York for a meeting involving equipment purchasing. I told him more about the gym and what I do every day. Then we started talking about movies and that's when it really got fun, because I love movies and so does he. I don't know if we have similar tastes, though. I told him about that new French film I've wanted to see called *Breathless*. It's playing uptown, I just haven't had the chance to go. Lucy and Peter say it will change the language of cinema. Leo said he doesn't like subtitles.

We had great seats for the show, center aisle, about thirty feet from the stage. Leo tipped the usher extra to take care of my crutches. He's so sweet! Mike Nichols and Elaine May were very funny. Leo and I both laughed so hard we had tears in our eyes. My side started hurting! I think I'll have to get their record.

Afterward, neither of us wanted the evening to end, so we went to a coffee shop on 8th Avenue. I insisted on walking with my crutches; I told him it was good for me. The place was crowded, since it was after theatre, but we managed to get a nice table in a corner. He bought coffee for both of us; I refused the offer for dessert, I was still stuffed.

We talked about the show and he brought up Los Angeles again. "You should move there," he said. "You'd love it."

"You said that last time."

"You could work at Flickers. Charlie even told me he thought you had class."

"Charlie doesn't even know me!"

"He saw you that first night, the night you and I met."

I laughed. "New York's not so bad."

"Maybe not, but with you here in Manhattan and me in L.A., you can't be my kept woman."

That shocked me. He gave me an enchanting smile and for a moment I believed what he was saying. Then I knew he was putting me on.

"Stop," I said, lightly slapping his arm. "You're terrible."

"Oh, I'm not so bad once you get to know me."

He helped me get a taxi and, in fact, he rode with me in it all the way to the gym. By then I didn't care if he saw where I lived and worked. After the cab pulled up in front, he asked if he could get a tour. I told him it was too late, maybe some other time.

"Hey, you want to go to a ball game?" he asked.

"Huh?"

"I have two tickets to see the Yankees on Saturday afternoon. Let's go. After the game we can go to dinner again. I have to go back to L.A. on Sunday."

I think I've been to Yankee Stadium less than five times since I've been in New York. It sounded like so much fun. Normally I'd be working, but was sure I could fix it with Freddie, so I said yes.

He told the cab driver to wait and he walked me to the front door. Then he put both hands on my head, drew me in, and kissed me. It was a wet, passionate kiss, and it lasted forever. Wow. I felt it from the tips of my toes to the top hair on my head, just like last time. Then he waited until I unlocked the door and got inside, and then he went back to the taxi and took off.

Well, there's no question that I like him a lot. He's got a show-business attitude, a little on the aggressive side, but that means he's very self-confident. I like that. A man who's sure of himself is attractive to me. That might put off some people, but I feed off of it. For such a little guy—and I don't mean that in a bad way—he's a bundle of energy. I know he's aware I'm taller than him when he kisses me, but there's no acknowledgment; it truly doesn't bother him.

He also makes me laugh. I sure laughed a lot tonight, and not just in the theatre.

I do sense, though, that there is something dark inside him. I've written this before. He has secrets. In the past when I've gotten involved with men who had secrets—and that's *all* of them—things don't always turn out so well. But in Leo's defense, I suppose everyone has secrets of some kind.

As do I. So there.

16
Judy's Diary
1961

April 16, 1961

Okay, dear diary, here we go. Judy Cooper has done it again. I'm head over heels. I'm smitten and I don't know if it's a good thing or a bad thing. Leo Kelly is a man of mysteries and complications, but he's also a gentleman, he's kind, and he's terribly sexy. He's a fantastic lover too.

Yes, that's happened already. Last night I couldn't help myself. His charm and seductive powers won me over. Today—I don't know how I feel about it. A little embarrassed, perhaps? I want to think that I'm not the kind of girl who sleeps around. Believe me, I get plenty of propositions. The guys at the gym take care of that department just fine. Shoot, I've been approached by total strangers on the street, men who ask me for my name and phone number. I've become used to it, the way men look at me. All girls feel the same way, don't they? You can tell when a man is looking at you with *those* thoughts in his head. And that's practically *any* time a man looks at you, ha ha! Corky at the gym told a joke once: God gave man two brains, one in his head and one in his you-know-what—but God made it so man could only use one brain at a time!

At any rate, I don't want to be an S-L-U-T, but it doesn't mean you're one if you really like the guy, right?

Yesterday was Saturday and I got the day off. I was prepared to take the subway and meet Leo at Yankee Stadium, but he picked me up at the gym in a town car. It was kind of like riding in a limousine, only smaller. He said he hired it for the day. It must be very expensive.

Leo had told me to dress casually, but it was surprisingly cool out, so I wore a sweatshirt and a pair of Levis. The temperature was in the fifties, but it was sunny. Leo wore a short-sleeve shirt, black trousers, and a baseball cap. Since I didn't have one, he bought me a Yankees cap at the stadium; I wore it during the game.

Once I was seated and my crutches were stored under the bench, it was so much fun. I like baseball more than football or basketball. There's something about the sense of community that exists in the stands. Everybody is there to have a good time. I love how the vendors walk around shouting, "Hot dogs! Cold beer! Coca-Cola!" It's so exciting when the organ plays and the enthusiastic crowd yells in unison.

The Yankees played against the Kansas City Athletics, and it was a tight, tense game. The Yankees won 5–3. Everyone was talking about who was better, Mickey Mantle or Roger Maris. If you ask me, I thought Roger Maris stole the show.

After the game, the driver took us back to Manhattan in the town car. Leo asked if I wanted to have dinner at his hotel, the Carlyle. I thought we might not be dressed properly, but he said it wouldn't matter in the Café Carlyle that early in the evening. So I agreed. The hotel is on the Upper East Side on Madison Avenue. A bunch of Cuban protesters with placards had gathered outside the main entrance. The signs said things like, "6,000,000 Cubans ask to be liberated!" and "Give us weapons to fight the Reds!" and "Do something, Mr. President!"

"Oh my gosh, is Kennedy here?" I asked.

"I don't know," Leo replied. "Maybe."

Once we were inside the café, I did feel underdressed. Leo said not to worry about it. It was too early for the piano player, George

Feyer, to start, so the "jet set" wouldn't be arriving until later. It was a cute place with colorful, slightly risqué murals on the walls. The waiter told us they were by Marcel Vertes. I'd never heard of him, but apparently he's a big deal.

We just had burgers and fries for dinner, and they were delicious. Leo told me what he'd learned about Kennedy staying there.

"He has a seven-room duplex suite on the 34th and 35th floors. Apparently, he sometimes entertains young ladies there when he's in town without his wife."

"You're not serious!"

Leo shrugged. "That's what they say."

"Well, I always heard he was popular with the ladies."

"Did you know he sees Marilyn Monroe every now and then?"

"No!"

"Apparently, there are some underground tunnels beneath the hotel, and Kennedy uses them when he doesn't want to be seen. He also sneaks his girlfriends in and out that way."

"I don't believe it! Who told you that?"

He winked at me. "I have my sources."

I asked him where his room was, and he replied it was only on the 11th floor. "It's a nice room, but it's no duplex suite. Want to see it?"

Ha! The guy didn't give up. I gave him one of my sideways looks and wagged a finger at him. "Be nice, Leo. I told you I'm not that kind of girl."

At that point he poured some more wine. We'd already had a martini each, so I was feeling pretty good. I laughed at his witty remarks, and I admit I was intoxicated by those Paul Newman blue eyes. I asked him if anyone told him he resembled the actor, and he said, "Yeah, all the time. Actually, I think I'm better looking, don't you?"

Well, dear diary, thirty minutes later I was up in his room. It did cross my mind at the time that it was too soon, that I was being a "loose woman," and that it was a reckless thing to do. But the drinks, the atmosphere, and the good time I was having with him simply hypnotized me. Leo Kelly knows how to seduce a girl. I finally threw caution to the wind and said to myself, "Oh, why not?"

All I'm going to write here is that of all the times I've been with a man, this was the most intense. And it happened several times— in one night! Today I am very tired and very sore, and not just my ankle. But I feel *great*, if that makes any sense.

We were about to go to breakfast in the café this morning, but I told him I didn't want to be seen in the same place wearing the same clothes as last night. We found a diner down the street and had an oddly quiet meal of eggs and bacon. I think we were both a little dazed. He checked out of the hotel and then the cab dropped me at the gym before taking him on to the airport. Outside on the side-walk, Leo took hold of my upper arms and said, "Come to L.A."

"Is that a proposal?" I asked facetiously.

Instead of laughing, he answered, "No. I'm not the marrying type, Judy. I should probably say that up front."

"Then why come to L.A.?"

"For a change. Don't you want a change? From the way you talk, I think you do."

At the time I didn't think so, but now I believe he's right.

Before a very passionate last kiss, he repeated that I'd have a job and would make a dynamite hostess. He said I should "think about it," and know that "he'd be there." We said good-bye and I watched him return to the taxi and shut the door. As the cab moved on, he looked back at me through the window and waved. I did the same.

I must have been really shell shocked, because I barely remember going inside and seeing Freddie behind the counter, and all the morning regulars in the gym. I don't *think* it really happened, but it seemed as if everyone stopped what they were doing, turned, and looked at me. What's it called, the "walk of shame?" When you're caught sneaking home after spending the night with a man? That's what it felt like. But maybe no one noticed. Except Freddie, of course. He had that fatherlike frown on his face. *That* I remember!

It's bedtime and I'm just now writing all this down. I floated through the rest of the day, working in the gym. At one point, Freddie told me to get off "cloud 9." I swear he really *is* becoming overly paternal.

There's always an ache in the middle of my chest after something like this happens. I miss the man, the intimacy. It hurts, but it's a good hurt. It's very difficult to explain. Is that how love begins? With pain? So often that's what it *ends* with.

Whatever, all I know is I can't stop thinking about Leo Kelly.

17
Judy's Diary
1961

Worrisome news today. There was a military sea invasion of Cuba this morning, but it's not clear what's happening. The daily newspapers were already printed when we heard about it on the radio. Apparently, it's an anti-Castro force of Cuban exiles that's behind the attack. I guess we'll know more tomorrow.

I think I have my head on correctly today. Yesterday I was in a cloud. This morning Freddie asked me if I was all right, and I just grinned and said, "I'm fine." He went back to his newspaper and grunted, "Well, I hope you know what you're doing."

Isn't a man supposed to call a girl the day after he's slept with her? I didn't hear from Leo, but I suppose he's busy after flying back. I can't expect this to be like a real relationship. After all, he's on the West Coast and I'm here. I have no idea when I'll see him again. Maybe it was just a one-time thing. I don't know. I'm not particularly bothered by that notion, although I do miss him. Did I do the right thing by staying the night at his hotel? After a day to get a more realistic perspective on the weekend, I have a feeling Leo Kelly could be trouble, if only because he's such a charmer. But what can I say? He knows how to treat a girl and make her feel good. I still have his business card. I wonder if *I* should call *him*? Probably not. That's not the accepted thing to do. Then again, when have I ever done the acceptable thing?

My ankle is better and I'm able to walk without the crutches, although I have to limp. I was more active in the gym today, and that's a good thing. Maybe the sprain wasn't so bad. The swelling has gone down completely.

I was going to end my day at work after Clark's boxing lesson because I was invited to Lucy and Peter's for dinner and the Oscar Awards on TV. Clark didn't show up; I don't know why, he didn't call to say he wasn't coming. That's not like him. Oh, well, I spent the time spotting Corky and Jimmy on weights.

The Oscar show was fun. Bob Hope is always a riot. It wasn't a surprise that *The Apartment* won Best Picture. Burt Lancaster won Best Actor for *Elmer Gantry* and Elizabeth Taylor won for *Butterfield 8*. Lucy thinks she got it because she just had a tracheotomy due to pneumonia and almost died, but Lucy's down on Elizabeth Taylor because the actress stole Debbie Reynolds's husband, Eddie Fisher.

Going to bed now, hopefully to dream about Leo.

APRIL 18, 1961

The papers say the invasion in Cuba was definitely what we thought. An anti-Castro force made up of Cuban exiles attacked the country, but as of tonight it's not going well for them. A lot of talk today was whether or not the U.S. was involved; otherwise how could a bunch of Cuban exiles get the boats and planes and guns? Freddie thinks the CIA is behind the whole thing. Nevertheless, it sounds as if the Cuban army is smashing the invasion force to pieces.

Normally, I don't pay much attention to the gym regulars' schedules and whether or not they show up, unless I have a one-to-one lesson or training session booked. But Clark was absent again today, so I called the phone number we had on file for him. It rang and rang. I'm getting one of my bad feelings about this. The mother lioness thing. Somehow I sense something's not right with Clark.

Leo still hasn't called.

April 19, 1961

I'm about to go out as the Stiletto. I wanted to wait until dark, so I had a little time to make a diary entry.

Very bad news—Clark is in the hospital. When he didn't show up again today, I started to phone his home again. But a little Negro girl, maybe twelve years old, came in the front door of the gym. She was timid at first, but Freddie asked her nicely if he could help her. She said she wanted to see Judy.

Her name was Violet and she was Clark's sister. She was very cute, but she had sad news. Clark was injured in a fight. Her mother told her to come tell me because I'd want to know.

"Is he going to be all right?" I asked.

She didn't know. Freddie nodded at me so I went with her—actually I hailed a cab—and we went together to Beekman Downtown Hospital. That's where I went to visit Billy last November when he was hurt. Violet led me to the floor where Clark's mother and baby brother were gathered. The Intensive Care Unit.

I introduced myself to Clark's mother, Mrs. Raney. She'd been crying and was still very upset.

"What happened?" I asked.

She told me Clark had been beaten nearly to death on 3rd Street last Sunday night and she believes it was a group of white boys that did it. The police haven't bothered to arrest anyone because there were no witnesses. Clark has been in a coma ever since.

"How bad are his injuries?"

Mrs. Raney said he had broken bones all over his body, but the worst part is that he'd been hit in the head with a *baseball bat*.

She let me peek in the room to see him. He was wrapped like a mummy in white, but glimpses of his dark flesh peeked through here and there. My heart broke. I started to cry. After a moment, I went back in the hall and Mrs. Raney gave me a hug. She thanked me for being good to Clark.

"He's not going to die," I told her.

She said the doctors told her it could go either way; but even if he does live, he'll be a "vegetable." That's the word she used.

So that's why I'm going out as the Stiletto. It was Kraig, it had to have been. Even though it happened on 3rd Street and not 2nd, I know it to be so.

It's almost dark, five more minutes. I just heard on the radio that the Cuba invasion failed. They're calling it the "Bay of Pigs" invasion, because that's the Spanish translation of where the battle was, I think. The fighting is still going on, but by all accounts the exiles have lost.

Okay, I'm out the window. Wish me luck.

18
Leo
THE PAST

The trip to New York was a whirlwind. I got a lot of business done and I had fun, too. Saw a Broadway show, a Yankees game, and I got laid. What more could a guy ask for?

I met with Jules Krasny, Mookie Samberg's friend who had access to the special paper the government used to make dollar bills. They called them Federal Reserve Notes. Everything about U.S. money was secret. The paper it was printed on, the kind of ink, the special engraving machines—and it was becoming more difficult to copy them. But if anyone could do it, Samberg was the man. Krasny's prices were high, but Samberg warned me they would be. I had to get on the phone and clear it with Casazza, who in turn checked it with DeAngelo, and then I got the green light. We got the paper at a reduced price in exchange for protection in New York through DeAngelo's colleagues in another family. No problem. We'll just have to kick some of the counterfeit dough to New York, too. I didn't care—a little slice of the pie wouldn't hurt us.

As soon as I got home from New York, I checked in with Christina, who was doing some fella she picked up at a nightclub in Hollywood. They were in her bedroom upstairs making all kinds of noise. I didn't want to disturb them, although I was curious to find out who he was. What could I say? I was protective of my little sister, even though she could probably kick my ass from here to Sicily if she wanted. So I just made some noise in the kitchen and after a moment she came out of the room dressed in a bathrobe and descended the stairs.

"You're home."

I acted surprised. "Really? I am? How do you know?"

"Mr. Funny. How was the trip?"

"Excellent. Got all the business done and enjoyed myself, too."

"Business and pleasure."

"You said it. How are you? Sounds like you got company."

"Yeah, one of the Heathens. I don't think you know him. Met him at the pool hall where they hang out."

The Heathens were a motorcycle club Casazza did business with. He sold them guns that were imported from Africa. Like the Hells Angels, the Heathens were considered "one percenters," referring to the statement made by the American Motorcyclist Association that only one percent of all motorcycle clubs were "outlaw" MCs. The Heathens were made up of white guys, and their sworn enemies were Los Serpientes, an outlaw MC that acted as runners and soldiers for the Mexican Mafia. My plan with the counterfeit dough was to sell it to Los Serpientes because the funny money would pass easier south of the border. It was funny that DeAngelo considered them to be degenerate lowlifes with no class or morals, but money talked. The Heathens paid good cash for the arms and Los Serpientes would pay good cash for the funny money. The Heathens had a distribution machine in place, so the arrangement made sense.

So the counterfeit operation was going to be my test, so to speak, to see if I could handle it, run it, and steer it through to the payoff.

"I have to go see Mookie, and then I have a meeting with Carlos Gabriel," I told Christina. "I'll be back late tonight."

She put a finger to her lips. "We don't want my Heathen friend to hear that."

"Right." Carlos Gabriel was the L.A. chapter president of Los Serpientes.

"Want to go to the shooting range tomorrow?"

I shrugged. "I have to go to the office. You know, check in and pretend I still run the business. But we can go late afternoon. Is that okay?"

"Sure. Be careful with those Serpents. They're nasty."

"So are Heathens. You be careful, too." I pinched her cheek and started to leave.

"You get any in New York?"

I just turned and wiggled my eyebrows at her. She laughed and went back to her room.

After a quick meeting with Samberg at the place he was renting in Hollywood, I drove to Southeast L.A. to see Gabriel. It's a rough part of town, full of Mexicans and Negroes. Los Serpientes owned an auto-repair garage and an adjoining bar on Florence, near Compton. I didn't like the way the Serpents stared at us as Boone drove the Lincoln into their lot. Whenever I did business with tough customers, I always had Boone take me. I owned a 1959 Lincoln Continental Mark IV town car for those purposes. It made me look important. And it was a good thing that Boone had a permit to carry a gun.

I recognized Gabriel's right-hand man standing in front. "Hey, Chuy, how are you doing?" I asked as I got out of the car.

The man grunted and shrugged. Some of the other gang members spoke in low voices to each other in Spanish. I had no idea what they said, but it was probably insulting.

"I'm here to see Carlos. He's expecting me."

Chuy jerked his head to one of the other guys, and he immediately went around my back to frisk me. I was clean. Boone volunteered his gun, a Browning 9mm semiautomatic he wore under his jacket. The Serpent frisked him anyway, and then we were allowed into the shop.

Carlos Gabriel was in his thirties, but he looked much older. All MC members were like that. I guess it's because of all the wear and tear on the road and living a lifestyle on the edge. He sat in the shop's office behind a desk that was surprisingly clean of any paper or objects. Chuy joined him, but Boone waited outside in the garage. Gabriel's two attack pit bulls sat at attention by the desk and immediately growled when I walked in. They growled at everyone.

"Bala! Hoja! Quiet!" their master commanded. The dogs reluctantly stopped, but it was obvious they would tear a person to pieces if Gabriel let them. I didn't like them.

Gabriel and I shook hands and then I sat in front of the desk. "Everything okay, Carlos? How's your family?"

"Family's fine," he answered, but he didn't smile. He never smiled.

"Well, I've got good news. The money operation will be starting up very soon. I was just in New York negotiating a price for special paper that my engraver will need to make the bills. Sometime this summer we'll have product for you to take down south."

He nodded. "What denominations?"

"Twenties and fifties. Twenties are less suspicious."

"Can you make fives and tens? Nobody spends twenty dollars in Mexico. Fifty dollars is unheard of."

"I'll talk to the engraver. It's just we can move less of it at a greater profit when denominations are higher."

"I understand, but we can't use the high denominations. Fives and tens. You can do whatever you want with the twenties and fifties."

"I'll talk to my boss."

"We can discuss price when I have an answer."

"Fair enough." I started to stand and shake his hand again, but he just glared at me. "Is something wrong, Carlos?"

"One of my men was shot last night."

"Oh, I'm sorry to hear that."

"It was the Heathens."

"Really? Where did it happen?"

"It doesn't matter. But your people sell guns to the Heathens. That has to stop."

"Whoa, Carlos," I said, "that's not my department. I have nothing to do with that."

"You work with Casazza and his wops."

I bristled when he said that. "Carlos, I'm half Italian."

"Which half?"

Was he kidding?

"My mother was Italian, my father was Irish."

He shrugged. "What are you going to do about it, half-wop?"

"Why are you insulting me?"

"Because my man *died* last night."

"I'm sorry, I really am. But you have to understand, I'm not even part of Casazza's crew. I'm organizing the funny-money operation as a way to get more involved, you know what I mean? The business they have with the Heathens is an exclusive arrangement that goes all the way to the top. I really don't know much about it."

"You have DeAngelo's ear. Aren't you related to him?"

"No. My father was a friend of his. That's all."

"Don't you screw his daughter?"

I bristled at that, too. "No. We've gone out a few times. We're good friends." I may be a diminutive man, but I had a ferocious temper. I could fight as well as any of those biker bastards. When I was twenty-six, I bit off some shithead's ear when we got into it. I've never killed anyone—not yet—but I had respect. Gabriel wasn't giving me any and it was starting to piss me off.

"You talk to DeAngelo," he said, "and tell him the Heathens have to stay out of our territory. And the price for the counterfeit money has to be so sweet it'll melt in my mouth."

"Or—?"

"Or Los Serpientes will cause some trouble for Casazza. We know all the routes the Heathens take when they do runs. I'd hate for any of those guns to get lost."

I thought I'd throw the guy a bone, so I told him about Casazza's new guys that were handling the gun sales. Faretti and Capri.

Gabriel thanked me for that information. "I thought someone new was in charge, but I didn't know who."

"I don't like them, either, Carlos, but what can I do about it?"

"*Talk to DeAngelo.*"

I shrugged and agreed to pass on the message. Then we both stood and shook hands, although at that moment I hated the guy. I glanced at the two pit bulls, who stared at me as if I was their next meal.

Boone was admiring a Harley-Davidson that a Serpent had on display. It was from the 1940s and was in like-new condition. Boone looked up and said, "How would you like to have this between your legs, boss?"

I laughed and said, "I already have a hot rod between my legs." That made all the Mexicans around us laugh, too. They talked more in Spanish, this time with good nature.

As we drove away in the Lincoln, Boone asked how it went. I said it was all right, but I had to talk to Casazza. It could wait, though. On the ride home, I thought about that beautiful girl in New York. Judy Cooper. We had a great time. I figured I should give her a call soon, so she wouldn't think I was some kind of jerk, but that was really not my style. Leo Kelly had a reputation for loving them and leaving them, and it was intentional. If that was the definition of a playboy, then so be it. I didn't like the entanglements of a serious relationship, but I loved the opening moves. But with Judy there was something different. She had a lot of that small-town Texas girl thing that pervaded her personality, and it was sexy as hell. But while on the surface she was an energetic, smart, and friendly girl, behind those bewitching eyes was an anger and pain I couldn't put my finger on. I couldn't explain it, except that when she talked about herself, I felt she was holding back details. As if she had some big secret in her past. She was definitely street-smart, and I didn't think she would put up with any bullshit. I could tell she knew something about the underworld. Maybe it was because she lived on the Lower East Side and worked in a sleazy gym, and she'd met such characters. She was certainly passionate in bed. A wildcat, in fact.

She was the opposite of Maria DeAngelo. That last date with Maria at Disneyland was fun, but she could be a stuck-up bitch. She always wanted this or that. Money was nothing to her, because she's always had it on a silver platter. I wondered if I'd ever get her in the sack. She was awfully attentive toward me, and we kissed a lot, but she shrunk away when I tried to go farther. That could change with time, and, of course, she was *rich* and DeAngelo was her father. That was as attractive as she was physically.

If I had a choice between the two, whom would I pick? Judy or Maria? Well, I didn't know if I'd see Judy again. I doubted she was going to move to L.A., so why was I even thinking about her? It was a waste of brain cells. There was no way I was hung up on her.

Right?

Women. Sometimes I thought they were from another planet.

19
Judy's Diary
1961

APRIL 20, 1961

I can't believe I'm writing this on a train to Chicago. Yes, dear diary, I'm on the *20th Century Limited*, from Grand Central Station, and I'll arrive sometime late tomorrow. Then I change to the *Super Chief* to Los Angeles. That will take two and a half days.

It's all so terrible. My life is completely upended. I've been in tears for most of the morning and a lot of passengers stare at me until I look at them, and then they quickly avert their eyes. One woman asked me if I was all right, and I just snapped, "No!" I didn't mean to be unfriendly, but I didn't feel like being sociable. I'll have to sleep in my seat tonight, but I think when I get to Chicago I'll pay the extra money for a sleeper car on the *Super Chief*.

My hell began when I slipped through my window last night as the Stiletto, ran across the rooftops, and slid down the telephone pole to 2nd Street. My ankle still hurt a lot, but it didn't prevent me from going out. It was taped tightly. I headed east toward Alphabet City. I was so upset about what happened to Clark, I knew if I encountered Kraig and his hoodlums, no one would be able to hold me back. Kraig needed to be taught a lesson.

There was the usual number of people on the sidewalks. If someone was in my way, I diverted around them and kept running. As I crossed 1st Avenue, I heard someone yell, "Go, Stiletto!"

The trouble started when I got to Avenue A. As I sprinted across the intersection, a police car happened to be on 2nd, heading west on the one-way street directly toward me. I didn't realize it was a patrol car until I had completely crossed the intersection and was a good twenty yards east of the avenue. The red-and-blue lights flashed on and the siren beeped. *Uh-oh*, I thought, but I figured I could run right past them. They were heading in the opposite direction and wouldn't be able to turn the car around to chase me. So that's what I did. I shot along the side of the car just as it stopped and two policemen stepped out.

"Halt!" one shouted. I kept going and didn't look back, but I heard them return to the vehicle and speed toward Avenue A to turn left. They'd probably hook another left on Houston Street, head east, and try to intercept me at Avenue B. But I was faster. I had already crossed the intersection by the time they turned the corner of Houston and B. By then I knew my plan to find Kraig would have to be aborted. I was on his block, but with the cops after me, it was best for me to hide. I didn't think the patrol car would turn onto 2nd because it was a narrow one-way street going against them, but they *did*. A taxicab had to swerve to the side to avoid being hit, but it still collided with a car parked at the curb.

And then another patrol car pulled onto 2nd from Avenue C, right in front of me. Once again, I found myself penned in, trapped in the middle of a block with cops at either end. Luckily, I was on the north side of 2nd beneath a fire escape that appeared to be trustworthy. I uncoiled my rope, attached the hook, and quickly swung it up to grasp the bottom rung of the ladder and pull it down. I scurried up to the first landing, the second, and so on to the top. It was a bit of a body stretch to grab hold and climb over the eave and then roll onto the roof. By then, there were cops on the street below me, shouting at me to come down. They had bright searchlights aimed at the building. I didn't stick around, of course. I dashed across to the back of the roof and *leaped* over the six-foot gap between it and the rear of the slightly shorter building behind it on 3rd Street. The jump wasn't too difficult. From there I darted west across the structures, back toward Avenue B. As soon as I saw an adequate fire escape on 3rd that would do, I jumped from the roof to the top landing, and hurried down to the ground. The police knew what I was up to, so they were already moving around Avenue B to intercept me at the intersection. In order for me to get home, I had to cross B, Avenue A, and 1st Avenue. It wasn't going to be a stroll in the park.

I ran like the dickens, reaching the intersection just as the cops did. A car pulled up, lights blazing, attempting to block the road. Two men on foot rushed around the corner to meet me head-on. The only way around them was to take a running jump and push myself off the pavement onto the patrol car itself. I scrambled over the hood and bolted out into Avenue B traffic. Horns blared, but at least this time I didn't cause any accidents. I made it across the road and kept running along 3rd Street toward Avenue A. I'm a fast runner, dear diary, I could probably be an Olympic champion if I so desired, so I knew I'd reach the next intersection before the police got it together enough to chase me.

Crossing Avenue A turned out to be no problem. By then, though, sirens filled the air. One car pursued me on the street. More vehicles were most likely speeding west to cut me off at 1st Avenue. People on the sidewalks had no idea what was going on, and clusters of pedestrians shrieked as I shot toward them. "Out of the way! Out of the way!" I shouted. I was afraid I'd knock someone down, but they parted like the Red Sea in *The Ten Commandments*. When I reached the intersection of 3rd Street and 1st Avenue, I took no time to check for traffic. I figured there were going to be cars no matter what I did, so I tore across and hoped for the best. More horns and screeching of tires. A police car collided into a taxi to my left. I didn't stop to see how bad it was. If I could reach my telephone pole in time,

I thought perhaps I could make it across the roofs to 2nd Avenue and slip into my bedroom window above the gym before the cops got around there.

The pole stood in shadows, which was why I used it. I snaked up to the roof and laid flat on it just as the police swarmed the street below me. I heard calls of "Where'd she go?" and "What happened to her?" They hadn't seen me, so I thought I was in luck. I got up and crossed the top of each building until I reached the gym roof. I put a leg over and slipped down to the ledge below my window. I raised the sash and started to crawl inside—when I heard "Halt! You at the window!"

There was a lone policeman on the roof of the building immediately south of the gym. He had a gun pointed at me, although the angle wasn't very good. The problem was that he'd seen me attempting to enter the gym window. He'd know that building meant something to me and that I hadn't randomly picked it.

So I climbed back to the roof and took off east. As I hoped, the cop chased me. "Halt!" he yelled. "You can't escape! You're surrounded!" I thought I'd try leaping south over the gap to a building facing 1st Street. The space was a little larger than before, so I got a running start and imagined myself doing the broad jump back in school. I barely made it, but had to drop and roll with the landing. Once I was on my feet, I kept going east, desperately looking for an egress in the front of a building. I didn't think the cop would dare attempt the same maneuver across the gap, but he did.

He didn't make it.

I heard him cry behind me. "Help! Help!"

I'm pretty sure I cursed aloud and stopped. What to do? What to do? I had to see the predicament he was in. I rushed back to the edge of the roof and looked down between the buildings. The policeman was hanging onto the iron bars covering a back window, maybe thirty feet below me. If he fell, he'd drop four stories.

"Hold on!" I called. What else could I do? I uncoiled my rope and dropped a line to him. "Grab it and I'll pull you up!" The man was terrified. The rope swung back and forth near his body; he tried to catch it, but missed. He was deathly afraid of removing one hand from the bars, even for the second it would take to clutch the rope. He managed to grasp it on the third try, though, and then clung on with both hands. I then used all my strength to pull him up. He was heavy and it was slow going. "My hands are slipping!" he yelled, and I shouted for him to hold on. A couple of other cops showed up on the ground below us. I heard them talk into their radios, probably alerting their colleagues as to what was happening.

When the policeman was about fifteen feet below me, I saw the terror in his eyes. "Hold on, sir, you can do it," I told him. "Just a few more feet and you'll be safe." I strained on the end of that rope, dear diary; I *really tried* to pull him up. And we almost made it, until his hands slipped.

He fell.

There was a moment of stillness, despite the clamor of police sirens in the vicinity. Then one of the cops standing below pointed at me and yelled, "Cop killer!" Oh, my God, I was suddenly very scared. I thought they'd catch me and unmask me and charge me with the murder of a NYPD *policeman*. I knew I had to get away. Disappear. Run. I took off from the edge of the roof and headed back toward 1st Avenue. The only way I could avoid capture was to find a way down without being seen, slip on my trench coat, unmask myself, and blend in with some pedestrians or enter a restaurant. My telephone pole was relatively inconspicuous, so I returned there. A lot of activity buzzed below me. Curious residents emerged from their homes to see what all the fuss was about, and cops appeared here and there, up and down the block. If I dared to descend, would anyone see me? I thought perhaps if I moved slowly—crept like a cat—down the pole, I wouldn't be noticed. I'd just be a black shape against a dark background. The pole stood directly between two brownstones that seemed to never have lights on.

Normally, I can move up or down that pole from the roof to the ground in eight seconds. This time it took ten minutes. I grabbed the pole and inched down a foot or two and then stopped. I'd wait, assess the street below, and move on in a few seconds. At one point about halfway down, I had to remain frozen on that pole for four minutes. There was a sudden flurry of traffic, probably in reaction to news that the cops had the Black Stiletto trapped. I thought for sure someone would see me, but I must have appeared to be just a piece of utility line equipment. As those minutes ticked by, though, I was almost in tears from the fright. I've never been that scared of getting caught before, but last night I was.

Finally, it was safe to finish the descent. I stood in the shadows and waited for a handful of pedestrians to pass. Then I quickly removed the coat from my backpack, put it on, removed the mask, and walked out onto the sidewalk, carrying the pack. I did my best not to hurry. As nonchalantly as I could, I walked to 2nd Avenue, but I didn't go to the gym. I couldn't take the chance that someone was watching me. So I turned north and headed for the East Side Diner at 4th Street. I just knew some cops would jump out of nowhere and wrestle me to the ground. I'd never make it. I was doomed.

But no one bothered me. I kept my head down.

I sat in the diner for over an hour and a half. Ordered some food. Pretended I was just another New Yorker having a late dinner. To be safer, though, I went to the ladies' room and took off the leather jacket, rope, belt, and stiletto, and stuffed them all in the backpack. I wore a man's T-shirt under the trench coat, so I left the coat on, but unbuttoned. In the mirror I didn't think I'd come off as suspicious looking. As long as a cop didn't ask to look in my backpack, I thought I'd actually be all right.

During that hour, the sirens eventually died down. An ambulance must have come to take the fallen policeman away. At one point, a cop stuck his head in, spoke to Elaine, a waitress I know, and I heard her answer, "Nobody's come in or out for at least an hour." Seeing that everyone in the place had plates in front of them, he figured it wasn't possible anyone could be involved. His eyes did linger on me a little longer than the others, but I just ignored him and ate a piece of pie. My stomach was in knots, though. Finally, he left.

It was after eleven, when the diner closed, that I braved the walk to the gym. There was still a lot of traffic on 2nd Avenue, but I was pretty sure the police had given up. I unlocked the door and went inside, and there was Freddie. He had tears in his eyes. I just looked at him and said, "Oh, Freddie." And I burst into tears. He came to me and hugged me.

"I'm so mad at you," he said, sobbing and clutching me for dear life.

"I'm sorry, I'm so sorry," was all I could say.

We held each other and cried together. At last he broke away and gazed at me. "I'm afraid you can't live here anymore," he said.

"I know."

"The police came. They wanted to search the building. I told them they needed a warrant. They didn't like that. They'll be back in the morning, you can count on it. We have to get you out of here. I'm sorry, but if they know a girl lives here, they're going to put two and two together."

"I know."

Without another word, we both went upstairs and started moving stuff out of my room. Freddie found some boxes in the storage room, as well as my old battered suitcase I'd brought with me from Texas. I'd forgotten all about it. That was sure a long time ago.

"Do you have any money?" Freddie asked.

I told him about the savings I kept hidden in a dresser drawer. I've never used a bank except to cash checks. I had nearly $1,900.

"Do you know where you'll go?"

I knew then and there it was going to be Los Angeles, and I told him so. He hated to hear that I'd be that far away, but after he accepted the idea, he looked up train and bus schedules. The train was the better option, and if I could be at Grand Central by 7:00, I could be gone.

It was really hard deciding what I could bring with me, and, in the end, it turned out to be not much. I filled the suitcase with the money, some clothes, and shoes. My backpack held my Stiletto gear, as well as a few odds and ends I wanted to keep. My record player and record collection would have to stay, and Freddie told me maybe someday he could ship it to me. He was never an Elvis fan, so he made me laugh when he said he'd especially take good care of my Elvis records by never playing them, ha ha.

We then stripped that room of any sign of my presence. The photos on the walls, the sheets and blankets, everything in the dresser, you name it. The bathroom was worse; it was full of my junk. We worked all night until six in the morning. Freddie had a key to the building's storage room, not just the gym's, so he put it all in there. When we were finished, the room just had some bare furniture in it and appeared as if no one had lived it in for months.

"You'd better get going. There's no telling when they'll arrive," he said. "I'll call a taxi." I was a little in shock. I couldn't believe I was leaving. The gym had been my home for nearly ten years.

After he made the phone call, Freddie said, "I'll tell Lucy and Peter something. And all the guys."

"Oh, Freddie!" I cried again, hugging him. "You've been so good to me, I love you," I told him. He started bawling again and told me he loved me, too. Gosh, the tears are flowing as I write this. I'm going to miss him terribly.

The cab took me to Grand Central, I bought a ticket to Los Angeles, which comprised of two trains, the *20th Century Limited* and *Super Chief*. Before boarding, I grabbed a *Daily News* with the headline: NYPD VS. BLACK STILETTO. I desperately scanned it, looking for any news about the policeman. It didn't reveal much except that he was alive. The man was in critical condition in the hospital.

Oh, Lord, if you're really there, please help Clark and the policeman, and give me the strength to face whatever lies ahead.

Good-bye, New York!

20
Martin
The Present

I walked twenty blocks to Hell's Kitchen to take a look at Betty Dinkins's building. The area was pretty much what I expected, but not as bad. It consisted of old, brown brick structures that looked like they'd been standing since before World War II—and they had. That musical *West Side Story* supposedly took place in Hell's Kitchen. Nevertheless, the ethnic mix was all over the map now. There were blacks and Hispanics, for sure, but maybe more white people than any others. I had to admit that 47th Street actually had a lot of character. *I* wouldn't want to live there, but I'd seen worse neighborhoods in Chicago.

The woman's building was easy to find between Ninth and Tenth Avenues, just like Uncle Thomas said. As it was midday, the neighborhood was quiet. Kids were at school, I guess, and most folks were at work. I stood on the opposite side of the street and watched the place for a few minutes.

Last night I wrote a letter to Betty Dinkins. I used the hotel stationery and went through three different drafts before I was happy with it. It was all bullshit, but I simply wanted to scare her into not pursuing the Black Stiletto thing. I told her I was a journalist from the Midwest, and that my name was Jerry Smith. Not very original, but what the hell. The letter said that "respectfully" I knew she wasn't the real Black Stiletto, and she was making it up. I said I had proof she wasn't telling the truth. Then I wrote that some very bad men were out there and they would harm her. She should go back to Sandy Lee and the TV studio and admit it was all a hoax and that she was sorry. Otherwise, the consequences could be very dangerous for her.

I sealed the letter in an envelope, wrote her name on it, and I now had it in my jacket pocket. The weather was a bit nippy, so I couldn't stand around waiting for something to happen. I started to cross the street when, lo and behold, who came walking up the block from Ninth Avenue?

Betty Dinkins carried a grocery bag and waddled quickly toward her building. I recognized her immediately. She wore a big coat and appeared as if she'd just rolled out of bed. Her head turned this way and that, perhaps looking out for the paparazzi. Our eyes met, and she quickly averted them. I wondered if the sudden attention she'd had from the media may have ultimately unnerved her. Maybe kooks were coming out of the woodwork to bother her. I didn't know and I didn't care. I just wanted her to stop what she was doing.

She opened the front door and paused at the mailboxes. Using a key, she opened her box—it was empty—and then unlocked the inner security door. Once she was inside, I crossed the street and waited a minute for her to get up the stairs. Then I opened the front door and stepped into the little foyer with the mailboxes. Through a window on the security door, I saw the stairs. Dinkins was gone. I scanned the boxes and found hers, marked "Dinkins 4E." I took the envelope out of my pocket, folded it so it would slip through a thin slot, and started to stuff it in. It's not the normal way the postmen deliver the mail. They usually have a key that opens the entire cabinet of boxes, exposing all of them for easy access. But it was the only way I could do it. The envelope got stuck halfway in and I had to pull it out and begin again. Just as I was pushing the thick wad through, the front door opened. A man stood there, surprised to see me. His eyes jerked from my face to my hand, obviously catching me in the act of forcing the envelope into Dinkins's mailbox.

Shit.

I finished the task, heard the envelope drop into her box, and then I turned to go. "Hi," I said to the man, as if there was nothing unusual about what I was doing. He let me move past him to the sidewalk, and I started walking toward Ninth. I felt him watching me, though. I turned back and, sure enough, he stood in the doorway, giving me the squinty-eye treatment. Was he a tenant in the building? A member of the Neighborhood Watch? Maybe he was a friend of Dinkins. He'd probably tell her that I'd stuck an envelope in her mailbox. He'd describe me to her.

As for him, he was in his thirties or forties, dressed in blue jeans and a brown jacket. He had dark, rather long hair, was unshaven, and wore a not very friendly face.

When I reached the corner, I looked back and he had disappeared. My anxiety dissipated a little. I figured I was being too paranoid. So what if he saw me putting a note in her mailbox? It wasn't a crime. Big deal. I told myself to forget about it.

I had no idea if my letter would accomplish anything. I was flying by the seat of my pants. If Dinkins continued to "be" the Black Stiletto, then there wasn't much else I could do about it. I had to ignore it and move on. Maybe she'd take the note to heart and realize she might indeed get herself in trouble. At any rate, I felt as if I'd done my job, I'd made an attempt to dissuade her from pursuing the lies.

Whatever happened next was out of my hands.

21
Judy's Diary
1961

APRIL 21, 1961

It's nearly noon and I'm in Chicago at the LaSalle Street Station. I'm waiting to board the *Super Chief* to go to Los Angeles. Last night I slept poorly in my seat, so I'll be glad to upgrade to a sleeper car on the next leg of the journey.

Yesterday afternoon the train stopped in Albany for a short while, long enough for me to get off and use the telephone. I'd kept the number for Beekman Downtown Hospital, so I called to find out how Clark was doing. First they asked if I was a relative, and I replied that I was a family friend. They kept me waiting a long time, and I was afraid I'd have to hang up and get back on the train. Finally, though, a woman got on the phone and told me that Clark had died.

I started crying. I couldn't help it. That poor young man, he was a victim of racism and hatred. It was so senseless. There's just no need for that kind of violence in this day and age. This is 1961, for heaven's sake.

I still had three or four minutes before the train departed, so I called the gym. Freddie answered, thank goodness, and we spoke for a minute. He told me the police did indeed show up at the front door at 8 yesterday morning with a search warrant. They went all over the gym and in the upstairs rooms. When they asked about my old bedroom, Freddie told them he was considering renting it out, hopefully to a future assistant manager. A detective asked him point blank if he knew anything about the Black Stiletto. He said he didn't. Why was she seen trying to get into the bedroom window? Freddie replied that the only thing he could think of was that perhaps she'd noticed the empty room from outside the building and tried to get in to hide. He thinks the cops believed him. Luckily, they never asked to see the building's storage room and probably didn't realize there was one. They left, asking Freddie to call them if he ever saw the Stiletto or heard anything about her.

"Do you know about Clark?" I asked.

"Yeah. It's terrible."

"Are the police doing anything? Do they know about Kraig?"

"I don't know."

"Call them, Freddie. Call the police. Tell them about Kraig. At the very least, maybe they'll talk to him. Somebody had to have seen what happened."

"I will."

"Will you do me a favor? Could you buy some flowers and find out where Clark's funeral is going to be? Please put my name on them and get them there."

"I'll do that. I'll send some, too."

I heard the announcement for all passengers to board. "Freddie, I have to go. I'll call again soon. I miss you already."

"I miss you, too. Be careful, Judy."

The call was over so quickly it was almost like it never happened. Before I knew it, I was back in my seat and the train was rumbling on across the state. Tears ran down my cheeks and I kept my face toward the window. I didn't want anyone asking questions. I was so upset about Clark, about leaving Freddie and New York, about everything. I guess I was really feeling sorry for myself, dear diary. Everything had turned out so rotten.

Another passenger, an older woman sat near me and noticed my red eyes. "Are you all right?" she asked in a foreign accent. I hesitated, but then shook my head. "Man trouble?" she asked. I figured that was as good excuse as any for my behavior, so I nodded. She sighed and said, "That's usually what it is. Here. Have some of this." She pulled a metal flask out of her purse and handed it to me. "Go on," she prodded. So I took it and had a swig. It was brandy, I think. It was warm and *brown*. It burned my throat going down, but it felt good. I started to hand the flask back, but the woman said, "You go ahead and keep it a little while. I think you need it more than me." She introduced herself as Ursula, from New Jersey. I told her my name, but then said I really didn't feel like talking; but I thanked her for the booze. "It's all right," she said. "I don't feel like talking either!"

After a half hour or so, I felt a little better. I'd had maybe six or seven swallows of the booze, and then I gave Ursula the flask. She took a long drink out of it and then put it back in her purse. We both sat and stared out the window as the countryside flew past. I'm glad she didn't want to talk, but it was nice having her there.

Eventually she fell asleep, so I removed some paper and a pen from my backpack. I wrote two letters. The first one was to Lucy and Peter. I tried to come up with a decent explanation for why I left town so suddenly, but, in the end, I relied on the same lame excuse—man trouble. Only this time I spun it the other direction. I said I'd fallen in love with Leo Kelly and that I was going to Los Angeles to be with him.

The second letter was to Freddie, and I poured out my heart. I told him how sorry I was for any grief I'd caused. The last thing I ever wanted was for him to get in any trouble with the police. I told him I hoped I'd see him again soon, but I didn't know when that would be. Then I said he was the father I never had; the memories of my real dad had faded into oblivion. I called Freddie a saint and wished him well.

We stopped again in Buffalo yesterday evening, just long enough for me to rush out, buy some stamps, and mail the letters. I didn't see Ursula after that. She never said good-bye.

The seat wasn't the greatest for sleeping; I was awake most of the night. It wasn't long after dawn that the train pulled into Chicago. I had several hours to wait for the next train, so I bought my ticket and a copy of the *New York Times*. There was a piece in it about the Black Stiletto and the encounter with the police. Dear diary, I was relieved to learn that the policeman who fell from the building is going to be all right. It turned out he was in the hospital's critical unit for just a little while. He had some broken bones and a concussion, but otherwise nothing too serious. The good thing is that the man exonerated me. He reported that the Stiletto actually tried to help him, and that falling was his own fault. The police commissioner, however, was quoted as saying that the Stiletto was still wanted and that I caused great harm to the patrolman and the force. They were diligently searching for me and had reason to believe the Stiletto resided on the Lower East Side.

It's a good thing I'm not there.

The paper's front page revealed that the Cuban invasion had failed. Castro blames the CIA and Washington for being behind the attack, and it may be true. It doesn't make President Kennedy look too good, I'm sad to say.

While I waited, I found Leo's business card and held it for a while. I knew I should call him and tell him I was coming. For some reason, though, I was hesitant. I was afraid he'd think I was nuts. I was in such a blue mood that I actually believed he wouldn't remember me, or he wouldn't care, or whatever.

Well, my fears were unfounded. After I had a bite to eat, I got up the nerve to phone his office before I boarded the train. I knew it was two hours' difference in time, so it was just after 10:00 there. A woman answered the phone with, "Mr. Kelly's office." I asked if he was in. "Who may I say is calling?" I told her my name.

After a moment, his voice was there in my ear and it was like wonderful music.

"Judy! What a surprise!"

"Hello, Leo. How are you?"

"I'm fine. How are *you*?"

"I'm okay. I just wanted to let you know I'll be arriving in Los Angeles on the *Super Chief*."

"What?"

I checked my ticket and told him the time. The day after tomorrow. He said he'd be at the station to pick me up.

"I can't believe you decided to move."

"I can't believe it, either. Leo, I'm going to need a place to stay, and if that job at the nightclub is still open—?"

"Judy, don't you worry about a thing. I'll make sure everything is taken care of. I can't wait to see you," he said.

Who would have thought? I answered that I couldn't wait to see him, too, and it was the truth.

22
Leo

The Past

I was really surprised to get that phone call from Judy Cooper. She said she was on her way to Los Angeles, so I guess the old Kelly charm worked after all. Even Christina was impressed when I told her. "I hope you know what you're doing," she said. Then she added, "I hope *she* knows what she's doing!" Very funny, sister.

When the train pulled into Union Station, I admit my heart was thumping. All I could think about was that night we spent together in my room at the Carlyle Hotel in New York. Judy had a body that wouldn't quit. I wondered how she was going to fit into my life. I hope she wasn't thinking that I was going to be her *boyfriend* or anything like that. That's not my style. But I was willing to help her out, introduce her to some people, talk to Uncle Charlie about the job at Flickers, and so on. And if I got her in bed a few times for my efforts, hallelujah!

Even after traveling for almost a week on a goddamned train, Judy looked fantastic. Absolutely gorgeous. Since her sleeper car was equipped with all the amenities, she said she'd showered and put on makeup just for me. Holy Mother of God, she could be a Hollywood starlet if she wanted. Judy gave me a big hug and we kissed and all that, and then I led her to the Lincoln that my driver had parked in the lot.

"This is Boone," I said. "I think you might remember him." She shook hands with my driver and said in that endearing Texas accent, "Glad to see ya again." Boone put her luggage in the trunk and we got in the backseat.

Judy asked that we take her to a hotel, but I said, "Nonsense, you're staying at my house."

"I'm not sure about that, Leo," she answered. "I mean, I like you a lot, but I'm not shacking up with you."

It was a relief to hear that, but I pretended to be hurt. "What? You're not going to be my kept woman after all?"

She laughed and said, "Leo, I have to have my own place and my own money. Who knows what the future will bring, but at the start I have to be independent."

"Don't you worry," I told her. "I already had Christina make out a list of available apartments that you can see. We'll find you a place to live, but in the meantime, we have a spare bedroom, you'll have privacy, and I promise not to bother you." Then I winked at her. "Unless you want to be bothered."

"Leo, you're awful," she said with a smile, and then she kissed me again.

My split-level house was on Woodruff Avenue, just west of Beverly Glen and south of Sunset Boulevard. I had the ground floor that included my bedroom, bathroom, and a small office. The kitchen and living room was there, too, along with another bathroom for guests. Christina had a bedroom and bathroom upstairs, with a separate entrance on the side of the house by the garage. She also had a balcony on two sides of her floor, and she spent many an evening sitting there with a bottle of vodka. The spare bedroom was on the basement level, accessible from the outside through a door beneath the stairs leading up to Christina's abode.

"Wow, you live in a mansion!" Judy said.

"No, I don't. This isn't a mansion."

"Are you kidding? I don't think I've ever *been* in a house this big!"

"Honey, it's not bad, and I'm not some lower-class schmuck, but

Christina and I don't live in a mansion, at least by Hollywood standards. Take a look at some of the homes in Beverly Hills and you'll see what I mean. This was my parents' house. My Dad did all right with his business. They lived okay."

Boone parked in the driveway and we got out. I pointed out Christina's balcony and the stairs to her section. "She likes her privacy," I said, "so it's best not to go up there."

"I wouldn't dream of it."

I led her inside while Boone carried the bags. We went immediately to her bedroom and she flipped. "Oh, heavens," she cried. "This is great!" I guess she wasn't used to much, because the only things in there were a bed, dresser, a chair, a little table, and a bookcase full of books. What sold it, I suppose, was the view of the swimming pool out the back window. "You have your own pool?" Judy choked.

"Lots of people do in this town," I replied.

"You're really a millionaire and you're not admitting it."

I laughed and said, "I wish that were true!"

"Does Boone live here, too?"

"No, of course not. He lives nearby, though. He's always available when I need him."

I gave her the tour of my level, showed her where everything was located in the kitchen, and told her to make herself at home. Then I gave her the list of apartments Christina had found. "I've instructed Boone to take you around to look at them when you're ready." I gave her his phone number. "Just give him a call. If he's not working for me, he's at your service."

"Leo, I can't thank you enough!" She was so cute; she was like an excited little kid.

Then I told her I had to go away. I hated to leave her alone, stranded, but I was due in Vegas. I was supposed to take Maria to hear Dean Martin at her Dad's casino that night, and I was already running late. Then I had to go to San Diego on business to talk to a railroad company about leasing warehouses. Judy looked disappointed, but she said she understood.

"When will you be back?"

"Couple of days. But Boone will be here. I'm taking the Karmann Ghia. Give him a call if you need anything. There's plenty of food."

"What about Christina?"

I shrugged. "She's not here right now. If a blue-and-white '58 Corvette is in the garage or the driveway, you'll know she's in the house. If you see her, you see her. Don't take it personally if she's not very sociable. It's just the way she is."

"She doesn't mind me being here?"

"Not at all. If I want you here, then it's okay with her."

We kissed and I told her I was glad she was in L.A. She said, "Me, too," but I could tell she was uneasy about me leaving. Nevertheless, I had to run.

The Sandstone Casino was built in the mid-fifties, so it was still fairly new. Located in the heart of downtown Las Vegas, it was the Golden Nugget's biggest competition. Vincent DeAngelo ran it with an iron fist, but he was fair to winners. If anyone was caught cheating, though, God help them. The casino bosses would turn Rico Mancini loose on them, and it was possible the cheater might not see the light of day ever again. I'd heard tales of bodies buried in the desert. Mancini, while serving as DeAngelo's bodyguard, was also the number-one enforcer for the family. I still thought Boone could whip his ass.

He treated me differently when I was with the boss's daughter. Rico gave me a big grin when he saw me escorting Maria to the Sandstone Club inside the massive place. Dean Martin didn't sing just anywhere, so it was a big deal that they managed to book him.

I shook Mancini's hand, which always felt like sandpaper. "How you doing, Rico?"

"Fine, Mr. Kelly. Hello, Maria."

"Call me Leo, for Chrissake," I said. "How long have you known me? Mr. Kelly was my father."

"Okay, Leo." He nodded at Maria. "Your father's already inside, Maria."

"Thank you, Rico," my date said with a sniff. She treated the "help" in DeAngelo's employ with equal disdain. It didn't matter who they were. She was the princess of the house, and she made sure everyone knew it. She looked like a million bucks, though. She had on a frilly, wide dress that hung just below her knees, exposing those marvelous calves of hers. The high heels did wonders for them, too. The bodice was low cut, too, displaying more of her cleavage than I'd ever seen. What was she trying to do? Had she dressed that way for me or for Dean Martin?

We sat in the VIP section with her family, naturally. DeAngelo and his wife greeted me warmly, and Maria gave her daddy a kiss on the cheek and welcomed him home. Apparently he'd been out of town and had returned just in time for the show. Paulie sneered at me, as usual, but we shook hands anyway. I asked him if he'd been traveling with his father, and the guy frowned at me as if I was a bug. "Of course, I was," he said. He was a snotty kid, just like his sister. The prince and heir apparent.

Maria and I grabbed our seats and I told her again how wonderful she looked. She took the compliment for granted, as if I'd said, "Your hair sure is blonde." Our conversation consisted of nothing but her describing a shopping experience on Rodeo Drive and how she'd hobnobbed with Tony Curtis at some Hollywood party. Not once did she ask about me or my sister or uncle. If she wasn't DeAngelo's daughter, and if she didn't have the looks of a model, I wouldn't be wasting my time with her. Truth be told, I couldn't help thinking about Judy Cooper, all alone back at the house on Woodruff.

At one point before the show started, DeAngelo got up to go to the can. Mancini followed him, of course. I excused myself to Maria and went along, too. DeAngelo and I did our business at the urinals at the same time. He asked, "How's business, Leo?"

"Fine, sir, er, Vince."

He zipped up and went over to the sink to wash his hands, but he looked around the place to make sure no one else was in there. "I'm still working out the details of that thing I mentioned the last time I saw you."

He meant the bank job. I'd been wondering about that.

"Just let me know, and Christina and I'll be ready," I said.

The boss nodded at me, moved to the bathroom door, and said, "Treat my daughter good, you hear?"

"Sure, Vince. I like Maria a lot."

He paused, letting that digest. Then he opened the door and said, "Enjoy the show, Leo." Then he walked out.

23
Judy's Diary

1961

MAY 12, 1961

It's been a busy month, dear diary, and I haven't had the time—or inclination—to write. So much has happened since my last entry.

First of all, I now live in my own apartment in Los Angeles. Actually, it's Hollywood! It's a nice little studio apartment in a building on Franklin Street, near Highland, and it's a fabulous location. I can walk to Hollywood Boulevard and Grauman's Chinese Theatre. It was one of the places on the list of apartments Leo gave me. Boone drove me there to see it, and I took it immediately. I had to pay a first and last month's rent, so it's a good thing I have a job now, too.

Leo came through and spoke to his Uncle Charlie. Four days after arriving in L.A., I had a job as a hostess at Flickers. It's very exciting, because Leo was right—you never know who you'll see there. I've met Kirk Douglas, Jerry Vale, Mel Tormé, and Debbie Reynolds. I was starstruck. My job is easy; I just greet guests when they arrive and check the reservation list. If they're not on it, I hand them over to Butch, the maître d', to see if he can seat them. If not—tough luck. Flickers is a popular place, and Charlie's a nice boss. I see similarities between him and Leo, but they're really very different. Charlie's in his late fifties, and he's like a wise old man. He seems to know everything and everybody.

After I arrived in L.A. and Leo left me at his house, I felt a little lost. I made myself something to eat and unpacked. Leo had deposited a street map on my bed with a note pointing out areas of interest—the grocery store, liquor store, movie theaters, bus stops, and so on. I ended up staying at Leo's for five days before I settled on the apartment I have now. I never saw Christina once, but I heard her. One time I was in the kitchen and I heard voices—a woman and a man—upstairs behind her closed door. And they weren't just talking, if you know what I mean. I find her very mysterious. She came and went as she pleased—I heard her car outside my window at all hours of the night—and she avoided me the entire time. I would say that's not very friendly.

As for Leo, I barely saw him either! I was a little miffed at him, but he's since made it up to me. I suppose you can say we're dating hot and heavy. Sometimes I spend the night over at his house—not in my old bedroom, but in *his*. I really like him and I think he likes me. Is it love? I don't know, dear diary. He has some secrets and I'm curious as to what they are. Then again, I have secrets, too, so I guess we're even. At any rate, he's out of town an awful lot. His main office is in the Wholesale District, just south of downtown Los Angeles. He took me there once. It's kind of an ugly area. Mostly Negroes live in the neighborhoods. His office is in a plain brick building adjacent to a warehouse. Christina works there, too. When I visited, it was the first time I'd seen her face-to-face since my arrival in California. She was cordial and said hello. I told her that I hope I didn't disturb her when I was in the house, and she replied, "Not at all. I barely knew you were there." That's because she didn't make an effort to see me!

Anyway, Leo travels on business a lot. He frequently goes to Las Vegas, and I've asked him to take me there someday. He says he will. In the meantime, in the past month we've been together only twelve times. Despite the sporadic contact, those dates are always wonderful. Leo really is a charmer and he's so good looking. He's a terrific lover, too, if I may be so bold to state!

Some of the waitresses at Flickers are not so fond of him, though. Helena, a pretty brunette who is my age, told me that Leo is a "love 'em and leave 'em type," and to be careful. Well, he has as much admitted the same thing to me, saying he doesn't want to be seriously committed to anyone. I don't know what to think about that. Does it mean he sees other girls when he's not with me? I think I'd be able to tell. I have that ability, you know, of discerning lies and deceit. Frankly, I do sense that he doesn't tell me everything and that his life is made up of "compartments." I happen to be in just one of those compartments. What are in the others? Therefore, I *am* being careful. I think. I do like him, though. And I wish he wasn't gone so much. And I miss him when he's not there.

Darn, it sounds like I'm not being totally honest about my feelings here, huh.

Another thing that's going on in *my* life is that I'm taking driving lessons! L.A. is so different from New York when it comes to getting around. You really need a car. Depending on the buses and taxis for transportation is slow on the one hand and expensive on the other. So, on April 24th I started lessons at the Hollywood Driving School, and I've just completed three weeks' worth. Next week I'll graduate and can take my driver's test. If I pass, I'll have my first driver's license! And I already have a car picked out. Leo helped me with that, since I don't know anything about cars. It's a slightly used 1961 Ford Galaxie Sunliner convertible! And it's *black*, of course, ha ha. It's beautiful, and I can't wait to get behind the wheel. I paid half the price, cash down, so the dealer would hold it until I got my license. It's so exciting!

In a little while, I'm going to walk down to Hollywood Boulevard, get something to eat, and buy the new Elvis record at the shop near Coffee Dan's. The song is called "I Feel so Bad." Freddie came through and shipped my record player and records to me. I got them just a few days ago, so now I'll be able to play it. I couldn't live without my music.

I like going out on the nearby streets. I've done a lot of sightseeing—alone—and shopping. The weather is beautiful and I love it here. Sometimes I feel like a starlet. When I walk down Hollywood Boulevard, men turn their heads to look at me. I've been asked more than once if I'm an actress. Many men flirt with me, especially at Flickers. I feel more attractive here than in New York. There's something about the sunshine and air that makes me feel pretty. Some days I feel like I'm flying above the earth in the Mercury *Freedom 7*, just like astronaut Alan Shepard, the first American in space. I watched that happen on TV last week. It was unbelievable.

I do miss New York; but mostly it's Freddie and Lucy and Peter that I miss.

Do I miss the Black Stiletto? I haven't thought much about her. My outfit and equipment are safely hidden in my apartment.

Freddie wrote in a letter that the police have left him alone, so he thinks my secret is safe. He said he's going to rent my old room to a man who will be his new assistant manager. Freddie wants to retire and sell the gym sooner rather than later. Maybe move out of the city, to Brooklyn or Long Island. He believes he hasn't been the same since his heart attack, and I suppose he's right. I'd hate to see him "give up," although rest and relaxation is probably what he needs to take care of himself. I worry about him.

I haven't heard from Lucy. I think she's mad at me for not saying good-bye in person. I hope someday she'll understand and forgive me.

I'm supposed to see Leo tomorrow night. I may have to ask him about *us*, but I'm pretty sure he won't want to talk about it. He says when a man and woman try to define their relationship, it goes wrong.

He may be right.

MAY 14, 1961

Leo and I had our first fight last night. We went out to dinner at a fairly new club called P.J.'s on Santa Monica Boulevard. It's a very "hip" place. They have live jazz music, and they provide a wood-burning tool to carve your name on the white oak tabletops! I inscribed "Judy Cooper" on the table for posterity. Leo refused to do it. We sat in what they called the "Junior Room," as opposed to the "Main Room." The Junior Room was smaller and more intimate. A band called the Barney Kessel Trio played in our room, and they were wonderful. A young Mexican singer named Trini Lopez was on vocals, and he was marvelous. I predict big things for him.

Everything was going fine until we left the club. Leo asked me if I wanted to come over to his house—and spend the night, presumably—and I said, "I want to talk about us, first." He said, "Uh-oh," and clammed up. I told him I didn't know what was going on between us. At times I thought we were in love and were serious about being a couple, and other times I felt as if he was just using me as a plaything. He told me again that he's not the "marrying type," and if I was thinking in that direction, then I should forget it.

"Well, I'm beginning to feel like I *am* your kept woman," I said. He had joked about it, but now I think he really meant it.

"Aren't you happy?" he asked. "You have a great job, a terrific apartment, and we have a lot of fun together. Why would you wreck it by wanting more?"

"I'm twenty-three years old, Leo, and I'm smart enough to know what you're doing. I'm an open-minded girl, but I do have morals. There has to come a time when it's not just fun and games anymore."

He took me home. I pulled out a bottle of bourbon that I had in the kitchen cabinet, and I poured myself a long, stiff drink. I don't really remember going to bed, but I woke up this morning in my jammies, under the sheets.

I think I'll go to Santa Monica and sit on the beach all day.

LATER

It's bedtime and I'm nicely sunburned and I feel hot and tired.

Leo called me and apologized for last night. He asked if he could come over and kiss me. I shouldn't have said yes, but I did.

He'll be here any minute. I'd better get ready.

JUNE 3, 1961

I don't know why I haven't been writing in the diary. Usually, in the past, if I went through spells of not making entries, it was because I was depressed about something. That's not the case here. I'm actually pretty happy in L.A. I'm having a good time. Am I changing? I mean, as a person? Maybe. One thing's for sure—I haven't thought about the Black Stiletto or had a desire to put on the outfit. This city has a completely different dynamic. Getting around on foot as the Stiletto would not be the same as it was in New York. It wouldn't be as easy to hide, slither up fire escapes to roofs, or run across town.

Maybe the key to being the Stiletto in L.A. is my new car. Yes, I'm driving now. I have my license and I spend a lot of time in my Ford Galaxie. When I'm not working, I drive all over L.A., getting to know where everything is. I've explored all of Hollywood, I've been up to the San Fernando Valley, I like to go to Santa Monica and Venice and spend time on the beaches, and I checked out downtown. I even drove down to San Pedro to see the Port of Los Angeles. I've been tempted to drive to Las Vegas myself, since Leo still hasn't taken me there. I haven't done it yet.

I enjoy working at Flickers. Last week Rod Serling and his wife were there. I told him I was a big *Twilight Zone* fan and watch it every week when I can—I recently got myself a television. He was very nice. We're not supposed to ask celebrities for autographs when we're working, but I sure wanted to that time.

One thing I've noticed is that every now and then some shady men congregate at the club. They look like mobsters. They're Italian, and I'm pretty good at recognizing the type. There's a man named Sal Casazza who gets a lot of attention from Charlie and the rest of the staff. He's really fat and acts like he's some kind of big shot. A couple of scary-looking guys are always with him—obviously body-guards. Leo is chummy with them, too. One night Leo was at the club while I was working. He comes in sometimes to see his uncle and gets a free drink or two. It's weird—when Leo's there and I'm working, he treats me like I'm just one of the staff. I'm the girl working as hostess, not the girl he's sleeping with! It makes me a little angry, but he told me later that Charlie wouldn't appreciate it if I was perceived as dating a customer, or worse, his nephew. I suppose I understand, but it's still awkward.

I asked Leo how he knows Sal Casazza, and he replied, "They're just some guys I know in business." I said they looked like gangsters, and he winked at me and answered, "Maybe they are." So my instincts were right. It makes me uncomfortable that Leo is so friendly with crooks. He tried to explain it to me one night. Apparently, the Wholesale District is a haven for the criminal underworld. Leo swears to me that he's not a part of it, but that he has to deal with them because he has to. I said it was a shame that his business had to work that way, and I suggested that he get out and do something else. He looked at me like I was crazy. "This was my father's business and I took it over," he said. "I could never do that."

I still don't know what to think about Leo. In my last diary entry, two and half weeks ago, I left off that he was coming over to kiss me and apologize for our fight. He ended up staying all night, and I guess things worked out between us. Nothing was *settled*, mind you, but at least we put the argument behind us. He was very sweet and kind, and he's continued to be so the three times I've seen him since. And that's the thing—Leo is very mercurial. One day I think he really likes me—maybe even loves me—and other days he's just *not there*. When we're together and it's good, then it's *really* good. That's when I could say that I'm in love with him. I forget all about the doubts and frustrations the *other* times bring me. My intuition constantly warns me to be careful with Leo, but for once my heart stands in opposition to what is probably the more sensible course of action. So I've spent the last few weeks alternating between being hopelessly addicted to the man and getting so mad at him I could scratch his face! I wish Lucy was here, I could talk to her about the situation. I'm sure she would recommend that I leave him and just stay friends, if that was possible. But she was also the one who dated Sam for so long, and he abused her and beat her and sent her to the hospital. Why are so many women drawn to men with a dark side? I'm certainly guilty.

But I guess that's what makes life exciting.

JUNE 24, 1961

It's Saturday night and Leo has stood me up. He was supposed to be here two hours ago and we were going to have dinner and see a movie. When he was an hour late, I called his house and no one answered. I tried his office number, but of course it was closed. Needless to say, *I'm angry*.

Even Elvis can't console me. I got his new album, *Something for Everybody*, the other day when it came out. I was surprised to see a song called "Judy" on side two! I don't think it will be a hit, but naturally it's my favorite song on the record.

Okay, I just tried calling Leo again. Still no answer. That's it. He's in the doghouse. I'm seriously considering putting on the Stiletto outfit and going outside. It'll be her first appearance in Hollywood. Should I do it?

Why not!

24
Judy's Diary
1961

It's really just later Saturday night, about 1:00 in the morning.

I went out as the Stiletto in Hollywood! It started out strangely, but then I *liked* it!

It was around 10:00, so there were still a few people out on that part of Hollywood Boulevard. Wearing my outfit under the trench coat, I walked from my apartment down the hill to the boulevard and hid in the shadows of a closed storefront. I removed the coat, stuffed it in my backpack, slipped on the mask, and I was ready to go. I stepped out on the pavement and cautiously walked along the street. At first I thought I'd be some kind of freak, but the fact that actors were dressed up as Snow White and Superman and James Dean and Marilyn Monroe, posing with tourists for pictures, emboldened me.

Pedestrians pointed and laughed at me. "Look, there's the Black Stiletto, ha ha." One woman wanted her picture with me, so I let her husband take it. She gave me fifty cents for the privilege. I told her she didn't have to pay me, but she insisted. So none of these people thought I was the *real* Black Stiletto. They figured I was some hungry actress trying to make a few bucks on the street. I didn't attempt to convince them otherwise. It was a safe way for me to gauge reactions.

A lot of the action was in front of Grauman's Chinese Theatre, right on top of the cement with the hand and footprints. People were just coming out of the movie, and suddenly I was the object of everyone's attention. Men flirted with me, saying, "I bet there's a pretty face underneath that mask!" and things like that. Several folks asked me for an autograph! I was flattered and enjoyed the accolades, but then I realized it was all phony. It was a joke. It started to bug me that to them I was only a *pretend* Black Stiletto. That autograph didn't mean anything, it was just a Hollywood souvenir. I had to do something to make them realize I was the real thing.

So what did I do? I removed my coiled rope and attached the pulley hook to it, swung it in the air, and caught the top edge of Grauman's marquee! I tugged on the rope to make sure it held my weight, and then climbed to the top. Everyone gasped and applauded. I waved and blew kisses to the crowd.

Then they started to shout, "Do another trick!"

"Throw your knife!"

"Do a somersault!"

I was tempted to honor the requests, but the manager stormed out of the theater and shook a fist at me. "Hey you!" he yelled. "Get down from there this instant! I'm calling the police!"

Some of my audience members protested, but the man was adamant. "You clowns have no right to climb up there. They ought to outlaw all of you costumed idiots!" He meant the actors who dressed up as celebrities. Well, I had no choice in the matter. I didn't want the cops called on me, so I slithered down the rope and pulled the hook loose.

"Sorry," I said, "I was just putting on a little show."

"You want to get hurt and sue us, *that's* what you want! Are you in Actors' Equity? I bet you aren't! You do any kind of performance on our premises, you have to be in the union and you have to be paid. I don't want Actors' Equity coming after me. Now *get out of here!*"

Gee whiz!

I bowed to him and said, "Yes, sir," a bit too sarcastically, and then I turned around and headed east on the boulevard. The crowd dispersed and most of them chalked the scene up to a street performer getting told off by a property owner; however, a few men followed me with catcalls and taunts. I began to feel uncomfortable, but I did my best to ignore them. When the heat got to be too much, I started to run. I passed Superman and James Dean and kept going. The men shouted, "Where are you going, Stiletto?" "Is the Black Stiletto a coward?" and junk like that. Well, I wanted to put some distance between me and them, so I ran all the way to Cahuenga Boulevard, just past the big Florsheim Shoes store. I stopped to catch my breath. On that part of Hollywood Boulevard there weren't as many tourists, and it seemed as if the town was shutting down for the night. There were a handful of bums sitting on the sidewalk against the buildings and very few pedestrians on that end of the block.

I crossed Cahuenga when the light changed and went on until I was at Hollywood and Vine. Looking north, I could see the big old Taft Building and the Capitol Records Building, the one that looks like a stack of records. The streets were dead. Hollywood just wasn't as vibrant as New York at 10:30 at night.

But then I saw something fishy. Around the corner on Vine, near the El Capitan Theatre, I noticed a car idling in front of a liquor store. A driver sat at the wheel, his arm holding a cigarette out the open window. The lights were on in the store, but the rolling steel grate was halfway down in front, as if the place was in the process of closing. I don't know what it was about the tableau, but I had seen too many idling cars in front of storefronts in Manhattan. My senses recognized it as a robbery in progress, so I decided to check it out.

I positioned myself across the street from the liquor store to get a better view, but it was difficult to see what was going on inside due to the grate. When there was a lull in traffic, I stepped out onto Vine and crept closer. The driver of the sedan never turned his head to look at me, but he seemed nervous. He kept looking at the street ahead of him, glancing behind him in the rearview mirror, and gazing at the store. He didn't expect anyone to come up to the car on the driver's side, so I silently crouched beside the car and peered over the tail end at the shop. Sure enough, a guy stood inside pointing a gun at the proprietor, who was busy emptying a cash register.

Time to act. I moved to the driver's door and opened it, scaring the man out of his wits.

"No parking here," I said. He started to scream when he saw me in my mask, but I grabbed him before he could utter much of a sound. I pulled him out of the car and threw him on the street. Two swift kicks—one in the stomach and one in the head—silenced him. I left the man lying in the road and got inside the car. I honked the horn several times, alerting the other robber that it was time to get out of there. In ten seconds he had stuffed whatever cash the shop owner had given him into what looked like a woman's purse, and then he came charging outside. By then, I was waiting for him on the sidewalk. The gun was still in his right hand, so I focused my efforts on disarming him first. It was surprisingly easy. I delivered a simple *Mae-geri* front kick and knocked the piece out of his grip. This guy *did* scream when he saw me. He tried to run, but I shouted, "Hold it!" and caught him before he could travel a foot. I pulled him over my hip and used a *judo* maneuver to throw him to the sidewalk. He landed flat on his back. I drew my stiletto, shoved my right boot into his chest, bent over him, and pointed the blade at his face.

"You can start by handing over that purse."

The robber was too scared to defy me. The shop owner came outside, holding a baseball bat. He was an older man, gray haired, wide eyed, and open mouthed. He obviously couldn't believe what he saw. I handed the purse to him. "Here. Count it. Make sure it's all there." He did and nodded. "Now call the police." He said he already had.

To the thief I commanded, "Roll over and put your hands behind your back." He obeyed, so I took a piece of rope from my belt and tied his wrists together. To the proprietor I said, "That should hold him. When the cops get here, tell them it was the *real* Black Stiletto from New York who did this." The old man just stared at me; he was probably just as frightened of me as the robber was. "Did you hear me?" He finally nodded. I sheathed the knife and ran across Vine. Instead of retracing my steps on Hollywood Boulevard, I went north to Yucca Street and ran west. I crossed Cahuenga and Wilcox, and followed the curve of the road up to Franklin. There, I found a shadowy spot, removed my mask, put on my trench coat, and casually walked home to my building.

There you have it, dear diary. My first outing as the Stiletto in Hollywood was a success! I have to admit it was exhilarating. It felt so *good*; it was that wonderful sensation of having got away with something. I started laughing like a fool. It was as if I'd played a monumental trick on the world and it worked. I immediately put on my new Elvis album and danced alone in the middle of my studio apartment, singing along to "I'm Comin' Home," "In Your Arms," "Put the Blame On Me," and, of course, "Judy."

Hello, California! I HAVE FINALLY ARRIVED!

25
Martin
The Present

Today I couldn't think of anything better to do, so I went to Gina's Krav Maga studio to watch and observe. I figured I needed to get a handle on exactly what it was my daughter was doing with her life. In many ways, I wanted to crawl into a hole this morning. After leaving that letter in Betty Dinkins's mailbox, I felt foolish, as if I'd done something extremely silly. My intentions were sound—I simply wanted the woman to fess up and stop telling the world she was the Black Stiletto. The veiled threat that she might be in danger was probably bullshit, but if Uncle Thomas was to be believed, then I suppose there was an element of extortion in my letter. "Do this or else bad things will happen." Would Dinkins show the letter to the police? I doubted it. She probably wanted as little doubt as possible reflected on her story. For a while, I considered contacting John Richardson again to get his opinion, but ultimately I didn't want to open that can of worms. I'd just have to prevent letting Dinkins's antics get to me and allow her Black Stiletto claim to play out, so I decided to forget about it and go back to Illinois tomorrow. I had one day to kill in New York, so it was best to spend it close to Gina.

When I got to the studio, my daughter was on the mat doing the same kind of sparring with Josh I'd seen before. There was one other spectator besides me, a man who sat in a folding chair in the corner of the room with an iPad in his lap. He looked to be in his thirties and he wore a suit, which seemed really out of place. The man was watching Gina and Josh intently, and every now and then he'd type something on his pad. His eyes met mine when I came in and he continued to stare at me until I nodded at him and took a seat several feet away, against the wall. He must have figured I belonged there, so he went back to his iPad and continued to make notes, or whatever it was he was doing.

As the couple on the mat sparred, Josh periodically spoke words I didn't understand. He kept saying things like, "Protect your danger zone," or "*Retzev!*" or "Nice *secoul.*" In a way, the couple reminded me of wild animals I'd seen on TV nature shows. They'd circle, size each other up, and then *blam*—they went at each other with a barrage of punches and kicks and slaps and pushes. It looked to me like Josh wasn't holding back his blows, either. Poor Gina was getting pummeled. I almost stood and said, "Hey, take it easy!" but I knew that would be a mistake. When they stopped, Josh angrily scolded her. "You can't think about *retzev*; that has to happen automatically. You're *thinking* about it, Gina! When you move into action, whatever you do must be so natural to you that it's involuntary. By the time your brain has thought about it, you might already be dead."

Sheesh. This is what my daughter wanted to do?

"Let's take a break." Then he was all smiles, and the two of them walked over to me. Although she appeared to be mostly on the receiving end, Gina was undoubtedly good at this Krav Maga thing. I couldn't believe some of the moves I saw her make.

"Hi, Dad."

"Good morning, Mr. Talbot, er, I mean Martin."

I stood and shook hands with Josh and gave my sweaty girl a hug. "That sure looks like rough stuff," I said stupidly.

Gina laughed. "It is! But it's not really so bad. We were just working on instinctive defenses and a few punches."

"It looked to me like you were getting your butt kicked."

She shrugged. "I have a lot to learn."

"What's *retzev*?"

Josh answered. "That's a Hebrew term that means 'continuous motion.' One of the fundamental concepts of Krav Maga is the idea of *retzev*, that you don't think about your defense and then execute it; you have to train your mind and your body to seamlessly combine a series of defenses and strikes so that they happen automatically. It has to be second nature."

"And how's Gina doing?"

"Like I said before. She's a natural. Gina's the best student I've ever had, and I've never seen anyone progress as quickly."

"You're not just saying that because she's standing right here?"

He laughed. "I normally *wouldn't* say that in front of her."

"Most of the time he tells me how awful I am!" Gina said.

Josh excused himself and ran off to his office, leaving me with my daughter. She sat next to me and chugged on a water bottle.

"When are you leaving?" she asked.

"I figured I'd catch a flight tomorrow morning. I know now I'll never be able to change your mind about school and this crazy fight club thing you're doing, so I might as well go back to my humdrum life in Buffalo Grove."

"Oh, Dad, your life isn't humdrum."

"You sure thought it was when you lived there."

"That was then."

"Yeah, less than a year ago!"

That made her laugh again. She was so cute when she laughed. In fact, the way her mouth was shaped reminded me a lot of my mother when times were good for her.

"I talked to Mom last night," she said.

"Oh?"

"Yeah. I think I convinced her I'm doing the right thing. For me."

At that point, the man in the suit got up from his chair and walked across the studio toward Josh's office. When he was out of earshot, I asked, "Who's that?"

Gina shrugged. "Some guy who comes in and watches. A friend of Josh's."

"He looks like he belongs in a Fortune 500 boardroom."

"He has something to do with Josh's funding."

That made sense. "So what did your mom say when you talked to her?"

"She just said she believed in me and she'd support whatever I wanted to do with my life."

Hmpf. Carol was becoming much mellower since getting married to Ross. She used to be worse than me when it came to worrying about Gina.

"You want to have breakfast in the morning before I leave? My flight isn't until noon."

"Sure. What time? I need to be here by ten."

"Eight? Eight thirty?"

"Let's say eight thirty."

Josh and his corporate friend emerged from the office. "Break time's over!" Josh called out in coach mode. Gina took another gulp of water and stood.

"Dinner tonight?" she asked.

"Why not?"

"Come over to our place. We'll treat you to a nice Jewish meal."

"Who's doing the cooking?"

"Josh and I share those duties. His mother's meatloaf recipe is to die for."

"You talked me into it."

She joined Josh on the mat, and I stayed put. The man in the suit walked toward the chair in the corner, and I held out my hand. "Hi, I'm Martin Talbot."

The guy stopped and hesitated, but then he shook it, and said, "Frederick Page."

"And you're here because—?"

He smiled and gave a dismissive shrug. "I like to watch."

"What are you, a talent scout or something?"

"Something like that."

End of conversation. He resumed his seat and ignored me for the rest of the time.

For the first time in a long while, I had a nightmare about my mother. A few months ago, I experienced debilitating anxiety attacks and ugly dreams involving the Black Stiletto. I woke up this morning in a sweat, and I had to take one of my emergency-only tranquilizers to settle down.

Last night was pleasant enough. I'd gone over to the apartment on Central Park West where Gina and Josh lived. It was a one bedroom with a sizable living room and kitchen. There was a doorman downstairs and an elevator and a laundry facility in the basement. A very nice place. I arrived at 7:30 on the dot, and was greeted with welcome cocktails. We didn't waste any time with chitchat; they were hungry and so was I. We sat at an elegantly set table covered in candles. It was Friday night, so Gina and Josh celebrated Shabbat, by lighting two center candles, after which Josh said a short prayer in Hebrew. This was followed by sharing sips from a cup of kosher wine and another brief prayer. There was another prayer and then Gina cut a piece of challah. We passed it around, each of us taking a bite.

"So, are you converting?" I asked Gina as Josh served dinner.

"I don't know," she said with a smile, as if it would be the most awesome thing in the world to do.

"Do you, like, go to a synagogue or something?"

Josh answered that one. "I belong to a reform synagogue but I'm afraid I've lapsed in attendance. Gina accompanied me to a service in February, isn't that right, honey?"

"Yeah. It was very interesting. I think we'd go more often, but we're too busy."

"You're too busy beating each other up?" I asked facetiously.

They laughed. "Maybe," Josh answered.

The food was delicious and Gina was right about the meatloaf.

I probably had too much red wine and was a little tipsy by the time it was all over. It was a nice evening, though. I said good-bye to Josh and confirmed with Gina our breakfast date. Then I went back to the Empire Hotel.

My sleep was fitful, I remember that, but I don't recall much about the nightmare. The one thing I do recollect was coming into my mother's room at the nursing home and seeing her dressed as the Black Stiletto in bed. It was a frightening sight: my mom—old, weak, pale, thin—wearing that costume. There were rips and holes in the leather, as well as several bloodstains on the surface. I tried to speak to my mom, but for some reason she couldn't open her mouth. I could see her terrified eyes through the holes in the mask, though, and it scared the hell out of me.

I felt okay after showering and getting dressed. It was 8:15. Gina would arrive in fifteen minutes. I was packed and ready to go. To kill some time, I turned on the television and sat to watch the news.

My heart suddenly started to race when I realized that I'd just tuned in to a very disturbing lead story. An old photograph of the Black Stiletto flashed on the screen, followed by a picture of Betty Dinkins.

The woman had been found murdered in her Manhattan apartment.

26
Judy's Diary
1961

JUNE 28, 1961

Interesting evening tonight! I didn't have to work at Flickers, so I went out as the Stiletto again.

My appearance on Hollywood Boulevard on Saturday caused a bit of a stir. Several photos of me were in the newspapers. One headline posed the question, "Is This the Real Black Stiletto?" The eyewitnesses at Grauman's couldn't make up their minds. Some of them thought I was the real McCoy, while others were convinced I was just a copycat with Tinseltown stunt experience. The liquor store robbery was reported, too, and the owner told police that the Black Stiletto foiled the crime. The police were befuddled as to how a woman in a disguise had managed to disarm and immobilize the two thieves. So there was a lot of speculation about the "masked vigilante."

Now I wanted to prove I was the real deal.

I went out around 9:00 in my trench coat—I must look a little weird wearing a coat in the middle of summer in L.A.!—with my outfit underneath. This time I walked down Highland to Hollywood Blvd. but kept going south to Sunset. It's a nice walk. I passed Hollywood High School on my right. I heard the list of alumni includes such celebrities as Lon Chaney Jr., Johnny Crawford, who I currently watch on *The Rifleman*, Judy Garland, Lana Turner, Mickey Rooney, Ricky and David Nelson, Alan Ladd, and a bunch more I can't remember. It was across the street from the school that I found a dark spot where I could make my transformation.

When I hit Sunset Boulevard in full regalia, I nearly stopped traffic. Like the avenues in New York, Sunset is very busy. It's one of the main drags through Hollywood, and besides hotels and shops, there are a lot of nightclubs. Most of the fancy places are farther west on "the Strip," but I found myself in the midst of a lot of activity. People on the sidewalk did double takes and pointed at me. So as not to attract a crowd, I began sprinting toward the Strip. I even ran by a policeman. He actually smiled and gave me a wave. He, too, must have figured I was just a Hollywood weirdo. Well, by the time I got to La Brea, I needed to stop and rest. I was out of breath. So far I hadn't seen any crimes in progress, and I didn't think I would on such an active street, so I turned around and headed east. Before long, I was back at Highland. I figured the night was a bust, so I started to head home—but then something drew me to make a right turn on Selma. I thought I saw a trio of Negroes who were nervously looking around. Were they up to no good? I decided to follow them.

Nothing happened, though. When they got to Cherokee Avenue, they simply got inside a car that was parked on the curb and drove away. Oh, well, I thought. Maybe in the future I'll get in my car and drive to a completely different section of L.A., park it, and then do a patrol. But at the time, I thought I'd go home, so I turned up Cherokee and walked north. And then I came to a bar called Boardner's. I was in the mood for a drink, so I stepped inside—dressed in my mask and all—and was immediately struck by how much atmosphere the place had. It hits you as you walk in. The interior was pretty dark, lit with old-fashioned lamps and such, and old-fashioned booths covered in leather or similar material. There weren't a lot of people inside. I counted eleven, all men. They all looked up from their drinks and their jaws dropped. The bartender stared at me, too, but he got hold of himself and I became just another customer. It didn't matter what I was wearing or who I was. Just another freak show in Hollywood.

"What'll you have?" he asked as if he no longer noticed my outfit.

I ordered a gin and tonic and paid for it. Then I sat alone in a booth against the wall, trying to ignore the gawks. The drink was good and the ambiance was pleasant. I thought perhaps Boardner's might become "my bar."

After a few minutes, a man sauntered up to my table. He appeared to be in his late 30s or maybe early 40s. He had on a rumpled jacket and tie, and he was probably slightly inebriated. But he seemed friendly when he asked, "So, are you the real Black Stiletto?"

I answered, "Yes, I am, but no one wants to believe it."

"Mind if I sit with you a minute?"

His accent was one I hadn't heard in a while. I gestured to the seat across the table. He slid in and asked if I wanted a second drink. "I'm still working on this one, thanks."

"You sound like you're from my part of the world."

"Oh? What part is that?" I asked, but I knew what he was going to say.

"West Texas."

"You're right." I was right in recognizing his drawl.

"From what town do you hail?"

I laughed. "It's not much of one. Would you believe Odessa?"

He smiled. "That's where I'm from, too. How about that?"

I couldn't believe it. "You pulling my leg?"

"As much as I'd like to pull on one of your legs, no, I'm telling the truth." He held out his hand. "Barry Gorman."

I removed my glove and slapped his palm. "Hi, Barry. I'm the Black Stiletto."

"I guess you're not going to tell me your real name."

"I guess not."

"How do I know you're the real Black Stiletto?"

"You'll just have to trust me. Do you read the papers?"

"Sure do."

"Did you read about that liquor store robbery the other night?"

"I did. That was you?"

"That was me."

"Well," he lifted his glass, "here's to fighting crime." I raised my drink as well and we clicked them together. "That's my line of work too."

"Oh?"

"I'm an unofficial private investigator. Former LAPD homicide detective."

"Former? Aren't you too young to retire?"

He shook his head. "My employment status, um, changed. Not by choice."

"I see. What happened?"

Barry shrugged. "I don't mind telling you. Everyone else knows. I was doing things I shouldn't have been doing. Working with some crooks down in our old neck of the woods."

"Odessa?"

He nodded. "The Dixie Mafia. I helped smuggle weapons down to Texas, and I was caught. So the LAPD cut me loose, and I spent eighteen months in San Quentin. When I got out, I wanted to become a P.I., but I couldn't get a license, being an ex-con and all. So I do it on the sly, so to speak. And, frankly, I find it suits me much better than wearing a badge. I guess you could call me a paid, glorified informer."

"Do you get a lot of work?"

"Actually, I work exclusively for the D.A., believe it or not. Bill McKesson and I are old friends. He took pity on me and hired me to look into organized crime here in L.A. You see, I had—*have*—a lot of connections in the underworld. What with my association with the Dixie Mafia and all, I know a lot of riffraff in town."

I found all of this very interesting. Since his glass was empty, I offered to buy him another round, but he told me to stay seated; he wanted to treat. So Barry got up and in a minute brought back drinks for both of us.

"You know, I followed all your exploits in New York," he said. "What are you doing here?"

"I left. The heat got to be too much. The police there wanted to throw me to the wolves."

He nodded. "Yeah, I know. It's a shame. They couldn't see what an asset you were. They should've given you a medal."

"Thanks."

"How long you been here?"

"Not long."

"You want a job?"

That threw me. "What?"

"You want a job working for me? I could use someone like you. You have—abilities—that I don't. You have unconventional ways of getting in and out of places."

"What are you talking about?"

"D.A. McKesson—Bill—he gives me carte blanche when it comes to my investigations. I have permission to hire anyone I want to help me. The money's pretty decent, too. I'm paid very well. You could do some good here in Los Angeles, actually working on the side of the law for once. What do you say?"

I wanted to laugh. "Are you serious?"

"Honey, if you're *the* Black Stiletto, then, yeah, I'm dead serious. Are you really her?"

"What do you think?"

"I think you are. No one else would have the ba—er, guts—to come waltzing in here in that getup and ask for a drink. Even the wackos on Hollywood Boulevard don't do that."

The drinks were making me a little tipsy, so I thought I should get home before I did or said something stupid. Nevertheless, Barry's proposition was intriguing. "What would I do?"

"I'd give you assignments. Sneak into here or there, find evidence of crimes, that kind of thing. I'd give you a camera, you could take pictures of mob bosses having secret meetings and such. I bet you could do that."

"I *could* do that. I did it in New York. And I already have a camera."

"See there? You're perfect for the job."

He reached into his jacket and pulled out his wallet. He removed a business card and handed it over. "You think about it and call me."

The card said: Barry Gorman, and it listed his office address on Fountain Avenue and a phone number.

"All right," I said. "I'll think about it."

"Thanks." He stood and held out his hand again. After I shook it, he left the bar. Not too long after that, so did I. Coincidentally, I stopped a crime right there at the corner of Cherokee and Hollywood Boulevard. I was walking up to the corner when I noticed a teenager grab a woman's purse. He started to run toward me, but I was in the shadows and he hadn't seen the Black Stiletto standing on the sidewalk in front of him. I caught the kid, and shouted, "Hey!" I scared the thief so badly he nearly peed his pants. I pinched the boy's earlobe and ordered him to accompany me back to his victim. I made him give back the purse to the distraught woman and apologize. Then I let him loose. The woman thanked me profusely, and then I heard a pair of hands clapping. I turned to see none other than Barry leaning against a dark-green car parked at the curb. The vehicle had seen better days.

"Bravo," he said. "You really *are* her. I knew it all the time."

"Told you so."

"Can I give you a lift somewhere?"

"In that? What is it?"

"Fifty-seven Ford Fairlane. Ain't she a beaut?"

"Sorry, Barry, but it looks way older than that. But, thanks. I prefer to walk. Or run, as the case may be."

"Suit yourself. Call me, okay?" Then he got in his dumpy car and drove away. I changed back into "Trench Coat Judy" when I got back on Highland near my apartment building. Now I'm back home, safe and sound, and Barry's card is sitting on my kitchen counter.

I *will* have to think about his offer.

27
Leo
THE PAST

I've been so goddamned busy it's driving me nuts. I can't sit still in one place before I have to go somewhere else. With overseeing the warehousing business and the counterfeiting operation together, I barely have time to relax and see Judy or Maria or maybe even someone else.

Christina was stepping in at the office to help out. She always had a place in our father's company, she just never had any interest until she was released from prison. My sister threw herself into the business then and earned the respect of her fellow employees. I think everyone was afraid of her, too, and that's funny because it helped! Now that she was also on the management team, it freed me up to pursue my other activities.

The money paper arrived from New York, and we set up shop in a warehouse I own off of Alameda. It was empty and for rent, but I created a dummy company and rented it from myself. Now the space was owned by "A-1 Outriggers Inc.," although it looked like no one worked there. More discreet that way. The equipment was set up in a remote part of the building, and the rest of the property was dark.

Now that everything was in place and the up-front money paid, production could begin. The plates were finished and Samberg tested them as soon as we got the paper. We decided to try and make fives and tens to sell to Los Serpientes. The bills weren't bad, but they weren't perfect. We knew that would happen on the first try. Casazza didn't think they'd pass in this country, but Gabriel took them anyway. Samberg was in the process of perfecting the plates, so it won't be long before we're printing the big stuff.

I've also been placed in the middle of touchy situation between the Serpents and the Heathens. I didn't ask for it either. The Heathens and Los Serpientes have escalated their beef with each other, and there's been bloodshed. The other night, a Serpent was killed by the Heathens. It was getting nasty. The problem was that the war was affecting DeAngelo's business running guns. So I was unwillingly elected mediator since I knew Carlos. I had gotten close to Carlos Gabriel for the sake of selling funny money, but I wasn't involved in other deals.

The closest I've ever gotten to the gun business was that I leased warehouses to Casazza and, in turn, DeAngelo. I didn't know what they used them for, but I guess I had a pretty good idea. Now Casazza thought I had Gabriel's ear and he told DeAngelo that. The word came down that the boss wanted me to try and smooth things out with Gabriel so he'd make peace with the Heathens. It made me extremely uncomfortable to be put in that position, and the likelihood of making peace now was a big fat zero.

Nevertheless, I delivered the Mexicans' funny money personally so that I could suggest to Gabriel that the feud would end up hurting everyone's businesses, including ours. My speech didn't work. Two nights later, a Heathen was shot to death in downtown L.A. As a result, the cops stepped up patrols and started targeting suspected motorcycle club hangouts for surprise raids. I just hope my name stays out of it. Several Serpientes know who I am. I wouldn't want the Heathens getting a whiff that I'm doing business with the Mexicans.

Besides dealing with all that, I don't know what to do about Maria. She's been getting more affectionate, flirting with me, and making suggestions. We've gone out a couple of times in the last month, and on the last date in Vegas she came over to the hotel where

I always stay, and we spent some time in my room. She wouldn't go all the way, but we went far enough to make it interesting. When I took her back to DeAngelo's ranch, she told me something I didn't expect.

"Leo, Daddy keeps asking me if you and I are serious."

"He does?"

"I think he wants to know if he should include you in more of his business."

"Really? He said that?"

"In so many words." She looked at me as I was driving and added, "I guess it depends on what happens with us."

Christ. The opportunity to be a part of DeAngelo's inner circle was mighty attractive. The problem, though, was that I sure as *hell* didn't want to get married to Maria. I wanted to get her into bed, no question about *that*, but I did not want to live with her for the rest of my life. There was no woman alive that I'd be willing to sacrifice my freedom for. Judy was a lot of fun, and with her I got some action every now and then, but I didn't want to commit to her either. Everyone loved her at Flickers. Charlie said she's been a draw for repeat customers, just so they can see her pretty face and fantastic figure again. I couldn't blame them. Judy is one hell of a girl. It was probably a good thing I didn't get to see her very much. I didn't want her becoming too attached to me, but I thought she might be already. She's hard to read. Once she asked me if I saw other women, and I told her no. She didn't need to know about Maria. As long as I kept Judy away from Las Vegas and avoided her when Maria was in town, then I'd be okay.

So far it had worked.

28
Judy's Diary
1961

July 3, 1961

I called Barry Gorman and said I'd work for him. I figured—why not? It would be some extra income and it would allow the Black Stiletto to do some good on the right side of the law. And it might be easy as pie.

It was best that we weren't seen together again, so we agreed to meet in his car, which he'd park on the same block as Boardner's. Cherokee was dark enough, and I was able to creep along the street without attracting too much attention. When I spotted Barry's beat-up car, I first made sure no one could see me, and then I knocked on the window and opened the door.

We sat and talked for a few minutes. I told him I wanted to work for him, and we ironed out the relationship. First off, he gave me $200 in cash to start! I'd be paid per assignment for a fee no lower than that, but it could be a lot higher, depending on what the job is. Then I asked him what my first one would be.

"Judy, organized crime runs a little differently on the West Coast than it does in the east," Barry said. "It's not so much family controlled because the territory is vast and spreads across several states. There're a lot of smaller organizations here, whereas in New York you have the Italian families, you know?"

"Okay."

"It's not just the Italians here, although they are still powerful in the L.A. underworld. We have Mexican and Negro and Asian gangsters, and white gangsters that don't belong to any particular ethnic group. You know what a motorcycle club is?"

"I think so."

"Have you heard of the Hell's Angels?"

"Oh, okay, and I saw *The Wild One* with Marlon Brando. Sure, I know what you mean."

"We have a lot of that kind of thing to contend with in this state. Anyway, cooperation between these various factions is essential for anything to happen. They do deals with each other—you know, for distribution of whatever illegal product they're selling, or maybe for knocking off the leader of a rival gang. That said, there are some organizations stronger than others and they tend to be at the top of the pecking order. We're going after those."

And then he shocked me, dear diary.

"Have you ever heard of a man named Sal Casazza or Salvatore Casazza?"

Of course I had, but I couldn't tell Barry how I knew him. I said, "I've heard of him. He's some kind of mafia boss?"

"You're right. We believe him and his crew are responsible for smuggling foreign arms through the Port of L.A. and distributing them far and near. They get stored in warehouses around the city before being moved. We're talking serious weapons, here. The kind that kill people."

Dear diary, my sensory antennae perked up when he said, "warehouses." Leo runs a warehouse business.

"Don't all weapons do that?"

"All right, these kind *over*kill people. We have to trace the pipeline up to the top. That's the goal. Sal Casazza actually works for a bigger fish in Las Vegas, a very wealthy man named Vincent DeAngelo. He's more of a New York–style gangster, his family members have big roles in his organization, and he's a somewhat public figure because he owns a big casino downtown. That's who we want to get."

"So why don't the police just arrest him?"

"There's no evidence. It's all speculation that he's involved. And that holds true pretty far down the pipeline. We have no evidence of the link between DeAngelo and Casazza, although we believe DeAngelo had the former L.A. boss whacked so Casazza could take over. Beneath Casazza on many levels are hundreds of smaller outfits that are hired out to perform tasks. It's a huge network that spreads all the way to Texas and across the southern states to Florida. In some circles we call it the Dixie Mafia. Have you heard of it?"

"You mentioned it before. So you're saying this DeAngelo guy is the leader of the Dixie Mafia?"

"Not at all. But he's a part of it. If the organized-crime network was a human body, he'd be an important organ."

"A vital one?"

"Pretty vital. Taking him down would hopefully have a domino effect across America." Barry lit a cigarette and rolled down his window. "Another thing. Recently a couple of these motorcycle clubs got into a feud, a very violent one. People are getting killed, and we're afraid civilians might get caught in the crossfire. Something has to be done to stop the war."

"What are they fighting about?"

"Again, we have no proof, but we believe Casazza's people are doing business with an MC called the Heathens. These are some really bad boys on motorcycles, and I advise you to stay away from them. We think that when weapons leave the Port, the first stop is with the Heathens. Then, they and their connections distribute them. Okay, that's one side. Los Serpientes is a Mexican gang, they actually boast being connected to the big Mafias south of the border, so they're responsible of getting stuff to and from Mexico and America. The Serpents are also working with Casazza, but it's not in weapons. We're not sure what it is, it could be narcotics, it could be counterfeit money, or both, or any number of things. From interrogation of guys arrested from both clubs, we know that they're fighting over territory, but mostly it's because the Heathens are trying to develop their own routes to Mexico, and that steps on Los Serpientes's toes, er, tails."

"So, what's my first assignment?"

"There's a warehouse in the Port of L.A. that I've had an eye on for some time. I think it's one of the places the mob uses to store the guns after they're off the boat and before they're shipped to the Heathens. How would you feel about sneaking in and having a look? If you find guns, the D.A. could then get a warrant for probable cause—and believe me, the police can come up with some pretty creative probable causes—and then they'd raid the place. But if it turns out to be a false alarm, the D.A. doesn't want us playing our hand, tipping them off that we're looking for them. So we want to be sure before we send in the troops."

"How well protected is it?"

"Not very. There are guys there, not very many, most likely armed, but they stay inside. When you get in, you'll want to keep pretty quiet as you look around."

He offered me $350 for the job and I took it. We set a date for Thursday night, because I'm off work then and it would give Barry time to go to his D.A. pal. The police will assemble a small backup team for me, in case I get into trouble. Can you believe that, dear diary? How many policemen in New York would act as my backup? So it will be me, Barry, and two or three plainclothes cops on the mission. It sounds so exciting! I feel like I'm part of a secret spy ring and I'm actually working for the good guys.

Tomorrow is 4th of July and I'm spending it with Leo. Can't wait to see him. I also might have to ask him a little more about his work.

JULY 5, 1961

Last night was magical. Leo took me to a wonderful Italian restaurant in San Pedro, near the Port. Then, we went into the Port of Los Angeles and up to the top of a building they call Warehouse #1, one of the oldest and largest facilities. He had lots of friends who work at the Port since he's in the warehousing business. He controls some of the buildings there, but most of his properties are in the Wholesale District. Leo said Warehouse #1 was built in 1917, and it's on a rectangular piece of land that sticks out into the water. Big ships load and unload there. We went up to the roof to watch the fireworks over Los Angeles Harbor, and that was *amazing*. There were other people on the roof, too, mostly longshoremen, but I felt as if I was in a privileged spot. We sat in lawn chairs and drank beer. It was a lot of fun.

When I asked, Leo told me more about his business. It finally became clear to me that Leo's company works with union longshoremen and warehousemen and staffs warehouses, hiring them out to shipping or railroad companies. He also is a liaison between property managers and warehouse owners, and he leases buildings. He said things are changing with what they call "containerization." Those are big, colored, rectangular blocks of steels that hold stuff, and the heavy machinery used to pick up and move them. Slowly, the container system will replace the old "break bulk" operations that have existed since seaport cities had docks. That's where they use cranes to pull pallets out of cargo vessels and load them onto shore. Sometimes Leo's work takes him down to the Port, which is why he has access there.

When I asked him if Sal Casazza has anything to do with his business, he said, yes. It's how Leo knows Sal.

"So you have to work with him?" I asked.

"Sometimes, but not him directly. Usually I deal with other people, but Casazza has a stake in what they do. So, being friendly to Sal at Flickers and so on, that's just business, Judy. I'm no mobster."

I believe him, I think. He's still not telling me everything, but I don't think he's involved in what Barry was talking about.

As if the dinner and fireworks weren't enough, the evening ended up being even more romantic. He drove me home, which took over an hour, but when he pulled up in front of my building, he asked, "Would you like me to come up?" I suppose I was taken away by the evening's spell, so I said, "That would be nice."

There were more fireworks in the bedroom, and that's all I'm going to say about that.

We fell asleep and he got up to leave around 5 in the morning. I asked him why he didn't stay for breakfast, but he said he had to be at work. So I said good-bye and went back to bed. I wasn't upset or anything. And I don't think I'll get pregnant. I still use the diaphragm, but that's not foolproof. The best thing is for the man to wear a rubber. That's what Leo does. Gosh, I sound like some kind of experienced courtesan, ha ha.

I sure do like Leo, but am I in love, dear diary? It's hard to say.

29
Judy's Diary
1961

JULY 6, 1961

Tonight the Black Stiletto made her debut fighting crime for the City of Los Angeles. It wasn't easy as pie, but I'm home and it's not even midnight.

The operation was on for 9:00 p.m., after dark, and when it was supposed to have been "quiet" at the warehouse. I drove to San Pedro following Barry's directions. Luckily the route was somewhat familiar after visiting the Port with Leo on the 4th. I parked my car on a side street off of Palos Verdes Street, a block away from the harbor. In the darkness, I put on the mask, removed the trench coat and stuffed it in my pack, and then made my way to the fence that surrounded Port property. My destination was a building not far from Warehouse #1, on City Dock One. The chain-link fence was easy to climb over, and it wasn't difficult to run between pools of shadow to keep out of sight. I was glad I didn't have to go to Terminal Island, the largest section of the Port, because the only way to get there was by ferry. All of the buildings were big and old, but I had no trouble locating the warehouse in question. At that time of night, it appeared that no one was around. I wasn't supposed to see Barry or the two cops, but they were out there somewhere, watching. When I was within rock-throwing distance of the place, I stopped to survey the location. Luckily, the spot wasn't well lit, although there were two spotlights, one directed at the front and the other at the back of the building. My goal was one of the shadowy walls on the sides of the place, where there were also checkerboard windows. Barry was right—there were no guards or anyone watching the warehouse outside, but I could detect faint light through a few windows, originating from somewhere inside. Someone was definitely there. I risked dashing across an illuminated open space to the building. It was the only way to get there. A flash of black probably wouldn't register to anyone that might see me. I've learned from experience that people usually *don't* believe their own eyes.

I crouched against the side of the building and caught my breath. I was bathed in darkness; my own vision enhanced the starlight above to allow some degree of illumination, enough for me to discern everything. The stars reflected off the water, the harbor that emptied into the vastness that was the Pacific Ocean. There were trash Dumpsters and stacks of wooden pallets on the ground by the warehouse. Two cars and a motorcycle were parked nearby. They most likely belonged to whoever was inside. The checkerboard-shaped windows gaped at me like dozens of eyes. I have to admit I was nervous. This was all very different from what I'd done in New York. The warehouses in Manhattan were not as big as *this*.

I don't know why I thought of it, but in hindsight, I'm sure glad I did. Barry hadn't told me how long it would take before a backup force would arrive, so I wanted to make sure that any crooks inside wouldn't be able to flee. I drew my stiletto, went over to the cars, and punctured two tires on each vehicle. They wouldn't be going anywhere. Then I studied the side of the building to determine my best course of action.

Obviously, the top windows would be more difficult to reach, but the bottom ones, unfortunately, seemed to be too close to the men inside. I watched the light in the bowels of the building for a while and caught a shadow moving across it. By standing on the stack of pallets, I could put my ear against a pane and listen; I heard faint voices. So that was a good reason to reject the ground floor. The top windows probably overlooked the entire interior, gymnasium-style, and one of them appeared to be already broken. The only way up there was to climb, so I threw the rope and hook to grab the eave of the roof, which didn't stick out very far from the wall. In terms of stories, the building was maybe four levels high. It was a high pitch, and the first try didn't make it. The hook came crashing down, but thankfully it didn't land on the Dumpsters, which would have caused a racket and blown the job. I had to be deadly silent for the plan to work.

Climbing the rope hand-over-hand was easy, although my arm muscles screamed at me a bit for not having used them like that in a while. The windows were approximately three feet square, and a little over half of the broken one's pane was still intact. A hole the size of a football occupied the bottom left corner. It was unapparent how the window got broken, as it was made of sturdy, thick glass. I needed to make the hole bigger, and while it'd be a tight fit, I thought I could then slip through. I could get away with maybe one bash on the glass; any more attempts would be too noisy. So I clung to the rope with one hand and formed a *karate Hiraken*, a perfect flat fist, concentrated on the invisible energy that existed between my arm and the window pane, and delivered a firm chop. My blow didn't shatter the pane, but instead formed a spiderweb of cracks across it to the other end, and made very little sound doing so. It was easy then to grasp edges of the glass sections, wiggle them free, and drop the pieces below me. Now the entire square was a big hole. Lifting my legs, I thrust them through the opening, hanging onto the rope as I went. Once I had slithered inside, I was able to perch precariously on the bottom of the windowsill. I released the rope—it remained hanging outside—and took stock of my surroundings.

It was indeed a long way down to the floor. I felt like an insect that happened to fly in through a very high broken window. The question was what I was going to do next. If only I could walk on the wall or ceiling like that fly! I was in an unsteady position; it wasn't the most comfortable "seat" and I had to control my balance while I studied the situation.

Directly above me and spread across the upper building was a series of metal latticework trusses. The floor was covered with crates and boxes. A "wall" of them had been built between the front door and the center of the space, from where all the light was coming. I saw three men there. Two of them stood at a table working with tools. The other sat in a chair, reading the newspaper. Then I realized it—those weren't tools. The men were assembling rifles. I removed my camera from a pouch on my belt and, using my right elbow on the side of the window to anchor myself, snapped a few pictures. I didn't know how they'd turn out from that high up, but it was worth trying. I put the camera back and figured I'd done my duty. There were definitely guns in the warehouse.

But then a darned *dog* started barking. He appeared right below me. Somehow it had spotted or heard me. The thing was huge, too, a German shepherd. I quickly grabbed the rope through the hole and wormed my way off the windowsill and hung outside; but not before I heard a man shout, "Look! Up there!" Then it became a race. I rappeled down the side of the building in seconds and hit the ground. I quickly jerked the hook off the roof, let it fall to the ground, then gathered up the rope and started running. I shot toward the road and got a good fifty feet away before one of the men let the dog burst out the front door. It galloped after me, and it was fast, too, barking like it was going to eat me alive. I didn't look back, but I didn't know where I was going. My car was some distance away, and there wasn't any place in sight that might protect me from the beast.

Behind me, I heard the man shout, "Get him, Ralph!"

Then a gunshot echoed on the street and the dog yelped. I dared to slow down and turn my head. Ralph ran, limping, to the dark safety of the side of the building. The man in front had stopped following us, not sure what had happened to his guard dog, but then he turned around and darted back to the warehouse.

One of the plainclothes cops trotted up to me out of nowhere. "I'm Sergeant Ross. Are you all right?" he asked.

"Yeah," I said. "The dog all right?"

"Nicked his leg. I had to do it. He was three seconds away from tackling you. You'd be dead if I hadn't shot him."

"Thanks." Normally I would've felt bad about a dog getting hurt like that, but not this time.

I told Sergeant Ross what I'd seen inside and how many men were there. He got on his walkie-talkie and called it in. By then, though, the crooks knew they were in trouble, and they weren't going down easily.

The roll-up door on the building's loading dock opened a few feet. Gunshots erupted from the dark slot.

"Get down!" the cop shouted. We hit the ground as bullets sliced the air above our bodies.

The three gangsters then raised the door higher, bolted out, and ran for their cars. They jumped in one and started it—but they couldn't go anywhere, of course. The flop-flop sounds of the slashed tires shattered their hopes of a quick escape. The men panicked, poured out of the car, and jumped to the other one—but then they saw the tires on that one, too. With nowhere else to go, they started to run away. Sergeant Ross pulled a gun and shot at them. They fired back. Another plainclothes officer appeared from behind a building, and he fired a weapon at the running men. Then, like magic, two police cars pulled out from behind other warehouses with lights flashing and sirens blazing. They screeched to a stop close to the running men. Four cops piled out to the opposite side of the vehicle as the three gangsters shot at them. The policemen returned fire and hit one man. His body twisted grotesquely and fell to the ground. The other two turned around and retreated to the warehouse. The cops kept shooting, but the gangsters made it. Once they barricaded themselves inside, the cops stopped shooting. I went over to them and crouched behind one of the cars.

"Miss, you need to get out of here," one of them said.

"Why?"

"There's going to be more gunfire."

As if on cue, the gangsters started shooting at the policemen from the building's lower windows. The cops returned fire and the noise was deafening.

"Don't you need help arresting them?" I shouted to the man who'd spoken to me.

"No! Backup's on the way!"

So I waited until there was a bit of a lull in the gunfire, and then I ran back to the fence I'd climbed and clambered over it. I walked toward my car and found Barry's Ford parked around the corner. He sat in his driver's seat, smoking a cigarette with the window down.

"You done good, Stiletto," he said.

"I could've been killed, Barry," I said. "Where did those cops come from?"

"They were part of the team all along. They were hiding around the corners, just in case something went terribly wrong. Sorry about the dog. You sure you're okay?"

"I'm fine. Now what happens?"

"The cops have called for more men and the guy who's bringing the search warrant. We have a friendly judge who signs the warrant ahead of time so the cops have it in hand. They'll get inside and arrest the other two bad guys—or kill them. They'll flush 'em out. Your job is done. Rick said you saw guns inside."

"Rick?"

"Sergeant Ross. One of our plainclothes—"

"Right. I saw a lot of guns."

"Okay. You go on home before the press gets wind of this."

"Barry, that was a little more dangerous than I imagined it would be. I really could have been dog food."

"I'll make it worth your while. Go on, let the police handle this. I'm getting out of here, too. Call me tomorrow."

So I got in my car and drove home. There was something anti-climactic about the evening. The Black Stiletto went in and stirred up the hornet's nest, all right, but then the police arrived to fumigate and clean things up. I was used to doing it all myself.

Still, I felt good about what I'd done. Maybe it made a dent in Sal Casazza's operation.

JULY 30, 1961

Gosh, I can't believe my last diary entry was nearly a month ago. Time has flown by and it seems I haven't had a moment to myself except to sleep. First of all, I found a gym where I can go and exercise! I'd really been missing that part of my life. It's a small, grimy kind of place, so it's perfect, ha ha. It's in East Hollywood, closer to downtown L.A., on Sunset, in what is primarily a Latino neighborhood. It's creatively called "Gym" and is run by a Spanish guy named Luis. Some tough-looking men go there, but there were tough-looking men at Second Avenue Gym, too. I know how to handle myself. When I first joined, Luis asked me if I was in the right place. There were no other women there, naturally. I told Luis to watch me a minute. The first thing I did was get on the speed bag, and I think I impressed everyone. After five minutes of pounding that thing, all the men stopped what they were doing and came over to watch. They'd never seen a *girl* do that. From then on, they just accepted me. Some of them tried to come on to me, ask me out, flirt with me, get a little fresh. I had to lightly pop one guy in the nose for putting his hand on my rear end, but after that they all left me alone. I come and go as I please.

So I've been going to the Gym every day until I report to work at Flickers, which is usually 5:00. I get home around 1:00 in the morning, unless the show that night is something special and runs longer. I'm paid overtime if that happens. Charlie's real nice about that. I might have one or two nights off per week, so that's when I try to see Leo, or I do something fun like go to a movie. The other night I saw *The Guns of Navarone* and it was very exciting!

Or I go out as the Black Stiletto and work for Barry and the D.A.

The morning after that first assignment at the Port, I learned from Barry that the three men in the warehouse were arrested. The one that got shot was all right. Twenty-four cases of illegal weapons were seized, so the D.A. was happy. Unfortunately, no evidence was found that linked the operation to Sal Casazza or Vincent DeAngelo, for that matter. They did discover that the arms were about to be sold to the Heathens Motorcycle Club. The more I hear about them, the more I hope I don't run into any of them. I've seen a few riding through town, though. They wear black leather jackets with all kinds of patches on them, like you'd expect. They're pretty scary-looking guys, and I don't like it that a couple of them have Nazi swastikas on their clothing.

The newspapers reported the raid and arrests, and the Black Stiletto was credited for helping the police. I was amazed to see that. Such an about-face from what I experienced in New York. For days after that, the Black Stiletto became big news on the West Coast. Photos of me that were taken before were now being published, and much of the skepticism that the real Black Stiletto had moved to L.A. had diminished. I don't know what the papers in New York were saying; I'll have to find out from Freddie. It's high time I give him a call or write. I'm afraid I've been neglectful.

I finally heard from Lucy. She said she forgives me for running out without saying good-bye, and that she understands. I guess she bought my "had to be with my man" story. She asked about Leo and how things were going. With her it sounds like everything is the same, except she and Peter don't have me around anymore to be a third wheel.

I haven't seen Leo at all. I've been busy, he's been busy. We managed to bump into each other one night at Flickers while I was working. There, of course, he treats me differently, like I'm just part of the help instead of my lover. If that's what he is. I don't know any-more. Just when I'm getting fed up with his absence and think I'm not going to see him anymore, we'll connect and his charm wins me back. I do love being with him. He makes me feel good; he reminds me that I'm *alive*. So I'm taking it as it comes, dear diary. In the grand scheme of things, I've been in L.A. a little over three months. That's not very long.

I've done two more assignments for Barry. They were very sim-ilar to the first one. He uses me to sneak into a building—in two out of the three cases they were warehouses—and the third one was an auto-repair shop supposedly owned by one of the motorcycle clubs the Heathens deal with. The shop job turned out to be a false alarm, so nothing happened. I didn't find anything and the police didn't raid it. The other warehouse was just like the first. It was located near the Port, in San Pedro, and had a few more men inside than the first one. I had no trouble getting inside and finding a cache of guns, and I was able to skedaddle without anyone knowing. The police raided the place and arrested the men.

Right after that I saw Sal Casazza at Flickers. He and his hood-lum bodyguards sat at a table and barked orders at the waitresses as if he was the King of Persia. Two new fellows have been showing up with him recently. I know them as Mr. Faretti and Mr. Capri. They're younger, probably in their thirties, and look more like Ital-ian businessmen than tough guys. They're very friendly with Casazza, so I figure they're now a part of his crew.

Anyway, usually Casazza is pretty decent to the staff, including me, but that night he was in a foul mood and wanted everyone to know it. When he got up to go to the bathroom, I corralled him and asked if he was "feeling all right." He snapped at me, saying, "Of course I'm all right! Why do you want to know?" I put on my best sexy hostess act and put my arm around his Humpty Dumpty body. "Sal, is something wrong? I hate to see one of my favorite customers in a bad mood. Tell Judy what happened."

Ha ha, he kind of melted. He looked flustered and said, "Oh, well, I just, I just lost some money in a business deal. Not a big problem. Happens all the time. Sorry if I'm taking it out on anyone."

I leaned in and kissed him on the cheek. "There," I said, "I hope that makes it better."

He brightened and said, "It certainly does, my dear. Thank you." Then he went on to the bathroom. I think he was embarrassed.

So apparently my work with Barry is doing some good. Chip by chip, we're making a dent in Sal's organization.

It's good staying busy.

30
Martin
The Present

Gina still hadn't arrived, so I sat in horror and watched the television story about Betty Dinkins. Her grown son had found her body and called the police late last night. She hadn't answered the phone or been seen since the night before. That was the day I'd spotted her on the street and left that letter in her mailbox.

The news show didn't have a whole lot of details, so the anchor spent the time interviewing people from her neighborhood. "Well, she must have really been the Black Stiletto if someone wanted to kill her." "Maybe an old enemy wanted revenge." "I don't believe there ever was a Black Stiletto." The anchor reiterated that Betty Dinkins had a million-dollar deal for a book and that her son was supposed to write it. And now this had to happen to her.

I was pretty freaked out. The police would certainly find my letter, if she kept it. I didn't put my real name on it. Would they have handwriting analysis that could identify the writer? I didn't think so, they couldn't be that advanced. There was no way they could trace me, and I was leaving on a plane in two hours. Surely, I had nothing to worry about.

Then I felt my heart freeze as I realized—I'd written that stupid letter on Empire Hotel stationery.

As if on cue, there was a knock on the door. I breathed a sigh of relief. Gina had arrived, we'd go to breakfast, and I'd get the hell out of Dodge. I went to the door, opened it, but my visitor wasn't Gina. There were two of them, men wearing long trench coats.

"Good morning, sir, we're the police. Can we come in?" one of them said. Only after he'd spoken did I realize he was the same guy I'd seen outside Betty Dinkins's apartment building. The one who saw me deliver the letter and watched me walk away.

Oh, my God, I was suddenly very nervous. "Do you have badges?" I had the presence of mind to ask.

"Sure, let us come in and we'll show them to you," the man said as he started to enter.

I said, "Hey, wait," and made a feeble attempt to close the door on him, but the guy was a lot stronger and bigger than me. He pushed his way inside, his partner followed him, and they shut the door behind them. "What's going on here?" I protested. "You can't just wa—"

A punch in the nose interrupted my sentence. The pain was incredible. Blinded and completely disoriented, I felt myself hit the carpet. I don't think I'd ever been hit in the face before, and I couldn't believe how badly it hurt. I was truly in agony. After a moment, I discovered my nose was bleeding.

The men hoisted me up and into a chair. I groaned and attempted to yell, but the guy slapped my cheek and said, "Shut up, don't make any noise or we'll kill you."

That's when I went into panic mode. I was in a fight-or-flight situation, and it scared the holy shit out of me. I was on the verge of tears, and I'm pretty sure I cried a little from the now-broken nose. But I didn't bolt and run for the door. I was too frightened. I'd never experienced anything like what was happening to me. Were they going to hurt me? Would they kill me? I believed the guy's threat. He and his pal were big and scary and mean. They certainly weren't cops.

The next thing I knew, I was tied to the chair. I don't remember them doing it. My ankles were tied to the front legs of the chair, and my chest and arms were tied to the back.

The man I knew spoke again. "This is Bernie. My name is Stark." He wasn't from around New York. He had a southern accent, Texas, maybe? It was similar to the way my mom talked! "And you must be Martin Talbot, right? I have ways of getting that information from the front desk, you see. We've been watching you, Mr. Talbot." When I didn't say anything, he leaned in closer and growled, "'Cause your name ain't really *Jerry Smith*."

Oh my God. It *was* about the letter.

Stark indicated his friend. "Bernie has a gag. Show it to him, Bernie." The other guy held up an ugly leather S&M-type ball gag. It covered the entire face, with a large ball that fit uncomfortably in the mouth. I didn't want that on me. "We can play this cool and not have to use that, what do you say, Mr. Talbot?" Stark asked.

"What do you want?" I managed to croak.

"We want to know why you wrote that letter to Mrs. Dinkins."

I could have played dumb and asked, "What letter?" but I knew that would just get me a slap. It was no time to be cocky or cover up anything. So I said, "I didn't want her to say she was the Black Stiletto, because she's not."

"And how do you know that? Why would you make that claim?" He waited for me to answer and then he grabbed my hair roughly and jerked my face up to his. "You know something about her, don't you? The Black Stiletto. You see, we've been looking for her. When we heard about Mrs. Dinkins, we came up to New York to check her out. At first we thought she really was her, but now we don't think so. Your letter also makes us believe Dinkins was full of shit. So you're gonna tell us your story, or you won't be telling stories ever again."

My heart was beating a mile a minute. Anxiety attack, full-blown. "There is no story," I gasped.

Slap. "Liar."

There was another knock at the door. The men stiffened. Stark put a finger to his lips and gave me the evil eye.

"Dad?"

Gina.

She continued to knock. The men realized she wasn't going away, so Stark went to the door. "You got the wrong room," he barked.

Silence. Then, "No I don't. Dad?" Another knock.

Stark cursed under his breath. "Go away, you got the wrong room!"

"I'm going to the front desk," Gina announced. Stark knew he couldn't let her do that, so he opened the door with the chain on it.

"Run, Gina!" I shouted.

But she had already known something was wrong. As soon as it was ajar, she kicked the door hard, breaking the chain and slamming it into Stark. She burst in the room and saw me tied to the chair.

"Dad!"

She immediately turned to Stark and started to *clobber* him! What I'd seen her do in the Krav Maga studio was nothing compared to what I witnessed in front of me. The man put up a good fight, but Gina pummeled him with fists and feet—and he went down quickly. I think she kicked him in the nuts and demolished his Adam's apple. By then, though, Bernie had drawn a gun. He was directly in front of me, but he was aiming it at her.

I think I cried, "Gina, look out!" before everything went black.

31
Judy's Diary
1961

AUGUST 12, 1961

I'm listening to the new Elvis record in my apartment. It's called "Little Sister," and the other side is "His Latest Flame." I predict it'll be another number one, but frankly I think I like side B better. I saw previews to his new movie *Blue Hawaii*, which is supposed to come out later this fall. I can't wait. *Wild in the Country* was okay, but it wasn't my favorite movie he was in.

I talked to Freddie today on the phone. He's doing well. The gym's business is up and the new assistant manager is working out fine. Freddie told me there was an article in the paper with the headline, "Has the Black Stiletto Moved?" Another front page asked, "Where is the Black Stiletto?" Well, too bad. New York had its chance. They ran me out of town and now Los Angeles is benefitting. I told Freddie about Luis and my new gym, but that I'll always miss the old place. Oh, another thing—Freddie told me that Kraig was arrested by the police for Clark's murder, but then he was *let go*. Unbelievable. Something about there not being enough evidence. Well, what goes around comes around, as they say, and guess what? Kraig met a bad end himself. He was shot and killed by a policeman during a convenience store robbery. So I guess justice was served after all. I don't think the world will miss that boy.

The other day Leo asked me if I wanted to try the pill. I didn't think it was available yet, and he said it wasn't, only to doctors who could prescribe it to married women. But he said he could get me some if I wanted them. To tell the truth, that offended me a little. He sounded like all he wanted from me was to go to bed, and the pill would mean he wouldn't have to wear a rubber anymore. I told him I'm happy with my diaphragm, it seems to work, and then I told him I'd see him later. He asked, "What's wrong?" but I ignored him, left his house, and drove home. He tried calling me, I'm sure it was him, but I didn't answer. I decided to let *him* wait for *me* for a change! I admit I enjoy sex, but I don't want it to be the only thing between us.

I'd hate to lose him, though. I'm not sure what it is we have together, but when it's actually happening, I really like it. When it's not, which is most of the time, it's frustrating. The other night a very handsome man at Flickers asked me for my phone number. He's an actor, but I'd never heard of him. His name was Jack-something and he was in that silly monster movie, *Little Shop of Horrors*, last year. I never saw it. I don't think he's as big an actor as he thinks he is. Anyway, it might have been nice to go on a date with him. But I answered that I was already seeing someone. That's crazy, though, because I hardly ever see him.

More and more, I've been curious about what Leo doesn't tell me. I think he has loads of secrets. He's supposed to be out of town this week. Since tomorrow is a Sunday, I'm going to drive to his office in the Wholesale District and see if I can use a lockpick to get inside. He won't be there, and I doubt Christina or anyone else would either on a Sunday morning. I don't know what I'm looking for or what I'm going to find, but I just want to make sure Leo's not a crook. He sure keeps company with a lot of crooks, and if he's one, too, then it's better I found out now rather than later.

Oh, my gosh, dear diary, I had a close one this morning!

I drove to the Wholesale District and parked near Leo's building on 7th Street, west of Alameda. The place appeared to be deserted. I left the car and walked across the road, feeling the sun beat down on me. It was hot, but a nice hot. New York has hot summers, too, but not like this. New York is more humid. L.A. has a hot that you can stand. I was dressed in shorts and a white short-sleeve blouse. I used to never wear shorts, but here I do all the time when I'm not working. In an area where no one but longshoremen and greasy manual laborers frequented, I must have stood out something awful. Actually, I mean I stood out something pretty nice, if I say so myself. A pretty white girl with long black hair and long, muscular legs. I do attract the stares and whistles, thank you very much.

The front door of the building was unlocked. There were people there after all. Kelly Warehousing Enterprises was on the second floor, so I bounded up the stairs like I knew what I was doing. I didn't run into anyone, though, but I heard male voices in the distance, somewhere in the building. Suddenly I was nervous and thought maybe I should have done the task at night as the Black Stiletto. What would Leo do if I was caught?

The door to his outer office was marked, "Kelly Warehousing Enterprises." There were a couple of ladies that normally worked in there, secretary-types, who guarded the way to his private office. His office was marked, "L. Kelly, President." I knocked first, just to make sure I was alone, and then used a lockpick to jimmy open the door. It was dark and empty inside, so I started to enter when *I heard Leo's laugh* on the stairs, down the hallway. Then a woman's laugh. Heading my way.

I froze. I didn't know what to do—I couldn't very well go into his office if he was coming. So I quickly closed and locked it again—just as Leo and Christina appeared at the end of the hallway.

"Hi," I said.

"Judy!" Leo was incredibly shocked to see me. "What are you doing here?"

"I, um, came to find you."

They approached as I deftly stuck the lockpick in my shorts pocket. Then I noticed they were both carrying *rifles* inside canvas cases. "Hello, Christina," I said.

"Hello," she answered with no warmth.

"Honey, why are you looking for me? I'm working and—"

"You *said* you were out of town." Then I had a bright idea. "Actually, I didn't come here looking for you at all. I was looking for Christina. I thought she'd be at work, but I forgot this was Sunday."

Leo and Christina exchanged looks. "Why were you looking for me?" she asked.

"Because I thought maybe we should get to know each other better. I was going to take you to lunch. After all, we 'share' Leo, don't we? It'd be nice if we became better friends."

"Really? How nice of you." Christina smiled, but I didn't believe her sincerity for a minute. I think she was smiling because she was laughing inside at the absurdity of my excuse.

Leo produced a set of keys and unlocked the outer office. "Actually, I'm leaving a little later today. I had to stop by the office to pick up some things. Christina came in to work a little bit, didn't you, sis?"

"That's right."

"Come in, Judy, we'll talk in my office."

So I followed them through the outer space. Christina sat in one of the secretaries' chairs while Leo unlocked his private inner sanctum. The door had a foggy-glass window, so you really couldn't see anything on the other side except light and shadow and shapes. He held it open for me and I stepped in.

"Judy, this is not like you," he said after shutting the door and putting his rifle case on the desk.

"I'm sorry, Leo. It's just—I don't know what I'm doing with you. You're never around. I thought maybe Christina could tell me a little more about you, how I could convince you that our relationship is more than you seem to think it is."

"Oh, Judy." His blue eyes twinkled when he raised the venetian blinds to let the sunshine in. Then he took me in his arms, and I let him kiss me. "I don't need convincing. I'm crazy about you, Judy."

"You don't act like it."

"I don't? Judy, don't we have great times together?"

"Of course, we do."

"I'm good to you, aren't I?"

"Yes, but—"

"But I work too much. I know. I know. Believe me, I know. But you have to understand my responsibility to the company, Judy. I have an important job and it requires my attention. I have to travel, it's part of the business."

"What's with the guns?" I asked, gesturing to the case.

"I've told you that Christina and I go to the shooting range sometimes. Christina loves guns. She has quite a collection. We were at the range this morning. I promised her we'd go before I left town."

I broke the embrace and slowly moved toward the window. Dear diary, he wasn't lying, but the crazy radar in my brain indicated he was holding back.

"So, are we just going to continue like this forever?" I asked. "I see you every once in a while, we *sleep together*, and then you go away? Leo, a girl needs more than that."

"Judy, I've told you before, I'm—"

"You're not the marrying type, I know." I turned back to him. "I suppose I'm not either. Not yet, anyway. But there's something unfulfilled here, and I don't know what it is. I don't have the words to describe what it is I need."

He held out his hands. "Well, maybe we can figure out what it is together."

That was a pretty good answer. I leaned against his desk and noticed a beautiful jeweled box next to his telephone. It appeared to be Asian. "This is pretty," I said. "May I?"

"Sure. That's my Chinese jewel box," he said. "It was my mother's."

I picked it up, examined the intricate craftsmanship, and shook it. It felt empty.

"I keep objects of great beauty inside it," he said, as he pulled the key chain out of his pocket again. For the first time I noticed a bright gold key on the chain, and he used it to unlock the jewel box. "This key is the only thing that will open it. The Chinese made the locking mechanism very intricate; it can't be broken into except with a sledgehammer. See, it's empty." He showed it to me; the inside was lined with red velvet. "I've never had an object beautiful enough to earn a place inside."

"Will you ever find an object that's worthy?"

He shut the box and locked it. "Maybe someday," he said with a smile. He replaced the box on the desk, adding, "It's just my good luck charm. That's all."

There wasn't much else to say. Whenever I tried to talk to Leo about us, the conversation always ended in the same place. I said, "Okay, I guess I'll go back to Hollywood. Have a nice trip, wherever you're going."

"I'm flying to New York this afternoon."

"Wow, New York."

"You miss it?"

"Sometimes. Want to take me with you?"

He took me in his arms. "I can't. Strictly business. But we'll do that someday soon. We can go and you can see your old friends."

"That'd be great."

He kissed me again and, like usual, the electricity went from my lips all the way to my toes. I don't know what it is about Leo Kelly, dear diary, but he has charisma in spades and magic in his touch. At that moment, all of my concerns flew out the window.

I said good-bye to him and Christina. She said, "We'll have that lunch someday soon, okay?" And I drove home.

Did he believe my story that I had come to speak to Christina? I doubt it. At least he hadn't caught me breaking in. That would have been a little more difficult to explain.

Just like our relationship.

32
Leo
The Past

I was surprised to see Judy at my office yesterday morning, and not in a good way. In fact, I was pretty angry, but I did my best not to show it. I didn't believe for a minute that she was there to be "girl-friends" with Christina. Was she snooping? It didn't make sense. What did she think she was going to find? I know she wants more out of our relationship, but I can't give it to her. Especially, not now. Not after last night.

I had told Judy I'd be out of town over the weekend; that was only partially true. Saturday I had things to take care of. Sunday morning Christina and I went to the shooting range. My God, she's good. My sister is a regular Annie Oakley. She's a goddamned expert sharpshooter. During our entire session, I don't think she ever missed the bull's-eye. Not once. She hit every target perfectly. Even Bobby, the manager, came over and watched her shoot. He rarely did that, because a lot of people were good shots. But not too many girls. He asked her if she wanted to enter a competition, but Christina just scoffed. That's not her style.

The incident at the office with Judy rattled me a little, but I was pretty sure I smoothed things over. She is such a honey, such a gorgeous, sexy girl. There's no way I could be mad at her for long, and it would be impossible to stop seeing her. So I won't. It was going to be tough, though. I would have to pull out all my resources, all of the Kelly allure, to pull it off.

After Judy left the office, I said good-bye to Christina and drove to Vegas. I was supposed to have dinner with the DeAngelos. Maria was expecting me, and Vince wanted to talk to me. I couldn't say no, nor did I want to. Maria had been dropping hints that she might be ready to, you know, go a little farther than first and second base. I wasn't about to pass that up.

So I took the Karmann Ghia and got to DeAngelo's ranch around five. I spent the next two hours with Maria out by the pool. She's a knockout in a bikini; she looks like that French dame, Brigitte Bardot. Oh, my God.

Dinner was a barbecue outside, overlooking that magnificent lawn. Vince offered me a drink—I had a martini—and pulled me over to the side so we could talk before we sat down to eat. Paulie was there, of course, and he was privy to our conversation. Maria was in the house helping her mother with stuff for the meal. They had servants and all that, but Carlotta liked to prepare some meals herself. She's a great cook. Maybe some of that'd rub off on her daughter, which would make Maria an even better catch.

"Remember that thing I asked you about a while back?" DeAngelo began.

"Sure, Vince."

"Well, we're ready to talk about it. How's your sister?"

"She's great."

"Is she working?"

"At my company. I made her office manager. She's a quick learner."

DeAngelo rubbed his chin and looked at Paulie. His son shrugged, so the old man continued. "You think she still has the stuff for a bank job?"

"Absolutely. I think she's itching for it."

"She's not worried about going back to jail?"

"Nah. She'd make sure she doesn't *go* back to jail. Christina's tough as nails, Vince."

"And what about you, Leo?" He poked a finger hard into my chest. It hurt too. "Are you tough enough for a serious bank job?"

"Yeah, Vince. Sure."

"How many did you do with your sister?"

I lied. "A bunch."

"Yeah?"

I held out my hands. "Hey, she's the expert. I was the bagman."

"You weren't with her when she got popped?"

"No. That was pure dumb luck. Two beat cops happened to come into the bank just as the job went down. Her two companions were shot and killed."

"I remember now."

"So what have you got, Vince? Tell me about it."

He handed me a cigar. I didn't smoke them, but I let him light it anyway. It tasted like horse manure. I think it was from Cuba.

"You ever heard of a guy named Frank Santorini?"

"Sure. He was a big mob boss in Chicago back in the '40s, wasn't he? I read that he died a few months ago, in L.A."

"Yeah. Heart attack. He moved to L.A. after he served some time. The guy was in his seventies then. He was a widower and lost two sons in World War Two and a third on the streets of Chicago. Frank was ninety-five when he died. I knew him, he was a good man. He ran his business like an admiral, but he handed it over to his crew and walked away in 1947."

"He must have been a tough old guy," I said.

"He was. Anyway, you ever heard of the Florentine Diamond?"

"I don't think so."

"It's a big yellow diamond, around a hundred and thirty-seven carats, cut very intricately. It originally came from India, but its travels are the stuff of legends dating back to the fifteenth century. The Medici family owned it, because we do know that a French jeweler and traveler named Tavernier saw the diamond among the Duke of

Tuscany's treasures and sketched it. It eventually passed to the Haps-
burgs of Austria, because the Grand Duke of Tuscany married Em-
press Maria Theresa in Vienna. The diamond became part of the
Hapsburg crown jewels in their palace, the Hofburg. Have you ever
been there?"

I had no idea what he was talking about. "No."

"I have. What a palace. Those people lived like kings."

"They *were* kings, Dad," Paulie said.

DeAngelo frowned at his son. "Shut up, I'm telling the story."
He puffed on the cigar a moment and continued. "After the fall of
the Austrian Empire at the end of World War One, it's believed the
diamond was taken by the imperial family into exile in Switzerland,
but it was stolen along with other gems and possibly brought to
South America. However, it's a long-standing rumor that the Florentine somehow found its way to America in the 1920s, and then it
disappeared. As of today, no one knows where it is."

"Really."

DeAngelo held up a finger. "But I do. Our friend Frank Santorini bought it on the black market, brought it with him to Los Angeles, and hid it in a safety deposit box at the Security First National
Bank on Hollywood Boulevard."

"The diamond is in L.A.?"

"Yes, it is. You may ask how I know this. I will tell you. Frank
Santorini and I were close friends. He revealed his secret to me
shortly before he died. He was planning to take it out of the bank
and sell it, but he passed, may he rest in peace, before he could do it.
All this time I've been trying to find out if it really is in the bank. I
had to pay off a bank manager to confirm it."

"How much is it worth?" I asked.

"Depending on the fence, it could fetch up to five million dollars.
Maybe more."

I whistled. "And it's sitting in that bank?"

"Yeah. And the thing is, Frank didn't leave any next of kin who
can inherit the contents of the safety deposit box. I've learned that if

the box goes unclaimed by the end of September, they'll open it and reveal its contents. If that happens, all hell will break loose. The diamond would be analyzed and identified, and most likely it would go back to Vienna and sit in the Hofburg Treasury, useless to anyone."

"That's quite a story, Vince."

"It is, isn't it? But the final chapter involves you and your sister."

I felt a shiver go down my spine. "We're gonna snatch the diamond?"

He nodded. "I've hired one of the best bank men in the business. Marco Maroni, do you know him?"

"Christina does. She's worked with him before."

"Perfect. He's the boss of the operation. You and your sister will join his team and do whatever he says, understand?"

"Sure."

"He has one guy already, but he needed two more reliable people, and I suggested you and Christina."

"I appreciate it."

"Marco is doing all the planning. The job will be sometime in September. You're going to break into that safety deposit box and take the Florentine Diamond."

"Wow." I swallowed hard. "You can count on us, Vince."

"I hope so. That diamond is going to be a Christmas present for Maria."

What? A five-million-dollar diamond—for *Maria?* "That's wonderful, Vince. I'm sure she'll love it."

"Okay, we'll talk closer to the day. I'll have Marco contact you directly. Not a word to anyone."

"Of course, Vince."

We shook hands and had another drink together. Then Carlotta called us to dinner. Maria had changed into a sundress that amplified her bosom and bare arms, and we sat together. The food was out of this world. Even Paulie was friendlier than usual.

*　　*　　*

Later on, Maria and I took a nighttime walk around the grounds. We stopped in the gazebo and talked about stupid stuff—her car, her dog, her clothes, her this and that—the same old superficial self-ish stuff. I especially can't stand her little foo-foo dog. Mitsy. A toy poodle. All it did was yap at me. I'd like to kick it into the swimming pool and watch it drown.

But as we sat in the gazebo and Maria kept talking and talking, I decided to do something about it, so I leaned in and kissed her. She responded enthusiastically. Lately, she hadn't minded when I put my hands on her breasts, so I did that and she started breathing heavier. This went on for fifteen minutes or so, and I was getting all hot and bothered. Finally she said, "Let's go to my bedroom."

Really?

She opened the trap door in the gazebo and we climbed down to the underground tunnel that connected to the wine cellar. From there, it was easy to climb up into the house and sneak past her parents to her room. She closed and locked the door and then she took me to bed.

I hit a home run and scored.

33
Judy's Diary
1961

AUGUST 28, 1961

The Black Stiletto had an exciting night. I finally came face-to-face with the Heathens. It was pretty scary, but I did all right. They're not so deadly after all. They're just a bunch of big, burly, tough, angry white men. Kind of reminded me of Neanderthals; I saw pictures of what they supposedly looked like at the Museum of Natural History, except the ones tonight wore black leather jackets, ha ha.

I met Barry in front of Boardner's, as usual, and he asked me point-blank how I felt about infiltrating a Heathens haven. I asked him to tell me more. There was an auto-repair shop on Wilton, near Santa Monica Boulevard, that the Heathens owned but didn't operate, although members had been seen there. The police were aware that the manager had served two stints in prison; otherwise, it was a garage that wouldn't normally be under scrutiny. Barry's investigation indicated the shop might be a storehouse for the weapons. All I had to do was get inside, see if I could find any guns, and get out. Sure.

So I drove to the neighborhood, parked the car on Santa Monica, walked a block, huddled in an alcove, and then slipped on my mask. I figured as long as no one saw me *as* the Black Stiletto getting in or out of my car, then my identity couldn't be traced through the license plate. There's quite a bit of light on Hollywood streets, so my foot traveling strategy has changed a great deal since the New York days. There it was fairly easy to dart between dark areas, closed store-fronts, and brownstone entries. In L.A. the streets are very different. Instead of brownstones there are houses. Instead of storefronts lining a street, they're gathered in little strip mall parking areas. So now, since I have a rather good relationship with the LAPD, I'll run down the streets in plain sight if it's necessary. Sure, I prefer to stick to the shadows when I can, but it's rarely possible. Running is more diffi-cult because the streets, in many cases, are long and I get stopped by traffic lights. Manhattan had long blocks on the streets going east and west, too, but the north-south avenues were very short between intersections. It's very strange being stuck on a street corner here with ordinary pedestrians, all of us waiting for the light to turn green so we can walk. In some cases I get a bit mobbed if people try to fol-low me. That's where the autograph seekers and picture takers catch up with me and crowd around. I try to indulge them while the light is against me, but as soon as it changes, I say, "Gotta go!"

The auto-repair shop was well lit, too. The place was surrounded by a high chain-link fence with barbed wire along its top. I guess they didn't want their motorcycles and cars stolen, or they wanted to keep trespassers out, or both, but I wasn't sure how I'd get over it without being seen. The main garage and its several car bays faced Santa Monica and another building was built at an L to it, which was probably the offices and customer entrance. The large gate in the fence was locked, as the shop was closed for the night. Still, lights were on in some windows and the garage doors were open, and I saw a couple of men working on cars.

I headed for the back side of the L-shaped section, moved in be-tween the fence and the property next door, and found a nice pool of shadows next to a pickup truck where I could crouch out of sight. I examined the fence and back of the shop and determined that my only access was from the front—which obviously would be a bad move—or through a door that stood on the back wall of the garage section. It was ajar, propped open, so that a breeze would blow through to the open bays. The two problems with that were the mechanics inside doing a late shift. I'd performed more difficult tasks, so I figured I might as well try. At that moment, no one was outside the building. I approached the chain-link fence and climbed it as quickly as I could. When I got to the barbed wire top, I grabbed the hook off my belt and used it to pull the wires down far enough for me to swing my legs over. By the time I'd dropped to my feet on the other side, maybe ten seconds had elapsed. Not bad. No one had seen me. I darted to the side of the building near the open door and flattened myself against the wall. I faced an alley and the edge of a small lot full of wrecked cars and pieces of vehicles. A five-foot-tall stack of tires stood a few feet away like a tower of black, rubber donuts.

The sound of hammering and clanging tools drifted out from the garage, along with music on a radio. Johnny Cash was singing "Folsom Prison Blues." That was an old one; I hadn't heard it since the days when Lucy and I played the jukebox at the East Side Diner. But the tune was somehow appropriate for the situation.

I inched toward the door; it opened away from me, so I was partly masked by the door itself. When I was directly behind it, I heard footsteps close by inside the building. A man shouted, "Byron, what are you doing in there? I gotta go, too!" A more muffled voice called, "I'll be out in a minute! It was that Mexican food, man." I almost laughed, but then those footsteps came nearer. The man on the other side of the door muttered, "Oh, f—- it," and then he *walked outside* and stood with his back to me, not four feet away. And what did he do? He unzipped and peed on the pavement in front of the wrecked cars. Ewww, how gross! But you know what they say about catching someone with their pants down? I crept up behind him and locked him in a choke hold before he knew what was happening. He was a big guy, too, and he struggled hard. After twenty seconds or so, he grew weaker and finally collapsed in my arms. I quickly gagged him with the cloth I keep in my backpack, and tied his feet and hands with the rope. Dragging him behind one of the junky cars was the hardest part; he was heavy! The man was already starting to wake up, but the gag and bindings would keep him subdued. When he was safely hidden, I went inside the garage.

The place smelled of grease, oil, and sweat. The radio was louder and echoed in the space. I didn't see the other guy—he was still in the bathroom, which was behind worktables, tools, parts shelves, and a sink. An old Studebaker was up on one rack, and a pickup truck sat on the floor of the second bay. Three motorcycles stood in another one, and the fourth bay was empty. Access to the other part of the building appeared to be through double doors on the wall perpendicular to the tool shelves. I spied a spindle of chain on a worktable, so I pulled the end of the strand, unrolled it long enough to reach the bathroom, and tied it around the doorknob. Then I tied the slack around the pickup truck's front bumper. Now there was no way the guy was going to open that door. My last act in the garage was turning up the radio much louder so no one could hear Mr. Toilet calling for help.

The guns couldn't have been in the garage. There weren't any secret storerooms that I could see, and there was no place to hide them. They had to be in the other section, so I went through the double doors and found myself catty-cornered from a large room where customers could sit and drink coffee while they waited for their vehicles to be fixed. No one was in there. The counter window was unmanned as well. A door reading "Employees Only" stood next to that. There was another men's bathroom door along with a women's. A glass door opened to the front of the lot, a small customer parking area, and the spacious drive to the gate. I moved to the employee door and listened. Two voices in the back. One guy was heading toward me, saying, "I'm gonna open the gate. They'll be here any minute."

Oh, my gosh, *who* would be there any minute?

I heard his steps just behind the door, so I scooted behind it as it opened. A man with gray hair and overalls walked out and went straight to the double doors without looking back. He hadn't seen me. I quickly slipped through the door and into a hallway. I saw a couple of offices, the doors to which were open, and another closed door. Again, I thought I'd hit a dead end. The guns *couldn't* be hidden back there. There simply wasn't enough room. Was Barry wrong?

Outside, the noise of motorcycle engines rumbled onto the lot. I went back to the employee door and peered out to see what was going on. The gray-haired man had opened the front gate, and four motorcycles had rolled in. The headlights brightened the front of the shop like daylight.

Heathens.

The smart thing would've been for me to get out of there fast, but I was too curious to see what the motorcyclists were up to. I watched as they pulled their bikes near the front of the building and stopped. I heard them greet the old man, but I couldn't understand what they were saying.

Then a bullet nearly took my ear off.

A Heathen, wearing a black, sleeveless leather jacket and sporting tattoos on his bare arms, stood at the other end of the hall behind me. He held a pistol pointed in my direction, and he fired again. Luckily, I was already jerking my body to the side, and the round splintered the door just a few inches away from my chest. Nothing else to do but run! I burst out the employee door and into the waiting room, only to run in to the gray-haired man, who in turn was followed by the Heathens! They had heard the two shots.

I was surprised. They were surprised. Everyone was surprised. And then it was chaos. I tried to run for the double doors to the garage, but one of the Heathens grabbed me. I made short change of him, first by easily breaking out of his bear hug, and then by using one of my invented *wushu* moves to jab him hard in the solar plexus. Throwing him over my hip was then child's play. By then, the others were drawing weapons. I had maybe two seconds at the most to do something, so I lashed out at the closest guy with a *Mikazuki-geri* "crescent moon" *karate* kick. It's similar to a roundhouse kick, only the motion of the foot is in a flatter arc, like the flat crescent of a new moon. The pistol flew from the Heathen's hand before he could squeeze the trigger. Then they all ganged up on me, but Soichiro's training saved my life once again. With a combination of *karate* punches and kicks, and my *wushu* fluid-movement offensive and defensive tactics, I became a whirling dervish and hurt them badly enough to give me the opening I needed to rush through the double doors.

As I ran by the bathroom door, I heard the poor fellow inside screaming, "Get me out of here! Help! Somebody!" I would have laughed as I shot toward the back exit, but I knew I wouldn't have time to scale the chain-link fence and round over the barbed wire before my pursuers caught up with me and put several bullets into my skin. Frantic for a hiding place, I wasted three precious seconds considering whether or not to try and hide inside the pickup truck, but rejected that idea. I heard the Heathens coming through the double doors, so I ran out the entrance from whence I came. I figured I could hide with my tied-up friend behind the wrecks—that was a tempting possibility—but then I noticed the stacked tires again. Without thinking about it, I leaped for the pile, scrambled onto the top, wormed inside the column, and ducked down. I squatted in the middle of the tires—a very tight fit—but as long as no one looked in them, they wouldn't see me.

A second later the men poured outside. "Where is she?" "Where'd she go?" "Danny?" "Danny, where are you?" "Hey, Sam's chained in the bathroom!"

Over the next five minutes, I heard them release Sam, but they couldn't find Danny, presumably the guy I tied up. Police sirens soon approached the lot; the Heathens cursed and started telling everyone to get rid of their weapons. They went back to the front of the shop, giving me the opportunity to climb out of the tires. I stopped briefly to check on my buddy behind the junk car. He grunted and mumbled at me through the gag. I patted his head—then happened to look inside the decrepit vehicle next to me. The seats had been taken out and a wooden crate sat within the body—the same kind of crate I'd seen at the Port warehouses. I quickly moved to some of the other wrecks and discovered similar crates.

The guns were hidden right out in the open, inside the junky cars.

I got over the fence and crouched in the same shadowy spot beside the pickup truck where I'd been before. I could hear a little of what was happening in front. The cops had arrived and were asking about reports of gunshots. The gray-haired man said something about an "intruder." After a few minutes of arguing, it was apparent that the cops found one of the men's weapons. "That's an illegal firearm," I heard a policeman say. About five minutes later, more police cars arrived. The raid was on. That was my cue to appear and tell the cops about the guns in the wrecks behind the shop. Because they were out in the open, the police didn't need a search warrant.

My task was done; as soon as I could do so, I scooted away from the site. I removed the mask and put on the coat, made it to my car, and drove home.

It was a satisfying evening, but it left me hungry for more.

34
Judy's Diary

1961

AUGUST 29, 1961

I talked to Barry on the phone this morning. He told me that the police arrested everyone at the Heathens' auto shop on illegal gun possession. Unfortunately, the motorcycle club members and the old man were bailed out yesterday morning. The D.A. argued that they were a flight risk, but the hoodlums had good lawyers. No charges were dropped, though, so that's a good thing. Barry wanted to know if I'd come by his house in Laurel Canyon to pick up my payment and talk about what's next. He'd been asking me for some time, saying how beautiful it was there. His house is isolated, in the hills. I'd been putting him off, but I finally said okay, mainly to pick up the $350 he had for me. We made a date for tomorrow night, because tonight I had to work at Flickers.

Leo is missing in action, but Christina was at the club tonight. She was alone, as usual, but she flirted with men she knew at the bar. It seems she never sits at a table to watch the show, no matter who's performing. Tonight it was Al Martino, who sang his hit version of "Summertime."

Gosh, the last time I saw Leo was about a week after that morning at his office. We went out to dinner and to a movie—he took me to see *Breathless* because I hadn't seen it yet. What a strange movie! It was very—different. I don't know what I thought of it, but it was very interesting and that French actor in it was very good looking, in a bad boy sort of way, and he was a *very* bad boy. Leo hated it.

Still, we had fun. Leo continues to make me laugh, and I enjoy his company. I didn't go back to his house or let him come to my apartment, though. He was disappointed, but I told him I was tired and was having my period. That dissuaded him. We talked about how busy he was, and he apologized for not being around much. I sometimes wish he'd take me with him on his business trips, wherever they are. I wouldn't get in his way. I'd find something to do while he was busy. It's just that I really want to know what he does with his life when he's not with me. I sense something darker about him lately, as if he's *really* hiding something. I'd resolved to talk to him about it the next time I saw him. But then I saw Christina, and I sidled up to her at the bar when I had a few minutes away from being a hostess.

"Heard from Leo?" I asked.

She lit a cigarette and smiled at me. "Hi, Judy, nice to see you too."

"Oh, Christina, you know what I mean. Hello to you, too. It's just that I haven't heard from him in a couple of weeks. Where is he now?"

She shrugged. "I think he's in San Francisco."

"Really? I'd *love* to go to San Francisco."

She shrugged again. "It's a nice town." Then she looked at me with ice-cold eyes and the hint of a sneer and said, "He has something going in Las Vegas, too, so he spends time there."

I think most people would have taken that literally, dear diary, but my internal alarm went crazy. Christina meant something entirely different.

Another girl?

"What's in Las Vegas?" I asked.

She puffed on her cigarette and answered, "A business opportunity. Oh, there's Shrimp, I need to talk to him. Would you excuse me?"

"Sure."

She went over to the end of the bar, where Sal Casazza's man stood with an empty glass of something. They greeted each other like old friends.

Leo and Las Vegas. I would have to think about that.

AUGUST 31, 1961

Last night I went to Barry's place in Laurel Canyon. He was right— it *is* beautiful there. He lives in a tiny cabin that sits all by itself on a hill, and you can see the lights of Hollywood from his front porch. I drove there, following his directions, but I still got a little lost. I retraced my path and started over, and then I found the right road near a country store.

It was strange, him sitting there in civilian clothes and me in my Black Stiletto outfit, but we had a nice dinner and talk. He made burritos with refried beans and ground beef, and we drank beer. The food reminded me of Texas. I'm not an avid beer drinker, but I'll have it on occasion.

He smoked a cigarette afterward and we stared at the enchanting vista. I asked him if he ever got lonely, and he replied, "Sure. But I enjoy my privacy more, so I don't socialize much."

"You ever been married?"

"Once. That didn't turn out too well."

"Where is she now?"

He laughed wryly. "I have no idea." Then he looked at me and said, "Do you know how famous you are now?"

"Oh, go on."

"You are. The D.A.'s office loves you. There's now a Black Stiletto Fan Club in Hollywood."

"There was already one in New York, or maybe it was national. I lost track of it after the first year."

"Someday you might have to reveal who you are, you know."

"Why?"

"Think of the money you'd make selling your story."

"Remember, I'm still wanted in New York. I don't think I'd get off that easily."

Barry shook his head. "I bet D.A. McKesson could fix that for you."

"The money's not that important, as long as I have enough to live on and be comfortable. I don't think I'd want my private self to be subjected to that kind of notoriety. I like things the way they are."

We talked some more about mundane stuff and then he brought up business. He said the guns they found at the auto-repair shop were only a small portion of a larger cache. Somewhere in the greater Los Angeles area there were a lot more, and he was working on other leads.

"Someone in Casazza's organization is making counterfeit money," Barry said. "The feds arrested a Serpientes member on his way to the border, and he was trying to smuggle five grand worth of fake five- and ten-dollar bills. They were very sophisticated, the best printing job they'd ever seen. Counterfeiting is not as bad as running guns, but it's still against the law and hurts our Treasury Department. The D.A. wants me to see if I can find the source of the funny money so we can take them down." He lightly hammered his fist on the arm chair and said, "God, I'd like to nail that S.O.B. Vince DeAngelo."

"You sound like it's something personal." That made him pause. "You don't have to tell me if it's—"

"No, no, I'll tell you. You know I served some time because of some smuggling I did a few years ago when I was a cop."

"Yeah?"

"I was smuggling guns for DeAngelo. It was years ago, before his operation was as sophisticated as it is now. Because of my connections with West Texas, I had a foolproof pipeline to the southern states. Anyway, when I was caught, I stayed mum. I wasn't a rat. I thought DeAngelo would pull strings and get me off, but instead he sold me down the river. He didn't lift a finger to help me. My actions made the LAPD look bad, and that meant more to him than having a cop in his pocket. So I lost my job, went to jail, and became a pariah. The most ironic thing is that DeAngelo took over my smuggling route and contacts in Texas, got rich, and became who he is today."

"Gee, I'm sorry," was all I could think of to say.

"That's not all. I have a brother in Odessa. Skipper, Skipper Gorman. Four years younger than me. He was working with me when I was doing all that criminal activity, and DeAngelo *shot* him."

"Oh, my God!"

Barry held up a hand. "He lived, but he's crippled. Has to stay in a wheelchair and is in constant pain. Two bullets destroyed his hip."

"That's terrible."

"He's okay. Skipper works as an accountant or investment counselor or something like that. Got himself a straight job. I don't understand stocks and bonds and taxes, but he does."

I laughed. "Me neither. I'm terrible at math."

"So, anyway, you asked. That's why I'd like to get DeAngelo. Eh, we'll get him eventually."

Dear diary, I'd been thinking of asking Barry this for some time, so I rustled up the nerve to do so. "Have you ever heard of a guy named Leo Kelly?"

The name didn't seem to excite him much, but Barry replied, "Yeah, I know who he is. He's in the warehouse business, or something like that. Why do you ask?"

"Let's just say I know who he is."

"He's a friend of Sal Casazza's, we know that, but he's not on our radar. He's kind of a playboy about town. A hit with the women. He has an uncle who owns a hot nightclub in Hollywood."

"What else do you know about him?"

"Nothing much." He snapped his fingers, trying to remember. "Wait, he has a sister who was a bank robber. Went to jail, if I recall correctly."

That I didn't know. "Really?"

"Yeah. Oh, and I know Kelly is chummy with none other than DeAngelo's daughter, Maria."

That made the hair on my head bristle. "Oh, yeah?"

"Their families were close for a long time. I knew Leo's father when I was on the force. He was a powerful guy down in the Wholesale District. I'm pretty sure Leo and Maria grew up knowing each other."

I didn't know what to think of that. "Does she live in Las Vegas, too?"

"Yeah, with her daddy. Spoiled bitch, if you ask me, but she's pretty."

Uh-oh. Do I have any reason to worry about that information? I could be imagining things. Maybe Leo was indeed *just* friends with her.

"So you don't suspect him of being involved in any of Casazza's or DeAngelo's activities?"

"Like I said, his name has never come up in that regard."

"You care if I check him out?"

Barry looked at me with a furrowed brow. "You really know him, huh?"

I didn't say anything.

He lit another cigarette, and said, "Well, if you want to on your own dime, go ahead. He's probably clean, but I guess it couldn't hurt to have a look at him. After all, he works with all those union guys, knows people at the Port, and that's where the guns come in from overseas."

We eventually called it a night. Barry said for me to contact him in a week and he'd let me know what we'll do next. I drove home from the hills—in the *dark*, and it was a little nerve-wracking—but I made it safely and reentered the world of Judy Cooper.

Now I'm thinking about how I can investigate Leo more thoroughly.

35
Gina
THE PRESENT

Oh, my freaking god, I'm in freaking *jail* and my dad's in the freaking hospital in critical condition and I'm in a freaking lot of trouble. I'm sure my legal problems will sort themselves out, because I did *nothing wrong*. It was self-defense. I was protecting my father, who was *tied to a chair and about to be tortured*. The man aimed a gun at me, I leaped for it and knocked him sideways, but the damned thing went off—at Dad.

I'm worried about him. The bullet went through Dad's *neck* and he was in surgery for nearly seven hours. Something called the vagus nerve was severed, but that's all I know. I have no idea what that means, if he's going to be paralyzed or impaired or what. He was fortunate that the carotid artery wasn't hit or he'd be dead. I'm so upset. I pray that he's going to be all right.

I've been in a 20th Precinct cell before. The place hasn't changed. Detective Jordan couldn't believe he was seeing me again in his station. He's the detective who handled my assault case, and again later when I was accused of stalking. Detective Jordan is a pretty nice cop. He's a handsome black man in his forties or fifties. Kind of like Denzel Washington. He took a shine to me back when I was nearly killed. He was doing his job and abiding by the law throughout his actions, but I think deep down he sympathized with me later when I was charged with stalking that rapist.

I've been arrested for assault on the two men who were about to kill me and my dad. The cops who arrived at the scene had never seen anything like it. After all, it was a nice, Upper West Side hotel room. It's just that the guest was tied to a chair and had blood all over him, and his assailants were lying on the ground unconscious, one seriously injured. The guest's visiting teenage daughter stood in the middle of it all, unharmed, claiming she had saved her father from torture and murder. The cops didn't believe me. Actually, they found me holding a towel tightly against Dad's neck, attempting to stop the blood. Luckily, ambulances came quickly and picked up my dad and the two creeps while the police questioned me. Dad's now at St. Luke's-Roosevelt, where I once spent some time, too.

Detective Merrill, whom I didn't know, asked me to come to the station for more interrogation. At the time, I wasn't under arrest. I said I wanted to go to the hospital to see about my father. When I refused to come along cooperatively, *then* Merrill said I was under arrest for assault.

It's now the next morning, and I'm sitting in this stupid jail cell with a gross little toilet and an uncomfortable mattress on the poor excuse for a bed. Needless to say, I didn't sleep well. The meals have been okay, but nothing I would normally eat. I wouldn't be able to keep my body in shape if I had to eat that high-calorie crap every day.

Right after breakfast, which was a strange concoction of rubbery scrambled eggs, leatherlike bacon, and a biscuit as hard as a stone, Detective Jordan came to see me. "Why are you always getting in trouble, young lady?" he asked. I couldn't tell if he was joking or not. He wanted to go over my story again. He and an officer brought me into an interview room, and I went through the whole thing for the zillionth time—how I'd come to meet my dad for breakfast and found him a prisoner of two strange men, one of whom was armed. I used what I've learned of Krav Maga to disable them, but the gun went off during the fight. My dad was shot. I tore into the shooter, and then I called 911. Then I attended to my dad and waited. And I've been waiting ever since.

Jordan checked his notes and said, "Gina, I'm sorry Detective Merrill brought you here and you had to spend the night in a cell. It wasn't right. His actions will be reviewed. I believe your story, but we can't completely drop the case until we talk to your father and get his side of it. He obviously can't speak right now, so until we *can* interview him you'll be released on your own recognizance. You'll have a hearing this afternoon in front of a judge. If you want to get a lawyer, you can. It's all bureaucracy and stuff, otherwise I'd just let you walk out of here. But you can't leave town, understand?"

"What about my dad? Have you heard how he is?"

"Only that the operation was successful and that he's still in ICU. But maybe your visitors outside can tell you more."

They were my mom and Ross, who had flown in from Chicago early this morning. After a few tearful hugs and kisses, Mom told me that Dad had a serious injury and it may take months or years for him to fully recover. The surgery repaired the wound, but only time will tell how badly the vagus nerve was damaged. Apparently, it has branches to the larynx, among other places, so his voice will most likely be affected. It's too early to know if he'll be able to speak again. Hopefully, he'll just be hoarse for a while. If you can call it "lucky," Dad was hit on the left side of his neck. If he'd been hit on the right side, he could suffer rapid heartbeat and hoarseness for the rest of his life. Instead, he'll have some gastrointestinal problems like reflux and loose bowels, as well as the hoarseness, for some time—but it's possible these will improve with time. Dad will be in ICU for at least another day, probably more. Right now he's drifting in and out of consciousness and can't speak. He's been told I'm "all right."

Ross asked me if I knew *anything* about the two men who attacked Dad. I told him the truth—I had no idea. It turns out the shooter has a broken neck, so he will be paralyzed forever. Maybe I got a little carried away on him. The other guy has a concussion, a broken arm, and a broken collarbone, but he'll eventually be okay. Frankly, I don't care if the shooter is paralyzed; I was fighting for our lives.

Mom said I had another visitor outside waiting—Josh. I was so happy to see him. He and Mom had been talking by phone since yesterday, so he met them when they arrived in New York. When Josh walked in the room, we didn't leave to the imagination how much we care for each other. Mom raised her eyebrows and said, "Well, it looks like you two are close."

Ross took care of hiring a lawyer for me. Again. They would surely drop all charges against me, but it was best to have one in the courtroom. I wasn't allowed to leave yet, so Mom and Josh stayed with me in the interview room while Ross went to take care of the red tape.

"What about Dad?" I asked. "Shouldn't someone be at the hospital?"

"Maggie flew in this morning, too," Mom said. "She's there now."

That's good. I like Maggie. I hope Dad will be all right and they'll get married. Dad needs someone like her in his life.

We waited a long time. At one point, Josh went to get coffee for all of us, and Mom said, "Ross and I like him a lot." That made me happy. She said she'd been disappointed that I'd quit school, but when she met Josh and heard him speak about me, she knew I should follow my heart.

Finally, Ross returned, and during lunch a nice lawyer named Mr. Drake came to talk to us. An hour later, I was in front of the judge and the whole thing was over in five minutes. I was free.

"Do you want to go home and bathe?" my mom asked.

"No," I answered. "I want to see Dad."

36
Judy's Diary
1961

SEPTEMBER 12, 1961

Today's events certainly distracted me from what's going on in my world. The main thing is the building of a wall between East and West Berlin, which is going to cause all kinds of political problems between us and the Soviet Union. The "Cold War," as it's called, is getting hotter.

That was on my mind this morning because I was listening to a story about the "Berlin Wall" on the radio in my car as I drove from my apartment down to Hollywood Boulevard so I could go to a Laundromat. The one in my building was under repair, and I badly needed to do a wash. I knew there was one on Cahuenga, so that's where I was headed. I also had my Stiletto outfit with me, because I was supposed to go see Barry in the afternoon and planned to change somewhere. But then the day took an unexpected turn, and I helped foil a bank robbery. I think. To tell the truth, I'm not sure exactly what happened or what the thieves got away with.

The Security First National Bank is an old 7-story building on the northeast corner of Hollywood Blvd. and Cahuenga. Barry once told me that Raymond Chandler's character Philip Marlowe was supposed to have an office inside. The ground floor was a bank, though, and there appeared to be some kind of commotion going on as I drove by. A police car with flashing lights was double-parked in front, but no one was inside and the doors were wide open, as if the patrolmen had rushed out. A crowd of people stood on the sidewalk. From their demeanor, it was obvious something bad was happening in the bank. My windows were down and I was sure I heard gunshots. I didn't even think about it—I turned right at the next street, Cosmo, and luckily found a parking place. Not having time to dress completely, I donned just the leather jacket, the mask, and my belt. I had on blue jeans and tennis shoes below. I took my stiletto and strapped it on my leg, and got out of the car. It was a risk because people were on the street, but everyone's attention was directed toward the boulevard, where all the excitement was happening.

As I darted across the intersection of Cosmo and Hollywood, I saw that the crowd had grown in front of the bank. I shouted, "Out of the way! Move! Let me through!" There were the usual cries of surprise, but they opened up for me. I halted briefly at the door so I could take stock of the situation.

It was a robbery in progress. I saw two gunmen wearing Halloween monster masks holding customers hostage on one side of the room. One was Frankenstein and the other was the Bride of Frankenstein. In fact, that robber was a woman, I could tell by the shape of her body. The civilians and bank employees were lying facedown on the floor with their arms spread. Bride of Frankenstein covered them with a handgun. A policeman lay on his back in a pool of blood. A second cop was nearby, lying facedown with arms spread-eagle—he had given up. Frankenstein had the patrolman's weapon in his belt. The robber was watching the cop and the other door that was the exit to Cahuenga.

Were more police on the way? I couldn't count on it, so I bravely burst into the bank. Frankenstein swung his pistol at me and fired—people screamed—but by then I had dropped, rolled, and crouched behind the cover of a free-standing station where customers could fill out forms. Frankenstein kept firing, but the Bride shouted, "Don't waste your ammo!" The gunman stopped shooting. The hostages sobbed in terror. I heard the Bride say, "Watch them," so I knew she was coming around to attack. I got up on one knee as if I was about to run the 50-yard dash, and perked up my ears to listen to her steps. I made a judgment call on exactly how far away she was standing, so I pushed up and charged around the station and slammed into the woman's waist. Her gun went off over my head, but I tackled her and we both crashed heavily on the hard floor. The weapon flew across the room and miraculously slid inches away from the living policeman's hand. Seeing his opportunity, he grabbed it, and, while still lying facedown, aimed the gun at Frankenstein. He fired and missed. The robber, who stood a few feet away, slammed his shoe down on the cop's gun hand, causing the patrolman to release the weapon. Then Frankenstein aimed his pistol at the man's head and squeezed the trigger.

Click.

He had emptied his rounds firing at me. Frankenstein dropped his weapon, pulled the policeman's gun from his belt, and aimed it at the man, but the cop courageously leapt for the thief. Frankenstein fumbled the policeman's weapon and it slid somewhere out of sight. The cop slugged the thief and the fight was on. Meanwhile, I was busy wrestling with the Bride, who was surprisingly strong and vicious. She punched me hard in the belly, knocking the wind out of me, and then she used that opportunity to roll away from me. The woman tried to jump for her gun, which the policeman had dropped nearby, but with my left hand I grabbed her by the ankle and twisted it. She yelped but kicked my hand hard with her other foot. I wasn't wearing gloves, so her shoe ripped the skin on the back of my hand. It hurt like the dickens and I started bleeding.

The Bride made it to the weapon and picked it up, but instead of shooting me, she grabbed a female hostage from the floor close by and pulled the woman to her feet. While that was going on, I stood and drew the stiletto. The female robber pointed the pistol at the woman's head and shouted, "Don't move!"

Meanwhile, the cop and Frankenstein were still grappling, but the policeman was receiving the brunt of it. The robber delivered a powerful punch to the patrolman's face and knocked the man out cold. He crumbled to the floor like a ragdoll. Frankenstein retrieved his empty gun and started to reload it.

The Bride addressed me, "Stay where you are or I'll blow her brains out!" The hostage sobbed uncontrollably, tears running down her face.

At that moment there was a small explosion somewhere in the back of the bank. Several hostages screamed again. A thick cloud of smoke issued from a hallway. I figured the robbers' colleagues were in the vault or another area where the money was kept, and the blast was their handiwork.

"Let her go," I said to the Bride.

"Back off, bitch!" the woman spat. "Drop the knife and lie down on the floor with the rest of them."

I eyed Frankenstein—he was seconds away from finishing his reload. I glanced at the fallen cops. One was dead and the other unconscious. The rest of the bank employees and hostages were prone on the floor. I was all alone, although I heard police sirens in the distance. Help was on the way, but not quickly enough.

The risk I took was a serious one. An inch off-target would have been a disaster. With the speed I'd practiced for years, I threw the stiletto, flinging it like I did when Fiorello taught me how to hit a bull's-eye without thinking about it. In a split second, the blade was imbedded in the Bride's right shoulder, causing her to flinch and release the woman. I followed through by charging her. Grabbing the hostage, I flung her out of the way—perhaps a little too roughly— and then walloped the Bride with a series of *Seiken* fist attacks. The hilt of my knife wobbled grotesquely from her wound as she attempted to defend herself, but I now had the upper hand. I desperately wanted to reveal her face, but the Bride mask was secured tightly.

Frankenstein fired his newly reloaded weapon at me. He missed again; the bullet ricocheted off the wall behind the hostages and hit a man lying on the floor. His cry convinced me to back off as

Frankenstein yelled, "Freeze or I start killing people!" I raised my hands and stood still, panting.

Two men appeared out of the smoke. One wore a Dracula mask and the other wore the Wolf Man.

"We have it!" Dracula shouted. "Let's go!"

They joined their colleagues, but Frankenstein kept his gun trained on me. The Wolf Man noticed the Bride's shoulder. "Oh, my God!"

"Shut up and pull it out!" she ordered him.

"We have to—"

"Pull the damn thing out!"

So he did. She jerked in pain as blood spurted from her shoulder. The Wolf Man dropped the stiletto on the floor.

"We have to *go*!" Dracula commanded.

The four robbers made their way to the Cahuenga side door, Frankenstein moving backward while continuing to point his gun at me. Dracula peered outside and said, "The van's here! Move!" Then I sensed that Frankenstein was going to try one last time to put me down. I leaped for the floor just as he squeezed the trigger. The round hit the wall somewhere behind me, and then the four-some was gone. I got up and ran to the door, opened it, and saw a black van zooming up Cahuenga. It took a quick right on Yucca. The police sirens were louder; the cars would be at the bank in sec-onds. I returned inside, retrieved my knife, and went to the woman I had rescued.

"Are you all right?"

"Yes, thank you. Please, help him." She pointed to the man who'd caught the wild bullet in his leg. He writhed on the floor, moaning in pain. There was nothing I could do for him but say, "We'll get you help, sir. Try to stay calm." By that time, hostages were standing shakily. Bank employees sprinted to their stations and immediately picked up telephones.

"Call an ambulance!" I called out to them, stating the obvious. "The police are already on the way."

The cop who had been knocked out started coming to. I helped raise him to a sitting position and asked if he was okay, calling him by the name on his uniform—

Garriott. He was still dazed, but he had the presence of mind to thank me.

"I have to go," I told him. He nodded and gave me a little wave.

I rushed to the door I came in, broke through the mob gathered outside, and dashed east to the corner of Cosmo and Hollywood. I kept running, past my parked car, until I found a safely concealed alcove, where I removed my mask, jacket, and belt. From there I walked as calmly as possible back to my Ford, threw the items inside, and went back to the corner to see what was happening at the bank. Three police cars had arrived and an ambulance was just pulling up. There was nothing more to do, so I got in my Sunliner and drove home.

I called Barry to tell him what happened and asked for a rain check on our meeting. I'd had enough excitement for one day.

37
Leo

The Past

DeAngelo always throws a big New Year's Eve party at his place in Vegas. Like the birthday party, sometimes I've been invited. This year I'm pretty sure I will be. Both Christina and I should get invitations, especially after what we did for him and what my sister went through. I'll have to drop a hint to Maria next time I talk to her and suggest that she makes sure her daddy puts us on the list.

Christina had to get several stitches in her shoulder and was in bed for two days. She lost a lot of blood, and Marco, Tomás, and I had to scramble to get her medical attention after that bitch the Black Stiletto threw a knife at her. Luckily, Marco knew Sal Casazza's doctor, a guy who did patch-up work under the radar. He lived in goddamned Venice Beach, so I had to keep my hands pressed on Christina's wound for half an hour or more in the back of the van while Geraldo drove like crazy. He had to take side streets to make sure we weren't spotted. The police were out in droves looking for us. The doctor had a garage, though, and we made it there safely. It was a damned good thing the man was home. Marco persuaded him to get to work on my sister immediately.

She's a tough girl and is going to be fine. She'll have a sore shoulder and arm for a few weeks. A major muscle was cut a little, but it could have been much worse. Physical therapy and exercising will help build up strength again. Christina's worried that it'll affect her aim. I told her she would have to learn to compensate for her injury, and her brain would do it for her with practice.

It's been nearly two weeks since the robbery, and she's now resuming her normal routine. She came back to work at the office the other day with her arm in a sling. At first I was concerned that someone might report it to the police—it was on the news they were looking for a woman with a knife wound in her shoulder—but Christina told everyone who asked that she tore a ligament. We went to the range for the first time over the weekend and she was disheartened. She only made bull's-eyes three out of ten shots. I tried to tell her most people never hit the bull's-eye at all, and that she was still a first-class sharpshooter.

We're going to get the Black Stiletto. If it's the last thing we do, we're going to hunt her down and feed her to rabid dogs. It's *unbelievable* how that masked freak of a woman has messed up everyone's business. Casazza and DeAngelo are completely fed up with her. They want her dead, top priority. There's no question that she's had an impact on their livelihoods. I don't have anything to do with their gun selling, but I know all about it. Since several of the distribution points in L.A. have been busted, the flow of product and money has stopped. I think the police are using questionable search-and-arrest tactics, and good lawyers and honest judges will surely throw the cases out of court, but at the moment the Heathens refuse to run the merchandise. DeAngelo thinks they'll get back on board if we stop the counterfeit operation with Los Serpientes, which is one of the MC's beefs. There's no way I want to do that. It's just getting started and it's going well. Mookie's new plates are outstanding. The funny money is passing smoothly here in the States. Big bills, too. So far the Black Stiletto hasn't bothered me in that regard; she and the D.A. seem to be concentrating on the guns. Maybe they don't know about the counterfeit currency that's circulating.

Still, I couldn't believe that she showed up at the bank, right in the middle of the heist. Christina and Tomás were doing a great job taking care of the tellers and customers. They even dispatched two cops who happened to come in. Marco and I were in the safety deposit box room, oblivious to what was going on out front. Once we were inside, it was easy to find the correct box. Marco had to figure out how much explosive to use—too little wouldn't work and too much would blow up the whole thing, including the diamond.

Well, there was a reason that Marco had the reputation he did, because his calculations were perfect. We opened the box and lo and behold, there it was, inside a large black velvet jewel case. Both of us gasped when we saw the size of the thing. The Florentine Diamond was the most beautiful object I'd ever set eyes on. The yellow color practically glowed like the sun.

And I knew then and there I had to have it.

But the diamond is now in DeAngelo's hands, and he was going to give it to Maria for Christmas. What a goddamned waste. Four or five million dollars with the right fence, according to DeAngelo. I'm sure I could find a fence of my own who could sell it. I know plenty of those guys.

It's crazy, but as we stood there and gaped at that magnificent jewel for a few seconds, a plan started forming in my mind. It involved New Year's Eve and Maria.

Of course, stealing it from DeAngelo—or his daughter—would be suicide. I tried to put it out of my head.

He paid us all well for the job. He also took care of paying the doctor for Christina's patch-up. That was nice of him, but afterward he told me that the operation was messy. I said that if the Stiletto hadn't shown up unexpectedly, everything would have gone more smoothly. How did she know the robbery was going down? The newspapers speculated that she just happened to be in the area because two photos taken of her in the bank revealed that she wasn't in complete costume. The incident sure added to her mystique. Of course, there were some newscasters who believed she was part of the heist team all along, which was a goddamned joke.

As a result of our actions, banks in Hollywood and Beverly Hills were beefing up security. That's all right with me, because I'm out of the bank-robbing business. That was enough for me. I hope it was plenty for Christina, too. What happened was too close to being a disaster, and my sister would have gone back to prison had she been caught. Hell, *all* of us would have gone to jail.

I told my sister about the counterfeiting operation, so she wanted to help me with that. I could use her assistance. It was getting complicated. Last week we had to kill one of my men. Executed him in cold blood. A bullet in the head. Casazza's guys caught him embezzling some of our dough from the funny money. Sal said to me, "You're the boss of this deal, right, Leo? Then act like the boss." He handed me a gun. But I couldn't do it. I don't know why. I aimed the goddamned thing at the man's head, but I couldn't pull the trigger. Casazza jerked his head at Shrimp, so he came over, took the gun out of my hand, and did the dirty deed. Casazza told me afterward that I'd never be a part of the "men's club" if I couldn't act like a boss. That pissed me off, but he was right. If it ever happened again, I'd show him what I'm really made of. At any rate, Christina would be able to spot inconsistencies in the books. She had a good sense when it came to numbers and records. I thought she'd be an asset. She wanted to be useful, have some kind of purpose. Jail taught her that life was too short to be idle.

Judy didn't have an idleness problem. I hardly ever saw her. She now went to a gym and exercised with men—she claimed it was what she did in New York, too—and she worked at Flickers a lot. Her attitude toward me has cooled, and I know why. She wanted me to make more of a commitment to her, which I can't do. This thing with Maria, it was heating up. The other day when I was talking to her father about something, he said something like, "—and after you and Maria get married then we'll get you involved." Hell, we weren't even engaged and he was talking about marriage? I thought he knew he'd made a slip, because a minute later he actually said, "I didn't mean to imply that you and my daughter were, you know." Well, if he said it, then it must have been on his mind.

I'm not giving up on Judy, though. As long as she'd see me in L.A. and I kept Maria in Vegas, everything should be fine. I'd have to start putting on the Kelly charm again and convince Judy that what we had was for real. I mean, it *was* for real. I am addicted to her.

She is like a goddamned drug.

38
Judy's Diary
1961

OCTOBER 10, 1961

I'm listening to Elvis's new album, *Blue Hawaii*, and it's wonderful. It has such an "exotica" feel, like that music I was listening to in New York for a while, although the ballad "Can't Help Falling in Love" is different. I predict that will be his next hit single. The movie doesn't open until next month, around Thanksgiving, but it's nice to have the record so I can be familiar with the songs before I see the picture. Actually, everyone's talking about the movie *West Side Story*, which comes out next week. It's supposed to be spectacular, and I'm excited to see it. I love the music.

This afternoon after I exercised at the Gym, I went to see Barry at his cabin in Laurel Canyon. I didn't dress up completely as the Stiletto, I just wore the mask and jacket. He laughed when he saw me. "Dressing casual, are we?" he asked.

Things have been quiet with regard to illegal guns. Barry's investigations have produced no worthwhile information in the past few weeks. The D.A. believes that my actions, along with the arrests, have curtailed the mob's activities. For a while, Barry thought the Heathens weren't cooperating with Casazza's organization because of all the heat that was on them.

"Actually, I think it's mostly about something else entirely," he said. "The Heathens are still at war with Los Serpientes, but their differences are not just about territory. Last week, border agents caught some members of Los Serpientes trying to enter Mexico carrying a load of counterfeit U.S. money. Remember I mentioned that? Customs officials have suspected that a pipeline between L.A. and the border has been in place for several weeks; some of the fake bills have already shown up down there. Counterfeit money is difficult to detect in Mexico because for the most part they aren't as familiar with what our money looks like as we are."

"And you think Casazza has something to do with it?"

"I do. The Feds sweated one of the Serpents down in Chula Vista. He said that the Heathens weren't doing business with Casazza anymore because they were pissed off that the Italians were making counterfeit dough and selling it to Los Serpientes and not to the Heathens. The Serpents want guns, too, but Casazza's deal was only with the Heathens, and the Heathens won't sell to the Serpents."

"Do you have proof that Casazza is behind the counterfeiting?"

"Only by this guy's word. We need physical evidence. That's where you come in."

"I figured you'd say that."

"It might be dangerous, possibly more dangerous than breaking into one of the Heathens' hangouts."

I waved him off. "Do your worst, Barry."

"We need to find where the stuff's being made. Maybe there are clues at Los Serpientes's hideout, so we'd like you to go there and see what you can find."

"Where is it?"

"In a rough part of town. Southeast L.A., on a street called Florence. It's another auto-repair shop, but it also adjoins the Serpents's clubhouse and a commercial bar that caters to Mexicans. Their leader is a man named Carlos Gabriel. He's Mexican, but he's an American citizen. He's been in and out of jail so many times you'd think his wardrobe would consist of nothing but striped pajamas.

He's a very bad man, and his men are killers. I suggest you take a look at the place during the day, come up with a plan, and let me know. Then we'll coordinate a night when we can get plenty of backup. You might need it."

He gave me the address, and I said I'd be in touch.

OCTOBER 13, 1961

Today I went to Los Serpientes's auto-repair shop. Barry was right. The neighborhood was not somewhere I'd normally go, but I'm fearless, ha ha. The place was called Tijuana Auto, and the bar next to it was named La Cantina. Like the Heathens's shop, it was surrounded by a chain-link fence with barbed wire on top. The front gate was open, allowing access to the garage during hours of operation. La Cantina didn't have a fence, of course, the dive was always open to the public as long as the clientele was Latino, I suppose. Scary-looking Mexican bikers were all over the lot. Yes, it was intimidating, even in broad daylight. But I had a plan.

I drove my Sunliner right through the gate like I knew what I was doing. Did I stick out like a sore thumb? You bet. A pretty white girl in a Mexican neighborhood? No women around that I could see, just big, burly Latinos with tattoos and scars and bad teeth. After parking the car in front, I got out and said hello to two men who stood gawking at me, and walked inside the shop. Two ugly dogs immediately started barking with the ferocity of lions. They were pit bulls, I think, a breed known to be vicious attack animals. They were leashed, thank goodness, tied to a post, so they couldn't get at me unless I moved closer. I had no doubt they would have bitten me had I done so.

A man wearing greasy work clothes came in through the garage area and spoke to me in Spanish. I said, "Sorry, does anyone speak English here?"

The dogs kept barking and he shouted at them in his language.

They shut up and then the man answered, "Yeah, I speak English." He said it as if the phrase was beneath him.

"Oh, great. I'd like to get new hubcaps for my car." I gestured outside. "The Ford out there. I want something classy." I pointed to the wall where several styles were mounted. There was a set of "dog dish"-style caps that were shiny and smooth that I thought would look great with a black body. "How about those? How much are they?"

The man looked at me as if I was crazy. What was a white girl doing in an outlaw motorcycle club's HQ? Buying hubcaps? Really? I knew that was what he was thinking.

"Hello? Did you hear me?" I asked after he said nothing.

"Yeah, I heard you. Why did you come here, lady?"

"A friend said you guys do great work." I shrugged. "I live down the street." I acted like it made no difference to me who I shopped with.

Another creepy man came into the sales room. He wore a Serpientes leather jacket that had a patch proclaiming him as "Presidente." There was an intensity about him that was palpable. He was Carlos Gabriel, no question about it.

"May I help you?" he asked. No smile, no indication that he was there to be of assistance.

"Oh, do you work here? I want to buy those hubcaps for my Ford outside. Is that a problem?"

Gabriel looked at the other man, who spoke rapid Spanish and shrugged. Gabriel looked back at me and asked, "Would you like us to install them, too?"

"Yes, please. How much are they?" I reached into my purse. He quoted me an acceptable price and I paid cash. The other man asked for my keys, so I handed them over. He went outside, got in the car, and drove it into the garage bay. In the meantime, I squatted in front of the dogs. "What beautiful animals. I love dogs."

They growled.

"Careful, they bite," Gabriel warned.

I spoke baby talk to them. "Aw, you wouldn't bite *me*, would you? What are your names?"

"Hoja and Bala," Gabriel answered for the dogs.

"Aren't they friendly to people they know?"

"Sometimes."

"Introduce me. I'd love to pet them."

Warily, Gabriel spoke Spanish to the dogs and indicated me. I carefully reached out and scratched Bala's head. His tail wagged. I did the same to Hoja. After a few minutes of neck and back scratching, they were my best friends. "Do you feed them any treats?" I asked.

Gabriel must have been impressed that a white girl like me would take to such horrible-looking and dangerous beasts. He reached up to a shelf, plucked two dog biscuits from a jar, and handed them to me. Bala and Hoja immediately started drooling and eyeing me with anticipation. I held the cookies above their heads. "Sit!" I commanded. Nothing happened. "Sit!"

"*¡Siéntate!*" Gabriel ordered. The dogs obeyed, so I fed them the treats. In doing so, I got a good look at their big, sharp teeth.

"Could I try it again?"

Although he wasn't smiling, I think Gabriel appreciated that I gave so much attention to his attack dogs. Most people were probably so scared of them that they shied away, trembling. He retrieved two more biscuits and handed them over. I quietly repeated the Spanish word to him to make sure I got it right, and then I stood, displayed the cookies over the dogs' heads, and commanded them to *siéntate*!

It worked. Bala and Hoja sat, wagged their tails, and drooled. I dropped the biscuits into their mouths, and they gobbled them in one bite.

"Are we friends now?" I asked them. I squatted again, scratched their heads, noses, ears, necks, bellies, and I let them smell me and lick me, which is exactly what I wanted them to do.

"Are they good watchdogs?"

There was a hint of a smile on Gabriel's face. He was probably thunderstruck that a white girl would be so friendly to him, be unafraid of the neighborhood, and take so kindly to his attack hounds.

"They'll kill anyone they don't know who tries to get on the lot after 9:00."

"Really? What happens at 9:00?"

"We close."

"Oh, right."

But he shrugged a little and allowed more of a smile. "But most nights we're right next door having a few drinks."

Was he *flirting* with me?

"Is it a good bar?"

"*Sí.*"

"Would it be safe for me to go in there some evening?"

The man stared at me for a long time. The hint of pleasantry had vanished. "Probably not," he said.

I kept petting the dogs for several minutes until the other man returned and spoke Spanish again. Gabriel interpreted, "Your car is ready." I stood and looked out the front glass window. My car was sitting there with the new adornments, and they were gorgeous.

"Wow, they look good, don't they! Well, thank you, er, *gracias.*" I turned to the doggies and said, "*Adiós, amigos.*" I petted them one more time and walked outside. Gabriel followed me and waited beside the car as I got in. After I started it, I rolled down the window to thank him again. He leaned in and said, "I don't know why you came here, lady, you can get those hubcaps most places. I suggest you don't come back." Then he walked back inside.

Fine. I won't be going back as Judy Cooper, that's for sure. But now I know exactly how the Black Stiletto's going to pay a visit.

39
Gina
The Present

I'm out of jail and at the hospital with Dad. Mom, Ross, and Maggie are here, too. Yesterday he was still recovering from the operation and slept practically the entire time. Today Dad is awake and lucid. His neck is bandaged and he has bruises on his face where those guys hit him. Since he can't talk, he uses a pen and paper to write stuff down. They're giving him liquid food, but he complains that it hurts to swallow. The doctor said that's to be expected for a while.

When he saw me, he got tears in his eyes and we hugged each other. He wrote, THANKS FOR SAVING ME on the pad. I answered, "What are daughters for?" and he smiled.

Maggie is very attentive, and when she and the doctor spoke in their language—medical talk—it was obvious she was in her element. She had a tendency to boss around the nurses and tell them what to do until Dad wrote to her, RELAX, LET THEM DO THEIR JOBS, DR. McDANIEL. She laughed at that and said, "You're right."

The police came to the ICU to see if Dad was willing to answer questions. The doctor told them they could try for just a little while. He didn't want Dad to get upset or overextend himself. He still needs a lot of rest.

There were three men. One of them was Detective Jordan, and one was that bastard Detective Merrill, who barely met my eyes. He didn't have the wherewithal to apologize for arresting me. Late yesterday, just as I was being released, Detective Jordan told us that it was pretty clear that the two men who assaulted Dad were responsible for killing some woman on the West Side. I didn't know anything about that. He said forensics tests still had to be done, but he was pretty certain what the results would be.

The men's names were William "Stark" Simon and Bernard "Bernie" Childers. It was Childers who was the shooter and now had a broken neck. They were both being charged with the murder of that woman and other crimes against Dad and me. I was tempted to go find them and give them a piece of my mind, but I didn't. Detective Jordan also warned me to leave them alone. Simon was being released from the hospital today and taken to jail. It wasn't clear how long Childers would be in the ICU. If he survived a week after paralysis, there was a good chance he'd continue living. He'd have to go through months of rehabilitation and spend the rest of his life in a wheelchair or a bed. I suppose I should feel remorse for doing that to him, but what can I say? *He played with fire and got burned.*

Mom and Ross went out of the room while the cops were there, but Maggie and I stayed with Dad. The police didn't mind.

"Mr. Talbot," Detective Jordan began, "we're glad to see you're alert. We're trying to get to the bottom of this, and we appreciate you answering some questions."

Dad: OK.

"Can you tell me what happened that morning?"

Dad: I WAS WAITING FOR GINA TO COME TO MY ROOM. WE WERE GOING TO HAVE BREAKFAST AND THEN I WAS FLYING HOME TO CHICAGO. THERE WAS A KNOCK AT THE DOOR. TWO MEN SAID THEY WERE POLICE. THEY BARGED IN, HIT ME, TIED ME UP, AND THREATENED TO KILL ME. THEN GINA SHOWED UP AND SAVED ME.

Detective Jordan pondered that answer. "They didn't say what they wanted from you?"

Dad: NO.

When he wrote that, I knew he wasn't telling the truth. Those men definitely knew who my father was. Why was he lying?

"Mr. Talbot, do you know a woman by the name of Betty Dinkins?"

Dad: NO.

"Never heard of her?"

Dad: NO.

"Maybe you have and don't realize it. Recently in the news she claimed to be the Black Stiletto. Were you aware of this?"

Dad: MAYBE. I DON'T PAY ATTENTION TO THAT STUFF.

"Did you know that the two men who assaulted you are suspected in the murder of Ms. Dinkins?"

Dad: I DO NOW.

"Did they ask you about Ms. Dinkins?"

Dad: NO.

Again, I could see Dad's face and I knew he wasn't being honest. I don't know how I can read people's faces that way, but I can. I've been able to do it since I was in junior high school. It was one of the strange things that happened to me and my body when I first got my period. My eyesight and hearing improved, and I had a weird sixth sense that I'd never noticed before. When kids at school lied to me, I knew it. When Mom or Dad told me something I didn't believe, it was because they were not telling me everything. I've never been able to explain it, and I've never told anyone about it.

I wanted to say something. I didn't think he should be lying to the police, especially about something as serious as this. I glanced at Maggie and she had a concerned expression on her face. *She* knew something, too! I could tell. What was going on? She and Dad had some secret together, and they weren't sharing it.

"The men who attacked you—William Simon and Bernard Childers—are residents of Odessa, Texas. Do their names or does that town mean anything to you?"

Oh, my God, my grandma Judy was from Odessa, Texas. Could this be related to her somehow? And for heaven's sakes, why would it?

Dad: NO.

"The men went by nicknames—Stark and Bernie."

Dad: NOPE.

Why didn't he tell the detective that his mother was from Odessa?

"Can you write a statement of what happened in the room when your daughter arrived?"

Dad nodded and put pen to paper. It took him a few minutes to write nearly a whole page of words. He said that I tricked the men into opening the door by threatening to go to the front desk—true—and that I attacked the guy called Stark—true—and quickly beat him badly enough that he fell unconscious—again, true. Then he said that he saw a gun in Bernie's hand, and that's all he could remember.

"So you don't know if Mr. Childers deliberately pointed the gun at you and pulled the trigger?"

Dad: NO.

"He was trying to shoot *me*," I said, "and I tried knocking the gun out of his hand. That's when it went off and the bullet hit Dad."

Detective Jordan held up his hand. "Gina, please, we have your statement. I need to hear what your father has to say."

Dad: IF GINA SAYS THAT'S WHAT HAPPENED, THEN THAT'S WHAT HAPPENED.

Jordan looked at the other two men. "Anything else for now?"

Dad: WHAT DO THE MEN HAVE TO SAY?

"Well, Mr. Childers is paralyzed. Your daughter broke his neck. He's not saying anything yet. He's barely conscious. Mr. Simon has lawyered up and isn't talking."

After that, the detectives wished him a speedy recovery and said they'd need to talk to him again when he's better. Detective Jordan said good-bye to me and told me to "be careful."

When they were gone, the nurse came in and said Dad needed to rest. His eyes met mine. He knew I was questioning some of his answers. I leaned over and kissed his cheek and said, "Get some sleep, I'm not going anywhere."

Mom and Ross left the hospital for a while. Maggie and I remained in the room. She read a magazine and worked on her iPad while I sat and stared at the IV and the tubes and monitors around Dad. I missed Josh and thought I'd go out in the hall to call him, but then I saw that Dad had closed his eyes and was slumbering. I moved closer to Maggie and whispered.

"What's going on?"

"What do you mean?" she asked.

"Something's not right. Those men were after Dad for a reason. Do you know what it is?"

She hesitated and didn't look at me when she answered, "No, I don't." Another lie.

"What's Dad's connection to that woman? Maggie, my grandmother is from Odessa, Texas. Dad's mother! Doesn't that mean something?"

Maggie closed her eyes. She was obviously struggling. She and Dad knew the answers to my questions, and they didn't want to tell me.

"Is my dad in trouble?" I asked softly.

"Gina. Gina, your father and you need to have a talk. It's not my place to say anything. I promise you that you'll understand everything soon. Please, I beg you, let your father answer your questions when he's ready. Let him heal. Let him get back to Illinois. I'm sure he'll tell you what you want to know, but you'll have to be patient. Please. I'm sorry. Just know that your father loves you very much. I do too, Gina, so please don't hold it against me. I made your father a promise and I intend to keep it."

"So there *is* something you're both hiding from me? And the police?"

"Gina. Trust your father. He will tell you when it's time."

I then looked over at Dad—and his eyes were open. He'd heard everything Maggie and I had said. He then picked up the pen and paper and wrote: I PROMISE. GIVE ME TIME. We held eyes for a moment, and then I said, "Okay."

Dad: I LOVE YOU.

"I love you too, Dad."

40
Judy's Diary
1961

OCTOBER 16, 1961

Monday was a day off from Flickers, so Barry and I set up the Serpientes shop raid for tonight. Well, it turned out that I got in place but never received a signal from Barry or the police backup team that they were ready. In fact, they didn't show up! I waited nearly a half hour, then got out of my car and went to a pay phone. Barry was glad I called. The cops had to cancel the operation because of some other problem in town, and Barry couldn't reach me—he can't, I always have to call *him*. When he said we'd have to reschedule, I said, "Forget it, I'm here. I'm parked two blocks away from La Cantina and the garage, as we agreed. I'm going in alone." He tried to talk me out of it, but I had an ace up my sleeve—I had a couple of friends inside.

Even so, it was a close one, dear diary.

The Compton Street area in Southeast L.A. was indeed a rough neighborhood and much more sinister at night. If I saw a white person, it was usually an old bum sitting against a dark building with a bottle in a paper bag, and they were few and far between. Mostly the streets were populated by Negroes and Mexicans. From what Barry told me, the two groups didn't get along. There was always trouble.

I could *feel* tension in the air, an electric pulse that warned me danger could be anywhere.

It was around 10:00. Once I was out of the car and found a shadowy spot in which to finish dressing as the Stiletto, I hit Compton and started running south toward Florence. People on the sidewalk—mostly men—shouted or said something as I flew past. At one point a couple of guys thought they could chase me and see what I was up to, but I made a quick left onto 70th Street and then shot up an alley between the backs of houses. It was plenty dark there. The two men ran past, soon realized they didn't know where I'd gone, and gave up. Again, it struck me how different traveling on foot in L.A. is compared to New York. I would have thought my exposure would be more subtle. In fact, it's the opposite. The streets of L.A. are wide open, they're not bordered by tall buildings that create a tunnel effect like the ones in Manhattan, and the sidewalks are sometimes set a good distance from the houses or buildings, especially in residential neighborhoods.

La Cantina appeared to be hopping. Men and women from the Mexican biker world congregated in and out of it. The Tijuana Auto lot, however, was dark and deserted. Everyone was at the bar, if what Gabriel said was true.

Circling the perimeter closest to the shop, I found an appropriate spot where I could climb the chain-link fence. I'd need my hook again to pull down the barbed wire, so I got it ready. I wanted to spend as little time as possible getting over to the other side, but I wasn't fast enough. As soon as I reached the top and bent down the wire, my friends Bala and Hoja came running out of the garage, barking like demons. But I was prepared. I dug into my jacket pocket and pulled out two dog biscuits. Earlier in the day I'd gone to the market and bought a bag of Milk-Bones, the same kind that were in the shop office.

"*¡Siéntate!*" I ordered, holding up the treats. The animals were maybe thirteen feet below me, baring their teeth, and making a tremendous racket. "*¡Siéntate!*" The command didn't work. I was afraid I might have to forget the job after all and go home; my plan hadn't worked. "*¡Siéntate!*" I tried again, to no avail. Then I tossed the two biscuits to the dogs, and they snapped them out of midair. That shut them up and they chomped the cookies and licked their jaws. I dared to bound over the fence and land on my feet right next to them. The dogs growled again, but they weren't barking. I held out more treats and spoke in my best "friendly" voice, "Bala! Hoja! Remember me? Hi!"

The snarling stopped and they looked at me suspiciously.

I removed the mask and shook my hair out. "See? It's me!"

That did it. The two animals leaped at me, tails wagging and tongues licking. I rubbed them and scratched them and spoke baby talk to them. I fed them more treats. They knew I was their master's friend who was so nice to them the other day.

Now they were quiet and happy, but the only problem with that was that they wanted to follow me wherever I went. I put the mask back on and slowly crept toward the shop. The dogs panted at my side. Every now and then I'd pat them and say, "Good boys!" A treat every so often didn't hurt either.

Los Serpientes were fairly careless about leaving doors open. I guess they figured no one would be crazy enough to try and get past Bala and Hoja. One garage bay door was up, allowing access inside the building. The place was greasy and messy, just like the one the Heathens's owned. Two cars occupied the other bays—a beat-up Cadillac and a crummy Oldsmobile. Several shiny motorcycles lined one side of the garage. An unmarked door led to the sales office, where I'd been the other day. Before entering, I pressed the side of my head on the door to listen for any voices. When I was satisfied, my pets and I entered. A quick look around led me down a hall and to an office that I presumed was Gabriel's. There was motorcycle imagery all over the room, and there was a desk with a skull and a framed picture of a pretty Mexican girl on it. She resembled Gabriel. His daughter?

Barry told me to look for boxes or bags full of bills. They would all be the same denomination—5s or 10s or 20s—and I shouldn't be surprised if they appeared very real to me. The police needed samples and photos to prove the counterfeit money came from the shop.

I spent fifteen minutes searching. I went in every room, even the disgusting men's bathroom. There was nothing.

Just as I was about to call it a night, the dogs perked up, barked happily, and ran out to the garage. I heard a whistle and a man's voice greeting them. *Carlos Gabriel.* He and two other men were walking from the bar back to the shop, and he'd just opened the front gate.

There was nowhere to go. The only way out was through the open garage door, and there was no question that they'd see me. I could possibly hide in one of the two offices, or the parts storage, or one of the bathrooms. The women's bathroom? Did I even see one?

The voices grew louder. I had to move, so I dashed to the Oldsmobile, opened the back door as quietly as possible, climbed in, and shut it. Then I curled up in the floorboard and hoped for the best. The windows were down, so I could hear the men talking. I thought something was unusual about their conversation and didn't know why, and then it hit me—it wasn't in Spanish! They were speaking English.

"Where are they?"

"Here, against the wall."

"Oh, man, they're beautiful!"

Gabriel was showing them the motorcycles. "That's a '51 Harley, looks brand-new, huh?"

"I'll say."

Gabriel's two visitors were not Mexicans. I took the risk to raise my head far enough to see out the window.

Los Serpientes's leader stood with two white men I recognized. They were Italians. I'd seen them at Flickers with Sal Casazza. It took me a moment to remember their names, because I'd greeted them as a hostess. Mr. Faretti and Mr. Capri. Bala and Hoja stood obediently by their master, but they were looking at the Oldsmobile. The dogs knew I was in there; I just hoped they didn't come over looking for me and give me away.

Could I get a photo? I plucked the Brownie Starmatic from my backpack and readied it, but I didn't have a good shot of the three men together.

"You want to come inside?" Gabriel asked.

"Nah, we'll wait here. I want a closer look at this thing."

"I'll be right back."

Gabriel left them and went inside the offices. Faretti and Capri squatted by one of the bikes, touching parts of it, and admiring it. Then they moved to the next one. Capri sat on the seat and proclaimed how great it felt. That's when Bala and Hoja got bored with the newcomers and trotted over to the car. I got down in the floorboard again as Hoja pawed the side of the vehicle. Bala whined. More scratching. I was going crazy. From inside the car I tried to will them: *Go away!*

"Hey, what are those dogs doing?" Faretti asked. I heard his footsteps come nearer—and suddenly the two animals viciously turned on him and barked. "Whoa! Easy, dogs!" He quickly backed away and joined his buddy. By then, Gabriel had returned. The dogs kept growling.

"Tell your dogs to heel, Carlos," Faretti said, not enjoying the canine attention.

Gabriel gave a command in Spanish and the animals shut up and sat.

"They must not like you," Gabriel said. "Here is what we agreed on."

That I had to see. I raised my head again and saw Gabriel hand Faretti two stuffed envelopes. The men were in a perfect composition. *Now!* I raised the camera and clicked a picture.

The dogs heard the snap. Again they trotted over to the Oldsmobile scratched on the side. I dug down into the car. *Oh no,* I thought, *I am dead.*

But the men ignored them and kept talking. "The delivery will be on time?" Gabriel asked.

"Like horse poop." The two Italians laughed boisterously at that one. Then Faretti said, "Carlos, I have a message from Casazza."

"What's that?"

"You have to stop the war with the Heathens."

"I've heard that before. It's the Heathens's fault. Tell *them*. As long as you sell guns to the Heathens, there will be war."

The dogs sensed their master's agitation. They barked and ran back to him, ready to devour the other men at Gabriel's command. The growls were louder than a motorcycle engine.

"Hey, don't kill the messenger!" Faretti said. "Tell them goddamned dogs to heel, Carlos!"

"You tell Sal Casazza that I made promises to my people in Mexico," Gabriel said. "Los Serpientes can make things very, very difficult for him—and his *boss* in Vegas—if you screw with us."

Capri said to his partner, "Come on, let's go."

But Faretti held his ground, even in front of the snarling pit bulls. He stared at Gabriel and the Mexican glared back. Finally, he laughed. "You got *cojones, señor*."

I was pretty sure I knew what that meant, ha ha.

There were no good-byes or handshakes. The two Italians left the premises. Gabriel stood in the garage bay and watched them, his dogs now quiet and at his side. After a moment, he spoke to the dogs in Spanish, and then he left for La Cantina. Bala and Hoja immediately ran to the Oldsmobile and scratched on the door.

"Okay, I'm coming," I told them. I got out and thought I had enough information to give to Barry. I peeked out of the garage and scanned the lot. I saw Gabriel standing with his cohorts in front of La Cantina, smoking cigarettes, talking, and laughing. It didn't look as if they were going to move any time soon. Would they see me? If I slipped out and sprinted to the side of the building where I'd climbed over the fence, I'd be visible for less than five seconds. It was worth the risk.

"Come on!" I whispered to the dogs, and the three of us shot out of there and ran. Since I was dressed in black, there was a good chance I'd blend in with the darkness or be mistaken for one of the dogs. At any rate, I made it to the fence and started climbing. Bala barked, not wanting to see me go.

"*¡Siéntate!*" I ordered, and they obeyed. I was getting pretty good at that command!

I pulled down the barbed wire with the hook, swung my leg over, and then somehow caught my jacket's armpit in the barbs. They started ripping the leather. I managed to balance myself, clinging on to the hook with one hand, the chain-links with the other, and my legs straddling the entire fence. I had to try and unsnag my jacket, or it would tear badly or, worse, not tear at all. And the latter was what appeared to be happening. I couldn't move! It was as if that barbed wire had a grip on my clothing and wasn't letting go.

The dogs barked.

"*¡Siéntate!*" They were already sitting, but that was the only command I knew. I wished I'd learned "Shut up!"

Then I heard Gabriel whistle for the dogs. They wouldn't go to him. Bala barked at me again, followed by Hoja. The irony of the situation was that they were probably trying to get their master's attention so he could come and help me out of a predicament.

Curious as to why the dogs weren't obeying, Gabriel and a couple of his men headed back to the shop. They'd see the dogs—and me—at any second. I tugged on my jacket and heard the material rip loudly.

One of the men shouted excitedly, and then they started running.

There was only one way to get free. I unzipped the jacket and pulled my arms out. There I was, suspended on the fence in my black pants and a *white* T-shirt, which stood out like a beacon in the dark. The men were inside the lot. I rolled over the wire and clung to the opposite side and removed the hook. The wires took my jacket with them as they rose to their normal position. I had to pull and jerk and finally crack my jacket like a *whip* before it separated from the barbs.

There was a terrible ripping sound, but I got it free. I dropped to the ground and ran, just as one of the men *fired a gun* at me. The bullet missed. I was sure they would get on their bikes and try to catch me, but I had my escape route mapped out—down an alley, across a street and into a different alley, and then a long block around to Compton, where I changed back to Judy Cooper and casually walked to my car. I never heard the cycles though. Once I was safely in my Ford, I examined my jacket. A foot-long piece had torn out of the lower arm and part of the shoulder. It must still be hanging on that barbed wire. Maybe they'll think it was from a Heathens jacket. So now I have to spend the next hour repairing it with needle and thread.

All in all, I was proud of myself for a job well done.

41
Leo
THE PAST

It was the first Monday in November and I was at work when I learned that two men were at reception requesting to talk to me. They identified themselves as representatives of Sandstone Incorporated. I knew that meant the Sandstone Casino, so I let them in. I didn't know them, but they were faces I'd seen at DeAngelo's parties. Muscle guys.

Apparently the boss wanted to see me *immediately* and they were there to see that I cooperated and came along as quickly as possible. So I did. I let Christina know where I was going, and asked the men if I needed to follow them in my car so they wouldn't have to bring me back. One said, "Don't worry, Mr. Kelly, we'll bring you back."

That didn't sit well. Frankly, the limo ride to Vegas was torturous. I don't normally get nervous or rattled, but I was then. I didn't like the idea of being in Vegas without a ride home. Was DeAngelo angry at me about something? The counterfeit operation had to halt because of the stupid war between the Heathens and Los Serpientes. Had it to do with that? Or was it about Maria? Did he find out we slept together and he wanted to kill me?

When we got to the ranch, I passed Paulie in the corridor, and his eyes shot daggers at me. What the hell was wrong? My escorts ushered me directly to DeAngelo's office, a library of sorts where he spent most of his time. It resembled a room in one of those elite English men's clubs with Victorian leather furniture.

Finally, the door closed behind me and I was alone with Vince in his inner sanctum. He stood with his back to me, looking out the window at his back lawn and the desert landscape beyond that. The boss wore a smoking jacket and had a lit cigar in his hand.

"Vince?" I managed to say. When he didn't answer, I asked, "You wanted to see me, sir?"

The man slowly turned around and looked at me.

"Do you love my daughter?" he asked.

Shit, he *did* know about us going all the way.

"Yes, sir."

"You know she's crazy about you."

"Yes, sir."

"Then why the hell are you carrying on with a girl in L.A.?"

What? "L.A.?"

He moved to his desk and picked up a piece of paper. "Judy Cooper," he read. Then he showed me a photo of her taken at Flickers. "I understand you've been seeing this girl for a few months now."

My stomach lurched. Several people in L.A. were aware I was dating Judy, but I didn't think they knew about my connection with Maria. How did DeAngelo find out?

He read my mind, saying, "You're wondering how I know. You think I wouldn't have a future son-in-law checked out? You don't think I have eyes and ears in all the territories I control? I know what my people are doing."

Crap. I was in a serious situation. Sweat started to break out all over and I felt clammy. I was about to get whacked. I'd never walk out of the DeAngelo mansion alive.

"*Well, are you going to admit it or not?*"

"I'm sorry, sir. Yeah, it's true. But I've been trying to break it off."

"So break it off already! How could you be sleeping with my daughter and making her believe you're going to marry her, and at the same time you're plugging some whore that works in your uncle's nightclub?"

I almost said, "Judy's not a whore," but thought it best to remain silent. He made me feel ashamed and angry. On the one hand, my feelings for Judy were genuine. He was right; I should have stopped seeing her a while ago after I began to get serious about Maria. But I couldn't. Judy was incredibly special. I liked being with *her* more than I did Maria. On the other hand, hooking up with Maria was a means to an end. Marriage into the DeAngelo family would be my ticket to paradise. I was hoping I could set up Judy in L.A. as my mistress while being married to Maria in Vegas, but now that Big Daddy knew about Judy, that wasn't going to work.

"Does Maria know?" I asked.

DeAngelo stared at me a few seconds to make me squirm. "No. Thank God. And you better pray she never finds out. Maria's a good Catholic girl, even though she went and did with you what she did, before marriage. Yeah, don't look so shocked. I know. In the past I'd kill anyone who took my daughter to bed without marrying her first. But it's different times. I understand that. The thing is, she did it because she really thought she'd be marrying you. You understand? How do you think she'd feel if she knew you were screwing another girl?"

"I'm sorry, Vince."

"You're damned right, you are." He kept his eyes on me a long time before he gestured to a chair. "Sit down." Then he went around his desk and sat in his leather rocker. I took the seat and waited for him to speak again. It seemed as if an hour passed by.

"Okay, here's the deal. You don't see her anymore. Ever."

I figured that one was coming.

"Two. You don't break my daughter's heart. The reason you're not in the hospital right now is because you mean a lot to her. And since you're doing a competent job with that counterfeiting thing, and since you've got all those warehouse connections and influence, and because you're the son of one of my best friends, may he rest in peace, I believe you'd be a welcome addition to our family."

He waited for me to respond to that. I was slow at realizing he'd just complimented me. "Thank you, sir. I'd really like that. I never meant any disresp—"

"I know you didn't." He waved a hand at me. "I'm a man, too. We're all the same. Dames are dames. I've had something on the side, too. But this is my daughter we're talking about now."

"Right."

"So you're going to marry her, and then I'll bring you into the business. We're going to be building a casino on Las Vegas Boulevard. That's the hot real estate in Vegas now. In ten or twenty years, downtown Vegas will be antiquated. The future of the city will be 'the Strip.' What would you say to fifty percent of the new casino? And a hundred grand dowry? I'd say that's a damned good deal, considering the alternative."

A great sense of relief washed over me. For a moment I thought I might start believing in God. "Thank you, yes sir, it is."

"What do you say about a Christmas wedding?"

Gulp. "Christmas?"

"Carlotta and I love Christmas."

"Isn't that a little soon? It's less than two months away."

"Oh, that's plenty of time to put together the wedding to end all weddings. It'll be here at the ranch, of course. But first you gotta propose to her. I'll take it for granted that you've asked my permission to do so, and you have it."

I stood. "Is she here?"

"Out by the pool."

"I don't have a ring."

"You can give that to her later. Just let her know you want to marry her."

He got up and put his arm around me. "Leo, I loved your father. Your recent behavior in L.A. disappointed me, but my own son sometimes disappoints me, too. You're solid, Leo. You like the ladies a little too much, and that's gonna have to stop, but otherwise you're okay. Now get out there and do your stuff."

"All right. Thanks, Vince. I appreciate it." I started to leave, but thought I'd show him I was still concerned about our business. "We should talk about the operation. This war between the motorcycle clubs—"

"We'll talk about that another time."

"Okay."

So what did I do? I went out to the pool and spotted Maria lying on one of those recliners. She had on sunglasses and a bikini. Magnificent body. Golden-blonde hair. Yeah, I thought maybe I could live with that. It actually made my plan for New Year's Eve a little more interesting. I'll have to get Christina's take on it. It was a good thing her arm was healing nicely.

The biggest problem was how I was going to tell Judy the news without breaking her heart.

42
Judy's Diary
1961

NOVEMBER 2, 1961

I'm depressed. Saturday is my birthday, and I have no one to celebrate with. I don't know what's happened to Leo. He knows the 4th is my birthday. The last time we were together we talked about it, about how I'm going to be 24, and how he was going to take me to dinner. Something is definitely wrong. Is he seeing someone else? Has he decided to drop me? Without *telling* me?

Christina was at Flickers tonight. She was dressed in a sleeveless, tight, black cocktail dress, but her arm was in a sling. I wanted to ask her about Leo, but to be polite I made it a point to inquire about her injury first.

"This?" she said. "Oh, I hurt it at work. I was trying to do a man's work with some heavy machinery. Tore a ligament in my shoulder."

"Sorry to hear that."

"It happened several weeks ago, so it's nearly healed. In fact, beginning tomorrow I can stop using the sling. Hell, I think I'll stop now." She slipped her arm out and flexed it several times. "There, that's better. Free at last. And how are you, Judy?"

"Fine, but I haven't seen or heard from Leo in a while. What's he up to?"

"Oh, you know, he's a busy man. Sometimes *I* don't know where he is, and I work in his office and live in his house!"

I didn't believe her. She knew exactly where Leo was. I really disliked Christina. She's always been very snooty to me. I don't think she was fond of her brother seeing me.

"Well, is he in L.A., is he traveling, or what? We'd talked about getting together for my birthday on Saturday and I haven't—"

"Oh, your birthday is Saturday? Happy birthday."

"Thanks." *Bitch*. When she didn't say anything else, I added, "Well, if you talk to Leo, please tell him to call me."

"Sure will."

Then I resumed my station and she continued to drink a martini at the bar where she always sat. What a very strange, unpleasant, but undeniably beautiful girl. A lot like her brother, come to think of it. Leo Kelly is also strange and undeniably beautiful. And he's beginning to be unpleasant now, too.

NOVEMBER 4, 1961

Dear diary, today is my birthday, and at first I thought I'd be spending it in the dumps, alone and depressed. I have to work tonight at Flickers, too, so I wasn't looking forward to that when I started the day. I'm dashing this off quickly before I leave my apartment.

Freddie called me this morning from New York to wish me Happy Birthday. He woke me up, but I didn't mind. It was great to hear his voice. Things are the same there. I told him I missed him and that I was having man problems. Freddie said, "If he's not treating you right, then forget him!" I thought it was good advice.

I was hoping Lucy might call me, but by noon she hadn't, so I called her. She'd forgotten it was my birthday. I didn't remind her, but we had a nice chat anyway. It sounded like things are pretty much the same with her and Peter, too.

Then I called Barry to find out what was happening with our cases. He told me the war between the Heathens and Los Serpientes isn't getting any better. Apparently, the Serpents firebombed the Heathens's clubhouse and garage and there was a gunfight. Two Heathens were burned badly and are in the hospital. One Serpientes was shot to death. No, it didn't sound like things were going to ease up any time soon. Barry said the gunrunning activity and the counterfeit money smuggling had probably halted indefinitely. Now the police were simply concerned about the violence occurring in civilian-populated neighborhoods. Innocent bystanders were going to get hurt. It was a mess.

"I could go back to the Serpientes's place and have another look around," I suggested.

"Don't you dare. You won't be able to get near them."

"I'm not afraid."

"Well, you're mad, but I love you that way."

"You *love* me, Barry?"

"As much as I can love a masked vigilante who won't reveal who she is."

"Aw, you're sweet. I love you, too, Barry."

After we hung up, I realized Barry is my closest friend in L.A. I haven't made very many. I like a lot of the people at Flickers, but I've never grown close to any of them. I wonder if I could reveal my identity to Barry someday. I think he could keep a secret. It helps to have someone I trust who knows, someone like Freddie.

I put on my exercise clothes and was about to drive to the Gym, when out of the blue there was a knock at the door. When I asked who it was, I heard Leo's voice.

"It's Prince Charming and I've got this magic slipper I'd like you to try on."

My heart leaped into my throat. On one hand I was happy he was there. On the other, I wanted to clobber him!

"Why should I let you in? Give me one good reason!"

"Because it's your birthday?"

He remembered. Or Christina reminded him. It didn't matter; I guess I sort of melted. I couldn't resist—I let him in.

Leo was full of kisses and hugs and apologies. It was like he'd never been away. He handed me a delicately wrapped gift and told me to open it. "Then we're going out to lunch. I hope you haven't eaten."

"I was about to go exercise. I had a snack an hour ago."

"Forget exercising. We're going to celebrate."

I wanted to protest, but after I opened the present, I was ready to do anything he asked. Dear diary, Leo gave me the most beautiful silver heart-shaped locket on a chain. There are three diamonds on it—he said they were each a carat—one on the point of the heart and the other two on top of the "mounds." Inside is a space for a small photograph.

"You can put a picture of me in there and I'll be with you all the time, even when the real me is out of town," he said.

The locket really is gorgeous. I didn't know if I'll actually put a picture of Leo in it. I'm not sure *what* I'll put it in. It really doesn't need *anything* in it. The outside is dazzling.

I put it on and he said, "It goes really well with your dark hair." I looked in the mirror and he was right. The locket hung down to the top of my cleavage. That was certainly going to draw a lot of eyes in that direction, ha ha!

"Oh, Leo, thank you so much." I gave him a hug and a kiss, and then added, "But I'm mad at you, too."

"I know, honey, it's been crazy. I swear some day I'm going to sell the business and run away with you."

"Promise?"

"Yeah."

He took me to Musso & Frank because I requested it. Even though it was the middle of the day, we had a romantic meal. When it was over, we didn't have much time to do anything else. I had to get ready to go to Flickers.

"Why don't I pick you up tonight when you get off work?" he asked.

I thought that was a good idea.

November 24, 1961

It's Thanksgiving and I'm alone. As usual. I'm about to go to Barry's house to have turkey dinner—in my outfit and mask. Even I have to admit that's weird.

Gosh, I can't believe the last time I wrote was on my birthday. I haven't made diary entries. I've done nothing but exercise—a *lot!*— and work at Flickers.

I've seen nothing of Leo since my birthday. After that wonderful afternoon and a romantic night after I got off work, he left and I haven't heard from him. He doesn't return calls when I leave messages at the office for him. I don't know where he is. I've become like a compulsive high school girl and driven by his house several times, hoping that I'd catch him there. No sign of his car, either. The lights were sometimes on in Christina's part of the home, but never in Leo's. Where *is* he?

Maybe he wasn't as serious about me as he said. I still wear the locket, though. I love it. I really do. But now it's a bittersweet gift, and wearing it actually fits my melancholy mood.

What am I doing in L.A.? Was it a mistake to come here? I'm beginning to think so. But if I go back to New York, I don't think I could be the Black Stiletto anymore. It got to be too dangerous. So that begs the question—do I need to be the Black Stiletto? Can I do without her? Before, I didn't think so. She was as much a part of me as my arms and legs. She was a narcotic I couldn't give up. Now? I just don't know.

I'm leaving for Barry's now. I plan to eat a lot of turkey.

And get plenty drunk.

43
Judy's Diary
1961

December 10, 1961

As you can see, time has passed and I haven't written a word. I've had no desire to do so. Leo is apparently out of my life. Or is he? Who knows? I still wear my locket. To tell the truth, it doesn't remind me of Leo. I believe it represents my *own* heart—I like to think that the organ pumping in my chest is made of silver and has diamonds on it. Why not? I don't know whether it's broken or not. My heart is very confused. It's become par for the course that just when I think I'll never see Leo again, he appears out of the blue. Still, I haven't seen him since my birthday, over a *month ago*, and it's gotten to where I don't care. I realized I can't be down in the dumps forever. I've been drinking too much lately. I have cocktails at Flickers while I'm working—Charlie doesn't care—and I keep whiskey and wine in my apartment. The other night I drank too much and got sick. Yuck. I hated that. I don't like it when you lay down and the room spins. It makes me want to throw up just thinking about it. So maybe I'm turning a corner. If Leo is gone, then he's gone. Maybe I should get rid of the booze and symbolically pretend it's Leo.

The other day I went to see *Blue Hawaii* and stayed through it twice. It didn't cheer me up. Elvis is losing his bad boy image with each passing year; I hate to say it, but he's becoming too sweet. I enjoyed the movie, though. It passed the time.

I talked to Barry today. He said the D.A. thinks the guns are moving again, but the police don't know who the mules are. Casazza and DeAngelo aren't using the Heathens anymore. A recently arrested gangster who allegedly works for Casazza told them that DeAngelo got fed up with the Heathens causing trouble with Los Serpientes. The war was clearly being escalated by the Heathens, so Casazza cut them off. This made the Heathens angry, and now they try to kill any Serpent they see on the street. The violence has increased tenfold. The D.A. wants to find out how the guns are now being distributed. Could the Italians be dealing with Los Serpientes now? Barry said there's no evidence of that. He believes Casazza is still in the counterfeit money business, too, and the Serpents are continuing to smuggle the stuff to Mexico. But very sophisticated counterfeit bills of higher denominations have also been showing up on our side of the border, so apparently that operation is going full steam.

I'm not working tonight, so I think the Stiletto will pay a visit to Tijuana Auto and see what I can find out.

It's a good thing I still have that box of Milk-Bone dog biscuits!

Later—actually, early morning December 11, 1961

I'm glad to be home and in one piece.

The night started out with rain. The weather is usually great in Southern California, but every now and then it decides to rain, and when it does, it can be a downpour. Tonight was one of those.

Nevertheless, I drove my Sunliner—top up, of course—to that questionable part of town where Tijuana Auto is located. First, I simply drove by the shop to see if anything was going on. Surprisingly, there was a lot of activity. The Serpents were going in and out of the shop and clubhouse. Their motorcycles were lined up in front next to a small truck. I parked my car across the street, but down a little ways where I could still see the open front gate of their lot, and I waited to see what would happen. I had on my outfit, covered by the trench coat, but hadn't donned my mask.

Sure enough, after twenty minutes or so, nine Serpents left the lot on their bikes, followed by the truck. Carlos Gabriel was one of them. I recognized him, even in the rain, which had dissipated to a drizzle. The cyclists wore helmets to protect their heads, but I'm sure they got soaking wet anyway. I had a hunch they were on a mission of some kind, so I started the car and pulled out after them, following from a safe distance. Barry had taught me how to tail someone without attracting attention. The trick was figuring out a distance between you and them that was far enough to be unnoticed, but close enough that you wouldn't lose them. It's not easy.

The bikers and the truck took Florence east a long, long way to Garfield Avenue and turned north. I'd never been that far east. After a while we were in the community of Alhambra. Then the caravan kept making turns, headed farther northeast, toward the San Gabriel Mountains. They were headed for canyon territory, where there wasn't much civilization, although there were signs of new development along the way. Much of it is mountainous with very few roads. The way the Los Angeles suburbs were expanding, I figured the area would be heavily populated within a decade. For now, though, I felt like I was in the boondocks. I was afraid the bikers would notice the lone car behind them, so I slowed down until I could barely see their taillights. If they turned off onto some remote street, they'd be gone.

I managed to keep them in sight, though, and eventually we were in the wilderness, surrounded by mountains and trees. It was dark, too, dear diary. I had the inclination to turn around and go home, but I didn't. They finally took a turn on a dirt road and descended into a canyon. I didn't want to follow in my car, so I stopped, stepped out, and watched the taillights descend the winding path to a level plateau that was probably a half mile away. I couldn't drive there—they'd see me—so the next best thing was to creep down on foot. I got back in the car and drove it off the road to a patch of trees and parked behind them. It was safely obscured from view. I put on my mask and started the trek into the canyon. Before long, two more vehicles appeared on the road and headed toward the plateau. It was a good thing I'd hidden my car! They were two big vans, but it was too dark to see who was inside. I kept going with only the moonlight to show me the way. It was cold and wet, but the drizzling had ceased. My boots got very muddy. In ten minutes, I was on the edge of the meeting place, perhaps forty feet from the vehicles. I crouched behind a clump of brush that concealed me. Were there snakes or other dangerous creatures out there? Probably! My enhanced eyesight helped me make out shapes and objects on the ground, but I couldn't be terribly sure I wouldn't step on something. Perhaps the rain drove the critters away.

The bikers kept their headlights on, providing much needed illumination on the scene. That allowed me to clearly see what was happening. The men's voices drifted easily to my position as well, and my acute hearing picked up bits and pieces of conversation.

A white guy got out of each van. They wore rain slickers, which was quite incongruous compared to how the Serpents were dressed. They shook hands with Gabriel and a couple of his men. The newcomers looked familiar, but their backs were to me. When they turned to open the backs of the vans, though, I saw their faces.

Mr. Faretti and Mr. Capri. Casazza's men.

Two Serpents opened the back of their truck and my two canine friends, Bala and Hoja, jumped out. The dogs started romping around the spot, smelling the ground, and lifting their legs. Otherwise the truck was empty. Then I saw what the two vans contained. They were full of guns—rifles, handguns, and what appeared to be machine guns, the kind the army uses. The Serpents started removing the merchandise from the vans and loading them into their truck. Every now and then a biker would take a weapon, try it out for size, look through the scope, and pretend to shoot something. Gabriel snapped at them to stop fooling around.

I dug out my camera. At that distance and with the poor lighting, I didn't know what kind of pictures I'd get, but I started snapping away. I was sure to capture the men carrying the weapons, and I even caught Gabriel handing Faretti a large, thick envelope. I wondered how much money paid for two vans full of illegal arms.

Then the dogs froze and turned in my direction—and started barking. Stupid me. They must have heard the clicking of my camera. Gabriel probably figured his pets had caught the scent of an animal, so he commanded them in Spanish to stop. They didn't. The dogs crept forward, growling and snarling, indicating to their master that a threat was nearby. Gabriel ordered them to stop once more, but then he had second thoughts. He spoke to two of his men, who drew handguns from beneath their jackets. After another charge to the dogs, the beasts started trotting toward my hiding place, followed by the gunmen.

I didn't wait for them. I took off running, which, of course, caused the dogs to bolt and chase me, barking like mad. The two men each fired shots in my direction, but luckily it was dark on the side of the canyon. To them I was just a black shape moving against darkness. The dogs could see me, though. I was pretty sure they were in such a frenzy that they wouldn't recognize me as their old friend. I was about to become their next meal.

Rather than scurry up the dirt path, which would have been suicide, I climbed up the side of a large boulder and made it to the top just as the beasts appeared at its base. They jumped and scratched and made all kinds of racket, but they couldn't ascend the rock. The men could, though. I heard them shouting to the dogs, coming closer. One man fired his gun again. He had no idea what he was aiming at, for the round ricocheted off the side of the cliff several feet away. I couldn't stay there, though, so I reached into my pocket, pulled out some dog biscuits, and tossed them to Hoja and Bala, literally showering them with cookies. That certainly surprised them, for they stopped barking and started gobbling up the treats. Then I moved on, climbing up the side of the cliff to a ledge. I heard the men talking to the dogs. The animals whined when they realized they'd lost me. Nevertheless, there was another gunshot, this time striking a little closer. The men were firing blindly, hoping for a lucky hit. The bullet broke some of the ledge in front of me. Against the background of the illuminated meeting site, I saw the silhouette of a man climbing up the same boulder I had traversed. Nothing to do but keep climbing. Dear diary, I was used to climbing ladders and buildings and fences. A rock cliff face was a different ballgame altogether. My boots kept slipping on the wet surface, and it was extremely difficult to get handholds.

My best bet was to slip around an edge of the cliff, out of sight of the men. To do that, I had to reach another level. Looking back, I saw that my pursuer had made it to the top of the boulder. With no time to lose, I scurried over an outcrop of rock and stood on it. About ten feet above my head was a tree branch that seemed to stick out from the side of the canyon wall. I don't know why I hadn't thought of it prior to that, but I suddenly remembered I had a coiled rope on my belt. With the hook attached to its end, I swung the rope round and round like a lasso, and then cast it high. The hook latched onto the branch in one throw, thank goodness. I pulled on the rope to test my weight against the branch's strength. It held, so I climbed hand over hand until I slithered over the branch like a snake. I wormed my way into the thick of the tree, which was embedded oddly into the rock. After pulling my rope in and coiling it, I perched there, trying to keep as silent as possible. I could no longer see the plateau, the vehicles, or the men, but I could hear the dogs barking and whining and the bikers shouting. They knew someone had seen them.

The man who had climbed the cliff after me was directly below. I'm sure he saw the branch, but figured there was no way I could have reached it. He kept going laterally around the cliff face. After several minutes, I heard Gabriel call to him. The man shouted back.

He'd lost me. He eventually made his way back underneath me and returned to the boulder. Angry voices filled the air. Gabriel wasn't pleased. I don't know Spanish, but I'm sure some of the words he used weren't very nice, ha ha.

I was in that tree for thirty minutes before the bikers packed up and left, followed by the two vans. The procession moved up the road to the top of the canyon, and disappeared. I waited another fifteen minutes before slowly making my way out of the tree and down the cliff side. I was all alone. For a moment I stood there and took in my surroundings. In one way, the dark, wet canyon was creepy; in another, it was incredibly beautiful there in the moonlight. After thanking my lucky stars that I was in one piece, I made the trek back to my car along the muddy road.

Barry is going to be happy about my findings: the Casazza crew was now selling the guns to Los Serpientes.

DECEMBER 12, 1961

I met with Barry today and gave him the roll of film from my camera to develop. I warned him that the pictures might not be very good, but he said the police technicians would do what they could to make them clear. A lot of magic can be done in a darkroom. He paid me $300 and thanked me. That made me feel good, the best I've felt in a month.

But I still miss Leo. I wish I didn't, but I do. And that's all I have to write today.

44
Judy's Diary
1961

Leo called today. I wasn't sure if I wanted to speak to him, but I did anyway. He said he wants to talk to me—in person. I'm off tomorrow night so I suggested he come over. He said he would. I'm a little nervous about it. Well, what happens is what happens. My heart's been broken before. Or maybe he's going to keep his promise to sell his business and run away with me, but I think that's highly unlikely. He said that facetiously.

It's been a dreary month since Thanksgiving. I went out as the Stiletto once for Barry to check out an abandoned building in San Pedro that was suspected of being the counterfeit operation headquarters, but it was a bust. There was nothing inside but cobwebs. Otherwise, I've worked at Flickers and continued my exercising at the Gym. Frankie Avalon was in Flickers the other night. I also met Eli Wallach and his wife, Anne Jackson. You never know who you'll see there.

Christmas was nothing special. I worked on Christmas Eve, and the club was closed on Christmas Day. I spent a lot of the day on the phone with Freddie and Lucy. There were no presents under the tree. I went to see two movies—*Judgment at Nuremberg*, and wasn't *that* a fun time at the picture show, sheesh—and I finally saw *West Side Story* and it's marvelous! I don't think I've seen a musical quite like that one. Everyone is saying how it breaks new ground, and I think I know what they mean. It's made me want to *dance* down the street, snapping my fingers and singing that bit, "Da dee da da daaaa!" What if I dressed as the Stiletto and did it?

People really *would* think I'm crazy, ha ha.

DECEMBER 29, 1961

I feel like going to Santa Monica beach and walking into the ocean to drown. It's not my style to think of suicide, but it's how I feel. I've spent most of last night and today in tears. I have to go to work in a couple of hours and my eyes are puffy and red. I won't be the "hostess with the mostess"—as Charlie calls me—tonight.

Leo broke up with me. We had *sex* and then he broke up with me, the bastard. And I took a big risk, too, because I was caught up in the heat of the moment and didn't even think about putting my diaphragm in until later, after he'd gone. I'm probably okay, I just had my period last week—ish. Ten days? Can't remember.

Dear diary, it's painful to write this down, but I need to document it.

Leo came over to help with the tree, as promised. I wore my locket, and he was happy to see it around my neck. Why couldn't I have stayed angry at him? How does he have the uncanny ability to break down all my defenses when I see him? Well, I figured out the answers to those questions. I love him. As badly as he's been treating me, as missing in action as he is, and as secretive as he is—I'm addicted to the man.

Now, I have to go through withdrawal.

He brought a bottle of expensive champagne. It was already cold, but we put it in the fridge while we spent a little time taking the decorations off my Christmas tree. He told jokes and made me laugh, he was as sweet as can be, and he apologized for the millionth time for not being around.

I'd made some spaghetti with meat sauce, and we had a candlelight dinner here in my studio apartment. Not the most romantic place in the world, but it felt good at the time. We broke out the champagne after that. I left the dirty dishes in the sink and we tried putting away the tree decorations, but we were feeling tipsy and silly. We laughed and messed around and suddenly we were kissing. That led to the other thing. And it lasted into the night and I thought all was right with the world again.

This morning, he was still in bed with me. We were both naked. I got up to go to the bathroom, and when I came back, he was sitting on the edge of the bed with his head in his hands.

"What's wrong?" I asked. "Hangover?"

He revealed his face and I saw that he had tears in his eyes.

"What is it, darling?" I asked, sitting next to him. I put my arm around him. "Tell me."

Finally, he got up the courage to speak. "Judy, something has happened in my life that's changing things."

I didn't like the sound of that. "What do you mean, Leo?"

"Judy, remember when I said that someday I wanted to sell my business and spend the rest of my life with you?"

"Yeah?"

"Well, that's still true. I want you to believe that. I want you to know that I will be back for you."

"Back for me? What do you mean? Where are you going?"

"There's going to be a period of time when I can't see you."

"What?"

"I can't see you anymore, Judy. For a few months."

"Are you leaving town?"

"You might say that. Yeah, I'm leaving town. Think of it that way."

I was totally confused. "Leo, what are you saying? Don't be so cryptic. Just tell me the truth, okay? What's going on?"

He stood and started to dress. "I can't, Judy. You'll just have to trust me. But in the meantime, please don't try to contact me. I really can't be with you for a while."

Dear diary, I felt my heart splitting in two. A ton of bricks fell on my chest. I'm usually a tough girl, but I started to cry. I don't think I've ever cried in front of a man, but I did. I'm ashamed, but I couldn't help it. The tears just flowed. All the frustration and uncertainty about Leo over the past few months just reached a critical apex. The dam broke.

"Judy, please don't cry."

Then I let him have it. I stood and I started beating on his chest. "You bastard! You son of a bitch!" I cried. "Tell me your secrets! Tell me your secrets!"

He grabbed hold of my wrists to stop me, and then he held me close while I sobbed into his chest. "I'm sorry, Judy," he said. "I truly am."

After a moment, I got hold of myself and pulled away from him. I threw on a bathrobe and told him to get out.

"Judy."

"Get the *hell* out of here, Leo!" I spat. "How *dare* you come over and pretend that everything is fine between us. How *dare* you take me to bed. That was your plan all along, right? One more *screw* and then break up with me? Well, go to *hell*, Leo! And take all your dirty secrets with you!"

He silently finished getting dressed. Then he walked to the door, turned to me, and said, "You've got secrets, too, Judy."

And then he was gone.

I bawled like a baby. I threw things. I broke the empty bottle of champagne and ended up having to sweep up the shards.

What did he mean by that last accusation? Did he know about the Stiletto? How could he?

I wish I was back in New York.

Later

I got through work all right. No one said anything about my puffy eyes. I probably seemed a little less energetic than usual because

Charlie asked if I was feeling all right. I told him I thought I was coming down with something, so he sent me home. He didn't want me getting anyone sick. That was fine with me.

I felt like trouble, so I dressed as the Stiletto and went out. It was around 11:00. I walked up and down Hollywood Boulevard. People gawked and pointed, but I ignored them. I wasn't in a friendly mood.

Up near Vine, I found a couple of familiar winos who always sat against the buildings, drinking themselves into a stupor. Three white men were harassing them, telling them to "get jobs" and calling them names. One man kicked a wino in the stomach.

"Hey!" I shouted, approaching them.

When the three men saw me, they grinned. "Lookie here, it's the Black Stiletto!" the kicker proclaimed. "You come to clean up our street?"

"Yeah." I punched the guy in the face. And then the stomach. He fell to the pavement.

"What did you do that for?" one of the other men growled.

"'Cause he's a bastard and shouldn't be picking on the helpless."

"They're f—ing *winos*!"

The man on the ground was struggling to catch his breath. "Get ... her!" His two pals took a step toward me, but I performed a perfect *Mikazuki-geri* crescent-moon kick and slammed my boot into one guy's chest. I didn't kick him too hard, just enough to scare them. Then I drew the stiletto and held it up.

"Don't mess with me, and I mean it!" I snarled.

One guy held up his hands. "Whoa, whoa, fine, we'll leave. C'mon, Gus, let's go." They helped their pal to his feet, scooted up Vine, and disappeared.

I went to the wino they'd kicked and asked, "Are you all right?"

The old man, who looked like he was as ancient as Moses, and hadn't taken a bath in years, just nodded and shot me a toothless grin. Then he held up a half-empty pint of Jack Daniels.

"Are you offering me a drink?"

He nodded.

So I sat between the two smelly drunks, took the fellow's bottle, and had a swig. What pedestrians who were out that late either didn't notice us or ignored us. Maybe it didn't register that the Black Stiletto was sitting with a couple of bums on Hollywood Boulevard, drowning her sorrows in booze.

But that's what I did.

45
Gina
THE PRESENT

The past two weeks were filled with me taking care of Dad, going to the studio, and trying to sleep when I could. I haven't had much time for Josh, except when we're working. On a professional level he says I've changed since the hotel assault, that I'm now exceptionally driven during exercises and spars, almost as if I'm taking the instruction much more seriously than I used to. I've always been serious about Krav Maga, but I think I might know what he means. The drive comes from anger. I'm angry at what happened to Dad. I'm angry that it's the second time I've been involved in a violent assault. I'm angry that the law often can't do anything about it. It makes me want to go after the people who did this to Dad. There's a connection between those men and Dad, and it's my intent to find out what it is.

He was in the hospital for a week, and then he stayed with us at our apartment. Our sofa bed is pretty comfortable, so Dad camped out in the living room for a while longer until the doctor said he could fly. We got the green light today, so I'm taking him back to Chicago tomorrow, staying for a few days to make sure he's going to be okay, and then flying home. Josh said it's all right that I miss work, but I should continue to do exercises at least an hour a day if possible.

The patient has improved considerably. The first week was iffy, mainly because Dad found it very difficult to swallow and talk. It eventually got better. The swallowing pain isn't as severe as it was, but the doctor says it's possible he'll be sore for a long time, maybe a year or two or more, before it goes away—*if* it does. Dad's voice is coming back, but he speaks in a hoarse whisper right now and can't do it for very long before it becomes uncomfortable. That, too, will take a lengthy period of time to heal, and his voice may never be the same.

His sense of humor is coming back, so that's a good sign. I told him he sounds like a cartoon character, and that made him laugh.

We spent the day packing and getting things ready for the trip, and we had a date to call Maggie at the nursing home and maybe talk to Grandma Judy. We've kept Maggie up to speed on my dad on a daily basis. He's been able to speak to her himself since last Sunday. They don't talk too long because of his voice, so I end up relaying most of the news between them.

My grandma is stable, no changes in anything since Dad was last there. Maggie explained to her that Dad is in New York with me, but no one's ever sure how much she comprehends. It's so sad to see Grandma Judy that way. She used to be so vibrant and energetic. I love her so much. There's a lot I don't know about her, and I think there's a lot Dad doesn't know about her. And we also don't have a clue about my grandfather. I once asked Grandma about him, and she just said he died early in the Vietnam War, shortly after Kennedy first sent "advisors" over there. She won't talk about him. All my life, she'd change the subject if I ever brought him up. I don't know why she keeps no mementos from their marriage. I once asked Dad what Grandma did for a living. He said his father left them money. Well, if he did that, then why didn't Grandma acknowledge it? Heck, maybe she *wasn't* married to my grandfather! Maybe he went to Vietnam and then she realized she was pregnant, and then he never came home. Was Grandma Judy so mortified by that experience that she would bury it? I suppose back in 1962 that would've been scandalous, but I can't imagine it's the only time something like that ever happened. Still, it's a mystery. The whole thing is very weird, but I've learned to live with it. Now it's normal for our family that there's a hidden secret or two.

I know *I* have a couple.

We phoned Maggie on time while she was on a break at Woodlands. She was in Grandma's room, on her cell.

"Hi, Gina, how are things?"

"Fine, Maggie. We're just getting all of Dad's stuff together, it's spread all over the place. I have to figure out what I'm going to take since I don't know how long I'll be there."

"Don't you worry, Gina. It probably won't have to be too long. I'll be there to take care of him, you know."

"But he insists on going home to his own house."

"I know. I'll come over and move in with *him* when you leave. But I think he's going to be stronger and more independent very quickly."

I told Dad that and he rolled his eyes. "She would say that," he croaked.

"Here," Maggie said, "let me put someone on." I heard her say, "Judy, it's your granddaughter, Gina." Noise of shuffling the phone went on for a few seconds. Sometimes Grandma doesn't quite understand what a cell phone is and has to be told to put it to her ear.

"Hello, Grandma?"

"Wha—hello?"

"Hi, Grandma. It's Gina. How are you?"

"Oh, okay." Her voice had that slow and resigned, but not necessarily unhappy, tone she always exhibited.

"Are they treating you nice where you live?"

"What?"

"I said are they treating you nice where you live?"

"Yes."

"I'm coming to visit tomorrow! How do you like that?"

"Oh, that's nice."

"I'm bringing Dad with me."

"That's nice."

I wasn't sure if she really understood what I was saying, but she did a good job of faking it. "That's nice" was an all-purpose response for her.

"I'm going to put my dad on the phone, okay, Grandma? His voice sounds funny, he's hoarse."

"What?"

"Dad's voice is hoarse. Uh, he has a sore throat."

"Oh."

"Here he is." I handed the phone to my dad.

"Hi, Mom," he whispered. "Mom? Mom, it's me, Martin. *Martin*. Yes, your son Martin. My voice sounds different, Mom, I, uh, have a sore throat. But it will get better. I just wanted to tell you that I love you and I'll be home tomorrow to see you. All right? Gina and I will see you tomorrow. Okay? I love you! Give the phone back to Maggie, all right?"

To me it didn't sound as if Grandma comprehended much of that at all. Dad and Maggie spoke for a minute about Grandma's condition and then he asked her a bizarre question.

"Maggie, how long is a normal pregnancy? I know it's nine months, but how many weeks? Uh-huh. I just want to know. Oh, don't be silly, I haven't gotten anyone pregnant, geez. What? Really? Well, what about a forty-two week pregnancy, is that unusual? Really. So it's uncommon but not rare. Uh-huh. Okay." The expression on his face indicated that whatever she'd said bothered him. "Thanks, here's Gina."

He handed the cell back to me.

"He sounds better," Maggie said.

"Yeah, with every passing day his voice sounds less like Boris the Toad." That made her—and Dad—laugh again. I made a face at Dad and he mimicked me, but I sensed he was covering up a bundle of different emotions.

"Well, we'll see you tomorrow. Be safe."

"Thanks, we will."

"When you get in I'll—what's that, Judy?" I heard my grand-mother's muffled voice in the background. "Okay, Judy, I'll tell him. Gina, one of those remarkable things that sometimes happens during Alzheimer's just occurred."

"What?"

"Judy said, 'Little Man Martin.'"

"What?"

"She used to call your father that when he was little. Tell him she said it. Out of the blue, after talking to him. She must have made the connection of who he was."

I put down the phone and relayed the message to him. His mouth dropped. "I never knew you were called Little Man Martin," I teased. "Can I call you that now?"

He waved me away, and I got back on the cell. "That's amazing, Maggie. Say good-bye to her for us."

We hung up and I asked Dad, "What was all that about preg-nancy?"

"Did you know women can carry babies up to forty-two weeks?" he whispered.

"So?"

He waved me away again—now his trademark "never mind" sign language—so I chalked it up to one of his kooky Dad-isms. We continued to organize his medications, clothing, and bandages. After a while, he went to the bathroom. I moved to the end table he was using as a nightstand to see if he'd left anything there, and I hap-pened to open the small drawer. Inside was an old book with a rub-ber band around it. It looked like a diary. I picked it up and saw that someone had marked "#4" on the spine. A bookmark was stuck in it toward the end. Too curious to pass it up, I removed the rubber band and opened it to the saved page.

The text was handwritten, and I was pretty sure it was my grandmother's penmanship. There was also a piece of paper from a small notepad stuck between the same pages as the bookmark. I un-folded it. Dad had written in pencil, "December ?–October 13" and

"Leo Kelly????" The only thing familiar about that was October 13th was Dad's birthday.

"Gina!" Dad's voice was loud and sounded like sandpaper. It made me jump, and I dropped the diary and note. He came over, angrily picked up the book and paper, and put them back in the drawer.

Well, I felt I had the right to ask, "Dad, what is that?"

He held up a finger, shook it back and forth, and then pointed to his throat.

"Oh, you can talk for a minute. Or you could write it down."

He shook his head at me. "Not now, Gina," he struggled to whisper. "Please. Don't ask me now."

That was weird. The book was actually something he hadn't wanted me to see. I shrugged. "Okay, Dad."

So we got on with the task at hand.

But *boy*, was I intrigued.

1961

DECEMBER 31, 1961

It's nearly 5:00 in the morning and I can't sleep. The last twelve hours have been a nightmare, dear diary. I'm in despair. I've been betrayed with such ungodly magnitude that I don't know if I'll ever get over it. I'm hurt, angry, and humiliated. I've been in tears since I got home. Damn, damn, damn!

All because of a man.

Leo Kelly.

The most despicable human being on the planet.

I have a lot to write down, and this is probably going to take me all morning. Then I'm going to call in sick to Flickers. Charlie won't like it, tonight being New Year's Eve and all, but I can't work. Not this night. I have a mission.

I'm going to Las Vegas to confront that bastard Leo.

Needless to say, I haven't been my best since he broke up with me. I've floated through the hours in a haze. I could barely concentrate at work, and then last night came the kicker.

I was at Flickers, attempting to put on my best hostess face. Charlie knew something was wrong and asked if I was all right, *again*. I told him flat out that Leo and I had broken up. He said he was sorry, and added, "You're not the first girl my nephew has hurt. He's family and I love him, but he's a cad, always was, and always will be. I hope you'll be able to move on and forget about him."

Everyone at Flickers had warned me. The waitresses. The bartender. Even Charlie. I didn't listen. I was too head-over-heels, dizzy with lust and love. I don't think I'll ever be able to watch another Paul Newman movie without thinking of Leo.

Work was a chore. I didn't know if I could get through the night. Sal Casazza was there with his two goons. They sat at his usual table. He was in a better mood than he had been in the past. He even took my hand and kissed it when I greeted him at the door. When he wasn't looking, I wiped my hand on my dress.

Everything was moving along in a dull fog until I saw Christina. She came in around midnight, just as Frankie Avalon was about to end his second set, and she went straight to the bar as usual. I wondered if she knew about me and Leo, so I purposefully walked in front of her.

"Oh, hi, Judy," she said.

I turned to her, but I didn't smile. "Hi, Christina."

There was the hint of a smirk on her face. She knew about Leo and me. "How are you doing?"

"Fine." I couldn't help the sarcasm creeping into my voice. "And you?"

"Oh, I'm fabulous. I went to a *marvelous* wedding on Christmas Day. Did you hear about it?"

"No."

"Oh, you haven't heard?"

"Heard what?"

"Leo got married."

The words stunned me. At first I wasn't sure I'd heard her correctly. "What?"

"Yeah, on Christmas Day. It was a beautiful ceremony."

I had trouble finding my voice. "T... to who? Wh... who did he marry?"

"Maria."

"Maria?"

"Maria DeAngelo."

My God, Vincent DeAngelo's daughter.

When I didn't say anything, she continued. "We were all wondering when they'd tie the knot. After all, they'd been dating since last summer." I swear she was gloating.

"Last... last summer?"

"Sure. Didn't you know he was seeing her, too?"

I walked away. I couldn't listen to her. Everything became a blur and I suddenly felt rotten. I went straight to the ladies' room, went into a stall, and vomited into the toilet.

How could he have done it? He came to see me after Christmas, and he *spent the night*. We had *sex*. And he was already *married?? Oh, my God!*

The next hour was a blank. I don't remember what I did. I think I went into the break room and sat for a while. I may have gone back to the hostess station, but I must have greeted guests without thinking about it. During my next break, I called Barry. I woke him up, but I didn't care.

"Did you know about Leo Kelly marrying Maria DeAngelo?" I asked him.

"Yeah," he said. "They had this big hullabaloo at DeAngelo's ranch in Vegas on Christmas Day. Why?"

"How do I find him?"

"Stiletto, what are you thinking? What's wrong?"

"Just tell me how to find Leo Kelly."

"I don't know. If he and Maria aren't in his home in Hollywood, then he's probably out there with the DeAngelo family. They didn't go on a honeymoon yet, they're probably waiting until after the New Year's Eve party."

"What party?"

"DeAngelo throws a huge New Year's Eve party every year. He must be really rolling in dough to be able to afford that wedding on Christmas and then the party tomorrow night."

"Where is that ranch, exactly?"

"Stiletto, don't even *think* about going there. It's heavily guarded, like a fortress. They'd shoot you on sight."

"Just tell me how to get there, Barry. I mean it."

He revealed the address and how to find it outside of Vegas. I wrote it all down. I thanked him and hung up. I went back on the floor just in time to see Sal Casazza and his two shadows getting their coats from the hatcheck girl. I overheard Casazza say to Shrimp, "Don't worry, it'll all be resolved tonight at the meet up." Then he looked at his watch. "We better hurry, or we'll be late."

They were on their way someplace significant, and I was pretty sure it had something to do with mob business. I figured doing some Stiletto work would get my mind off of Leo, and if I could take out my aggression on some gangsters in the process, it would do a lot for my mental health. I went straight to Charlie, told him I wasn't feeling well *again*, and said I was going home. Instead, I ran to my car and waited until I saw the valet deliver Casazza's Rolls-Royce to the front of the nightclub. The three men got in, and Shrimp drove it away.

I followed them.

47
Judy's Diary
1961

From Hollywood they took a route south and then east, toward downtown Los Angeles. But soon it became clear they were headed for the Wholesale District, southeast of downtown. It took quite a while, but eventually they stopped at a dark warehouse on Towne Avenue. It appeared to be completely derelict.

I circled the block and parked a street away, and then changed into my Stiletto outfit in the car. First making sure no one was around to see me, I got out and stealthily darted between shadows until I had a clear view of the warehouse from across the street. I crouched behind a parked pickup truck and surveyed the scene.

A handful of black sedans were lined up in the lot by the building, and over the next fifteen minutes, a few more cars arrived and parked. Men wearing suits got out of the vehicles; I recognized a few faces here and there from Flickers. They were Sal Casazza's people. On cue, a small band of bikers noisily drove up the street and entered the parking lot. Heathens. Men wearing sleeveless black leather jackets and sporting ugly tattoos on their forearms dismounted and went inside the warehouse. A few minutes later, Los Serpientes arrived. They were careful not to park their bikes too close to the Heathens's.

There was no doubt this was a high-level meeting. I snuck away from the pickup truck and frantically looked around for a pay phone. I spotted one at the corner, so I sprinted to it and called Barry.

I told him what was going on. He didn't think he could assemble a police backup team in time; the meeting would probably be over before anyone arrived. However, he asked if I could infiltrate the warehouse and find out what was going on. He would make sure one or two patrol cars were alerted to stand by. I didn't want them to jump the gun without some kind of a signal, so Barry said he'd instruct them to remain vigilant and not act unless they heard from me or trouble really broke out. He hoped there wouldn't be any violence; four cops weren't about to be effective against what sounded like an entire army of gangsters in the building.

So it was up to me.

I ran away from the parking lot, around to the opposite side of the warehouse, to look for a way in. A loading-dock door on that side was shut, but the back of the building looked more promising. The structure was the equivalent of three stories, but along the top, near the roof, was a series of windows. One was cranked open to let in air. My rope wasn't long enough to reach it, but there was a storm gutter drainpipe that led from the roof to the ground on the corner of the building. Those things are made of a flimsy material—aluminum?—but there were metal straps bolted to the building in increments that held the drainpipe in place. I approached the structure and put my boot on the first strap. Its width was negligible, but as long as I was careful, the tip of my boot fit. It held my weight, so I risked the ascent. It was like climbing a ladder with half-inch-deep steps on tiptoe. When I was about two-thirds the way up, I had a scare—one of the metal straps was loose and broke away. My foot slipped and I would have fallen had I not clutched the drainpipe with both hands. Because my gloves were made of leather, the friction held; otherwise I would have slid down the pipe like a fireman.

Once I was on the roof, it wasn't difficult to make my way to a spot above the open window and use the rope and hook to lower myself inside.

The warehouse was like a huge barn, and I was up in the trusses near the ceiling, above the work lights that hung from the ceiling on long electrical cords. I figured since I was behind the lights, the men on the floor couldn't see me. Nevertheless, I did my best to perch on a crossbeam bathed in shadow.

A number of folding chairs had been set up, and the men were milling around and taking seats. It looked like a neighborhood town hall meeting, ha ha, except they were all criminals. The Heathens sat to one side, the Serpents to the other, with a wide space in between. A line of chairs faced the two groups, and these were occupied by Casazza, Shrimp, Mario, and eight other men. Otherwise the place was empty and unused. The cavernous qualities of the building caused the men's voices to echo in the rafters, so I had no problem hearing the conversations. Right now, they were all talking at once, as the meeting hadn't begun. Apparently, they were still waiting on some people.

Over the next ten minutes, a handful of more bikers and men in suits arrived and took seats. I counted six Serpientes, seven Heathens, and eleven Italians. And then I got a shock.

Leo Kelly and another man entered and took seats near Sal Casazza. They shook hands with the others in the line, and then they went over and shook hands with Carlos Gabriel! After that, Leo and the other guy moved to the other side and shook hands with a couple of the Heathens, probably their leaders.

My heart was beating a mile a minute.

Leo was a gangster. All along, he had lied to me. He was part of Sal Casazza's—and in turn, Vincent DeAngelo's—organization. No wonder he married DeAngelo's daughter! He was ensconced in the thick of it! The bastard! The no-good, lying bastard! The betrayal just kept getting worse.

The other man with him was tall, blond, and good-looking in a country-boy kind of way. In fact, he wore cowboy boots and a Stetson.

Then the meeting was called to order. Casazza stood, all three hundred pounds of him, and addressed the attendees.

"Thank you all for coming to this important sit-down. Mr.

DeAngelo and I appreciate you putting aside your differences to come and hash out these problems we're facing. I know all of you want to get back to business as usual, and so do we. You all know who I am, right? But you may not know our friend from Las Vegas." Casazza turned to a tall, skinny guy who was probably in his thirties. He stood and joined the fat man. "This is Paulie DeAngelo, Vince's son. He's here as an emissary for his father."

Paulie raised a hand and said, "Hello," and then he returned to his seat. So there was the proof that Casazza was in bed with DeAngelo, and that the motorcycle clubs worked for them.

"And you may not know Ricky Bartlett." Casazza gestured to the cowboy, who stood, smiled, and waved. "Ricky's here from Texas. As you know, he has an interest in what happens here today. Thanks for coming, Ricky."

"My pleasure," Bartlett said. "I hope we can be in business again real soon." He sat down. I had to remember that name—Ricky Bartlett—and ask Barry about him.

Casazza resumed. "We all know the Heathens and Los Serpientes are at war, and this is hurting everyone's businesses. The police are all over us. The Feds are biting our asses. It has to stop. Now. We're gonna listen to each side's grievances. Bryson, you're up." He nodded to one of the Heathens sitting in their front row. The man stood and walked to the center, and then Casazza sat. I don't think I'd ever seen him before. He was big, bald, and had a swastika tattooed on his forearm.

"I'm Doug Bryson, president of the Heathens," he said. "We have enjoyed a long and fruitful relationship with Mr. Casazza and his crew. The product they've supplied us from overseas has always fit our needs. We have a damned good distribution machine in place, and it's been that way for quite some time. Recently, we opened up a route into Mexico, but the spics—"

The Mexicans didn't like that. They shouted in protest and two of the men stood to challenge Bryson.

"Whoa, hold it," Casazza said, standing again. "Watch the language, Bryson. We're all friends here, *right*?"

Bryson sneered and shrugged. "Sure. Sorry. As I was saying, the *Mexicans* here don't like us moving guns south of the border. They started attacking our runs. Then people started dying. One of our HQs was firebombed. That's number one. Second—we've heard that *our* guns are being sold to Los Serpientes instead of to *us*. That's unacceptable, especially since we were told you guys were suspending the exchanges while the heat was on. Third—we know there's a counterfeit money operation going on and Los Serpientes are benefiting. We want in on that action, too. The Heathens can move funny money of higher denominations all the way across the country, and you know it. Fourth—" Then he turned to Casazza and said, "I don't know why you want to do business with these greasy wetbacks. You might as well do business with niggers, too."

More shouts of protest from the Serpents. One of them bolted from his seat and tackled Bryson to the floor and started punching. Heathen members jumped up to protect their leader. It looked as if a full-scale gang fight would break out until Paulie pulled a handgun from underneath his jacket and fired a shot in the air. That got everyone's attention and the brawl ceased.

"Everyone shut up and sit down!" Shrimp hollered. "We're at a sit-down, for Chrissakes!"

"You want the cops to barge in here?" Casazza yelled. "Sit down!"

Bryson got up off the floor and brushed himself off, all the while glaring at the Serpents's side of the room. "I wasn't finished talking."

"I think you are finished," Casazza said. "Sit down." Bryson gave *him* a dirty look, too, and then resumed his seat. "Just for your information, Bryson, we *do* have business with the *niggers*. We do business with whoever Mr. DeAngelo deems to be a worthwhile partner." He then looked at Carlos Gabriel. "Señor Gabriel. Your turn."

Los Serpientes's leader stood and took the floor as Casazza sat.

"We gonna need a translator?" Bryson mumbled. There were chuckles from his side of the room, but Gabriel's icy stare shut them up.

"I speak English very well, thank you very much," he said. "Los Serpientes only recently started working with Mr. Casazza and Mr. DeAngelo. We welcomed the relationship, and up until recently everything was going good. We had our routes to Mexico in place, and they were established *decades* ago. Los Serpientes claimed them on behalf of *La eMe*, and we have made runs for them for two years."

I knew that "La eMe" was the Mexican Mafia. Barry told me that. Los Serpientes was a splinter gang that worked as their associates.

"It is our *right* to maintain these routes. Our people have always controlled them, and we always will. The Heathens recently started using them, doubling the chances of arrest. We all know that territories must be respected unless special arrangements are made. That's *my* number one. Second—we've been asking to be cut in on the gun deals for months. Our brothers south of the border need them. The Heathens always refused to sell to us, but other motorcycle clubs benefited. It's not right that the Heathens have been the first-line distributor. There are plenty of MCs that can do the job, including us. I say, share the wealth and we'll all be happy."

Gabriel took his seat and Casazza stood. "All right. Thank you, gentlemen. Now. Mr. DeAngelo has advised me to offer terms to reconcile this messy war. But first of all, I want to address Señor Gabriel's claim that we've been selling guns to Los Serpientes instead of the Heathens. We haven't. We haven't sold to anyone since the war started and the heat has been on everyone. The truth of the matter is that our supply of guns coming from overseas was being ripped off from under our very noses. We've had two such thefts, and it's *those* stolen weapons that were sold to Los Serpientes without our knowing about it."

That elicited murmuring among the attendees.

"I had my men look into it, and we identified the traitors. And we're going to deal with them here and now as a gesture of good faith to everyone present tonight."

He turned to Shrimp and Mario, who stood and left the meeting. They disappeared into the darkness against the back wall. I couldn't see exactly what they were doing, but it appeared they were handling a flatbed dolly. Sure enough, they rolled it out and into the space between the two factions. Lying on the dolly were two men who were bound and gagged. Two more of Casazza's crew helped Shrimp and Mario pick up the prisoners and set them up on the floor on their knees.

They were Mr. Faretti and Mr. Capri.

That reminded me of my camera! I dug into my backpack and pulled it out—and then realized it didn't have any film! I had given the last roll to Barry and hadn't bought any more. Ugh! I could have slapped myself. The camera was useless, so I put it back and concentrated on trying to memorize everything the men said.

"I was saddened to learn that my trusted colleagues, Mr. Faretti and Mr. Capri, had stabbed us in the backs," Casazza said. He looked at Gabriel. "Is it not true that these were the men who sold you the guns?"

Gabriel stood and answered, "Yes. That's them. But we thought they were acting with your blessing, Sal."

"I know. I'm not blaming you, Carlos. You get to keep the guns they sold you. We've already recovered the money you paid them. But traitors and thieves will not be tolerated in our organization."

Casazza pulled a handgun from under his jacket. He then turned to *Leo* and beckoned him to stand. Leo looked confused, pointed to himself, and mouthed, "Me?"

"Yes, you, Leo. You all know Leo Kelly, right? He's been doing important work for us. And he's also now a part of Mr. DeAngelo's family, isn't that right, Leo?"

Leo stood and said, "Uh, yeah. That's right."

"Your father-in-law has asked that you do the honors." He held the gun out to Leo.

Oh, my God, I thought. *Oh, my God*.

Leo hesitantly approached Casazza and took the weapon. There was a beat, and at first I thought he wasn't going to go through with it. Then, like an expert, he quickly checked the ammunition and tested the handgun's weight in his hand. He stepped up behind Capri and pointed the gun at the back of the man's head. Both Capri and Faretti struggled in their bonds and cried muffled pleas into their gags.

Seconds went by, but they seemed like hours.

Then—*bam!*

Capri fell forward. A pool of blood started to spread around his head and shoulders. That made Faretti panic and try to stand. Shrimp and Mario held on to him. Leo moved over behind the man, pointed the gun, and fired again.

My former lover had just murdered two men in cold blood.

Leo stood there, his arm still outstretched. I think he was a little stunned at what he'd done. Casazza approached him, patted him on the back, and took the weapon.

"You can sit down now, Leo." He did. Casazza gestured to some of his men, who picked up the two corpses, laid them back on the dolly, and rolled them away. "Now. Let me address your grievances. Mr. Bryson."

"Yeah?"

"The income we get for the counterfeit money helps pay for the weapons coming from overseas. That operation will continue. We agree to let you distribute the higher denominations at a 70/30 split. If the war between you and Los Serpientes ends tonight, we will resume the gun sales to you. However, you must deal with our Latin friends here and sell them whatever weapons they desire at your cost. We want to keep our funnel flowing into one receptacle only, and that's you, Bryson. The Heathens. You've done well selling the arms to other organizations who then distribute them around the country. We won't sell directly to anyone else, not even Los Serpientes, but *you* will. At no profit."

"Wait a minute—" Bryson said, starting to stand.

"Shut up and sit down!" He did.

"That's not negotiable. Finally, the Heathens will *not* utilize Los Serpientes's routes to Mexico, *except* through Texas." Casazza looked at the cowboy, who nodded approval. "*But*, Los Serpientes will pay the Heathens fifteen percent of their earnings from all sales south of the border."

Bryson looked confused. "We can't go to Mexico from California or Arizona or New Mexico, but we *can* through Texas?"

Bartlett stood. "If I may, Sal?"

"Sure, Ricky," Casazza said. "Go ahead."

The cowboy addressed Bryson. "The routes *must* go through Odessa. We're backing a good percentage of this operation, so we'll be getting extra shipments of both guns and counterfeit dough for our purposes in Texas and the Deep South, and the Heathens are going to deliver them. In exchange, you'll get a whopping twenty-five percent of what we move."

That seemed to satisfy Bryson. He folded his arms and sat back in his chair, as did Bartlett.

So Ricky Bartlett was from Odessa, Texas! I figured he must be a big shot with the Dixie Mafia.

Casazza continued. "In addition, regarding deaths of members and destruction of property, both the Heathens and Los Serpientes will call it even. There will be no retaliation for what has gone on prior to this day. Are we agreed?"

Silence. After a few seconds, Bryson stood and asked, "What about the Black Stiletto?"

Casazza nodded. "She has indeed caused a lot of trouble for our businesses. You have Mr. DeAngelo's permission to kill her on sight. The Black Stiletto is a dead woman."

That didn't make me feel too good.

"So are we all agreed?" Casazza asked again.

Bryson looked over at Gabriel, who stood. They both walked to the center—and shook hands. Everyone applauded.

The meeting broke up. Everyone dispersed. Leo left with Casazza.

I waited until everyone was gone before slipping out the window and climbing down the drainpipe. By the time I got home it was 4:00 in the morning. I couldn't sleep. Now it's 7:00. I'll wait an hour and call Barry to tell him what I learned.

Then I'm going to get out my road map and drive to Las Vegas. It's a six- or seven-hour drive. Vince DeAngelo is going to have an uninvited guest at his New Year's Eve party.

I can't wait to confront Leo and tell him what a lowlife he is. Such betrayal. Such lies. All along he was a *criminal*. I should have trusted my very first instincts, and Lucy's, too! The bastard. I hate him. I hate him. *I hate him.*

There will indeed be fireworks tonight. Wish me luck, dear diary.

48
Leo
THE PAST

I was a little nervous about tonight, even though everything was in place and ready to go. The party would start at eight, the fireworks at midnight, of course. Apparently the soiree would be limited to a hundred people, tops, as DeAngelo wanted to keep it more "intimate." It'd be mostly family and close friends and a few business associates. That was good.

I knew what we were doing was a risk. A goddamned big one. If we failed, we'd be dead. If we succeeded, then we'd be set for life. Christina thought it would work. She was confident it was a good plan. She was excited about it. When it's all over I'd be in a strong position within DeAngelo's organization. If only Paulie would slip on a banana peel and break his neck, then who knows?—I could be running the business sooner rather than later.

Christ, I can't believe I'm gonna do what I'm about to do. Especially, after last night. That rattled me. I hadn't expected Sal to hand me that gun to whack those two goddamned traitors. But I did it. I didn't hesitate. I had to do it. I was family now, as well as part of the Family with a capital F. It was the only way I could gain respect. And tonight was how I was going to return it.

It had to work. Or I was a dead man.

It was one hell of a week. On Christmas Day, I got married to

Maria. She looked beautiful in her white satin wedding dress. 'Course, she ain't no virgin, but we were all Catholics, so what the hey. It was a real nice ceremony, too. My best man was Boone, because I didn't have anyone else to ask. I had approached Charlie, but he acted all huffy and said I treated Judy badly. Yeah, I know, but I'll come to that in a minute. Maria didn't ask Christina to be in the bridal party, which didn't make me too happy, but I could live with it. Christina didn't give a shit. She hated weddings. Maria's maid of honor was that cousin of hers from Santa Monica. There were about fifty people in attendance.

It damned near didn't happen! Maria found out about Judy, and it wasn't pretty. We had a huge fight and she spent a day crying in her room, but then we made up and she forgave me, mainly because I think she didn't want to go through the embarrassment of canceling the wedding. Some asshole bitch friend of Maria's in Hollywood told her. She had heard the skinny from someone at Flickers that I'd been seeing Judy. When Maria confronted me about it, I told her, yeah, I *had* been seeing Judy Cooper, but that was over and I hadn't seen her in weeks. Maria wanted to know if I'd slept with her, and I was honest and admitted I had. That's when Maria got all upset. The next day, though, Maria asked me if I loved *her* and I answered, "Yes." Then she told me that if my fling with "that whore" was truly over, then the wedding was still on.

I'd bet Maria told her daddy about it. It's probably why DeAngelo ordered Casazza to make me pull the trigger on those two bastards last night. I'm glad I stepped up to the plate and handled it like a man. At least now the war between the Heathens and Los Serpientes would be over, and business would be back to normal. We were producing counterfeit dough now like chickens laid eggs. It was going to be very lucrative, now that our deal with the Texans was solidified. Everything would be great as long as the cops and the Black Stiletto stayed out of my hair. And I'd be dealing with her shortly too.

So we got married. I was mostly interested in my father-in-law's gifts. Maria's daddy gave her the Florentine Diamond for Christmas, just as he said he would. He'd had it set and put on a silver chain to wear as a necklace. My God, it was beautiful. And worth a fortune. I asked her to wear it tonight at the party. Vince gave me fifty percent of the new casino he was going to start building this year, plus the hundred grand he promised. With his connections to "investment advisors," I wouldn't have to pay any taxes on the cash. I was learning all kinds of things about hiding income from the government.

But all that for what price? I knew I didn't want to actually be married to Maria. I'd known it all along. She was a spoiled, snobby, rich daddy's girl before the marriage, and she remained a spoiled, snobby, rich daddy's girl afterward. She refused to move out of the ranch house. I had to live with my in-laws! Sure, it was a nice place, it was a mansion, and we had servants and luxury, but it wasn't my idea of how I wanted to live. And, besides, I couldn't abandon Christina. When I brought up the subject of Christina moving into the ranch, too, Maria was dead set against it. As far as Maria was concerned, Christina was beneath us. It's gotten to where I can't stand my new wife, no matter how gorgeous she is. The marriage wasn't a week old and already the situation was driving me crazy.

I missed and wanted Judy.

I'd foreseen all of this. It's why I've been planning tonight's job for months. Some people were going to get hurt, no question about it, but it had to be done. Beginning January 1, 1962, it was going to be very different around here.

I wanted to somehow convey the message to Judy that I would return to her in the future. I went to see her, even though I was a married man by then. I thought—screw it, lots of guys had candy on the side. Judy and I had a fantastic night together; the sex was as good as it got, even though she was mad at me for being "missing in action," as she called it. But the next morning, I had to tell her the truth—that I couldn't be with her for a while. I didn't admit I was *married*, I'm not that dumb, but I supposed I felt a little bad that I wasn't telling her everything. The main thing was that I *would* be back, if she'd have me. That wasn't a guarantee. Judy was the type of girl who might hold a grudge. And if that was the case, well, there were other fish in the sea.

Now, for tonight.

I was a little nervous.

49
Gina
THE PRESENT

Dad and I flew home last night and took a cab to his place. Maggie came over and I went and stayed at Mom's house, but this morning I drove one of her spare cars, a VW, back to Dad's so we could have breakfast together and then go see Grandma Judy at the nursing home. Dad wanted to drive his own car, but Maggie didn't think that was a good idea just yet. He kept whispering that he was fine, that the only thing wrong with him was that he sounded funny and it was still uncomfortable for him swallow. He joked that now he could go on that diet he always wanted to do but never could manage.

We got to Woodlands—Maggie drove her car separately—and the three of us went to Grandma's room. They'd already dressed her and she had finished breakfast. She sat in the rocking chair she liked so much, and someone had put on a CD of Elvis music for her. When we walked in, she was rocking with her eyes closed, dreaming away to the music with a slight smile on her face. She looked peaceful and happy. Many times when I first walked in the room, she appeared old and sad, but usually she lit up when she saw me.

"Hi, Grandma!"

That startled her and she flinched. But then she recognized me and grinned widely and held out her arms. I went over to her, bent over, and gave her a big hug and kissed her cheek. "Mmm, you smell nice, Grandma."

"They gave her a bath and shampooed her hair yesterday in anticipation of your arrival," Maggie said.

"Hi, Mom," my dad said as best as he could. Grandma Judy looked up at him and her brow wrinkled. "It's me, Martin."

"That's my dad, Grandma," I reminded her. "He sounds funny, doesn't he?"

There was authentic concern in her expression. "What… what …" she tried to say, not quite knowing how to express it.

"What's the matter?" I prompted.

"What's the matter?" she mimicked.

Dad pointed to the bandage on his neck. It was smaller now, not so scary-looking. "I had an injury to my throat, Mom. I'm okay. I'll be hoarse for a while, that's all. It'll get better with time. How are you doing?"

"What?"

"How are you doing?" I repeated.

"Oh, okay. I was—" She looked over at the boom box and struggled for the words.

"Listening to your favorite music. I know!"

She beamed.

"Who is it, Mom?" Dad asked. "Who's singing?"

She thought for a moment, blinked, and then answered, "Elvis."

"That's right!" I said. We all looked at each other and smiled. Dad had told me she'd taken a turn for the worse, but it seemed to me she was doing just fine. "I'm going to turn him down a little so we can talk."

Dad and Maggie sat on the bed, and I pulled up one of the chairs to sit near her. "So, Grandma, I'm here for a few days from New York. You remember New York, right?"

"New York."

"I love it." I told her about Josh and how great he was. "You'd like him, Grandma. He's very handsome. He's from Israel, but he lives in the United States now."

"That's nice."

"Oh, and I'm taking Krav Maga lessons and I'm getting good. Do you know what that is?"

Dad said, "Honey, I don't think she does. Mom, it's like *karate*. You know what *karate* is, don't you?"

She looked at him and nodded. "*Karate*."

"Well, Krav Maga is another martial art self-defense system." I stood up and struck a stance and demonstrated a few moves, punching the air. Grandma watched me intently, her eyes growing wide. Then I laughed and said, "See, I could probably be the next Black Stiletto."

Grandma reacted weirdly to that. The smile remained on her face, but her eyes welled with tears. It was as if she was crying with happiness. I noticed Dad's and Maggie's eyes meet as if something was wrong. "What?" I asked. "It was a joke." I sat back down and said, "What's wrong, Grandma?" Dad and Maggie stood and he went to her side.

"It's okay, Mom. We're here."

And then the strangest thing happened. Grandma took my hand and looked at me with a combination of sadness and earnestness, and she said as lucidly as possible, "I quit for Little Man Martin."

"What?"

"I did it for—he was the baby." And then she got agitated and looked around the room. "Martin? Martin?"

"I'm right here, Mom," he said. "I'm perfectly safe. I just have a sore throat."

She gazed at his face and narrowed her eyes.

"I'd forgotten you used to call me Little Man Martin," he said. "What made you remember that?"

Before she could answer, I interrupted and asked, "What did you mean, Grandma, you 'quit' for him? What did you quit?"

Maggie said softly, "Maybe we need to let Judy rest for a little while. She might be getting a little upset."

"It's okay, Mom," Dad said to her. "Everybody's here and we all love you."

"We sure do," I echoed. "I think about you all the time, Grandma."

That seemed to shake her out of the little funk she was in. She smiled broadly.

"Why don't we come back a little later today?" Dad said to her. "Would you like that?"

"Yes."

Dad and Maggie went out of the room for a minute, and I stayed with Grandma and talked to her about what she was wearing and how she had her hair fixed. I liked the fact that it was still long, although it was all white now. I saw her tattered robe and said, "I think you need a new robe, Grandma. I'm going to buy you one for a present. What do you think about that? Wouldn't you like a whole new outfit?"

She replied, "The outfit will fit you."

I thought she meant what she was wearing, which was a pair of loose slacks and a blouse and sweater. "I don't know, Grandma. I think I'm a size or two bigger than you now. You're still tall, but you're pretty thin. See, I bulked up." I stood and showed her my arm muscles.

Dad came back in and said, "Okay, honey, let's let Grandma rest."

"We'll see you later, Grandma. I love you!"

"I saved it for you."

I was confused. "Saved what?" I looked at Dad.

He said, "I love you, Mom. Get some rest, okay? Let's go, Gina."

"Bye, Grandma!"

"Good-bye." Then she smiled and gave us a little wave.

As we walked out of the room, I asked, "What was all that about? What did she mean?"

"I don't know," Dad answered. "Alzheimer's gibberish, you know. Sometimes she says things that just don't make a lot of sense."

Hmm.

Once again, I sensed that my father was lying.

When we got to his house, everything that I'd been feeling since the assault sort of bubbled up and exploded. First of all, there was the shock of walking into a hotel room and seeing my father—beaten, gagged, and tied to a chair—with two scary-looking gangster types. Then I found myself putting into practice what I'd learned of Krav Maga in the short time I'd been studying it. I put two men in the hospital, one seriously injured. Was I crazy, or didn't that mean something was going on with my dad that he wasn't talking about it? And it involved *Grandma Judy*. Those men were from her home-town. Third, there was Grandma Judy herself, a mysterious woman I have loved my whole life, but never knew much about. She was always a socially shy woman, but a powerhouse when she was with her family. I had no idea what her love life was like or even if she dated. The enigma surrounding my grandfather was even more bizarre. So there's *that*. Then there were the little things recently, like that book Dad desperately didn't want me to see, and Maggie telling me that he would tell me some things when he's ready.

I wanted to know what the hell was going on.

"Dad?" He had gone straight to his comfy chair in the living room, reclined, and turned on the television with the remote.

"Yes, honey?"

"What the hell is going on?"

He blinked and his eyes betrayed that he knew what I was talk-ing about, but he answered, "What, what do you mean?"

"You know. Why did those men attack you? You *know*, Dad. You're keeping it from me. I'm not a child anymore, you can tell me this stuff."

"Until you're twenty-one, you're not *really* an adult."

"*Dad!*" Now he was annoying me. "You *do* know. So tell me. Does it have anything to do with Grandma?" When he didn't say anything, I knew that was my answer. "It does, doesn't it!" Dad just stared straight ahead, obviously fighting an internal struggle of some kind. I sensed he wanted to tell me, but was afraid to.

"Are you in trouble, Dad?" I asked softly. "Because if you are, I—"

"Gina, no, I'm not in trouble, not now. Please don't worry. Nothing's wrong."

"Dad, I can tell you're ly—er, you're not telling the truth."

He blinked and looked at me. "You can?"

I thought that was funny and laughed. "You're not very good at lying, Dad. Mom could see right through you. I can see right through you. Grandma used to be able to do it. I bet Maggie can, too."

"Great."

"Dad, I can see that you're carrying some kind of burden. Was Grandma some kind of criminal at one time?"

"No! Gina, *please*."

He appeared tortured. His eyes watered and it was palpable how conflicted he was. Best to let it go, *again*.

"Well, Maggie said you had something to tell me when you're ready, so when you are, I'm here." I turned and started to walk out of the room and into the bedroom I used when I was at Dad's. It's funny how that room was always nice and made up, and his own was a complete mess. How did Maggie tolerate it when she came over?

"Gina."

I looked back. "What."

He stared at me a long time.

"*What!*"

He sat up in the chair and slowly stood. "Wait here. I'll be right back. Please sit down." He left me, went to his bedroom, and shut the door. Okay. We were getting somewhere. I turned off the TV and sat on the couch.

In a moment, Dad returned. He carried a bundle of books, the same type I'd seen at the hospital. They had a rubber band around them. He stood and held the package up for me to see. I reached for them but he pulled back.

"These are your grandmother's diaries. She kept them hidden until Uncle Thomas—you remember Uncle Thom—"

"Yes."

"He had them and wasn't supposed to give them to me until Mom was either dead or incapacitated. About ten months ago, he presented them to me. If the world learns what's inside them, I have no doubt it would cause a global—" He searched for the right word. "—sensation."

He really had me going. My heart was pounding and I reached for them again, but he wouldn't let me have them yet.

"Gina, I was hoping that you wouldn't find out about any of this until, well, later, when you're older. But seeing as how with recent events—" He paused and lowered his voice. "—and how you saved my life and all—I've been thinking about it and thought maybe it was time."

"Gosh, Dad, I can't imagine what this is."

"Gina, you have to promise me—and I mean a solemn, hand on a stack of Bibles, cross your heart, Scout's honor, sworn oath—that you will not reveal this to *anyone*. Not even Josh. Not yet. If you two stay serious about each other, then maybe we can bring him in on the secret if he becomes part of the family."

"What secret?"

He held up his hand. "Patience, honey." Then he added, as an aside. "I do like Josh, sweetheart. He's a terrific guy."

"Thanks, Dad. But, sure, of course, I promise." I held up my hand like I was saying an oath. "You have my word. My lips are sealed."

Then he handed them to me. "Be careful with 'em. They're very valuable. I've read only the first four—I'm a slow reader, you know. I want to start the fifth one while you read the others."

"Okay."

"Oh, and after you get a few pages into that first one, you're going to wonder if my mom was crazy. That this is all bullshit. Well, I'll be in my room. Come and get me. And then we'll go someplace and I'll show you something."

So he went to his room and shut the door. Completely captivated, I pulled off the rubber band and picked up the diary marked #1 and opened it.

July 4, 1958

Dear diary, I thought maybe I should start writing all this stuff down. When I was a little girl I kept a diary. I wrote in it for about three years, I think. I don't know what happened to it. I guess it's still back in Odessa, sitting in a drawer in my old room. If my old room still exists.

I'm chronicling everything that's happened to me lately, just in case something bad happens. I'm not sure if I really want the truth to come out, but here it is. So much has occurred in the last six months. In a way, I'm more famous than the mayor of New York City! Well, not me, Judy Cooper. The Black Stiletto is. No one knows Judy Cooper is the Black Stiletto, and I hope to keep it that way.

WTF?

I read that second paragraph again. I swore my heart did a somersault and somehow got stuck in my throat. My stomach lurched the way it did when you were on a roller coaster.

No way. No freakin' way. This was fucked up.

I stood and stormed down the hall to Dad's bedroom and knocked. "Dad! Dad, can I come in?"

"Sure."

I walked in and he was lying on his back in bed. "I wondered how long it would take you," he said.

I pointed to the diary in my hand. "What is this? Is this true? Is this a joke?"

"No, honey. I thought it was at first, too. But it's not." He winced as he raised himself off the bed. "Damn, it hurts to lie down and get up. You'd be surprised how many neck muscles you use doing that. Let's get the car."

"Where are we going?"

"I'll show you. Come on. Leave the diaries here."

So we went out to my VW and we drove south to Arlington Heights, toward the old house where Grandma used to live. He directed me to a bank on Euclid.

"You gonna use the ATM or something?" I asked.

"No. Come in with me."

We went inside and Dad told the teller he wanted to get in his safety deposit box. They performed the ID-showing and signing-in routine, and then the teller led us around the barrier to the vault where the boxes were kept. Dad had one key, the teller had another. They both unlocked #225 together, and Dad pulled out a box that was about three-feet by two-and-a-half feet, and eight-inches deep, one of the larger varieties the bank provided.

"Would you like a private room?" the teller asked.

"Yes, please."

She led us to a small room with a counter and two chairs. No window on the door. "Just come on out when you're done," she said.

Dad closed the door and set the box on the counter. "Better have a seat."

I couldn't imagine what I was about to see.

He opened the box and started pulling out items and laying them on the counter.

Some old "Black Stiletto" comic books.

A pair of knee-high black boots.

Two pairs of black leather pants. One was thicker than the other.

A big belt that looked like something soldiers would wear. There were hooks and pockets on it.

A flashlight. A large pulley hook. A freakin' big coil of old rope.

A pair of black gloves.

A freakin' stiletto knife in a sheath.

Holy fuck, a handgun.

Two black leather jackets, again one thick, one thin.

A backpack.

And, finally, a mask. A very famous one.

When he was finished, Dad leaned against the wall and folded his arms in front of him. He had a ridiculous smile on his face. Despite the angst he'd experienced debating whether or not to reveal his mother's secret, he appeared to be very happy. I think he took great pleasure in showing me this stuff.

As for me, I was speechless. Stunned. Incredulous.

I picked up the mask and held it.

I pulled the knife out of its sheath and lightly ran my finger along the blade.

I fingered the jackets.

My hands trembled.

"Well?" Dad asked.

I couldn't move. I sat there in shock. The seconds went by until I finally, miraculously, found my voice.

"Oh, my freakin' God, my grandma was the Black Stiletto."

50
Judy's Diary
1961

DECEMBER 31, 1961

I suppose I should say it's January 1, because it's 6:30 in the morning.
I'm still a little shell-shocked. The drive back to L.A. from Las Vegas
was a blur. It's a miracle I didn't have an accident. I don't remember
much of the trip. But here I am in my apartment.

I don't know what I'm going to do next. Not today, not tomorrow, not next week. Things are bad, dear diary. *Really* bad.

Yesterday I tried to sleep a little before noon. I think I got three
hours' worth, but I was too anxious for any more. So I grabbed my
Stiletto outfit—which I hoped I wouldn't need—and got in the Sunliner to head for Nevada. I filled up with gasoline and I drove out to
the desert. It was a long, lonely trip.

I'd never been to Las Vegas. I scoped out where DeAngelo's
ranch was located, but since I was too early, I drove into town to have
a look around. It was dusk, so all the neon lights I'd heard so much
were just beginning to shine. I went to Fremont Street and saw the
big casinos there—the Golden Nugget, the Lucky Strike, the Mint—
and of course, DeAngelo's place, the Sandstone. I was impressed by
the famous "Vegas Vic" neon cowboy that was outside the Pioneer.
If I hadn't had a serious mission ahead of me, I might have parked,
gone inside one of the casinos, and tried my luck. But seeing as how

my luck hasn't been too good lately, I probably would have lost all my money.

I stopped to get some dinner at Biff's Famous Food because I hadn't eaten much all day. By the time I'd finished, it was after 10:00. The neon lit up the streets. It was indeed spectacular. I vowed to myself that I would return someday when I could have some fun and enjoy it. But it wouldn't be so great by myself. I needed someone to accompany me. Las Vegas seemed to be a glamorous, romantic destination. Who'd want to go alone?

DeAngelo's ranch was on the north side of town, just outside the city limits. It was easy to find, but only one road led to the big, stone fence that surrounded the property. I didn't have an invitation, so I knew I wouldn't be able to drive through the gate and park inside with the other guests. Getting in the party would be the hardest part, so I parked some distance away off-road and in the dark, turned off my headlights, and watched as guests drove up to the gate. There were two men on duty there, checking the identities of passengers before letting them through. There appeared to be not enough parking spaces for all the guests within the fence perimeter, so men were directing drivers to park on a flat, dirt space just outside the gate. There were already sixteen cars there. Once cleared and directed to a parking spot, guests walked from there through the gates.

I left the Stiletto outfit in the car and locked it. I didn't even bring the knife. I was Judy Cooper, and I was simply going to be a guest at Vincent DeAngelo's New Year's Eve party. I'd dressed in one of the cocktail dresses I'd worn in New York when Lucy and I would go to the Village Vanguard or other nightclubs. High heels. Black stilettos, as a matter of fact. I'd spent an hour on my hair this morning after I awoke, and made sure I looked fabulous. Even after the six-hour car ride and dinner, I thought perhaps I still did.

I walked along the road toward the ranch, but stayed in the shadows. My timing was perfect. I skirted around to the makeshift dirt parking lot just as a Rolls pulled in and parked. A man and two women got out, dressed to the nines. I didn't know them.

"Nice night for a party," I said, approaching them.

"Ain't it?" the man said. I could tell he liked the way I looked. His two companions were younger than him and very pretty. They smiled and one of them said, "Hello."

"Hi, I'm Judy."

"I'm Candy. This is April."

"Glad to meet you." I turned to the man. "And you are?"

"Stan."

"And I'm glad to meet you as well."

By then we'd started walking toward the gate together. I simply became part of their group as we chatted and passed right by the two gatekeepers, who gazed at me, Candy, and April, lasciviously. They figured I'd been in the Rolls, too. It was a gamble, but it worked. And my three companions must have thought I belonged there, too.

Guests were led into the house and then through a large foyer, a hallway, and into a space that was one of the most luxurious living rooms I'd ever seen. There was a beautiful, large, lit fireplace, a full-size polar bearskin rug, and a magnificent Christmas tree, its strings of lights brightly casting a rainbow over the room. Very few guests were indoors; everyone was outside where the food and drinks were. Apparently, there would be fireworks at midnight. Even though it was New Year's Eve, the weather outside was nice. Not terribly hot like it would be in the summer, but pleasant enough that you could have a party outdoors.

From there, we moved to a very large porch enclosed by walls with big screen panels, through which I could see the entire back-yard. I guess you'd call it a veranda, and there were a lot more people gathered there. The men wore tuxedos; the women were in formal gowns or cocktail dresses. They held glasses of booze and smoked cigarettes. No one I knew. I heard music from a band playing out-side, so I opened the screen door and stepped into what I feared would be a nest of peril.

The decorations and lighting were tasteful and lovely. Four rows of candlelit tables lined the area closest to the house. They were cov-

ered by a huge, open-air tent. A twelve-piece band was set up on a
platform beyond the tables, facing a "dance floor" on neatly-cut
grass. The band was in full swing, playing the kind of music that
was popular during World War II and the '40s. Glenn Miller stuff.

Behind the bandstand was a gigantic swimming pool. No one
was in it; this was a dress-up party. There appeared to be a tennis
court beyond that, and then the edge of the yard and the stone fence.

On the opposite side of the dance floor was the food. A long line
of tables jutted out from the tent, facing the bandstand. A buffet was
set up there; the bar was next to it, and that's where the biggest lines
were. Maybe six couples were dancing. Most people were sitting at
the tables, eating or drinking or talking.

Beyond the dancing area, the yard went on into darker spaces.
Guests could walk back there if they wanted, for it was romantically
lit with twinkle lights, providing just enough illumination to see
where you were going. I imagine that's where couples would stroll
if they wanted to engage in a little hanky-panky. I could make out a
gazebo in the distance; it, too, had strings of twinkle lights on it. The
fireworks would most likely be shot from that back section of the
yard.

I walked along the tables and spotted some familiar faces. There
was Sal Casazzo, Shrimp, and Mario, with three women. Their
wives? They looked too young to be their spouses. I didn't particularly want those guys to see me. They might wonder how I'd received an invitation. I'd never seen Vince DeAngelo before, but I
knew what he looked like. Barry had shown me photos. I found him
standing near the bar, holding court and talking to a group of men.
His son, Paulie, the skinny gangster I saw the night before at the
warehouse, was by his side. Ricky Bartlett was part of the group, too.
Barry knew who he was, and I was right. He's one of the top gangsters in West Texas, even though he masquerades as a legitimate
businessman in his part of the state.

My watch told me it was 11:40. I didn't see Leo anywhere. He
and his new bride were not on the grass. They weren't at any of the

tables. I hadn't seen them in the house. They had to be out farther, in the twinkle-light lover's lane of the yard. That suited me fine. I didn't really want to make a scene when I confronted him, although it was altogether possible that's what it would be.

First, I needed a drink. I walked past DeAngelo and stood in line for a few minutes, and then I ordered a gin and tonic from a handsome bartender who called me "Glamour-puss."

I walked back to the veranda entrance, so I could skirt around the perimeter of the yard, behind the pool and tennis court, and around the fence toward the gazebo. But suddenly, there was Christina. Right in my face. She'd been walking toward the porch to go inside the house.

I have to say she looked gorgeous in a strapless, low-cut cocktail dress that was shockingly short and revealed more cleavage than I'd ever dare to do.

Needless to say, she was surprised to see me.

"Judy! What... what are you—? How did you get invi—uh, I didn't know you were invited."

"Yeah, I was," I lied. "I got an anonymous invitation in the mail. You didn't send it, did you?"

"Uh, no."

I jerked my head toward Casazza's table. "Then I think it was one of Sal's friends. They *always* flirt with me at Flickers. They're constantly asking me out, but I'm not supposed to date customers. But I suppose at a party like *this*, that rule wouldn't apply. I'm trying to figure out which one of them did it."

She stared at me, trying to decide if I was telling the truth. "Does Leo know you're here?"

"Not yet. Do you know where I can find him?"

Christina's eyes narrowed. "Judy, you should leave. This is not your place. You know about Leo and Maria."

"Sure, I just want to congratulate them. Tell him we can still be friends." That was a tough one to say.

She leaned in, inches from my face, and, as menacingly as she could, whispered, "Judy, I don't know what you're doing here, but you better leave. *Now*." I wanted to punch her in the face and ruin her pretty makeup, but I controlled myself. I was Judy Cooper, not the Black Stiletto.

"Fine," I said.

"That's all I have to say." She turned and went through the screen door.

Well, nuts to her. I wasn't about to leave. In fact, that gave me the nerve I needed to stay on course. A quick glance at my wrist-watch told me it was five minutes until midnight. If I wanted to get it done before the noisy fireworks began, I had to get going. I maneuvered toward the bandstand, walked behind it, and headed into the darker area of the spacious yard. The twinkle lights did provide a pretty, holiday atmosphere back there. Three or four couples strolled along the edge, next to the fence, but they weren't my prey. At first, I was afraid I might not find them, but then I spotted Leo and a blonde woman standing near the gazebo. I was too far away to get a good look at her, but she was wearing a lovely brown cocktail dress that flattered her figure. They both held champagne glasses, and he had an arm around her waist. They appeared to be looking up at the stars.

How romantic.

So I approached them. Actually, the first thing my eyes went to was a huge, glittering diamond that hung around Maria DeAngelo's neck. It caught the lights beautifully, and was truly dazzling. I almost lost my train of thought, but I recovered quickly.

"Hello, Leo. Happy New Year," I said.

He reacted with horror. His eyes grew as wide as saucers and his jaw dropped. A cigarette fell out of his mouth to the grass.

"Oh, and congratulations on your *marriage*."

Leo was speechless. The blonde woman was indeed very pretty, but I really wanted to pick up that cigarette and burn a few holes in her face with it. She looked at me and at him and back at me.

"Leo?" she asked.

Finally, he found his voice. "Judy, what . . . what are you doing here?"

Maria's eyes narrowed. "Is this . . . is this *her*? That *slut* you were seeing in L.A.?"

"Judy, what—how did you get in? You can't—"

"Shut up, Leo. You goddamned *liar*. Did you tell your wife how you came over to my apartment on Thursday and spent the night?"

Then *her* mouth dropped. "What?" She looked at him. "Is that true?"

In the background, the crowd at the tables started counting down, "*10, 9, 8—*"

"Maria, no. I was—no, she's crazy. Judy, get out of here. I'm going to call one of Vince's men to—"

"It's true, Maria. He came over, *screwed me*, spent the night, and then broke up with me the next morning. And if I'm counting correctly, that was three days after your wedding."

"*4, 3, 2—*"

She kept jerking her head back and forth from me to him. Leo muttered protestations and looked as if he was going to hit me.

"Go ahead, Leo," I said. "You going to slug me? Punch me in the face?"

"Judy, *get out of here!*"

But before anything else happened, what sounded like a soaring *missile* split the sky, followed by a loud *pop*. A gigantic canopy of red-and-blue sparkles formed against the starry backdrop. There was a cheer from the crowd back at the tables.

"I mean it, Judy, *go!*"

Another firework went off. This one was louder, with a series of crackles, similar to exploding flashbulbs above our heads. Then there were more *pfffttt* sounds as bottle rockets flew into the air and detonated. Within seconds, a cacophony of bangs followed one another, over and over, as the grounds lit up from the colorful display in the sky. All eyes were on the magic formations filling the panorama over the ranch. The band started playing "Auld Lang Syne." Leo, Maria, and I could no longer hear ourselves.

And then it happened.

A dark figure appeared from the gazebo. I didn't know if she had been there the entire time and was hiding, or what. It seemed like she materialized out of thin air.

It was the Black Stiletto.

Well, of course, it *wasn't* the Black Stiletto, but a woman dressed like her. Same mask, same jacket—almost—a backpack, but no belt.

She leaped out in front of us and brandished a handgun. First, she pointed it at me and shouted, "Back away!" The noise of the fireworks was so loud I could barely hear her. I had no choice but to take a few steps back, although I considered attempting to disarm her. But that would give *me* away. I lifted my hands.

The phony Stiletto then pointed the gun at Leo and Maria. They both dropped their champagne glasses and raised their hands, too.

"The diamond! Let's have it!"

"No!" Maria cried. "Leo! Do something!"

He just stood there, probably too scared to move, but I saw his lips move. "Give it to her, honey. Do it now!"

I quickly turned my head to survey the rest of the yard. Nobody was watching us. The people near the house were all looking up.

The "Stiletto" didn't wait for Maria. She moved close, grabbed the diamond necklace, and roughly yanked it off the woman's neck. Maria cried out in pain, and then she started screaming. *Really* screaming, loud enough for people to hear.

The gun barked once. No one noticed. The bang blended with all the other blasts and pops.

The screaming stopped.

Maria fell.

"No!" Leo shouted. He immediately got to his knees to tend to his wife.

By then, the phony Stiletto had jumped into the gazebo, and I swear it looked like she sank into it. Snapping out of my shock, I bolted after her, and saw that there was a trapdoor in the gazebo's floor.

I went back to Leo, who was lightly slapping his wife's face. "Oh, my God. Oh, my God." Then he stood and shouted, "Help! Vince! Help! The Black Stiletto just shot Maria!"

That got some attention. Men started running across the lawn toward us. The fireworks kept going.

I backed away from the scene. *Who was impersonating me? Why would they kill Maria DeAngelo? Was it just for that diamond?*

Several men, including Vince DeAngelo, crowded around us. I became one of the bystanders. No one noticed me, so I slowly inched my way toward the house. But I was too mortified and stunned to leave yet.

DeAngelo cried to the heavens. "Mariaaaaaaaa! My God! Maria!"

Leo stood and helplessly watched his father-in-law break down. Men started running about, shouting, "The Black Stiletto! The Black Stiletto is here! She killed Maria! Find the Black Stiletto!" Some of the men opened the gazebo trapdoor and went down. More ran to the house.

The fireworks eventually halted. Paulie ran up and stopped when he saw his sister lying on the grass. I heard a man say that one of the servants was found knocked out in the wine cellar. I suppose that's where the trapdoor led. That meant the fake Stiletto was some-where in the house.

"Bring me her head!" DeAngelo hollered. Tears ran down his face. "Bring me the Black Stiletto's head! A million dollars to anyone who brings me her head!"

I figured I needed to get out of there fast. Leo had forgotten all about me. The place had erupted into chaos. Guests were trying to get close to the scene, but DeAngelo's men tried to hold them back; it was easy to weave my way through the crowd and reach the back to the house.

Just as I approached the veranda screen door, Christina emerged. "What's going on?" she asked.

"The Black Stiletto just shot Maria," I managed to say.

"*What?*" Then she bolted past me and ran toward the gazebo along with everyone else.

Had she been in the house the entire time?

I was literally shaking when I made my way through the mansion to the front door. I walked out the open front gate—the guards were no longer there—and stepped into the shadows to follow the road out to where I'd parked my car. I heard sirens approaching in the distance. Police? Ambulance?

My Sunliner was still hidden in the dark where I'd left it. I got in and sat, trying to make sense of what had just happened. An ambulance and two police cars, their lights flashing and sirens blazing, rushed past me on the road. When I thought it was safe enough, I started the car, left the headlights off, and drove away from DeAngelo's property. I waited until my taillights could no longer be seen from the gate before turning them on. Once I was back in Las Vegas, I stopped—I don't know where—and tried to get hold of myself. I'd found I had spontaneously started sobbing.

I wasn't crying for Maria. I certainly wasn't crying for Leo.

No, the tears were for me. Only me.

Happy New Year.

**Don't Miss
The Final Installment**

Endings & Beginnings

ABOUT THE AUTHOR

Raymond Benson is the author of over thirty books and previously penned *The Black Stiletto* (2011), *The Black Stiletto: Black & White* (2012), and *The Black Stiletto: Stars & Stripes* (2013).

Between 1996 and 2002, he was commissioned by the James Bond literary copyright holders to take over writing the 007 novels. In total he penned and published worldwide six original 007 novels, three film novelizations, and three short stories. An anthology of his 007 work, *The Union Trilogy*, was published in the fall of 2008, and a second anthology, *Choice of Weapons*, appeared summer 2010. His book *The James Bond Bedside Companion*, an encyclopedic work on the 007 phenomenon, was first published in 1984 and was nominated for an Edgar Allan Poe Award by Mystery Writers of America for Best Biographical/Critical Work.

Using the pseudonym David Michaels, Raymond is also the author of the *New York Times* best-selling books *Tom Clancy's Splinter Cell* and its sequel *Tom Clancy's Splinter Cell: Operation Barracuda*. Raymond's original suspense novels include *Evil Hours, Face Blind, Sweetie's Diamonds* (which won the Readers' Choice Award for Best Thriller of 2006 at the *Love Is Murder Conference for Authors, Readers and Publishers*), *Torment*, and *Artifact of Evil*. *A Hard Day's Death*, the first in a series of "rock 'n' roll thrillers," was published in 2008, and its sequel, the Shamus Award-nominated *Dark Side of the Morgue*, published in 2009. Other recent works include novelizations of the popular videogames, *Metal Gear Solid* and its sequel, *Metal Gear Solid 2: Sons of Liberty, Homefront: The Voice of Freedom*, co-written with John Milius, and *Hitman: Damnation*.

Raymond has taught courses in film genres and history at New

York's New School for Social Research; Harper College in Palatine, Illinois; College of DuPage in Glen Ellyn, Illinois; and currently presents Film Studies lectures with *Daily Herald* movie critic Dann Gire. Raymond has been honored in Naoshima, Japan, with the erection of a permanent museum dedicated to one of his novels, and he is also an ambassador for Japan's Kagawa Prefecture. Raymond is an active member of International Thriller Writers Inc., Mystery Writers of America, the International Association of Media Tie-In Writers, a full member of ASCAP, and served on the Board of Directors of The Ian Fleming Foundation for sixteen years. He is based in the Chicago area.

www.raymondbenson.com
www.theblackstiletto.net

CPSIA information can be obtained at www.ICGtesting.com
Printed in the USA
LVOW12s0539300615

444314LV00006B/7/P